VOICES

OF

THUNDER

Cover illustration (transposed) reproduced by kind permission of G Parachute Battery (Mercer's Troop), 7th Parachute Regiment Royal Horse Artillery, from the original 'G Battery Royal Horse Artillery - Waterloo 18th June 1815' by Major Thomas S Secombe.

A catalogue record of this book is available from the British Library

First Edition: August 2003

ISBN: 1-84375-047-3

To order additional copies of this book please visit: http://www.upso.co.uk/garethglover.htm

Published by: UPSO Ltd
5 Stirling Road, Castleham Business Park,
St Leonards-on-Sea, East Sussex TN38 9NW United Kingdom
Tel: 01424 853349 Fax: 01424 854084
Email: info@upso.co.uk Web: http://www.upso.co.uk

VOICES OF THUNDER

by

Gareth Glover

UPSO

FOR

MARY
SARAH & MICHAEL

MY MUCH LOVED,
LONG SUFFERING FAMILY

THE LANDING

A tattered red flag rose slowly above the decaying wooden fort that commanded the entrance to Ostend. The signal indicated that the depth of water within the harbour was now sufficient for the multitude of impatiently waiting craft to enter safely. Thomas Jeffrey, the Master of the merchant vessel *Sabus,* was a short dumpy man, his haggard features and dark sunken eyes told of many sleepless nights plying his exacting trade. He sported a two-day stubble which helped to conceal his cankered teeth, a stained jacket and trousers caked in grime completed his dishevelled appearance. As Master however, he was King of his vessel and bellowed the order for the helm to be set. He directed the helmsman to keep the bow of the vessel aimed at the point of a spire silhouetted against the grey sky of an overcast dawn. It peered above the low grass speckled sand hills, that lined the shore, the only indication of the great port that lay beyond them.

"Have to aim well up above the harbour because the current will set us down to leeward", he explained to Captain Alexander Mercer who stood nearby. Alexander continued to stare at the sullen morning sky in stony silence; he had little interest in such nautical niceties.

Alexander was a stout young man of average height, a quaff of light brown hair, thick long sideburns and sporting a magnificent drooping moustache whose points nearly reached his chin. He wore a navy blue tunic; heavily laced across the chest in yellow gold, contrasted by grey riding breeches and calf length black boots. He trailed a silver metal scabbard containing his curved cavalry sword, which continually clattered upon the wooden planking of the deck. A dark blue hussar style jacket with broad cuffs of scarlet and again laced heavily in yellow; was draped decoratively over the left shoulder. Under his arm he caressed a brass helmet surmounted by a great black brush of hair that curved over the crest. He was every inch, the epitome of high military fashion.

Alexander shuddered inwardly as the Masters' words finally struck home, the prospect of missing the harbour entrance was not an attractive one. The gloom of an overcast sky and a chilly light sea breeze was outdone by the worrying sound of the breakers crashing heavily upon the beach to the left of the entrance, it did not add to his feeling of comfort. The sails having been unfurled a little by the small band of chattering seamen that seemed to anticipate unerringly every order of Jeffrey's before he could speak, increased the ship's speed. The vessel slowly crabbed towards the gap in the wooden piled pier, which marked the entrance into the harbour. Even to his untrained eye, Alexander could see that the current was setting fast to the left where the roar of the waves dashing upon the sands and the great billows of spray warned of impending disaster.

Alexander now watched the crew intensely as they lay out a huge hawser in a coil on the fore deck, "What is the rope for?" he enquired. Jeffreys looked at him with a wry smile, curling his upper lip and with a knowing glint in his eye, "You'll soon see" a seaman answered nonchalantly, then turned back to watch the local Belgian pilot's handling of the ship.

Alexander watched the helmsman struggle incessantly to keep the bow pointing toward the spire, perspiring heavily as he fought with the great wheel in anticipation of the ship's movement.

Orders for the trimming of the sails made Alexander look up and survey the ship. The *Sabus* was a vessel of some two hundred and fifty tons, quite big for a merchantman. Two masts towered above him, both square rigged with their yards and rigging looking a jumble of ropes to a landlubber like him. He watched with bewilderment as orders from the Master caused the small crew to scamper through the rigging to furl the sails or to pull on great ropes that angled the yards that little bit to catch the breeze square on to the sails. He marvelled at the tough unceasing work for these sailors. They were an extremely hardy breed, there was no watch system here like the Royal Navy, these merchant seamen were up on deck whenever required, night or day, rain or shine.

A sickening scraping sound quickly followed by the heart wrenching noise of cracking timbers brought Alexander's meandering thoughts abruptly back to the present. Alexander felt himself impelled towards the deck as the vessel lurched to a sudden halt, only saving himself by grasping hold of the standing rigging as he plunged forward. Righting himself, he was aware that everyone was shouting at once, the utter confusion was self-evident. He caught sight of the Belgian pilot, jumping insanely on his small cocked hat and swearing vociferously at all and sunder, thankfully no one could understand Flemish. The ship had struck the pier just to the right of the harbour entrance; it's prow towering over the wooden sea wall;

obviously the current had not set them down as much as had been expected!

A handful of sleepy Belgian soldiers, burst out of a small wooden guardhouse on the pier. They were dressed in dishevelled blue jackets with white cross-belts and grey trousers. Judging from their state of dress, they had been sleeping on duty, following a heavy night. They appeared dazed and shocked to see the bowsprit of the *Sabus* towering above them, as they ducked underneath it to move to a safer location. Manic screams from the pilot accompanied by unintelligible gesticulations from the crew confused them even more. Eventually some of the soldiers began to comprehend the situation and managed to organise their comrades. The huge hawser that had been so carefully coiled upon the deck was now thrown from the bow onto the pier, one of the soldiers managed to catch the rope by the great eye in its end. With the aid of his companions they hauled on the hawser, it was obviously very heavy and they struggled despite their number. Eventually they managed to haul enough ashore to lay the eye over a great iron bollard set into the wooden pier. Seeing this, the sailors turned the shipboard end of the hawser around a pair of bollards on the fo'csle in a figure of eight pattern. Everyone seemed to visibly relax a little now that things were under some form of control.

Alexander suddenly noticed that during this distraction, despite the confusion all around, the seamen aloft had furled the sails to stop the wind driving the ship onto the pier causing further damage. The current was steadily pushing the *Sabus* to the left, towards the harbour entrance; the hawser was let out slowly to control the ship as it scraped along the wooden wall. The ship slowly set down to leeward and eventually cleared the end of the pier, the soldiers immediately released the rope, letting it fall into the sea and it was slowly hauled inboard. This bemused Alexander; surely they would now drift down and smash onto the opposite pier of the harbour amidships! But no, a new current had obviously taken control of the ship, the tide flooding in to fill the port carried the ship safely through the harbour mouth and with a few studding sails reset, she sailed gracefully into the port.

Alexander observed that they had now joined a slow procession of craft, all entering on the flood, many were local boats, fishing smacks and coastal craft, but interspersed among them were a number of large ocean going merchant ships similar to *Sabus*. They had probably all been hired by the Transport Board hurriedly over the last two weeks to carry the army to Belgium as quickly as possible. Indeed the *Sabus* had sailed from Harwich along with the *Adventure* and *Philarea* three days previously, all full of troops.

Transporting was a profitable business, so Mister Jeffreys had informed Alexander. Because of her copper sheathing allowing faster speeds, he would get twenty shillings per ton per month from the Transport Board, better than could be earned hauling coals down from Newcastle to London!

Alexander's thoughts now started to wander again; they drifted back to just seven days before, when he had been sat at his desk at the Royal Horse Artillery barracks in Colchester. The despatch rider had brought the order for his battery, 'G' Troop, to prepare for immediate embarkation at Harwich. Major Alexander Fraser, Commanding Officer of all the Horse Artillery at Colchester, had appeared whilst he was still cogitating over the order. Fraser was a stern disciplinarian who ruled by fear, he glared at Alexander and demanded.

"Well Mercer, you have your orders, how quickly can you be ready to march?"

Alexander was thrown into confusion by this sudden demand; he was not fully prepared for the question, something Alexander never liked. "A week at least Sir, some of the horses are not at their best either" he blurted out, red faced.

Major Fraser's expression told Alexander that he disagreed and was none too pleased with his answer. He looked sternly at him and ordered, "Take whatever equipment you need, and the best horses of all the troops here, but mind that you are ready in three days!"

Alexander took the hint and excusing himself, ordered his servant Millward to inform the other officers that they were to meet in the Officer's Mess in five minutes. It did not take them long to gather, they knew that something was in the wind. Alexander surveyed his five fellow officers as they stared intently at him, eager for the announcement. Robert Newland, his second in command, stood imperiously aloof, attempting to maintain an air of nonchalance and exchanging knowing glances at the other 'veteran' Lieutenant William Ingilby. They had been through it all before and were not going to show any signs of excitement at the call to war. The remaining trio, Lieutenants Leathes, Hincks and Assistant Surgeon Hichens held none of their emotions back, their eagerness for confirmation of the orders was obvious. They cared little for the disdainful looks of the seasoned officers, they yet knew only of the glories of war. Alexander could not conceal his own delight, he had little experience of campaigning himself and shared the latter's enthusiasm.

"Gentlemen, we are ordered to Belgium immediately, all must be ready to leave in three days, do whatever is necessary to achieve this." His grave demeanour whilst speaking, broke into a grin as Richard Hichens proclaimed, "I'll get my father that Cuirassier's helmet yet!"

Those three days were ones of complete haste, everybody urgently checking equipment and preparing it for use, but by the third day everything was arranged. The men were given leave to bid their loved ones farewell on the last night and to Alexander's intense pride, 'G' troop mustered the following morning complete in men and equipment. Nobody was missing, nor intoxicated.

Major Fraser had gruffly congratulated Alexander on such a fine turn out and had ordered them to march. They rode out onto the great post road from London to Harwich, all gaiety, and eager for glory. Alexander's black Labrador 'Bal' ran alongside his horse, mingling with the rest of the pack, as more than a dozen of the men had their dogs with them. It had been a glorious summer's day and they had stopped to water and refresh the horses at Maningtree. Proceeding, they had finally arrived at the bustling seaport that afternoon. The transport vessels were in harbour awaiting their arrival but the tides were not right to sail immediately. Some of the men and equipment had been embarked before dark; the rest spent the night in the local barracks. There were soldiers everywhere, some dusty and dirty from their long marches, many lounging outside the public houses, relaxing in their undress uniforms awaiting embarkation orders. It seemed that the entire British army was here awaiting transport to Belgium. Sailors passed regularly, many with a woman or two on their arms, others rolling along blind drunk, offering a fight to any landlubber crossing their path. The soldiers were wisely ignoring them, but Alexander knew there would be trouble later when the soldiers had also got a belly full of beer.

A thick fog had greeted them in the morning, but nothing would stop the embarkation. The horses were coaxed onto large wooden floats, slowly pulled alongside the ships, and hauled aboard in a canvas harness. The horses did not like the experience and the operation took hours, indeed some men were injured as horses fought out of their harnesses and fell into the sea, taking the seamen with them. All the horses were recaptured unharmed and were eventually safely settled in stalls built for them in the specially adapted hold.

For a second day, the wind had been blowing strongly into the harbour and they could not sail. Leaving the men and horses aboard, the officers had retired for a more comfortable night at the 'Three Cups' public house, where an excellent meal and bed were available. Sleep was a luxury not to be found with all night drinking and the creaking floorboards constantly plied by the clientele, but the transport would certainly be less comfortable.

They had finally sailed the following day with a favourable breeze but having cleared the harbour, they were forced to anchor as the fickle winds turned against them once more. It seemed that fate meant to delay them; they all feared that the great battle, which everyone was predicting, would be fought before they arrived.

The following morning, the wind swung at last and the passage to Ostend could begin in earnest. The Master had gauged the trip at some thirty-six hours; and sure enough, this morning, the third day at sea, the low sandy hills of Belgium had been visible low on the horizon. Having picked up a pilot, who jumped deftly from a small cutter that wafted briefly alongside, they had soon approached the harbour of Ostend where they had awaited the signal to enter, as the Master had informed Alexander that the harbour dried out at low tide.

The *Sabus* continued to glide through the harbour, with the few studding sails set, she was making little more than two knots, just enough to maintain steerage way. Outside on the open sea, this speed had seemed interminably slow,

Alexander thought, but in the harbour passing objects at close proximity, it suddenly felt much faster, almost too fast! Alexander watched the local inhabitants taking their stroll along the promenades for the air, all dressed in their Sunday best; they watched the ships with interest. In front of the *Sabus* were a number of jetties already thick with masts and Alexander could not see where the ship could berth, there did not seem to be any room.

Alexander ruminated on the adventures to come, he hoped that inexperienced as he was, that he could see them through their trials safely. He recalled his joining the artillery at the tender age of sixteen, when he had immediately been sent to help suppress the Irish rebellion of 1799. After that, apart from a very short and unsuccessful campaign in Buenos Aries in 1807, where General Whitelocke had been forced to capitulate, Alexander had always served in England. His professional abilities and knowledge was second to none, but he was aware from the warnings of his senior officers, that life on campaign was something that could not be taught in advance, he would learn by his mistakes, a comforting premise! Indeed, he was really only the Second Captain of G Troop, but his senior, Lieutenant Colonel Dickson, a Peninsula veteran and a favourite of Lord Wellington, was presently seconded to headquarters in command of the siege train.

Alexander surveyed his fellow officers, Lieutenants John Hincks; John Bretton; Henry Leathes a supernumerary officer awaiting appointment and who had seen a little of campaigning in Spain, and Richard Hichens the Assistant Surgeon. They were a fine set of young men and he was happy to know them as his 'band of brothers'. Then there was Robert Newland and William Ingilby; who were a totally different kettle of fish! Robert had only been promoted to Second Captain last year, reward for a successful term as a Lieutenant, serving for a considerable time on campaign in Spain. Ingilby had also served in Spain for many years. Alexander was clearly the senior Second Captain by time served in the rank, but Robert had much the greater experience of life on campaign, of which he never seemed to fail in reminding everyone, much to Alexander's irritation. Robert felt aggrieved at Alexander, he would normally have expected to be second in command of a troop with his promotion, not a third hand just because Lord Wellington had other work for Lieutenant Colonel Dickson. Their working relationship had so far been professional, but Newland regularly questioned Alexander's decisions and was supported by Ingilby, who continued to chase a Captaincy on Newland's coat tails. There was no love lost between him and them; this could become a major problem in the future.

Alexander's reverie was abruptly ended as the Master bellowed out a barrage of orders.

"Hard-a-larboard", caused the helmsman to haul the great wooden wheel fully over to the left, he puffed hard as he wound the wheel around a few times to its full extent even though helped by another seaman. Initially there was no movement of the ship, the bow still aimed straight up harbour, then, slowly, with an almost imperceptible movement, the bow started to creep to the left. The turn gained momentum and soon became obvious, but where were they going? There was only a beach to their left, were they turning back to sea? Soon the bow started to point directly toward the beach.

"Midships" brought the grunting helmsman into action again, turning the wheel back to the right. The speed of turn slowed and soon the ship settled on a course directly for the centre of the beach. Surely he wasn't going to run them aground!

"Brace yourselves" left them in no doubt, a loud scraping along the hull followed by a violent break in their momentum told them that they had beached.

Master Jeffreys turned with a smile, "Welcome to Ostend, Gentlemen". His job was done.

A noise ashore caused Alexander and his fellow officers to turn and look over the ship's side. A party of some twenty British sailors were running across the wet sands toward the ship, splashing through the shallow water and clambering up the wooden hull of the merchantman. Most were nearly naked but for tight pantaloons, besmirched in oil and dirt, soaked through. They were all young, well built and athletic, skin darkened by the sun, and eager for work. One of them, slightly older than the others and obviously in charge, said nothing, simply pointing out the horses and piles of leather equipment. The sailors simply commenced picking the stores up and hurling them over the ship's side onto the wet sand!

Alexander was dumbfounded, "Who is in charge here?" He demanded.

A voice behind him spoke firmly, "That would be me Sir, Captain Hill Royal Navy, at your service". Hill had a face ravaged by years before the mast, his face weathered and cracked by the salt air and sun. A few tufts of fine grey hairs above the ears were the only traces of a long forgotten head of hair. The crown of his scalp was clearly marked by a dark scar where a Frenchman's sword had failed to break his skull a few years before. His naval uniform had seen more glorious times, he was now retired from those 'wooden walls of old England' and forced to see out his days overseeing the landing of supplies for the army. He rarely had the joy of congenial company and held out his hand in friendship.

Alexander snubbed the proffered hand and haughtily

proceeded to lecture this ageing sailor, "This haste is madness Captain Hill, you must slow down the speed of disembarkation, to enable us to maintain the equipment" he demanded.

"Afraid not, can't help it Sir, Duke's orders are positive that no delay is to take place in unloading the troops as they arrive and the ships sent back again, so you must be out of here by dark". Hill was not a man to be trifled with.

Alexander became irritated with this officious man, "I urge you to stay your men, as the loss incurred in horses and equipment by such reckless haste is unnecessary, it is already three o'clock, we cannot sensibly disembark all before nightfall".

Captain Hill was unmoved, "Can't help it, no business of mine, Duke's orders are positive". He signalled to his team to continue. Soon the ship was a scene of utter confusion, horses being hoisted overboard and plunging into the water, then left to roam along the beach; equipment falling into the sea for the tide to claim and men clambering ashore as best they could.

Master Jeffreys had seen it all before, "Mister Mercer, they will not listen to you, but the tide is now full and will soon ebb, your men must reclaim their equipment before it floats out to sea".

Alexander ordered teams of gunners to recover the equipment and pile it further up the beach, the drivers attempted to catch and calm the jittery horses. He surveyed the scene, it was utter chaos, three other transports had now beached alongside and were rapidly spewing their cargoes onto the sands in similar fashion. Alexander watched in horror as the neighbouring ship discharged the beautifully kept chargers of a dragoon regiment unceremoniously into the cold sea, straight from the warm hold below. They were forced to wade or swim onto the beach;

Alexander shuddered at the loss of condition to these fine horses.

The beach itself was bedlam, nervous horses trotting all about in confusion. Dragoons chasing across the sands in an attempt to catch them looked a sight with great boots and spurs tripping them up. Soldiers and artillerymen dragged packs and equipment out of the water and piled them on the beach. Many women had travelled with their men-folk; they sat forlornly on piles of old trunks, with young children and dogs scampering around them, just waiting for someone to offer aid. The locals did not help the confusion, the local merchants crowded the area with little stalls offering their wares to the 'Ingleesh solljer', bakers with their breads and cakes; butchers with scrawny looking chickens and great ham joints; young lads hawking lemonade or beer; fine ladies offering beautifully worked lace items for their loved ones at home and a large number of not so fine ladies that offered company to those that could pay! Alexander had seen nothing like it and gawped at the madness for some hours in total disbelief.

Turning to Mister Jeffreys he asked, "How much longer do we have before the flood tide returns Sir, as they are still removing the horses".

Mister Jeffreys answered immediately "We have about four hours before the flood tide sets in properly, Mister Mercer".

Turning to the obstinate naval officer, Alexander shouted, "Then may I suggest Captain Hill, that it is impossible to complete disembarkation this day, for we have no more than a few hours, which cannot be sufficient to complete the horses and all the wagons as well. Indeed if we attempt to set the wagons down they are more likely to sink into the sand or be swept out to sea. What do you think Lord Wellington would have to say of that, Sir?"

Captain Hill was forced to submit to this argument, from this impudent officer, but did so with extreme bad grace. He ordered his team to finish all but the carriages that day and bid them speed this process to get quit of the damned ship! With little need for the hint, his men proceeded to complete the jettisoning of equipment with all haste and it now became a mass of knotted leather straps on the tide line.

Somehow a young man had wormed his way up alongside the artillery officers, he was dressed in a faded green livery jacket and ragged trousers, topped with a glazed black bicorn. He was about five foot six in height, a healthy youth with a very beautiful elfin face.

He spoke in French. "Gentlemen, may I crave your attention", this succeeded in stopping their discussions and making them listen. He continued in good French, "My name is Karl, I am twenty years of age, I have served in France with the famous General Vandamme for seven years, including marching to Moscow with him. Unfortunately, the General was unable to maintain my employment after the retreat; I was left in Saxony to make my own way back to my native Flanders. I wish to enter the service of a gallant English officer, as I can be very useful. I speak Dutch, French, German, Russian and Italian fluently and I speak Spanish tolerably, I am a faithful servant, I cook, I cut hair and I sing!"

They all laughed.

John Hincks turned to Alexander, "What do you think, do you wish to employ him?"

Alexander declined, "He sounds a good catch but I have Millward."

Karl interjected with a wry smile and a wink, "My master never goes hungry, either!"

Again they laughed, Henry Leathes stepped forward,

"Come Karl, you may work for me as I starved too often in Spain!"

Karl was soon set to work, Henry trusted that he would live up to his promises, in the evening he would be able to entertain the mess with his exquisite singing, he would hopefully be a very useful find.

Ordering his officers to organise recovery of the stores, Alexander decided to withdraw to the town, seeking his orders, but more so to escape the continuing madness.

With a little good fortune, Alexander identified his horse, saddle and a bridle. Mounting 'Cossack', he edged her through the throng and into the winding streets of Ostend, Bal scampered alongside. The crush was a little easier here but everywhere there were wagons and canon parked with drivers lolling over the barrels of the guns as if they hadn't a care in the world. After a very considerable time and with extreme difficulty, he eventually found the abode of the Town Major, in the Place d'Armee, a handsome square forming the heart of Ostend. Lieutenant Colonel Gregory of His Majesty's Forty Fourth Regiment of Foot seemed to have little idea why Alexander should seek him out and was irritated by his intrusion.

"I have no orders for you, nor anybody else, Sir. The only order I possess is for all units to march on to Ghent immediately. I am not able to furnish anything more, good day", and with that he closed the door in Alexander's face.

Alexander turned his horse back toward the beach front with no idea what he was to do for his men that night.

The words "Alexander, good to see you!" broke his train of thought; he looked around not recognising the voice immediately, and then beamed as he was confronted by an old acquaintance.

"Percy, perhaps you could advise me what to do."

Major Percy Drummond, a dashing young man in his

artillery uniform and sporting a black moustache twisted up to form fine points, soon eased his concerns. Percy was in charge of the Reserve Artillery of the Army, he was experienced of campaigns in Belgium and his advice would be readily accepted.

"There are some large sheds attached to a saw mill one mile along this road, just beyond the town barriers. My unit used it last night but we are now on route to Ghent. I would thoroughly recommend you take advantage of its shelter tonight. The shed will accommodate your troop with ease. I fear we will shortly suffer ill weather." He pointed skyward, the thick black cloud approaching from seaward on a rising breeze spoke of stormy weather; it was time to hurry back to the beach to organise his troop.

The view on his return was far from encouraging, equipment still strewn far and wide and pandemonium reigning throughout. Alexander took charge, ordering his men to reclaim the remaining bridles and saddles from the voracious sea. The flood tide was now rising fast and what was not collected rapidly would be lost forever. The skies darkened ominously, the winds rose, causing an eerie screeching and groaning in the masts of the myriad vessels in the harbour. Suddenly the skies broke, initially droplets the size of marbles fell spasmodically, then a huge fork of lightning lit the whole arena, which was closely followed by a cataclysmic crash of thunder and the floodgates opened fully. Alexander had never seen rain like it, they were drenched to the skin within seconds, vision was reduced dramatically but they had to continue. Somebody had the bright idea of borrowing storm lanterns from the nearby ships. By the lanterns glare they continued to search for missing pieces of equipment well into the evening. The lightning and rain added to the scene of madness, Alexander thought it reminded him of the views of purgatory and hell printed in the Bibles he had seen as a small child.

Eventually, all but two horses were accounted for and the last sweep of the beach had not revealed any other equipment lying on the sands. It was time to rest for the night, Alexander called out above the noise of the rain and the now less frequent thunder, for the troop to form up on the roadway and harness the horses. The tangled mess of harnesses took an age to sort and it was nearly midnight before they were ready to march to their shelter.

Alexander led the way, leaning forward on the neck of Cossack, into the wind and rain, his one hand holding the reins, the other resting on his helmet, which seemed to have no intention of staying upon his head. In the darkness, the way to the sheds was extremely difficult to find, everything had looked very different in daylight. Two men were stationed in front with a storm lantern each, to check the way and act as beacons for those following. Slowly they edged their way through the narrow streets of low brick houses that constituted Ostend. They passed across a rickety wooden bridge over what looked like a canal in the dark. They took their time, each team of horses passing over before the next started to cross; the bridge creaked and groaned with each effort. As the third team crossed there was an almighty crack and suddenly the bridge gave way in the centre. Horses and men plummeted into the darkness; the shouts and cries brought everyone running. Luckily, the canal was little more than a storm drain and as yet had only a little water flowing through it, but what it lacked in water it made up for with a great depth of black mud! Once it was quickly established that by a miracle no horse or man had been injured, the rest burst out laughing. Even the men struggling to extricate themselves and their horses from the putrid bog smiled, they had to laugh or go mad!

A patrol of Belgian soldiers policing the streets came upon the scene and with a smattering of French from Alexander they were eventually able to understand the need to find another way over this ditch for the remainder of the troop. They indicated another route and Alexander had them proceed with the tail of the troop toward a nearby stone bridge they knew of.

Once reunited, Alexander led his party on through the winding, dark, unlit streets, the only noise being the splashing of the rain, the rhythmic drumming of the horses' hooves on the cobbled streets and the clanking of metal scabbards on their legs as they rode along. They passed cafes still open, the lights on and groups of Belgians drinking and laughing in the warmth, it just brought their own miserable plight into sharp contrast. They were drenched to the skin, cold, famished and lost; the glory of campaigning seemed a distant dream now. The final insult came when they arrived at the outer barrier of Ostend, manned by a belligerent Belgian officer and a handful of troops.

He spoke in broken English "Dere gate is closed until de morning."

Alexander had lost all patience and glowered at this irksome official. "Open it, or we will push it aside."

The officer had no intention of agreeing so easily, but Alexander's obvious anger and his hand moving to grasp the hilt of his sword made the Belgian think again. He ordered his men to raise the barrier and the troop proceeded out into the countryside.

Here the ground was extremely slippery, the road seemed to run along the ridge of a dyke and the horses struggled to maintain a firm footing in the dark. Deep shadows either side of the road indicated that the banks fell away steeply, allowing no room for error. They proceeded gingerly, every few yards a horse would stumble and the column had to stop and wait. The road seemed to go on forever, they were progressing so slowly it might take all night. Job Price the Farrier brought worse news, "The oil is running out in the storm lamps, Sir."

Alexander despaired of finding the sheds, so he ordered the men to enquire the way at a house, shrouded in darkness hard by the road. The occupants took an age to wake despite the violent rapping at their door and it took a lot of persuasion to get them to answer at such a time of night. Eventually however, the door opened a crack and an old man thrust his head topped with a dirty nightcap around the edge of the door and informed them that they had come too far, the sheds were a mile back! The chill spring wind and freezing rain continued unabated. The cold seeped into their very bones; they hadn't known misery like it.

They trudged back, slipping and sliding again until more careful reconnaissance discovered a short lane leading off to the barns. At two o'clock in the morning they finally arrived and pulled back the huge door to reveal a large, spacious, dry, welcoming haven brimming with sweet smelling straw. The look of pleasure on the men's faces as they surveyed the scene before them would rival the happiness at finding Shangri la itself.

The horses were lined along one side of the barn, their saddles removed and a mountain of hay laid for their feeding. The men then lay on the remaining straw along the opposite face, soon all were snug and warm despite their saturated clothing and their troubles seemed a far distant memory.

Henry Leathes strode over to the adjoining house and woke the occupants by repeated knocking at the door. He managed to explain whom they were and that they would only use the barn that night. The house was that of a miller and his wife, they were more than happy to accommodate them and invited the officers into their humble abode rather than use the barn with the men.

Alexander eagerly agreed and crossed the yard to enjoy the hospitality of the miller. As they entered the cottage, the rich aroma of coffee brewing on the stove miraculously revived their worn frames. Having been restored by the steaming coffee and black bread, they were offered accommodation. Alexander declined the generous offer of a bed for the night; the thought of having to put those sodden clothes back on cold in the morning was more than he could bear. He plumped for a large high backed wooden chair in front of the roaring fire, where he could slowly steam himself dry. Only William Ingilby and Richard Hichens took up their kind offer of beds. The others sat around the fire and chatted for a while with their hosts in broken Flemish and sign language, but sleep finally stole up on them all, Alexander smiled faintly, in a perverse way he wouldn't forget today in a hurry!

THE CALL

Lieutenant Colonel Sir Andrew Barnard rode purposefully towards the silent ranks of the First Battalion of the Ninety Fifth Regiment, acknowledging the salutes of his officers as he passed. Removing his bicorn hat for a moment to run his chubby fingers through the thinning remains of his tightly curled quaff, he ran through his speech one last time. He knew that news of the messenger's arrival would have already swept like wild fire around the camp, and that there was an air of great expectancy. The troops had been awaiting orders to sail to Canada for weeks. The American's had taken the opportunity of attempting to wrest the Canadian Provinces from King George whilst the British Army was fully engaged in the life and death struggle with Napoleon's armies in Europe. However, three years of desultory conflict amongst the forests of the border territories, had failed to provide any clear victor despite the American's numerical advantages. Now that the war with Napoleon was ended, Wellington's veterans could be provided to finally defeat these upstart colonials and save Canada. This must be the order to embark at last.

Sir Andrew rode ramrod straight in the saddle despite the constant dull ache in his side, he was immensely proud to command this battalion in their distinctive green uniforms. He had shared their triumphs and sufferings throughout the late campaigns in Spain and Portugal, indeed they had seen him suffer with them. He still remembered their anguished faces and genuine concern for him when he had been shot through the lungs and then fallen from his horse upon his sword hilt. He had thought that he was dying as he had lain there, the acute pain searing through his mangled body, struggling to catch a breath as he coughed up blood. Lieutenant George Simmons had been first on the scene and had turned him on to his back; the wound had been to his left side smashing his ribs; indeed his lungs were clearly visible through the gore. George had some medical knowledge, having served as an Assistant Surgeon with the Royal South Lincolnshire Militia for four years before gaining his commission in the 95th and he viewed his patient with a professional eye. The hole in his chest had been large enough for George to insert the whole of his hand into the wound. There had been so much blood, that he had thought that there could not be much left in his veins and that he must surely die. His mouth was constantly filling with blood; eventually after some difficulty, George had managed to stem the bleeding, so that he could breathe more easily. Sir Andrew had looked up at him and asked, "George, speak the truth, have you ever seen anyone survive such a serious wound?"

"Of course I have, Mr Burke will soon have you sorted" he had lied. George had known that there was little chance of him lasting the hour. However, Simmons had ordered two men to carry him to the field hospital a little way behind the regiment for the surgeons to do their best. Following a long recuperation in France constantly being looked after by a devoted George Simmons, and then in England, he had eventually proven the surgeons wrong and recovered. He had gladly returned to duty when the battalion arrived home and they had welcomed him back heartily.

A short tug on the reigns compelled his faithful steed to halt in front of the six hundred men formed on the parade ground and pulling himself high in the saddle he summoned all his reserves to project his voice to the straining ears.

"The King has work for us again lads, but it is not to be Canada." The surprise on the faces of his audience was all too palpable and their sharp intake of breath was clearly audible. He would not keep them in suspense for long however. "The Ogre has slipped his cage. General Bonaparte is back in Paris, he has overthrown the legitimate government of the King of France and we are to join Lord Wellington in Brussels immediately!"

A great cheer arose; this was better news than they had ever dreamed of.

A smile escaped from the stern face of Sir Andrew, "Let's show Johnny Crapeau how to dance on the battlefield again, and this time we will let old 'Boney' himself watch".

'General Bonaparte' George Simmons mused, only the British still refused to recognise Napoleon Bonaparte's right to the title of Emperor of France with which he had proclaimed himself eleven years ago in 1804. He had controlled France since 1799, had completely rewritten their ancient laws and customs; overhauled the public finances and created an awesome military machine particularly on land. With these soldiers, Napoleon had destroyed all the massed armies of the ancient royal houses of Europe. They had fought against him in a vain struggle to halt France's revolutionary ideas spreading throughout mainland Europe. Victory had followed stunning victory for the ruthlessly ambitious Napoleon; he placed his relatives or his marshal's on the thrones that he had won or to the kingdoms that he invented out of the chaotic system of princedoms and free states that had plagued medieval European politics. His reforming zeal to eradicate the suffocating ancient feudal rights of these states had brought him huge support from the chattering classes of Europe. However, experience of French occupation had altered their views radically as the coffers of these provinces had been systematically looted to fund Napoleon's insatiable demands. The reforms that had released the under-classes from feudal tyranny had also freed their minds and they strove for a new order. Napoleon had unwittingly sewn the seeds of his own downfall by awakening feelings of nationhood. Underground movements had formed, working for a united Germany, Poland or Italy. Open rebellion had broken out in Spain in 1808 and the Spanish guerrillas were ably aided by Britain's only army, led by Wellington, eventually driving the French from the Peninsular. When Napoleon finally overreached himself and left the flower of his army frozen to death in the wastes of Russia, open revolt had broken out everywhere. The genius of Napoleon had miraculously manufactured a new army from seemingly nothing and held off the inevitable for a further two years, but eventually the combined forces of all Europe had finally led to the loss of Paris and Napoleon was 'persuaded' to abdicate by his Marshals. Napoleon was banished to the tiny Italian island of Elba. The war weary peasantry of France welcomed a return to monarchy, but more especially to peace. Napoleon was now so unpopular that he had to travel incognito to his new kingdom, constantly in fear for his life.

The Bourbon family had learnt nothing whilst in exile and rapidly lost the support of the populace as they cavalierly removed lands from those that had legitimately purchased property after the revolution, returning it to the nobles that had loyally fled with the King. These sycophants were preferred over the able ministers of government that Napoleon had placed in office; even the army became disgruntled at the advancement of royalist officers that had seen the war out from the drawing rooms of London, placed over the experienced officers that had fought bravely for Napoleon in every quarter of Europe. After a year in Elba, recognising the exact moment to act, Napoleon had landed in France with a mere eight hundred of his guard, but within two weeks he was back in control of France at Paris, the King having fled again. The allied powers were assembled at Vienna to redraw the map of Europe that Napoleon had torn to shreds. News of Napoleon's return caused the dissolution of the Congress with the agreement that all the countries of Europe would wage war upon Napoleon until he was defeated again. The declaration of war was specifically against the person of Napoleon and not the French nation, a particular honour to his genius. The armies of Prussia under Marshal Blucher and the conglomerate army of Dutch, Belgian, British and Germans under Lord Wellington sat upon the northern frontiers of France. The ponderous Austrians would take weeks to mobilise in the south and the fearsome Russians would take months to march from their homeland. It was therefore arranged that Wellington and Blucher would commence the invasion of France.

Reinforcements were to be forwarded to Belgium as quickly as possible to strengthen the British contingent of Lord Wellington's army. The men of the First Battalion of the 95th Regiment were delighted to rejoin their old commander. For five hard years they had fought throughout Portugal, Spain and Southern France under his leadership. He had always looked after their stomachs, never wasted their lives and best of all he always won! They were always confident of victory with Wellington.

Major Alexander Cameron, a tall slightly built man with a great quaff of jet-black hair topping a long dour face, stepped forward to order the battalion to dismiss. He had also been with the battalion throughout Spain, his thigh bore the marks of a musket ball gouging a furrow in the muscle at the battle of Vitoria and he still nursed a weakness on his left side where a French bayonet had nearly finished off him in Egypt, back in 1801.

The battalion roared their approval as Sir Andrew turned his horse slowly and rode off towards the stable block to settle his horse. Passing his Officers still drawn up in line on the edge of the parade ground, he snapped, "Gentlemen, have everything prepared to move at a moments notice."

Lieutenant George Simmons, a stocky Yorkshireman, looked on the ranks of the 1st Battalion 95th Rifles with pride and felt the emotion well up within. Together with many of these men he could see before him, he had fought for five long hard years, across Portugal and Spain; many showed the horrible scars collected during those tough fights. However, they had never faced the greatly admired Napoleon in person before, they held a grudging professional respect for him, but now they would see how they measured against his best. The boyish looks of the raw recruits intermixed with the veterans suddenly shook his confidence. Many had died in Spain and many more had finished with fighting when they came home in 1814, so the ranks were swelled with fresh faced innocents who had never experienced a shot in anger, could they cope with what was to come?

Scanning the ranks of the formed companies he picked out a few well known faces, Private Costello, a portly

Irishman, who had survived the terrible carnage of Badajoz, and became rich at the battle of Vitoria having found a sack full of gold coins in the French wagons abandoned after the battle; James Burke, a tall muscular man who had survived all the great sieges of the Spanish war and Sergeant Robert Fairfoot, a tall stocky man and with a presence that made him stand out in the crowd, he was a greatly experienced non commissioned officer, that kept the men fully in check. With men like these one could go anywhere and do anything, the new boys would learn fast or die.

Looking around at the officers, Captains Jonathan Leach the senior captain, Edward Chawner and William Johnstone a tough Scot, 'Willie' to his friends; Lieutenants Allen Stewart a giant of a Scotsman who had been slightly wounded at Badajoz; Orlando Felix and John Gardiner both other casualties of Badajoz; John Fitzmaurice who with only two other men had captured a cannon and its horse team near Vitoria and John Stilwell, 'Scamp' to his fellow officers, as he was rumoured to be an illegitimate son of the Duke of York, but then again who wasn't? They all stood out as his friends and brothers in arms throughout Spain. Their worn, lined parchment skin and sunken cheeks spoke of years of hardship and endeavour beneath a harsh Iberian sun. Many walked with pronounced limps from old injuries poorly healed but they stood proud and regarded them as badges of courage.

Even George walked with a severe limp, he had been shot in his fleshy thigh at the River Coa but the one he remembered vividly was the musket ball that fractured his right knee cap in 1814, he still felt a niggle there to this day and couldn't bend it properly.

The following days passed quickly in preparing the battalion for embarkation to Belgium. The men packed their haversacks, received rations for three days ahead and the tents, rifle ammunition, camp kettles and sundry other items which were brought out of stores, checked and packed.

The officers had their bâtmen prepare their travelling equipment including dinner services, tents and private stocks of fine foods and wines. One didn't know how long this war was to last, the previous conflict was supposed to last only a couple of years but had raged virtually non stop for twenty one years, with a phoney peace for a year half way through it. When fighting, they would have to travel light, leaving their supplies far behind in the baggage. Lord Wellington was very particular on this subject, woe be the man caught with his baggage wagon at the front! However, there would be plenty of time between the fighting, when the tedium of camp life was only to be eased by the enjoyment of fine foods and wines shared with the ladies of local society. Some officers even took their own cooks with them on campaign, many wives would insist on coming too!

The officers spent their time concluding outstanding business, ensuring their estates were in order, wills written and most importantly, horses purchased. Officers were required to purchase their own horses both to ride themselves and to carry their wives, servants and baggage, a very expensive luxury, which some less affluent officers would have to forego. A good riding horse could cost thirty guineas or more and a mere baggage horse, fifteen guineas. This was a huge amount of money when a Captain earned 5 shillings and 8 pence per day.

The old hands like Edward Costello started lightening the load to be carried, just as they had done in Spain. He explained to the young lads in his mess in his thick Irish brogue, "The army in their wisdom wishes to supply youze with everything you will ever need. Well the army tinks we is some kind of jackass, what they gives you will weigh you into the ground. In this here knapsack you are to carry, two shirts, two pair of stockings, a pair of shoes wid a spare sole and heel, t'ree brushes, blacking powder, a soapbox and spare trousers. You are also to carry your mess tins, canteen, greatcoat, powder flasks, ball bag, mallet, belt and pouch with fifty balls in it, a sword and roifle. That lot weighs eighty bloody pounds! On the march in the midday sun it feels loike a bloody hundred and eighty! Take it from me boys, have all your kit roight at muster, but in Belgium get rid of sum. Your roifle and stuff wull save your skins but bugger clean shirts and shoes, sell them lads and buy a drink on King George!"

Tom Crawley concurred, "Aye lads he's roight, listen to us an youze moight live to tell the tale."

Finally it was time to go; the packet was waiting in the harbour to embark the battalion. Lieutenant Colonel Sir Andrew Barnard watched his First Battalion parade ready for marching down the steep hill from the barracks at Dover Castle to the harbour well below. Five companies were to go to Belgium, each consisting of ninety-five men, every company allocated a Captain and two Lieutenants, they were to proceed directly to Brussels to join Lord Wellington's forces.

He surveyed his men with pride; they were not men of great stature, many being as short as five foot two inches, with the odd six foot giant looking ungainly and out of place, peppered through the companies. But his regiment was not about tall men in red uniforms with great towering helmets and plumes to increase the illusion of height, who must stand ramrod still and fight in rigid units unthinking and mechanically. To him, soldiers of the line just stood like skittles waiting to be bowled over and were expected to stand and die without a sound. He had come through that system and saw the merits of the rigid wall of red jackets which struck awe into the enemy, but he now preferred the freedom of light infantry tactics, where every man dodged and darted to obtain cover and fire on the enemy formations. He encouraged the men to think independently and take advantage of their surroundings, to use their intelligence.

It was an imposing sight, five hundred men all in fine new uniforms, dark green with black equipment and belts, a black hat, whose only adornment was a silver hunting horn badge with 95 above it, all topped with a green tuft. This was the first uniform in the British army designed for concealment. The men were quietly proud as well; they regarded themselves as the best in the army and had proved so in Spain, they would not let Wellington down this time either.

Sir Andrew turned to Major Alexander Cameron, "Very well Major, march them off"

The order given, the battalion marched along the precipitous road winding down from the castle to the harbour. The townsfolk lined the road to see them off, they cheered, some clapped, young ladies ran into the ranks to kiss and say farewell to their sweethearts, all was gaiety. The band played 'See the Conquering Hero come', what a send off. Some of the wives followed, many with children, determined to follow their man and share his hardships, after all, how were they to live with their man in foreign lands? They couldn't rely on the men sending money home regularly and the only other alternatives were going home to mother or the workhouse.

At the dockside, the men looked at the great forest of huge bare masts, ships packed in so tightly that it was said you could walk across the harbour without getting wet! The packet *Wensleydale* destined to transport the battalion to Belgium was waiting. The crew hurried the men and baggage aboard to catch the evening tide.

One man was missing; imminent embarkation for Belgium had not been to his liking. During the previous night at Dover barracks, the bugler, Private Thomas Foote, had deserted. The lads were singularly unimpressed; the coward had better not get caught, because no matter what punishment the Colonel ordered, it would be infinitely preferable to the punishment that would be meted out in the barrack room!

Alongside the band, who stayed on the quay stood the small cadre of staff remaining at the battalion depot, those new recruits too raw to send, the training staff, the sick and the lame. George Simmons turned to this group and approached the officer in charge. He held out his hand to shake his, but the officer grabbed the hand very firmly, pulling George towards him and embracing him warmly.

"Goodbye Joseph, I'm sorry that you can't come, but the family couldn't bear losing us both, they at least know that you're safe" George stammered.

"Take care big brother, I'll follow soon enough, just make sure you leave some Frenchmen for me." Joseph was the younger brother by some three years, but had served two years in Spain with George in the 95th. This time he was to remain to run the depot and send on drafts of replacement men as their training was completed. The Simmons's were a military family, another brother Maud was serving in Ireland with the 34th Regiment. Perhaps they would all meet up again on campaign as they had done frequently in Spain.

George broke away and boarded swiftly, it would not do to show any emotion in front of the men.

It was a beautiful spring evening with light winds on 25

April 1815, when the *Wensleydale* loosed her topsails and edged slowly out of Dover harbour. What did the next few months have in store? George pondered as he watched the white cliffs slowly disappear from the stern rail.

Ten hours with a favourable wind, the Captain had said! George thought about this twenty-four hours into the voyage as he vomited over the lee side for what seemed like the fortieth time. The wind had swung easterly, blowing off the Belgian coast and the ship could make little headway despite tacking back and forth for hours. The wind had got stronger and waves higher, most of the soldiers were seasick. He had learnt to use the lee side the hard way, the sailors thought it was hilarious to watch the soldiers vomit into the wind and see them spattered with their own bile, how they laughed! Many soldiers lined the rails; some too ill to move, vomited where they lay in the hold, where the near five hundred men had sought shelter from the storm overhead. The stench was awful, men who had faced death and laughed, now lay moaning like babies imploring somebody to put them out of their misery. Finally as dawn broke on the 27 April they could see the coastline of Belgium and soon got into the lee of the land, the seas smoothed, the ship ceased lurching and the men started to recover. Many came on deck to escape the foul odour below and were surprised and overjoyed to see the church spires and houses of Belgian towns. That morning they berthed at Ostend and the men wearily climbed ashore, some kissing mother earth at the sheer joy of arriving safely on terra firmae once more.

Johnny Kincaid a tall dour Scotsman with a great flat nose that ruined his features, was out shooting woodcock with his trusty retriever Alex, when Munroe, one of the servants rushed across the moor towards him.

"Munroe out of the way I nearly bloody shot you man."

Munroe gasped for breath.

"Sir, there is a letter from the regiment, marked 'With Dispatch'"

Johnny took the letter and opened it eagerly, reading anxiously,

'On route for Brussels, to join Lord Wellington, make all haste to join us. Captain Leach'

Jonathan as senior Captain had obviously been given the task of informing the men and officers away from the battalion of the turn of events. He must hurry or he might miss all the fun. He had been given permission for leave to recover from another weakening bout of Walcheren fever; like all those others that had come back from that pestilential pit, he just couldn't shake the flux off. Every so often he would collapse with the shakes and high temperatures, it would last for weeks, it had hit him again when he returned from France. Would he ever be rid of it? Mind you, thousands had succumbed to it permanently, he was a lucky survivor but it kept on trying to get him!

"Munroe pack my campaign chest quickly, I must leave tonight."

Johnny stood for a while pondering having to fight again; his fingers unconsciously felt the scar line across the top of his scalp. At Foz de Aronce a musket ball had entered his hat and cut a furrow across his head without damaging the skull at all. Doc had said he was lucky he hadn't been half an inch taller! He still didn't remember the incident at all; everyone told him that they had thought he was dead for sure, as he had fallen as if a sledgehammer had felled him. He had suffered from a severe headache for a week after, but that was all, he hoped his good luck would see him through again.

His family seat in Stirlingshire was a long way from the scene of action. How to get to Brussels quickly?

On returning to the house, Johnny discovered a notice in the 'Edinburgh Correspondent' that a ship was sailing from Leith to Rotterdam that evening. A messenger was despatched instantly to gain passage and he followed hard behind. The courier met him on the road, returning to confirm his passage and indicated that the ship's master had adequate provisions, which he could partake of. This was a relief, as it would save precious time, not having to obtain victuals before sailing.

Johnny arrived at Leith docks in the shadow of Edinburgh Castle at six o'clock in the evening and was shown the berth of the *Swallow* by an old lame seaman for sixpence.

On boarding he was met by the master, one Thomas Bryce, a rough and ready seaman, made comical by his attempts to speak in a refined accent. "Welcome Mr Kincaid, we will sail within the hour, James here will show you to your berth" indicating a black sailor standing to his left.

"Thank you Mr Bryce, how long may we expect for the passage?"

"With a fair wind we should reach Rotterdam in three days, but the wind doesn't look fair tonight."

Ten days later, the coast of Holland was just in sight! The weather had been awful and winds contrary throughout. But the worst of it, was that the 'adequate rations', had consisted of half a lamb and a few cabbages, to be consumed with five gallons of whisky! Johnny had forced some of this repulsive slop down his throat each day, washing it down with the whisky to kill the foul taste. Luckily he was a good sailor and was never seasick; he was just bored of the monotonous swaying of the ship, the regular commands of the master for tacking or calling for a depth being the only changes in routine.

Suddenly there was a horrendous grinding noise from below followed by the sounds of splintering wood, a solid jolt brought the ship's movement to a sudden halt and Johnny was hurled bodily from his bunk to the floor, hurting his shoulder slightly in the fall.

"What the devil was that?" he shouted

"Nothing to be a feared of Sir, we just run aground" came the nonchalant reply of Mr Bryce.

"Are we sinking?" enquired Johnny.

"Not to fret Sir, we does this pretty regular, ships have been known to be lost on these sand banks, but we didn't hit too 'ard we can float off at high tide."

Johnny was not reassured especially when Mr Bryce had a flaming row with the Dutch Pilot who came out to get them into Den Haag safely; he wanted double pay because the ship could be holed and sinking. Mr Bryce obviously lost the argument as the pilot stayed onboard and guided the ship into a local harbour for repairs. Mr Bryce retired below, he sat in his cabin pouring whiskies at a rate of knots, the repair fees would be more than the profit from this trip.

Once the ship berthed alongside, Johnny left immediately while the master was comatose drunk and hired a small boat that engaged to get him up river to Rotterdam in six hours. Previous promises should have made him wary, but no. They set off immediately and the journey lasted over twenty-four hours. There was no food in the open boat and mid morning hunger pangs took over from all other considerations. Johnny forced the boatman to land and enter a nearby house to beg for a morsel. He returned after what seemed an age with some coffee, the only sustenance they could spare. He gladly received this small offering but eventually forced the boatman alongside at an inn, where he gained a full meal. The innkeeper took pity upon Johnny; he advised him to seek an alternative method of reaching Rotterdam and saw him on his way to Brussels via Antwerp on the post chaise. The journey took two days, Johnny hated being constantly jostled by the rough roads in a poorly sprung post coach, but this was a huge improvement over the slow travel he had endured at sea. On arrival in the fair City of Brussels, he fought his way through the throngs as he sought his battalion's billets.

The battalion had transferred immediately from the packet at Ostend into small coastal craft called Schuyts, large open boats with a single mast carrying lateen sails. They formed a leisurely procession up the wide canal to Bruges, each boat pulled by a team of horses, which walked along the bank. Sergeant Robert Fairfoot, lounged at the rear of his barge enjoying the spring sunshine and listening to the lads joking time away. Fairfoot was a tall man, strongly built and well respected by both officers and men, he looked after the boys and they looked after him, it was a brotherhood. He surveyed the faces of the men in the barge, his eyes set on Edward Costello, 'Ned' to all his friends, he had a portly but muscular frame, he was intelligent, quick and rich! He looked on Ned kindly, as he had saved Robert from a court martial and the 'cat' back in 1813, without looking for favours in return. Robert still remembered that awful day with a chill, despite the warm sunshine he was basking in. He had just been made paymaster for his company and promptly lost thirty-one pounds, how could he get out of this mess? The army would never believe he'd just lost it. Ned had just walked up having heard through the battalion telegraph, and offered him the money to cover the loss. He had just found a bag in the French baggage after the wonderful victory of Vitoria, opening it he had discovered one thousand gold coins, more than he could earn in two lifetimes! Robert had kept a general lookout for Ned ever since and would watch his back this time round again. He was also very useful as Ned was an ex cobbler, issue boots wore out fast on long marches!

Robert Fairfoot's eyes next rested on a quiet, very thoughtful figure sat in the corner, keeping out of the general conversation. Thomas Maher was his name; he'd been captured at Barba del Puerco back in 1811 and had spent nearly four years in a French prisoner of war camp at Verdun. He'd had very severe treatment and had come back with a dark brooding depressive mood about him; everyone knew that this sultriness could explode into uncontrollable rage without warning at any time.

Johnny Castles was next to him, the great tub of lard! Mind you he had moved like a whippet back at Arcangues when he and a few others had been forced to rush back from their forward post where they had been enjoying their gin ration too much, as the froggies advanced. He surely ran faster than a cheetah that day and had never touched a drop of grog since!

Finally there was Thomas Grindley; he had disappeared one night at Arcangues when on sentry duty. The following morning he was returned by the French, completely drunk! Throughout the last war the two warring sides had not fought when in camp. Opposing sentries regularly warned each other of imminent attacks so they could move out of the way, a few useless deaths were to be avoided. Lord Wellington forbade fraternisation with the enemy but it still happened. The lads had food, the French usually had brandy, and so both sides regularly shared their goods across the front line. Grindley's escapade was hushed up and to be fair to the French, they had not attempted to take advantage of the situation.

These men were a bunch of rogues, but they were his rogues and they couldn't half fight.

George Simmons sat beside Robert; he meditated on the huge number of Irishmen in the regiment, bloody boggies everywhere! He had to give them their due though, although they never stopped drinking and cursing and brawling at every opportunity, they certainly could fight in battle and he was glad they were on his side. He still couldn't help wishing they used more surnames, in this battalion of five hundred men there were; four Kitchen's, three John Connor's, there were even three John Murphy's in the same company, it was bloody confusing! There was a strong contingent of Welshmen as well, there was Moses Blythero and John Davis from North Wales, Sergeant Thomas Morgan from a small town called Cardiff and Thomas Edwards from Swansea, both on the great post road to Milford Haven. Scotsmen abounded as well, indeed many of the officers were Scottish, and indeed barely more than a quarter of the battalion were English.

It started to grow dark as the barges neared the medieval town of Bruges. The boatmen stopped for the night and the men climbed out onto the towpath and quays beside the low artisan's houses intermingled with the towering medieval warehouses and town houses of the rich, with their steep stepped gables. They soon lit fires to cook up their rations of beef and brew their tea. The next morning they continued down a branch canal to the city of Ghent, where they parted with the barges, they would have to walk the rest of the way to Brussels.

They were to stay ten days in Ghent, but they would be busy, Lord Wellington was coming to review the regiment and God help them if he wasn't happy with what he saw.

There was however a little time to look around the beautiful Flemish city, some admiring the tall medieval buildings, more admiring the local ladies and fine beers.

The Officers and men were billeted on the local population, each house usually being allocated two men. Officers got the billets with the rich merchants and enjoyed a very good living. The men received their rations, which they gave to the householders to cook; often they would trade some of their rations for the families to use as their meal in exchange for more grog.

On the 30th April, the officers assembled and proceeded to the monstrously gothic façade of the fourteenth century great Stadhuis to be introduced to Louis XVIII, the deposed King of France, no less. The recently displaced King, wanted to meet the gallant British Riflemen and wish them good fortune in their efforts to restore him to his throne. They had heard stories of his overbearing ways, his fat gouty features and his inability to comprehend the needs of his people. This was said to be the main reason why Napoleon had been welcomed back so overwhelmingly. This made sense, as they had seen in Southern France in 1814 that the French were then heartily sick of war and 'Boney' and they could think of no other reason why these people had welcomed Napoleon back so enthusiastically within a year. However, Louis in fact, was charm itself, personable, interested in each of them and they were well pleased with him. Discussing everything afterwards they agreed that it must have been his government that was uncaring and if only Louis would show himself more to the people, maybe Napoleon wouldn't have come back so easily.

On 7th of May, the fatal day had arrived, Review day. Everyone was up and preparing the final touches to their kit at dawn. The order was given to form up at eight o'clock;

the battalion marched on to the square dominated by its Stadhuis and merchant's houses, where Lord Wellington, 'The Duke', was due to inspect them. At precisely nine, a small group of officers on horseback entered the square and Lieutenant Colonel Barnard rode over to report his battalion ready for inspection. There he was, Wellington with his bloody great hooked nose! You could spot that nose a mile off! The old hands knew him well from Spain where he always seemed to be everywhere at once. He was always a good omen to them, he was not a wasteful General with his most important asset, them! He made sure they were fed and didn't get them killed for little reason, like some other rash Generals. He was still happy to attack when he could win such as Salamanca; that was some victory that was. With him around, they were confident that everything would be all right and of course what was even better, he always won! The raw recruits stared at him in awe; so this was the great man! They wouldn't forget this day or that nose ever! But, it had taken a while to work out who he was; all the other officers were wearing their best crimson jackets, covered with gold and silver braid and numerous decorations on their chests. Wellington was dressed in a simple grey frock coat and a plain cocked hat, no great finery for him, unless he had to see the King! He rode down the lines with hawk eyes scanning every detail; suddenly he stopped and looked straight at Sergeant Fairfoot.

"Show me your rifle Sergeant"

Robert stepped forward and handed the rifle to him.

He scanned the weapon thoroughly, checking for any sign of dirt or rust, indicating neglect. He returned it.

"Excellent, Barnard your men are in fine condition, can they still fight like they used to in Spain?"

"I am sure of it, my Lord, we will not let you down." beamed Barnard.

"I'm certain of it" was Wellington's confident reply. With that, Wellington turned his horse and rode rapidly away, his Aide de Camp's had to ride hard to catch up.

Some of the officers that had arrived with Wellington remained and now moved in front of the battalion with Sir Andrew. Sir Andrew Barnard bellowed.

"Well done men. We are to be attached to the Fifth division in this army under the command of Sir Thomas Picton, who is presently on route. We will form part of the Eighth brigade within that division, commanded by Major General Sir James Kempt" indicating the officer beside him.

"Major Cameron, march the men off and issue a double ration of spirits"

The men smiled and let out a loud hurrah, but it was tinged with foreboding, as they would have to face 'bloody' Picton, the hardest bastard in the army, a foul mouthed Welshman, bad tempered and strict as hell! But, he knew his business well and he would look after them.

Two days later the order to march to Brussels came, all were assembled, and they set off marching in the early morning light and arriving at their stage for that day around midday. Instantly, rations were served, men collected wood for fires and tents were erected in perfect lines. Each company had thirty men in each of three tents, the men lying in a circle from the centre pole; officers had personal tents. Evening was given over to relaxation or repairing kit; there was no threat of immediate war and little guard duty.

After three such uneventful marches, they finally arrived at the fine city of Brussels on the 12th May. Their division was lucky to be one of those actually stationed in Brussels and everyone was keen to get good comfortable billets. The men were billeted around the City, no more than a mile from the bustling centre. Most of the men were country folk and the sights of the City drew them like bees to a honey pot. They marvelled at the stark contrasts between the great tree lined avenues cutting a wide path as they crossed the City and the twisted narrow streets overhung by tall houses that meandered confusingly immediately they left the avenues. They marvelled at the hidden treasures such as the Grande Place, with all its gaudy gold work on the grand medieval merchant houses, which they stumbled upon without warning whilst wandering through these back streets. The disparity between this and the large formal parks, wide streets and grand frontages of the new palaces jarred the senses, making Brussels a City of two styles. However, the locals welcomed the soldiers warmly into their homes and life was good.

On the 14th May the men cheerfully met their other company commanded by Captain Francis Glasse as they marched into Brussels. This company had been in Belgium since returning from Spain and many an old friendship was renewed that night! All six companies were now together again, ready for the start of any fighting, which would surely come soon. Presently, the joint allied armies were preparing to attack France simultaneously. However, they were not ready yet and Napoleon wouldn't dare attack, so they could relax and enjoy the sights of Brussels.

A few days later, Johnny Kincaid eventually arrived from his adventures and took up his office as Adjutant to the regiment. He had managed to buy a good horse soon after arriving at Brussels and started preparing the battalion for the orders that would surely come sooner or later, for war.

THE JOURNEY

Bright rays of sunlight falling harshly upon Alexander's face shattered his dreams; he felt the stiffness in his joints as he straightened his body in the chair that had formed his resting place. The grate was now dark and uninviting, there were no bright embers remaining to warm his exhausted frame. The others still slept, he quietly raised himself, squeezing between the somnolent occupants and stepped out of the stuffy house to fill his lungs with the sweet fresh air of dawn. He was very pleasantly surprised to find that at the rear of the dwelling, unseen last night, a small walled garden, beautifully kept, with all the spring flowers competing to bloom the most luxuriously. It was a sheer oasis of peace and beauty in a barren landscape of flat plains dissected by a multitude of watercourses. He took a few moments to fully absorb the scene and clear his mind of the previous day's troubles. He was reinvigorated by the bright dawn light that already warmed his body and heralded a more pleasant day than yesterday. Alexander sat upon a wooden bench and enjoyed these few minutes of serenity, he thought of his mother; father and sisters enjoying a carefree life at home in England. He wondered if they thought of him that morning or if they still slept. He remembered balmy days by the river at home as a youth with his village friends and wallowed in this indulgent nostalgia. Such happy times saddened him when he compared his current situation, full of cares and responsibilities. He tried to change his thoughts away from home and eventually sauntered back into the house to wake his brother officers. The troop must prepare to return to Ostend as early as possible.

The miller and his wife had produced a breakfast of the freshest bread, cold meats and gallons of strong black coffee. They all ate ravenously of this feast, having partaken of little sustenance the day before. Soon, they felt fully restored and ready to face the trials and tribulations that would undoubtedly be their lot in Ostend that day. With renewed vigour, everybody worked quickly to prepare the horse teams for the strenuous task ahead. As soon as everything was complete, the troop set out on the road back to the town. Alexander wished their hosts well and proffered a gold coin to pay for their victuals, it was politely declined. In daylight, the narrowness of the road running atop the dyke and the steep drop to either side of some twenty feet, made them all very thankful for their safe transit the previous night.

Within a mere ten minutes they arrived at the barrier of Ostend, the journey in the dark stormy weather last night had taken more than an hour. The barrier was closed until eight o'clock and the officious Belgian officer whom they had encountered the previous night, stood glaring at Alexander and his men. A small crowd of labourers that worked in the town and farmers with carts richly laden with their produce, waited patiently at the gate, the troop joined the orderly line. Alexander took the opportunity to observe the fine stonewalls that formed the defences of the town. The angular revetments protected from shot and shell by great banks of earth and crowned by rows of canon of great calibre which reminded Alexander of the works of that great fortress builder Vauban.

At the appointed hour precisely, the barrier was raised and the crowd strode on, allowing G Troop to proceed toward the harbour. The Belgian officer watched them pass with a thinly disguised smirk painted on his fulsome cheeks, he had won this time, they had been made to wait. Alexander would have loved to wipe the smile from his face, but the Belgians were allies and not to be upset at any cost, Lord Wellington's orders.

Arriving at the harbour, exactly the same scene of mayhem as yesterday was being re-enacted, further troop ships arriving continuously merely added to the confusion. Captain Hill's men had waited until this morning to unload the guns and carriages as promised, but they had obviously started at first light and a number of guns were already on the beach awaiting them. Alexander had previously detailed each officer and NCO to take charge of certain carriages or guns with their allocated horse teams. Having had the time to arrange the horses and to saddle and harness them properly, the operation went exceedingly smoothly.

Alexander found time to relax a little and took the opportunity to observe his surroundings. Groups of soldiers awaiting orders were already happily drinking ale in the morning sunlight, seated outside bars that had remained open throughout to capture the trade. Others were marching off, escorting baggage wagons; packhorses and mules tethered to the rear of the wagons strolling nonchalantly behind. A Field Artillery Battery that had presumably disembarked the previous night was still lined along the roadside, dying embers nearby told of fires lit to try and keep warm in the terrible weather. The horse teams were harnessed to the guns and stood throwing their sackcloth nosebags high into the air with a flick of the head to reach the oats lying at the bottom. The men lolled along the length of the gun barrels or across the ammunition boxes on the wagons, in an attempt to let the early morning sun dry out their saturated clothing. Small whiffs of steam rose from their bodies as the sun did its work.

The locals were back at honest toil this Monday morning and deliveries came and went. The Belgian delivery men wore blue smock coats, heavily embroidered with colourful ribbons, their heads adorned with a cap of white or red, not unlike a nightcap, they were invariably filthy. Most sported huge earrings as an embellishment. The men walked far behind their horse and carts, controlling them with a very long pair of leather reins. The women all wore lace caps and sported huge looped ear rings, blouses and long skirts heavily embroidered with colourful threads and they usually wore wooden clogs upon their bare feet.

Observing his own teams of horses, Alexander fretted to see such handsome creatures transformed into bedraggled, ill conditioned hacks so quickly. Their drooping heads and listless eyes told of the damage done to their condition by such hard service. Alexander realised the folly they were all guilty of; they mollycoddled the horses on garrison duty in England and when they were called into action on campaign, they were far too soft and lost condition very quickly. No wonder that Lord Wellington had sent recalled cavalry units home from Spain without their chargers. New horses could be procured at home, but those inured to the rough campaigning of Spain were irreplaceable and a great boon to newly arrived regiments. Before this practice became common place, cavalry regiments could often only field a few squadrons at the front line, as most of the new horses were either sick or died! The men had fared little better and obviously needed time to recuperate a little. He hoped they would get the time needed before any fighting commenced. Their equipment was already torn, dirty, the metalwork rusting, indeed some swords and scabbards had rusted solid.

A piercing scream rent the air; it was followed in rapid succession by further blood curdling screams and shouts for help. All eyes immediately turned towards the source of these terrible sounds; it emanated from a group of Belgian women who were stood at the end of the pier. They huddled together as protection against the stiff sea breeze, whilst pointing seaward, the anguish etched on their faces was all too obvious. Dark storm clouds had again started to roll in, accompanied by a very strong wind, which was rapidly gaining in strength and presaging a full-blown gale. A number of small fishing smacks and brigs that lay outside the harbour were running for the protection of the wooden pier as the wind and seas grew alarmingly. One brig had missed the harbour mouth and was being rapidly carried down towards the beach and its huge breakers. The sea had whipped up extremely quickly and huge waves were now crashing against the wooden piers sending vast plumes of spray high into the air. The waves looked much taller than the brig's masts and seemed to threaten to envelope it completely. However, each time a wave threatened to pass completely over it, somehow the brig mounted the crest and escaped submersion. The brig rolled heavily, the masts thrashing from side to side almost touching the water.

"If the masts touch the water, she will turn turtle and sink," John Hincks observed.

Alexander said nothing, Hincks was right of course, but such statements often became prophecy and he did not wish to be part of such a terrible disaster. The brig was now close to the beach and everyone ran along the shoreline to help. The ship was no more than a dozen yards from the sands where they congregated, the crew aboard were clearly visible pleading for help, but there was no way to aid them. The surf constantly swept over the hull, the crew clinging on to the rigging, holding on for grim death, some tying themselves to the masts in their efforts to stay onboard. The tattered shards of sail flapped violently on the yards making a thunderous noise, the creaking and groaning of the ship's timbers foretold her imminent death throws. Occasionally the sea lifted the vessel bodily as if made of matchwood, then hurling it against the sands in its determination to destroy the puny craft. As it crashed to earth, the whole hull shuddered and the masts vibrated wildly with the shock.

A small cheer of hope arose from the crowd as an oared boat pulled out from the harbour crewed by a few brave men prepared to battle the very sea for custody of the crew. As they closed with the brig, Alexander recognised amongst these heroes, the same pilot that had brought their own ship into port, he was leading the rescue team. The boat neared the stricken vessel, only to be swept disdainfully away by the disparaging waves. They made numerous attempts to close but were as often defeated by the scornful sea. Slowly however, they managed to manoeuvre alongside for short periods and individual crewmen were able to spring with a leap of desperation from the shattered hulk of the brig into the boat. Some hesitated to leap, but there was little alternative and eventually they all let go of their grasp on the ship to make the hazardous gambol. Most were eventually gathered in safely, but one missed the timing of his jump, plunging into the boiling sea. He was lucky enough to resurface alongside the boat and caught hold of the gunwale. With an extreme effort, two of the rescue team managed to haul him over the side, despite his heavy frame and saturated clothing. All seemed to be going better than could possibly have been hoped for as the boat closed for the last time. Tragically, by some terrible accident, the pilot lost his footing as the boat bumped alongside for the final crewman. He clutched for a hold of anything to save himself as his body fell across the boat. His head fell between the hulls of the two vessels at the precise moment of impact; his skull was instantly smashed to pieces. The crowd screamed in horror as the awful scene unfolded directly in front of them. Unnoticed during this drama, the last crewman had managed to jump across, landing safely in the boat. The cutter was now rowed with great urgency toward safety in the calmer waters of the harbour. They succeeded in pulling into the lee of the pier but there was no celebration of their success, they merely slumped in their seats from sheer exhaustion. Seconds later, a loud splintering noise dragged all eyes back to the brig as with a final sigh it gave up the unequal struggle and the vanquishing sea broke the hull into pieces. The triumphant waves raised the jumbled timbers of the stricken vessel, tossing them to the four winds in celebration of its great victory. The crowd ran toward the harbour and surged around the boat as it eventually landed safely. Some cheered the saviours of the crew, but most stood solemnly as all honours were bestowed upon the mangled remains of the brave pilot. His corpse was wrapped in a flag torn from a nearby ship and carried in stately procession to the local church. He had died a hero; they vowed to bury him as such and to care for his family, now bereft of their only provider. Once interred on hallowed ground to await burial, the crowd slowly dispersed. Alexander sat feeling very melancholy, however his thoughts were interrupted by a discreet cough, and he looked up into the face of the Quartermaster, John Hall.

Hall looked embarrassed, and sheepishly held out a small leather purse. "From the men Sir, for the Pilot's family."

Alexander choked back his feelings; he was proud of his men and happily added a few gold coins as his personal contribution before sending him to the town Mayor with the offering.

The excitement over, the troop was reassembled and settled back to await the Commissary with their rations before they could march. Eventually at three o'clock that afternoon, the wagons finally arrived and rations were issued to the troop. Finally, Alexander could order them to march for Ghent. The drivers took their positions on the wagons or the lead horses of each team and the gunners mounted their own horses. The orders given, the troop proceeded slowly through the narrow, winding, filthy streets of Ostend, the houses in daylight betrayed their dilapidation, how different it all had appeared last night. They marched past the foot artillery battery still waiting for orders on the quayside; Alexander noted the disdain shown by his men for the foot-sloggers. In the Foot artillery, the guns and carriages were provided with horses, which only seated the drivers, none of the artillerymen were mounted and had to march along behind, they were so clumsy and slow! Alexander looked at his battery with pride; they were the elite of artillery. In the army, they were often known as the 'Flying Artillery' because of their speed. Every man was seated, either on the carriages or provided with horses to ride alongside the guns. This meant that they would keep up with the cavalry and could gallop into action, unlimber and commence firing in minutes. They were the flexible, fast, hard punch of the army and were rightly proud of their high reputation. The horses were all dark brown or black and solidly built, they were trained to perfection in their teams, each reacting immediately to the driver's orders. The men in their dark blue figure hugging, hussar style jackets with myriad lines of yellow gold lace across the chest and grey breeches looked every inch the soldier. It was topped off by a great black crested helmet with peaked front, a brown turban wrapped around and thick black brush of hair running fore and aft over the top of the rounded helmet.

In full gallop, the six teams of horses with cannons, a numerous train of support carriages and gunners on fine chargers riding alongside, was an awesome and spectacular sight. Alexander had every reason to be proud of the unit, he just hoped that he could command them as well as they deserved.

Near the barrier at the entrance to Ostend, Gunner John Butterworth, known as 'Tuppence' to his fellow Artillerymen, on account of the current price that a pound of butter cost, called out.

"Lefftenant Ingilby Sir, I thinks that them two horses is our missing ones, I'd recognise Hero any where's"

William Ingilby rode over to the horses, which stood untethered, quietly munching on the grass at hoof on the earthen scarp of the defences near the barrier. He soon ascertained that they belonged to the Quartermaster's stores by the tell tale triangular arrow shape clearly branded into their hindquarters. The Belgian guard at the barrier confirmed that they had no idea whose horses they were as they had arrived alone during last night's storm. William gladly reclaimed them for King George. Alexander was pleased, his troop was now fully horsed again and the loss of equipment from yesterday's mayhem was now trifling.

As they cleared the outskirts of the town and left the

shelter of the formidable defences, they were struck by the wind, which had picked up in strength again. It beat them with great violence as they started out along the road cresting the dyke. The men now found their grand helmets cumbersome and a damned nuisance. Without a word spoken, each moved independently to protect themselves from the freshening breeze. The mounted gunners leaned hard into the wind, keeping their body low over their horse's necks, they held their reins in one hand and with the other they strove to hold their helmets on their heads. Those seated on the carriages sat with their backs facing the wind, burying their heads into their hands to be sure of retaining their helmets; it all struck Alexander as very humorous. He needed to lift his spirits, for the view in all directions was hardly appealing. For as far as the eye could see, there was an unbroken expanse of flat marshland. Small outcrops of reeds occasionally broke the monotonous scene that consisted largely of a sea of black pestilential mud, which was accompanied by a fetid stench. The road of mud and stones ran along the top of a dyke some feet above this marsh in a straight line for at least fifteen miles. Everyone concentrated hard on keeping the teams on the roadway; any that strayed would lose their footing and be lost in the quagmire.

Having travelled across this desolate and depressing plain for a few hours, they were all delighted with the sudden change of scenery. They were confronted with miles of flat, lush green pasture, populated by thousands of well nourished cattle and swine; indeed it appeared to be a veritable land of plenty.

Away from the sea, the winds eased and with a more cheerful outlook, the troop's spirits rallied. They started to relax and enjoy their sojourn, animated conversation and laughter started to break out. Alexander was pleased to observe that their spirits were unharmed after the last two trying days.

A small hamlet came into view; it consisted of a huddle of a mere dozen houses, ringed by a smattering of isolated farmsteads dotted sparsely over the plain.

Alexander turned to Robert Newland, his irksome fellow Captain.

"That should be the village of Ghistel, Newland, we are to billet on these good folk tonight."

Robert looked bemused, "We will struggle to find everyone a billet here. We will have to spread them far and wide in those farms. Not good for efficiency or control of the troop."

Alexander agreed but was irritated, Newland always managed to make his comments sound like criticisms.

As they approached the few houses hugging the road, a tall man dressed in a long black coat and wide brimmed hat, looking every inch the Quaker, greeted them. He introduced himself as a Monsieur Van Heyden; he was effectively the village notary. He read the official order to provide billets for the night, which Alexander had procured from the Commissary, with little joy, but rapidly issued notes for each homestead with the number of horses and men to be billeted on each. Staff Sergeants Parsons and Hall detailed off each group. Having formed a park for the guns and carriages on a green in the village, they proceeded with their rations to the houses allocated. Few homesteads had room for their visitors in their meagre, low cottages. Most occupants happily offered their barns, now virtually empty of winter hay, as accommodation, which was gladly accepted by the men.

Alexander and his fellow officers were happy to accept accommodation in the better houses in the village; they enjoyed an evening's relaxation in the company of their host's families, who entertained their English guests with good grace. Alexander did not fear for his scattered unprotected troop, they were way behind the lines and fighting had not broken out. He would revel in the evening, it was a pleasure not having any cares for a while and he was determined to enjoy himself.

At dawn, the local cockerels serenaded the men sauntering from the scattered farms to muster at the artillery park on the village green. Some had to travel in from farms more than two miles away and the sun was well above the horizon before all were accounted for and the troop could proceed. The march this day was short and very unremarkable; they simply enjoyed the view and soaked up the warmth of the sun on this pleasant spring morning. After a mere two-hour ride, the spires of Bruges, that famous town of lace and canals peeked into view, marking the end of the day's journey. They rode through its beautifully preserved medieval streets, crossing the multitude of canals on narrow stone bridges, just wide enough for the gun carriages. They passed through the impressive Markt, a wide square lined with ornate Guild houses, each painted a different colour. They craned their necks to view the octagonal tower that topped the Belfort, a thirteenth century bell tower rising over two hundred and fifty feet and dominating the square. On they went past towering churches blackened by age and then along streets of low stone cottages, through to the cavalry barracks, their home for the night. This was a much less attractive billet, with dark dank rooms for the men and poor cover for the horses, it was conceivably the worst building in Bruges. However, once the horses were settled for the night and the wagons and guns parked, the town beckoned, promising beer and congenial company for the men.

Alexander and the other Officers were billeted on the

Hotel de Commerce in the main square, a fine edifice but sadly dilapidated. This was however, a pleasing opportunity to clean themselves up, as there had been little chance for a change of clothing since sailing. The hotel was small, dark and dismally quiet, but it did offer good food, rest and hot water, they had no reason to find fault.

William Millward had been Alexander's servant for some twelve years and as has been said by others, no man is a hero to his servant; William proceeded with him to his rooms to collect his filthy shirt and necessaries for washing. Alexander wallowed in the luxury of the hot bath provided by the hotel. He reflected on the sudden changes of circumstances and wondered what further surprises were to come their way. Watching William shuffling around the room, laying out his clean uniform; he appreciated the loyalty and excellent service he had always enjoyed from this aging trooper. Millward was a proud man of some forty years, always upright and steady; he would never fail him. Alexander looked on their relationship as one of complete trust and hoped that William understood how completely he relied on him. He was the nearest thing that he had to a wife.

Finally, fully refreshed, he rose from the bath, and then leisurely dressed in his crisp, clean, spare shirt, starched to perfection, exactly as William had packed it in Colchester just over a week ago. Dressed, he met up with his fellow officers to enjoy a fine meal in the hotel restaurant. As they consumed their fair repast, Alexander took note of their surroundings; he observed the surfeit of staff with little to do and the general air of gloom pervading the hotel.

On enquiry, the Maitre d'hôte explained.

"Business is poor here for many years monsieur, because of Napoleon's blockade of goods from England. Now all trade has stopped again because they fear his armies will come and destroy everything!"

Henry Leathes attempted to reassure him. "Do not fear so my good fellow, Lord Wellington and our army will not let him come here."

The Belgian turned to Henry in all seriousness, answering. "I 'ope you are right Sir, but you Inglish have not fight with Napoleon 'imself before and he has beaten everyone else!"

Henry looked downcast at the truth of the answer, but William Ingilby chipped in, "Napoleon is a mere bludgeoner like his Marshals. Lord Wellington saw them all off, Ney, Soult, Massena, Marmont; he had the beating of them all. I'll wager thee Sir, that Wellington has the beating of Napoleon as well or I'm not a Yorkshireman!"

They all laughed, all knew that the fighting ahead would be hard, but they would not dwell on what might happen in the future and was out of their control. They would enjoy the moment and live for today, a wise lifestyle for a soldier!

Wine, Beer and Port flowed freely as they vied to outdo each other in their generosity of order for the table; they drank and cavorted until the early hours, when they slowly dispersed to bed.

Early morning saw them on the road again, having gained little sleep. The officers were sad to leave their comfortable berth; by contrast, the men were very glad to leave the dank, gloomy cells at the stables. Almost everyone suffered the pains of a hangover and conversation was sparse for the next few hours.

Two further days of light marches over similar countryside, halting each night at small villages similar to those previous, eventually brought the troop into the streets of Ghent. The City, sitting astride the River Scheldt, spoke eloquently of wealth. Fine merchant's houses were interspersed amongst the trappings of a grandiose past as a great medieval trading centre. A fine castle, ornate Cathedral and great Cloth Hall, all indicated great power and importance but all were now showing signs of age and wear.

They rode past a large building site; an eager army of labourers were laying the foundations of some great edifice. A passing gentleman informed them that it was to be a fine new University, due to open the following year, a symbol of Ghent's continued importance.

They proceeded on toward the cavalry barracks, which was to be their billet during their stay in this fine city. However, as they entered the gateway of dirty red brick to the barrack blocks, it became evident that someone else was already in residence and the troop halted abruptly. Alexander rode forward to discover who had taken their berth. As he approached closer, he could discern English voices and the semblance of Horse Artillery uniforms on some of the men busily feeding horses or mucking out stables. He stopped to observe the scene and to identify somebody in authority to inquire of. His eyes suddenly set upon an officer strolling across the yard, checking on his men's work. Alexander's eyes brightened and he called out in the pleasure of recognition of an old friend.

"Alex, how long have you been here?"

Second Lieutenant Alexander Macdonald turned and beamed a smile of welcome recognition. "Alexander Mercer, how the devil are you?"

Alexander Macdonald was Second in command of Major Norman Ramsay's 'H' troop of Horse Artillery. The two knew each other from long periods of tedious garrison duty in Colchester. Mercer looked upon Norman and Alex as the prefect Horse Artillery officers and had learnt much from them. Both had extensive experience in action and of campaigning, having served throughout the Peninsula war in Spain in various Horse Artillery units before joining together to make a formidable team.

"We are all well Alex, but I see you have our intended berth!" Alexander replied.

Alex looked apologetic, "I am afraid we have no room for your troop, we have been here ten days and do not yet know when we are to move on." Then recognising some old faces behind Alexander, he shouted "John, Henry, William, greetings, I trust we can expect your company at our mess tonight!" He bent to pat Bal, who sniffed around his boots in recognition of an old friend.

Alexander's brother officers returned the compliment and promised to visit once they were installed somewhere in the city. The horses and carriages were eventually ensconced within the cavalry barracks for safekeeping, but the men would have to be billeted elsewhere. Eventually, the local authorities allocated lodgings and the troop dispersed to locate their individual havens. They were to be spread all over the city, some more than two miles away; this would make the maintenance of discipline and organisation virtually impossible. There was precious little choice in the matter and with seemingly no threat of attack or urgency in their movements, he felt fully at ease.

Alexander rode slowly through the winding streets of central Ghent vainly searching for his own berth in Bruges Straet. Halting regularly to seek the aid of passing locals, he eventually drew Cossack up outside a tall four storey wooden house. Thin flakes of garishly coloured paints betrayed how strongly coloured the house had once been; it must have been a splendid sight with its rich carvings and ornate trimmings. Time had ravaged the facia, dirt and grime besmirched it, and it shouted decayed opulence. Alexander rapped at a low dark door, which was eventually answered after what seemed an age by a short rotund, elderly gentleman who accepted his billet papers with little enthusiasm. He did not proffer his name and Alexander did not pry, he simply accepted the rooms offered and the extremely valuable perk of the use of a cook to prepare his food during his stay. Passing this information to his brother officers via Millward, a mess was quickly set up at his rooms, which were undoubtedly the best of the officer's billets. With a pooling of their little stocks of food and a contribution from each for William to purchase further fine food, wines, and cigars, they soon settled into a luxurious lifestyle. There was precious little furniture to speak of, but with a little ingenuity and hardihood, the mess became a roaring success. Each evening they conversed whilst enjoying exquisite food and the finest wines and port. It was then the height of luxurious indulgence to relax and smoke their cheroots.

William Ingilby would utilise his wealth of great stories regarding the hardships of life on campaign in Spain as only a Yorkshireman can. He particularly liked to talk of Norman Ramsay, who had become famous throughout the army for his exploits at the battle of Fuentes de O'noro.

Norman was the beau ideal of all Horse Artillery officers, tall, handsome, dashing, brave as a lion, he was the hero of the corps.

"You should have seen him that day" he would say, "Grand it was. There was Norman with two guns in the middle of the battle suddenly surrounded by hundreds of French cavalry. Does he surrender? Not on your nelly! Out of the great mass of horsemen, dashing forth at breakneck speed with unstoppable force, Norman sword in hand forces a way through the surrounding Frenchmen and is followed closely by the two horse teams, guns and all. Never would I have believed it possible, if I had not seen it with my own eyes! Too bad he's a Scotsman, for he would make a bloody good Yorkshireman!"

Then he became serious, "However, Lord Wellington dealt with him harshly after the glorious battle of Vitoria"

They all nodded agreement; the story of Norman Ramsay's arrest was common knowledge throughout the Artillery and had embittered many against Wellington.

"Norman was ordered to stand ready at a certain point and await further orders. Well, some jumped up son of a Lord ordered him to enter the battle to help an Infantry Brigade, which was under pressure. Norman's answer that he dare not move unless expressly ordered by Lord Wellington was turned against him by this youth, regarding Norman's actions as that of a coward! I would not have hesitated to strike the youth from his horse, but Norman felt his honour impugned and moved to help, where his efforts did turn the tide and aided the victory. Trouble was, Lord Wellington had other important work for Norman's troop and sent orders for their timely intervention at the desired point. His fury at hearing that Norman's troop was not to be found, knew no bounds. Despite the general elation of a great victory, Norman was unceremoniously arrested for daring to disobey Wellington! Despite the efforts of all the senior officers with the army, he remained under arrest in his tent for three weeks, lost any chance of a mention in the battle dispatch and therefore did not gain a promotion in rank as all those who were mentioned did! Lord Wellington made a scapegoat of him, to make a point; after that, everyone knew the consequences of disobeying him. For pities sake do not cross the Duke!" he warned earnestly.

They all nodded solemnly, they recognised Wellington's success, but felt that he had always failed to appreciate the work of the artillery and was very slow to praise them.

Henry Leathes added "Not only that, Wellington ignored

all the senior artillery officers with the army, using Alexander Dickson to command the artillery. He transferred him to the Portuguese army, where Lord Wellington could promote officers without having to gain Horse guard's permission. He was promoted to Lieutenant Colonel so that he was the senior artillery officer in the joint army and therefore commanded all the artillery from Vitoria onwards, a very unfair use of power!"

They all nodded agreement, except Robert Newland who blurted "That's our Commanding Officer, you are talking of, mind your tongue, Sir!" Dickson was nominal head of their own troop, but he was seconded to command the Siege Train, the heavy twenty-four pounder cannons for battering fortress walls, they had seen little of him and they had scant loyalty for him.

The artillery officers were all pleased that they did not belong to the War Office, but to the Master General of the Ordnance's department. They were proud of the differences between them and their infantry and cavalry counterparts. Firstly, they were convinced that they were the only true professionals in the army, as they all had to pass out of artillery training at the Royal Military Academy before serving. The infantry had had no such training until recently, their Royal Military College being set up by the Duke of York just thirteen years ago and even now many officers served in regiments without any formal training.

Secondly, they were not allowed to purchase promotion, all advancement was by seniority, hence the rankling over the Dickson scam. They felt their system ensured supreme professionalism and avoided infants commanding troops as had happened a few years back in the infantry. At the time of taking command of all the allied artillery at Vitoria, the Ordnance Board rated Dickson as a mere Captain!

They were a disgruntled bunch, but thoroughly

professional, they would not fail in their job and trusted Wellington to uphold his famed fair play this time and give them their due credit.

The group ignored a loud rapping at the outer door, whilst they conversed; Millward went out of the room and following an animated conversation in the parlour, returned and approached Robert Newland to whisper a message in his ear.

Robert rose abruptly and bid the others excuse him a moment, then strolled out to the lobby where Quartermaster Hall was now standing. Following a short discussion, Hall left and Robert returned to the room. Standing in front of the group, he spoke.

"There has been trouble in the bars tonight, the Wee Gee's and Gunners have been brawling again! Hall has arrested a few ringleaders and broken it up, all have been ordered back to their billets and it is quiet now."

They sighed; this bickering rivalry was a constant problem. There was an awkward anomaly in the system; the gunners belonged to the ordnance, but the drivers, known throughout the army as the 'Wee Gee's' actually belonged to the Corps of Royal Artillery Drivers. The Transport Board ran this body and had their own officers but they rarely served with the men. Each battalion of drivers was broken up into teams of about eighty-four men and allocated to the troops of artillery, they then fell under the Troop Captain's orders but the rivalry between gunners and drivers was always there. The gunners looked upon the drivers as an inferior bunch. In Spain there had been many stories of the drivers selling equipment they were supposedly transporting to the army to Portuguese merchants. Indeed, working so far away from their officer's supervision did lead to many problems. However, there was no easy solution.

The moment of conviviality having been broken, they all

proceeded to their own billets and bed. They would have to talk to their teams in the morning and try to rebuild a rapport between them, hopefully sober they would settle down to work together again.

During that morning a messenger arrived; he carried orders for Alexander's troop to form a Guard for the displaced Louis XVIII, who was residing nearby in a palace at Alost. John Hincks, John Bretton and William Ingilby were ordered to attend with selected gunners on the finest horses, to form the Guard of Honour. Robert Newland had put William Ingilby forward; the brash Yorkshireman was a strange choice as he was a rough diamond, however he was an exceptionally experienced and professional soldier, he would not let Alexander down. They rode five miles out of Ghent to the chateau in a beautiful wooded valley, where they were introduced to the newly formed Garde de Corps, the King's Bodyguard.

"They are mere boys and fal-de-rah's" William whispered. The others fought to suppress their laughter; John Hincks could not speak for fear of releasing a roaring laugh, tears rolling down his cheeks.

The small unit, formed of youth's from the families of the gentry that had fled with Louis, hardly commanded the respect of seasoned soldiers. However, their military powers were unlikely to be tested, as Louis would not remain if Napoleon's army ever approached. They were a friendly bunch however, and joyfully welcomed the artillery officers into their mess. Duties were hardly onerous, as the corpulent Louis never travelled afar. Their time was spent drinking and indulging in mess sports as young officers always have, wrestling and fencing being particular favourites. They were destined to remain here in idle luxury for a week. Passing the exercise yard one morning, William nudged John Hincks and pointed to a grey haired officer putting his horse through its paces. "Do you know who that is, John?"

John peered at the rider, but had no idea, "No who is it?"

"That is the great Marshal Marmont, the toughest General we fought in Spain and France until Lord Wellington beat him roundly at Salamanca. He has stayed loyal to the King this time; he'll be highly honoured if we win the crown back for Louis, if not Napoleon will wring his neck!"

They stood and watched the old warrior in awe for some time; he did not deign to notice the prying English officers and eventually duty called them away.

All enjoyed this restful period at Ghent, but the order to finally proceed further towards Brussels on the 24th April, to a village named Dendermonde, was received with enthusiasm. A change of scenery was welcomed and bidding farewell to their hosts, the troop formed up on the appointed morning and set out on the road again.

They travelled along the muddy roads of Belgium at a steady pace, with little to occupy their time other than enjoyment of the beautiful countryside that they passed. Their first day's march ended at the tiny village of St Gille, where after some discussion with the local dignitary, the park of guns and horses was established in the only available enclosed area, the churchyard! Proceeding to billets on the local farms, a peaceful evening and sound sleep was enjoyed by all.

Morning broke and soon after dawn the troop reassembled at the churchyard to tend their charges.

Gunner James Putten approached the churchyard first and pulled himself up onto the stone wall, as if to gain a better view of something. Turning back to the others he shouted.

"Bloody 'ell, come and 'ave a butcher's at this, I don't believe it!"

The men rushed over to the wall, jostling each other to gain a better view; a great hubbub grew rapidly. Alexander pushed himself forward demanding access to view whatever had caused such consternation. He finally forced his way through the throng to the wall, where peering over the parapet he groaned at the bizarre scene that he beheld. The heavy horses and even heavier wagons had been too much for the deceased to bear. Hooves and wheels had sunk into the graves, the coffins having collapsed under the weight imposed on them. The horses had sunk to their bellies in these pits and in their wild attempts to extricate themselves, they had upset the contents of numerous graves. Human bones and fragments of clothing were sprinkled lightly on the dew-drenched grass, skulls with sightless eye sockets stared accusingly at them in remonstration. Alexander ordered the horses and gun carriages to be hauled out of the plots, which took fully an hour. The bones were thrown back into the holes with no certainty of which grave they had come from and all was re covered with sods of earth. The scene looked in relative order again and Alexander hoped that the locals would remain ignorant of the disaster. He also prayed that the spirits of the departed would excuse their incursion and as they did not require their mortal remains any further, that they would forgive the undoubted mixing of their bones. Alexander and many of his men crossed themselves in superstition before setting off on the road to Dendermonde.

They arrived at Dendermonde after a short march and remained there for some eight days, enjoying excellent accommodation with the locals. They were again spread over miles, at various farmsteads, but there was little option. Everything was peaceful, there were no urgent orders and they simply relaxed with the families that they had been put upon. The eight days passed slowly for Alexander and the other officers. They spent the time in riding around the countryside and in the evenings the entertainment consisted of cards or singing around the pianos of the better off families where they were billeted. The men, having fed and watered the horses and maintained the equipment, found solace at the local hostelry or partook of the fruits of the farmer's stills.

Orders suddenly came at midnight on the 1st May. The Sergeant Major awoke Alexander from his deep slumbers, "Sir, messenger just arrived" and handed over a small note which Alexander could hardly see.

Alexander read slowly in the dim flickering candlelight supplied by Staff Sergeant Parsons, 'Proceed immediately with all haste to Strytem', it read.

Alexander rose immediately and ordered Staff Sergeant Parsons to have the bugler sound 'Boot and Saddle', the cavalry reveille. Within minutes the harsh notes of the bugle broke the still night air. All was rush, confusion and noise as men stumbled out of their billets into the cold night air and hurried to saddle the horses. By the aid of lanterns, the men struggled to complete the strapping of the horses and then attach them to the carriages. It was difficult to work when the mind was stultified by a sleep so harshly broken, but within an hour the troop was mustered from the outlying farms and prepared to move.

The noise and confusion had woken all the inhabitants of the village. They hung out of the bedroom windows peering into the darkness or congregated in a huddle alongside the road in their nightwear to watch the troop form up. The lady of the house that Alexander had stayed in rushed up to him to enquire what was the cause of such a commotion in the middle of the night as he desperately searched for Strytem on the map he had removed from a book in his host's library,.

Alexander turned to the lady who was in her fifties dressed in only her night attire, her face betraying the fear she felt. She fronted a deputation of the village folk all looking just as afraid. Alexander sought to allay their fears and answered as best as possible.

"Madam, we are ordered to Strytem immediately, my orders do not state for what purpose, but I assure you that a midnight call would indicate urgency."

William added, "Lord Wellington only calls when there is a need."

This had done nothing to calm his hostess, so Alexander added kindly "It would appear that whatever is afoot is far from here, you will all be safe here." He hoped that this was true.

Robert Newman appeared to announce that the troop was ready to march and Alexander ordered the advance towards who knew what?

FALSE ALARM

The urgency of the midnight order had sent expectations soaring within the troop, as they moved on Strytem everyone conjectured on the reason for such haste. Was the Allied army about to advance into France or had Napoleon invaded, what was the emergency? As they felt their way through the Belgian countryside by the feint light of the crescent moon, tempers frayed. Alexander worried over his paltry map stolen from his hosts, he fretted over keeping to the correct road, Newland constantly goaded him for their slow progress.

As the early morning light finally broke, they began to pass other artillery units camping peacefully in the adjoining fields. On enquiry, they discovered that they had received no orders to move and it eventually became evident that there was no crisis looming at all. Eventually, Alexander surmised that the order had been routine but over zealously administered. Expectations crushed, the adrenalin surge that had maintained them lapsed and they rapidly became greatly fatigued, but on they must march.

By mid morning they had finally discovered their destination. After passing through the drab collection of hovels forming the village of Strytem, G troop marched alongside a high stone wall, which skirted the road for some considerable distance beyond the village. Dramatically, a sudden break in the stonework revealed the chateau of Strytem in its full glory.

Built of grey stone, its features were heavily masked by copious blankets of ivy, it boasted a high square tower with gothic roof and extensive ornately leaded windows; it stood magnificent in the sunlight. The house was formed of a central block with two small wings, the whole surrounded by a moat of malodorous stagnant green water.

"This is going to be an exceptional billet," Henry Leathes announced.

As the troop snaked up the winding driveway and drew up in front of the chateau, two figures emerged from behind the great wooden front door and approached Alexander. The one, a dishevelled old man bent by toil, dressed in an old military coat and dirty nightcap, who appeared to be a gardener. A fresh-faced damsel, dressed as a maid, accompanied him. The gardener spoke Flemish, which neither Alexander nor his colleagues could understand, but they caught the gist of his ramblings. His master was usually in Brussels and rarely called at the chateau, there was nothing here for them and they would be better moving on.

Alexander indicated that no matter what, they were staying and signalled to Newland to give the order. The troop drove the cannon and wagons through a narrow archway that barely allowed room for manoeuvre into a wide courtyard within the stable block. The officers would utilise the chateau and the men and horses would be spread throughout the nearby homesteads, a subdivision at each of the larger farms. One division was to be located at the farm of Mr Walsdragen, a gruff surly old farmer, none too pleased to have them, especially as his wife was heavily pregnant. Having settled the horses down, the men proceeded towards their separate billets.

The officers entered the chateau to be met with rather a bleak view; furniture was scarce throughout the house and drab faded tapestries darkened the walls; all appeared unkempt and dilapidated. Each officer chose a room for their stay; Alexander used his perk of seniority to choose first. He discovered a fine room on the ground floor, with views through the formal gardens to the woods beyond. This was to be his chamber for the term of their stay; he thought it would be delightful. Millward laid Alexander's bedroll on top of an old sofa, Bal jumped up onto the old flea ridden bed; it was obviously to his liking. Doors in the apartment led to each of the wings and another to the upstairs, a fourth hidden behind an old faded tapestry led into a delightful little private chapel, which Alexander had little need of.

A large room on the first floor was identified as an ideal location for the mess; the few chairs and tables sprinkled throughout the multitude of rooms were dragged together by the servants to furnish it to an acceptable standard. Meeting there in the afternoon, they relaxed after their night ride. William Ingilby was amazed, "By the Lord Gentlemen, you ought to think yourselves very fortunate in getting such a quarter, for in the Peninsula the Duke himself was often glad to get as good a roof over his head, indeed it was often much worse."

John Hincks and Richard Hichens smiled at each other, as all youngsters do at the hardships described by their elders; they felt like saying "Times change old man", but neither dared!

Henry Leathes lolled on the arm of a sofa and pointed towards the great arched window at the end of the hall. It extended from the floor to its apex some twelve feet high;

in the centre of the great window was a pair of French doors, which opened onto a balcony. From this terrace one could gain exceptional views of the formal gardens laid out below.

"That window reminds me of one such as that at the convent of Santa Augusta when we besieged the forts at Salamanca. The abbot had a beautiful dining room on the first floor with just such a window; its doors leading out onto a balustrade. It made a fine site for a gun to enfilade the forts. We hauled a six pounder up there and had excellent fun lobbing balls over the walls of the nearest fort. Every time we fired, the glass rattled in the windows and we constantly expected the next discharge to bring the shards of glass showering down upon us. We were very glad when the forts decided to surrender!" Robert mused.

William Ingilby shuddered at the reminder of old times in Salamanca. "I nearly lost my head there!" he exclaimed, "When ordering number one gun to fire at the forts, the NCO on two gun mistakenly thought that the order was for him and lit the fuse. The damned thing went off directly behind me. I fell to the floor unconscious, my hair singed and my ears pouring blood. They thought I was killed."

Robert Newland laughed, "I remember that, we thought that your head was clean off."

Ingilby grimaced, "On recovering somewhat, I propped myself up against a wall, my head throbbing. I sat dazed for some time. Who should approach me just then? It was none other than the Duke himself. Well, he conversed with me for a good few minutes then left no wiser for my answers, for damn me if I could hear a thing! Damned painful it was, but after three days my ears suppurated and the relief was indescribable. I am still a little deaf in my left ear to this day".

Newman looked at Alexander with a thinly disguised sneer. "Of course, you weren't there were you?"

Alexander chose to ignore the remark; he did however feel isolated by their reminiscences, which highlighted his inexperience, it made him feel vulnerable.

There was a loud rapping at the great door below and the servants allowed admittance to a small deputation of local dignitaries. The group ascended the grand staircase and stepped into the room where they lounged, the Belgians stood fidgeting, nobody plucking up the courage to speak. They were arrayed in their fancy full state uniforms consisting of long dark blue waistcoats and blue and white striped stockings. One of the visitors, a rotund grey haired fellow, who was obviously the leader, stood just in front of the others. A taller gentleman with a strong military bearing, dressed in a short green jacket adorned with gold buttons and matching green trousers stood quietly just behind the little fat man.

Ingilby grew impatient of their procrastination and bellowed "Well Sir?"

The leader, whom it transpired, was a Mynheer Evenpoel, attempted to address Alexander in Flemish, another interpreted into French for him. They claimed that the district was unable to support the troop and that they should move on. The Prussians had been here only last year and they now claimed that there was nothing left.

Alexander replied sternly, "Lord Wellington's orders are precise, that we should remain here. Your King has ordered that all of his countrymen are to aid us with whatever we need. Indeed gentlemen, it seems obvious that the land hereabouts is very fruitful and I am sure that any search authorised by me would yield ten fold what we require. You are aware that all requisitions for His Britannic Majesty's Army are receipted for and that you will receive payment from the Commissariat. Therefore gentlemen, I will order my men to visit your homes forthwith!"

Alexander called over Quartermaster John Hall who had escorted the Belgian party into the room.

"Sergeant, have a foraging party ready to proceed within five minutes."

Hall saluted, "Yes, Sir" and retired rapidly. Two of the Belgians followed Hall out and attempted to stop him, but the wily old Sergeant affected not to understand their protestations.

Hall proceeded to the courtyard where his barked orders for the men to assemble could be clearly heard in the room above.

"Gunners Putten, Butterworth, Death, Hunt and Springly, fall in."

This caused consternation amongst the dignitaries, they appealed for a stay whilst they applied to Brussels for the troop to move.

The others returned to report to their leader, their voices betraying severe anxiety as they vied with each other to speak first. Eventually Mynheer Evenpoel turned to plead with Alexander again, repeating their intention of writing to Lord Wellington. This would take at least a full day and they had no provisions. Alexander replied. "I offer you two hours to provide the requisitions, or my men will visit your farms and take all they find, good day." So saying, Alexander turned and walked away, moving over to the great window, he affected to gaze out at the preparations of the foraging party, surreptitiously glancing quickly at them. The Belgians argued vehemently between themselves, the tall slender man with the look of an old soldier stood aloof and had said nothing during the interview. He now spoke and the others immediately fell silent in awe; he simply indicated that they needed to comply in the set time or face the consequences and they left abruptly.

Just within the two-hour deadline, the door was again assaulted, this time only the tall gentleman had returned. He advanced directly toward Alexander to speak with him. He had come to apologise that his compatriots had not even attempted to collect the supplies demanded. He offered to ride with Quartermaster Hall and his team to obtain the supplies himself. Horses were provided and they rode off down the great drive, the Dutchman leading, looking extremely ungainly on the troop horse, Alexander could only liken it to a giraffe riding a camel!

The party returned within a further two hours bringing three cartloads of provisions, far in excess of what was demanded. It emerged that the tall Dutchman was the 'Garde Village', effectively the Chief of Police in the district, a roll Napoleon had given to many old soldiers. They were to run his affairs locally and ensure compliance with his decrees. The locals knew him as 'Petit Jean', he had served with the French in Catalonia until a musket ball had torn two fingers from his left hand, and he had been forced to retire from the Imperial Army. As an old soldier, he obviously sympathised with the demands of Alexander and had persuaded the locals to comply as the lesser of two evils. Alexander realised he could be a useful ally and ensured that he was treated with respect by all, indeed during their stay, he was to prove invaluable in smoothing over any complaints impartially which greatly aided the process of reconciliation.

The afternoon's excitement over; a pleasing supper, followed by port and cigars whilst being serenaded by the delightful voice of Karl, caused their tired bodies to demand sleep and they eventually proceeded to their rooms for the night.

It had been a warm pleasant day and the evening had remained sultry and humid. Alexander lay down to rest, fatigued from the strains of the day, Bal lay at his feet quietly content, and Alexander closed his eyes in search of a deep deep sleep.

But what was that dreadful din? Rising with difficulty from the warm comfortable bed, he stumbled over to the window in the darkness, catching his toes on a chair leg on the way. He hobbled to the window and pushed it wide to lean out. Now the noise was deafening! A cacophony of deep-throated croaks made him peer down into the moat glistening in the bright moonlight beneath his window. It was swarming with great bullfrogs and toads, all croaking their love chants on this hot evening. Closing the window and burying himself in his blanket helped little; he could not drown out the sounds of croaking. He tossed and turned for hours, covered his head with his pillows and stuck his fingers in his ears, to no avail; still the sound pervaded his brain. Eventually in frustration he arose; admitting defeat he climbed the steps up to the drawing room to read and smoke a cigar to ease his troubled mind. As he ascended the staircase Alexander noticed that the door to the mess was ajar, and a feint glimmer of candlelight shone from within. Pushing the door wide open, he discovered his fellow officers all-lounging around with dark, deep-set eyes from lack of sleep, loudly complaining of the awful billet. They had all admitted defeat, no wonder that the owner rarely came here, it was sheer hell!

Morning arrived to find them all lying uncomfortably around the drawing room, sleep finally having crept up on their exhausted frames. Alexander had curled up on a fur rug; Henry Leathes was stretched on a sofa; the others had lain on tables, chests, or tried to sleep in chairs. They were as stiff as boards, tired and wretched, but the delightful aroma of bacon cooking wafted in from the kitchens below. This began a revival, which culminated in a hearty breakfast and succeeded in restoring them thoroughly.

Alexander stepped out onto the lawn to seek the morning sunshine, which was rapidly burning off the morning dew; he stood enjoying the warm rays on his face as he planned a war of vengeance against the frogs that had now strangely gone quiet. His machinations were disturbed as he caught sight of the feint figure of a horseman riding slowly toward the chateau through the morning mist that still sat on the wide lawns. The figure dressed in a blue jacket and bicorn hat finally neared and the gentleman spoke.

"Good morning, Captain Mercer I trust?"

"Indeed it is Sir, Alexander Mercer at your service, but you have the advantage of me, may I enquire your business with me?"

The gentleman in his mid thirties with dark wavy hair and thick moustache held out his gloved hand in welcome.

"Joshua Coates at your service, your Commissary, I am to organise the local farm carts into a team of supply wagons for you and prepare fodder and ration stores ready for any advance."

Alexander was happy for this welcome addition to his team, the requisitioning of supplies was a thorny problem with the farmers and he relished handing over this aspect of his job. He took Joshua's hand and shook it violently in his delight.

"You are most welcome Mister Coates; I trust that you are well versed in this role?" Alexander was well aware of the horror stories surrounding the Commissariat department and its staff. They were run by the Treasury, not the Army, thus as civilians they were not under army discipline. Many in Spain had been untrained and inefficient or downright corrupt, but then who would take a career where your normal fifteen shillings per day on home service actually fell to five shillings when on campaign! However, some had done sterling work in the Peninsula and Lord Wellington had arranged for the worst to be sent home. Those that finished the tour of Spain had gained a wealth of knowledge and performed their tasks relatively efficiently.

Joshua smiled "I trust five years in Spain, providing for Lord Wellington's army, will have prepared me well for this task. Indeed, this is a fertile area, there are more carts and fodder within five miles of here, than I ever saw within a hundred in Spain!"

"Then I trust that you will form the stores as ordered and utilise my men for any task required to accomplish it. Come now and join our breakfast, there is plenty of good bacon, bread and coffee left."

Joshua dismounted, tethering his horse to a nearby stanchion and walked with Alexander to introduce himself to the other officers.

An hour later, Joshua Coates left to visit the local farmers to requisition the horses and carts necessary for feeding the troop for a few days. He expected opposition from the farmers, as the loss of their carts would be a serious inconvenience. The official forage allowance for horses was fourteen pounds of hay and ten pounds of oats per horse per day. Each man was allowed a pound of meat, the weight including any bone and offal attached, a pound and a half of bread, a quarter pint of peas, an ounce of butter or cheese, an ounce of rice and a pint of wine per day. All this weighed nearly three tons just for one day's rations for the whole troop! He would need to requisition quite a number of carts to supply the unit for any reasonable length of time.

Alexander had ordered the troop to muster fully equipped on the lawns of the chateau at 10 o'clock for 'watering parade' and a full inspection. It was vital that the horses were exercised and that the troop ran through their drills, to ensure that they had not become jaded during their long journey from Colchester. They would venture out to find a field where they could carry out manoeuvres. Alexander entered the stable block and mounted Cossack; he had been beautifully groomed by William. The beast was eager for action, snorting and pulling on his bridle in anticipation. Once mounted, Alexander pulled his legs in tight, silently ordering him forward. Cossack stepped out, head held high as he carried his master onto the lawn, to view his expectant troop. G Troop was fully formed up in fighting order, Alexander halted in front of the troop to cast a critical eye over the full team. The troop boasted six cannon, five six pounders and a single five and a half inch howitzer. Cannon were denoted by the weight of the largest solid iron ball that would fit down the muzzle to be fired. Their iron barrels gleamed in the sunlight, sitting on their grey painted wooden carriages with great spoked wheels. The carriage extended back beyond the barrel, angling downward to rest on the floor, this was termed the 'trail'. The trail formed the third contact point with the ground, which with the wheels formed a stable platform for the cannon. The gun carriages differed fundamentally in design from Continental armies; they used a trail that had two solid arms angling back in a V shape with cross pieces to give added strength and stability. British guns only had the single solid trail, which made the frame much lighter and significantly more manoeuvrable. The foot of the trails had a large iron hoop bolted on to them. When the hoop was attached to a hook on the back of the limbers, the horse teams could pull the cannon along. Cannon were designed to fire balls on a horizontal trajectory, which smashed through anything directly in its path. Unfortunately targets could often hide behind cover and thus be protected from direct fire, hence the introduction of a howitzer into the battery. These guns looked very similar to ordinary cannon but had the ability to angle the barrel upwards via a simple screw or wedge mechanism, to 'lob' their fire over intervening cover and reach their target. Howitzers were strangely designated by a different method, the simple diameter of the barrel, such as the five and a half inch one they used. All countries tended to use mixed batteries of cannon and howitzers, all the guns were fundamentally of similar design and performance, but the British had a secret weapon, 'shrapnel'. All nations fired shells from howitzers; these were spherical iron casings filled with explosive. The act of firing the shell from the muzzle ignited the shell's fuse, it arced high into the air and would land from a steep trajectory, often sitting on the ground for a few seconds hissing loudly, as the fuse burnt down then exploded. The explosion sent shards of the casing in all directions causing serious injuries. The problem was that shells often smashed on impact on rocky ground or sank very deeply into the soft earth, where they exploded, showering those nearby with harmless mud. Those that landed properly could also be disarmed before the fuse burnt down by some intrepid individual plucking out the still burning fuse, or more often they sat hissing for a few seconds giving warning of the imminent explosion, allowing everyone to lie down or take cover before the blast.

Captain William Shrapnel had invented an alternative, the Shrapnel shell, more commonly called 'spherical case shot'. He simply redesigned the common shell, thinning the casing and packing musket balls into the void along with the explosive. The fuse was cut by well trained gunners, timed to explode in the air at about head height, the casing and balls spreading outwards to shower the target below. One such shell could destroy a complete gun team or decimate a closely packed column of infantry. Amazingly, although it had been used with great effect throughout the Peninsula war, the French had never copied the idea and it remained a virtual 'secret weapon'.

The troop was also confusingly termed a brigade, each Captain could command a three gun 'half brigade' each, if required to divide. The three lieutenants commanded two guns each, termed a 'division', each gun within the division was commanded by an NCO, known as a sub division, therefore the troop could operate efficiently at an individual level.

The troop was drawn up in its three 'divisions' for the inspection, each lieutenant reporting his own teams of two guns. The guns were all harnessed onto their limbers, the box seats of which held emergency ammunition but also formed a seat where two gunners sat. The drivers sat astride the left hand horses to control the teams of eight horses. Ten gunners for each cannon rode individual horses and lined up in pairs behind their gun. Behind each cannon was a wagon filled with the cannonballs, shells and charges for each gun, here the last three gunners of each team sat with a driver controlling the six-horse team. Further back stood another line of 'reserve' ammunition wagons, one to each of the three gun 'divisions'. At the rear of all, stood the ancillary wagons, a cart for spare wheels; one set up as a travelling forge; another to transport an anvil for shoeing the horses and a wagon for the baggage; each cart was furnished with a driver and four horses. Thirty spare horses stood to one side; these were to replace any that may be lost in action. The Ordnance Board allocated each officer a horse and a pack mule, but most self-respecting officers had two more furnished at their own expense. The Surgeon, Mr Hichens was further issued a horse and pack mule for his chest. Alexander viewed this impressive array of military might and his emotions welled up within him, he was proud of his troop. One hundred and eighty nine officers and men and two hundred and twenty six horses and mules in total, it was a sizeable team with a powerful punch, he was awed by the responsibility. Four officers; a Surgeon; eight non commissioned officers; six bombardiers that cut the fuses to length; one farrier; three shoeing smiths; two collar makers; one wheel maker; one trumpeter; eighty two gunners and eighty drivers; that was his command. Only one man was absent, Gunner Rees Harris who had been sickly for months and had been left behind in Colchester.

He would do his best for them; he just hoped that it would be enough to get them through. He lifted his eyes and offered a silent prayer to the Almighty to give him his help, for now Alexander realised how little of campaigning he knew. Then he mentally upbraided himself for his fears, he must show total confidence, and they would get through somehow. He spurred Cossack forward to receive the salute and reports from the officers as he commenced a thorough inspection.

Alexander took an age to inspect every horse and their equipment to ensure that it had all been restored to perfect condition after the misuse it had suffered. The dousing in salt water had hardened the leather making it rub on the horses. All the leather had been dried, wiped to remove salt residue and repeatedly 'blacked' to regain its suppleness. The horses had been thoroughly groomed, their matted manes brushed through and having rested with ample rations, their eyes and coats gleamed, they were at their peak again. There was no evidence of long-term deterioration in their condition from their ordeal; they had come through their first major trial well. He was rightly pleased.

PRACTISE

Alexander led G Troop out onto the road in search of a practice ground. The troop marched about four miles through a number of small villages, until entering a tiny hamlet marked Denderhaut on his map, Alexander discovered a large pasture, that was not in cultivation and would suit his needs ideally.

He ordered them into the field, parked the reserve carts near the entrance and put the gun teams through their paces. The six guns lined up at one end of the pasture, and then Alexander ordered Henry Bowen the bugler to order the advance, at which they trotted forward, and then broke into a gallop. Without warning, he indicated again to Bowen who sounded the sharp notes of 'prepare to engage'. With scarcely a word uttered, the horses slowed, rapidly performed a full one hundred and eighty degree turn then halted. The cannon were now facing the 'enemy' and were unlimbered in seconds by the gunners, the trails striking the ground with a solid thud. The horse teams trotted to the rear and the gunner's horses were led out of the way. The caissons having also advanced were now in position fifty yards behind the guns; ready to issue further ammunition once the limber supplies were exhausted.

The 'aimer' quickly judged the distance to fire unless ordered at a set range. This time Alexander bellowed, "Target three hundred yards, engage at will". The aimers quickly looked through their sights, ordering the others to lever the trails left or right with their iron bars until the barrel pointed directly at the target; then turned the screw elevator to the desired range.

The men went through the routine like clockwork, the 'sponge man' swabbed the barrel out with a saturated fleece tied to a pole, which damped the hot cannon down, removed any burning embers still in the barrel and removed any carbon deposits that might impair it's effectiveness between firings.

As the 'Sponge man' worked, the 'Vents-man' stepped forward to place his right thumb, which was encased in a leather stall, over the touchhole to prevent ingress of air prematurely igniting the explosive charge as the cannon was loaded.

Another stepped forward with the pre packed charge. The ammunition consisted of a mass of gunpowder packed with a wooden disc at one end, this formed a divide between the iron cannon ball and explosive, the complete assembly was then wrapped in paper or canvas. The 'Charge-man' placed this parcel in the muzzle and the 'Sponge man', using a ball shaped tool on the opposite end of his pole rammed the charge to the base of the barrel.

The 'Vents man' then removed his thumb from the touchhole and inserted a metal spike into the hole, which penetrated the paper wrapper of the charge, releasing some of the gunpowder. On the order to fire from the NCO in charge of the gun, the 'Vents man' applied a lighted slow match, which was twisted around a stick, to the touchhole and the charge would ignite. The resulting explosion drove the cannonball out of the barrel at high velocity.

The operation of loading and firing, if done slickly, took no more than thirty seconds. Indeed, any half decent team would be able to sustain a rate of twice a minute for a reasonably long period of time. The other team members were employed in fetching the ammunition from the wagons or dragging the gun back into position after each firing as they had a severe recoil, jumping backwards many feet on firing. The constant dragging of the cannon back into position was usually the greatest exertion for the gun teams in battle.

Alexander timed the unlimbering of each team to the moment of the first shot discharged on his fob watch. They all achieved timings of less than two minutes, a good speed; obviously they had not lost their edge.

They loosed off a further five blank charges each, then using a decayed farm ruin at the far end of the field as a target, they practised three rounds each with real ball. Little was left of the barn walls following two excellent shots from Staff Sergeant Hall's team.

Alexander called out to John Hincks "Your division do you proud, Sir. The others need to learn from your team, such accuracy under pressure is essential, well done."

Alexander was highly pleased with the days practise and ordered the march back to the chateau, they would celebrate tonight!

Their return in the fading light of dusk was marred by the sight of a deputation of local farmers arguing with Mr Coates on the chateau lawns. The group spotted the returning troop and immediately turned to approach Alexander. He reined in Cossack to halt, as the troop continued past him, through the archway and on into the stables.

Alexander could see anger on the faces of the Belgian landowners.

"What is it Joshua?" he enquired.

Coates looked exasperated, "I have informed them of our need for carts, fodder and provisions, but they refuse to release them until you returned. I wish to form a park and magazine at Mister Walsdragen's farm, but they are not happy to comply."

'Petit Jean' was present and was obviously deputised by the others to put their case. He stepped near to Cossack, patting the horse as he spoke softly but with authority.

"Captain Mercer, the farmers cannot work without their horses and carts, they wish to keep them on the farms until needed, they promise to deliver them within an hour of you calling for them."

Alexander recognised their concerns and relented, "Please tell them that they may use them until we order them away, but they must hand them over immediately I order."

Joshua was horrified, "Alexander, you cannot do this, it will take far too long to form them when you need them. Their promises are rash, my experience in Spain tells me that we must requisition now, or hang the consequences. Indeed the rations we have accumulated so far for the horses are totally inadequate and I need to collect a great deal more. As the saying goes, 'the more flesh a horse carries the more he has to lose and therefore the longer privation he will endure'."

Robert Newman interrupted, "I think you should reconsider, it is a bad decision Captain Mercer."

Ingilby nodded his silent agreement with Newman.

Such a public challenge angered Alexander; his irritation with Robert was growing deeper daily.

"The decision is made and I stand by it, you will not question my decisions, Mister Newman," he snapped back.

Robert was not so easily diverted. "You must reconsider, it......"

Alexander raised his palm firmly, plainly indicating to Newman for silence. He was determined to crush this threat to his authority. "Captain Newman, you will retire or I will be forced to refer your challenge to a Court Martial."

Robert Newman rode off, crest fallen but indefatigable in his aim to undermine Alexander. His contempt for him had reached new depths, how could he not listen to his experienced opinion?

Alexander had decided to trust the farmers and he tried to calm Joshua. "It is my decision and I will be accountable for it as the senior officer."

He was aware that this was the first occasion that he had overruled his more experienced colleagues, and hoped that he would not live to rue his firmness. However, he could not now lose face by altering his judgement, he would tough it out. The deputation left in high glee having achieved their goal and peace was restored.

The days rolled by, some mornings, the low growling sound of distant cannon fire could be heard. It had initially caused some consternation, but the farmers had informed Alexander, that it was the Belgian artillery based at Mons carrying out regular firing practise.

Time passed monotonously in a continuous round of field practise followed by relaxation at the chateau. Occasionally when they arrived at the field, King Louis' Garde de Corps, whom they had known at Ghent, was already using it for drill, causing them to stand and wait. Other days they arrived before the Garde, when they were in turn forced to wait whilst G troop went through its paces. The Garde numbered some two hundred men, many little more than youths; they were dressed in the various uniforms of all the colours of the rainbow, which they had worn in the French army before fleeing with the King. They were put through their paces by the Duc de Berri the King's brother, a short, dumpy, surly character with a bellowing voice and a vocabulary consisting entirely of expletives.

One morning, one of the troop dogs took exception to the Duc's horse and barked constantly whilst nipping at the horse's legs. The horse was worried by the hound's antics, shying and kicking in an effort to rid it of this nuisance. The Duc lost his temper and drawing his sword, thrashed left and right in a determined effort to dispatch the cur. The antics amused all who watched, which made the Duc even more furious. The Frenchmen fought valiantly to control their stifled laughs through gritted teeth, sounding like so many engines releasing steam. G troop had no such problem with controlling their reactions and roared loudly. The dog was repeatedly called without success by Butterworth, until eventually the rascal grew bored of nipping at the horse and retired quietly to his master. The Duc slumped forward onto his horse's neck from sheer exhaustion. Eventually regaining some composure, he raised himself until he stood in his stirrups and with undisguised anger ordered his corps to march off the field.

Driver Thomas Dibbin shouted after them "I'd not be in their boots for one hundred guineas tonight!" everyone nodded their agreement.

"Aye, they'll be sorry for laughing at him!" added Gunner Death.

Alexander rode up alongside Butterworth, "Keep that bloody dog under control!" he barked.

"Aye Sir" he answered meekly.

Alexander turned away to ride back to the head of the troop and couldn't resist a small chuckle at recent events.

In the interminable days that followed as week followed week, the two units continued to meet at the field regularly, but little love was lost between the commanders and rarely a word was exchanged during the changeover.

Once inspection was complete, if it were not a practise day, Alexander would often ride out alone for exercise on Cossack or Nelly his second horse. Passing through the surrounding villages, he encountered numerous camps of the various cavalry and artillery units dotted throughout the neighbourhood for ease of supply of victuals. The area had rightly been chosen as a very fertile spot with plenty of forage for the vast number of horses belonging to the cavalry and artillery. At a number of these camps, he would stop to pass a few words with old acquaintances and to exchange news, not that there seemed to be much happening. Sometimes he rode near to Brussels itself and came across the Brunswickers practising in the fields and hedgerows. Their Duke was aware that they were largely raw recruits and had them camp with sentries out and guards formed, they were to constantly act as if the French were no more than a mile away, which helped them to learn and understand their trade quickly.

On the 19th May, Sir George Wood, the Commander of all the Artillery under Lord Wellington, had ordered an inspection of his horse artillery troops. It took place at G troop's practise field near Denderhaut, all six troops lined up alongside each other making an impressive display. Alexander was proud to stand as a troop commander alongside such men as Robert Bull commanding I troop, James Webber Smith of F troop, Norman Ramsay of H troop, Hew Ross of A troop and George Beane of D troop. Virtually all had served in the Peninsula and possessed great experience of command, this made Alexander all the more nervous, but made the accolade of the best turned out troop an even sweeter moment. Many of the officers in the various troops were old colleagues, Alexander and his team richly enjoyed the opportunity to rekindle old friendships. Alexander mused how they all sported non-regulation effects as Lord Wellington had little care for the fineries of dress code, he cared much more for the calibre of the man within. Ramsay sported a garish red and yellow striped light cavalry belt, Bull and Newland sported a 'full set' of moustache and beard; Alexander himself sported a fine non-regulation moustache. After the inspection, Sir George invited himself and Sir Augustus Frazer to their mess at the chateau where all enjoyed a convivial evening, the various servants being organised beautifully by Karl. Sir Augustus commanded the Royal Horse Artillery; he enjoyed a particularly high reputation, having served throughout the Peninsula War with distinction. He was a thorough gentleman, modest and a total professional, everyone's beau ideal. Talk turned to the current political situation.

Alexander dared to ask the question they all wanted answered. "Are we likely to move soon, Sir George?"

Wood looked thoughtful for a moment, considering his reply carefully. The general banter in the room quietened as everyone awaited his reply with interest.

"Latest reports from Grant in France to Lord Wellington do not indicate any threat from Napoleon's army at present."

Everyone knew of Colquhoun Grant and his daring exploits in Spain. Grant was probably the only man who had Wellington's utter trust; working as one of his 'Exploring Officers' deep behind enemy lines, but always dressed in his full scarlet uniform to avoid an ignoble death as a spy if caught. He and others like him hung around the edges of the French forces, collating reports from their own observations and those of the local landowners. Their only defence on being discovered was a remarkably fleet horse, to outstrip any French cavalrymen. If he was now in France gaining intelligence, Wellington was sure of ample warning of the French army's movements.

Frazer added, "It is planned that our army will march in concert with the Prussians in early July, when the Austrians, Russians and Spanish are ready to launch their own invasions from the South. Napoleon cannot win; he cannot hope to stand against over half a million men! We will have a pleasant stroll to Paris, mark my words Gentlemen!"

Robert Newland proposed a toast, "To the downfall of the Monster!" which was cheered by all,

Two days later, a messenger rode into the courtyard of the chateau; he was hot and thirsty from his hard, exhausting ride. Alexander eagerly took possession of the numerous reports and orders he had brought and bid William take the despatch rider to the kitchen for refreshments, whilst he saw if there were any urgent replies required that could return with the dragoon.

The first he opened was a very welcome order from Sir Augustus Frazer; he was to send the five six pounder cannon back to Ghent, where they were to be exchanged for larger nine pounders. Alexander was pleased to issue orders for Robert Newland to command the teams which would proceed to Ghent the following morning, as the nine pounders packed a much more powerful punch. The six pounders were a little weak for modern warfare, indeed the French preferred twelve pounders, which Napoleon, an ex gunner himself, called his 'Pretty girls', but many French units still carried 6 pounders as they did. They did indeed pack a punch, but had been no match for nine pounders with shrapnel shells in Spain. He could thank Sir Augustus Frazer for convincing Wellington of the need to improve their firepower.

Another official notification was from the Ordnance Board, which had decided that his troop was overborne with officers, and in their wisdom ordered that William Ingilby was to transfer to Sir Robert Gardiner's troop, which was short of officers. That had been Robert Newland's old unit, when a Lieutenant in Spain. It had the advantage of depriving Newland of his arch accomplice in his campaigns to undermine him. Alexander was not unaware that Ingilby often felt frustrated with him, but when all was said and done, Alexander would miss the miserable bugger of a Yorkshire man! Ingilby would have to set off in the morning, so they would arrange a good send off that night.

A letter from Sir George Wood brought news of a major review of the troops by Lord Wellington and Marshal Blucher the Prussian Commander in Chief, on the 29th May. The review would take place at Grammont and afterwards all commanding officers were invited to a grand banquet at Ninove, cavalry headquarters. Sir George also let slip that farmer Walsdragen had written a complaint regarding Alexander to headquarters, despite his decision to leave them with their carts, but not to worry, Sir George hinted that somehow it had been lost in the system! Alexander breathed a sigh of relief, as Lord Wellington was known to react violently to serious complaints from locals, he tended to side with them without seeking the officer's own version of events, at least that's how the officers saw it. He suggested that the division presently stationed at Walsdragen's farm be moved, Alexander immediately ordered them to move to another chateau farm about a mile further away at Ysingen, Henry Leathes as their divisional officer would have to live out there with them.

Having completed the official business, Alexander turned with joy to the two letters from his family in England, which Bombardier Masterton had sorted from the bundle of ordinary mail the messenger had also brought. Alexander could easily recognise the handwriting on the envelopes; the one was the untidy impatient scrawl of his father, the other the painfully perfect script of his meticulous sister. All at home were well, their letters spoke of family, friends, neighbours, horses and dogs, all trivial but read through three times over. He poured over every word, bringing thoughts of home flooding to the fore of his mind. It was a bitter sweet experience; the excitement of receiving news of loved ones soon succumbed to feelings of dejection, as thoughts of missing family life and friends washed over him. One was left with a good feeling from knowing that all was well, but tinged with a longing for the day that would bring them back together again. One could wonder why they put themselves through such torture, but the look of utter misery on the faces of those that did not receive any letters at all answered that. Some contact with that sane, normal world was infinitely preferable to no contact at all.

The next day was one full of fretting for Alexander, he worried that orders to move would arrive, or the French would attack, whilst Newland and his cannon were away in Ghent. Following a quick, formal farewell William Ingilby rode off to his new appointment, Alexander watched him ride out of the grounds and wished him well. He strolled along the path skirting a large wood on the edge of the estate with Bal tucked at his heels. He planned to take a long walk in the pleasant sunshine, partly to refresh himself following the heavy drinking of last night as they saw old Ingilby off; and secondly, as a futile attempt to distract himself from his worries. He did not even reach the gate at the end of the wood before his plans were destroyed. A very angry farmer Van Hyden, who owned the farm adjoining the chateau, beset him. Accompanying him was 'Petit Jean', who marched up to Alexander triumphantly hauling John Butterworth along by his collar.

Van Hyden tried to explain through his anger, but his Flemish was rushed and incoherent from rage, 'Petit Jean' explained succinctly in French.

"This man has been arrested, caught in the act of stealing potatoes from Mr Van Hyden's garden."

Alexander was angry; Lord Wellington would blame him for his men upsetting the locals, if this ever got to his ears.

Turning to Butterworth he spoke harshly, little concealing his frustration. "Well what have you got to say for yourself?"

John Butterworth showed no remorse, indeed he was indignant. "I did take some potatoes up, Sir, but they were just a few for to add to my meal and he does have plenty."

"That is no excuse, you know the penalty for stealing" Alexander warned.

"But, he struck me Sir, with his cane, there was no need for that!" indicating Van Hyden's walking stick propped alongside him.

'Petit Jean' understood and roared as his rage erupted!

"Merde, cochin!" he raged at Van Hyden and proceeded to strike the farmer across the head with his own cane. Alexander understood enough Flemish through the tirade of expletives to indicate that 'Petit Jean' was horrified that the farmer had struck a soldier, how dare he? Van Hyden fled, squealing like a pig, the policeman continuing to strike him, as they disappeared towards his farm.

The amazing scene had lightened Alexander's anger and there was little chance of a complaint going to Brussels now! Turning to Butterworth he warned, "You are a lucky man Butterworth. You appear to have got away Scot free this time........but do not fail me again!"

John Butterworth full of contrition meekly saluted and skulked away, professing his gratitude until he turned the corner of the chateau and was out of sight. He stopped to rest his head against the stone wall, a broad grin played across his face as he pulled dozens of fine new potatoes from his deep pockets. That had been close but he'd got away with it again!

Alexander continued with his walk in a vain attempt to ease his worried mind, but no matter what he did, he couldn't clear his head. He strolled around the neighbourhood until evening eventually came, when the chill in the air as the sun slipped below the horizon urged him to return to the chateau. With no alarm coming, he unwound a little as he lazed in the mess, but he did not completely relax until the sound of hooves clattering on the cobbled yard below, finally announced the return of the teams with the new nine pounders. He needed a cigar and a hefty bumper!

Each day followed another with the same monotonous routines, everyone longed for a move, something new to do. Eventually, they had even learnt to sleep despite the interminable racket of the frogs. The noise had become bearable with the windows all closed to dull the sound. However, now that the evenings were turning warm and sultry, windows had to be left open to avoid suffocating. The frog choir seemed to grow audibly each night and it became unbearable again, plans would have to be made to destroy or drive the frogs away. Striking them with wooden staves on the banks succeeded in killing hordes. The scene soon became disgusting, ooze and slime was splattered everywhere from their numberless corpses. All fell silent and they retired to the mess to celebrate their victory, but within half an hour it was obvious that they had not won the war! A few hardy frogs had reappeared, reconnoitred the scene of carnage and long before an hour had passed, thousands of relatives had joined the mourners, croaking their sorrow. Three evenings of this carnage did not improve anything, still they returned in greater multitudes. This led to more drastic measures being suggested in their desperation. Henry Leathes idea was explosive charges; Alexander declined it as too excessive! Richard Hichens and John Bretton had a theory that the frogs disappeared into the water whilst the attacks progressed; they would destroy them by using their cudgels from a rickety homemade raft. The men enthusiastically helped collect the spare butts and planking to construct the wooden platform. They were glad to relieve the boredom of the evenings, and they were amused to conjecture on their success. Launch day eventually arrived with great hopes of finally solving the problem. Having pushed the raft out on to the water gingerly, they were relieved to see it float unaided. The platform was just wide enough for the two to stand at each end, still allowing them the room to swing their weapons of death. They were cheered as John and Richard crawled onboard and the raft was propelled towards the centre of the moat. Having gained confidence in the solidity of the raft, they struck all around at the numberless targets that bobbed on the surface. They did kill huge numbers, but more seemed to emerge as quickly as they destroyed them. Exhaustion crept upon them but desperation drove them on, they struck out more and more wildly in a vain attempt to succeed. Their movements becoming more and more violent they rocked the platform wildly, until the inevitable finally occurred. One edge of the platform descended deep into the water and the boards slowly arced up and over as the raft turned turtle. Both occupants were propelled into the stinking waters! Having floundered for a few seconds, their splashing ceased as the realisation dawned that they could simply stand up in the moat. . The waters reached only up to the chest at its deepest. The cheers and roaring laughter of the spectators sent them into fits of apoplexy.

They dragged themselves through the stinking pool to the edge where eager hands helped haul them from the putrid waters. They stood dripping with ooze, their shirts green with slime.

Their servants ran into the chateau to order vast amounts of boiling hot water to allow them to bathe. Alexander stopped his roar for a few seconds to receive the parcel he had sent William to fetch from his room. With all seriousness he offered the box to Richard. Opening the package, Richard smiled in recognition; it was a large bottle of eau de cologne.

"You will need all of that to hide the stench!" he proffered, before resuming his roar. Everybody joined the fun; they would not live this one down for a good while!

Drastic action was going to be required to eradicate this frog problem Alexander thought as he mulled over the days occurrences, he would have to devise a better plan.

Next morning, he called for the old gardener and ordered him to let the sluice open, to drain the moat and so kill the frogs. The Belgian argued against it, he claimed that the Prussians had tried it only the year before but had given up because of the stench. Alexander was adamant that it was to happen; the weather had turned cool and cloudy again, so the smell should be minimal. The gardener grumbled loudly as he closed the fill channel and opened the drainage sluices. The water levels in the moat started to drop very slowly and after two days only half the water had drained away revealing a thick layer of green slime and the bodies of thousands of frogs. Then the sun peeped out from cover again and the temperatures soared, so did the smell of putrefaction! The smell was unbearable; but still they struggled on for another day, walking around the chateau with handkerchiefs held to their noses. By that evening the frogs had diminished markedly in volume, they were winning! It was decided to continue for another few days to empty the moat completely, the stench would be worth it. However the following morning, the foul smelling waters ruined their breakfast and being unable to stand it any more, Alexander ordered the sluices reset to fill the moat again. The purgatory was not so easily finished, it continued for three whole days, whilst the waters rose high enough for the slime to sink beneath the surface and the air to begin to purify. At least the frogs had been defeated Alexander mused; the fetid stench had been worth it.

Late that evening Alexander lay in his bed enjoying the peace, his eyelids felt heavy. A croak! Then another! Soon dozens of the amphibians were vying for the accolade of loudest voice. Unbelievably the frogs had returned, in just as large numbers as before.

Alexander, like all the others, lay in bed infuriated by their inability to eradicate the problem. However, after a while listening to the interminable racket, sleep had finally stolen up on each of them. They soon realised that they had become acclimatised to the din at night and slept despite it, so they agreed to leave the frogs in peace. Alexander and the others were forced to admit total defeat!

THE REVIEW

Finally, the day of the grand review had arrived and at first light Alexander gave the order for the troop to proceed on the road to Grammont. Only the cannon and gun crews were required, the remainder were to stay at the chateau with Robert in command.

Alexander was happy to put a few miles between the two of them for a while. Following a poor map that he had removed from a book in the chateau's library, they had managed to find their way. They travelled some ten miles over pot-holed roads, where they had been forced to stop frequently to cover the holes with earth and brushwood before they could proceed. Eventually, the village and a large plain bordering the meandering River Dender came into view. Many cavalry regiments could already be seen on the broad plateau, they were grooming their horses after their long dusty journeys.

Alexander ordered his troop into the position indicated to him and ordered the three Lieutenants to organise their men. They had to groom the horses, clean all the leather work, shine up the brass cannon and fittings, then brush their own uniforms down to remove the dirt and grime from the dry earth roads. Horses were fed and watered; the men quenched their own thirst from their canteens, washing the dust out of their throats.

A group of horsemen approached and the alarm went up that Lord Wellington and his guests were arriving early!

"The Duke, the Duke, the Duke's coming!" blurted Death.

However, the consternation soon subsided once the riders had been identified.

"Ah 'tis only the Duc de Berri and his aides, Stand down lads" barked Staff Sergeant Hall.

The Duc must have preceded the official guests on purpose, to upstage them and to display his own importance.

It was not to go to plan, for the senior officer politely but firmly refused him a salute. The troops were not ready and he was not entitled to one, as he was not formally reviewing them. This answer was not to the Duc's liking, his face went puce as his blood pressure rose visibly; he argued, but got the same reply from the brave officer. Finally he snapped, let rip with an almost unintelligible burst of profanity, then turning his horse sharply he struck out at the poor beast with his whip and disappeared in a great cloud of dust, hotly pursued by his entourage. The troops had watched proceedings whilst affecting an air of total indifference to the Duc. His departure brought forth a great roar of laughter, which would not do anything to improve his temper.

Driver Thomas Dibbin stood just in front of Alexander cleaning a horse collar; he looked up as the Frenchmen dashed away and shouted a parting shot.

"I wouldn't be one of them there French fellows at drill upon the common tomorrow for a penny, if they're not proper bully ragged, I'm damned."

Alexander smiled, he was right, the Duc would be furious for a week!

The review was to be an impressive affair to reassure the Prussians that the British were serious in supporting them during the planned invasion of France to oust the usurper Napoleon. There were three lines of troops spread across the total expanse of the plain. The front rank consisted of lines of hussars in their garish, brightly coloured uniforms, with numerous rows of braid in strong contrasting colours stretched across their breasts. A jacket of matching bright colour was worn fashionably over the shoulder with the right arm out of its sleeve, the jacket was known as a pelisse. It was all topped off with a great felt or fur hat of black or brown. These light horsemen copied the colourful uniforms of the original Hungarian hussars that had struck terror through the Turkish hordes of yore. Interspersed between the hussar regiments were the troops of horse artillery including G troop. The second line consisted of heavy dragoons; great brutes of men on giant horses, all wore scarlet uniforms with vertical stripes of gold and navy running down the chest and copied in the cummerbund; white belts and grey breeches with a broad red band running down the leg. A great brass helmet with a flowing black comb trailing over the shoulders completed the dramatic outfit; they contrasted strongly with the hussars.

Between each regiment of the dragoons there were foot artillery batteries stationed with their nine pounders. There were also a number of massive twenty-four pounders of the siege artillery. The third line contained further foot artillery units linking light dragoon regiments. These cavalrymen sported dark blue uniforms edged on the collar and cuffs with various bright colours that denoted individual regiments. The regimental colour was repeated on a large central panel of the jacket covering the chest and also formed the colour of the stripes on the grey trousers. This uniform was topped by a large bell shaped shako; adorned with a red and white cockade and tassels of gold.

Alexander and his troop were not to be outdone, with their own uniforms aping the hussars in style. They were dressed in their jackets of deep blue with yellow-gold braid and matching off the shoulder pelisse, the sleeves and collar edged in artillery red. The foot artillery did not sport such an extravagant version of the uniform, their blue jacket had little braid, they had no use for a pelisse and their infantry style 'stovepipe' shako was not as impressive as their counterpart's fur crested 'tarleton' helmet.

The overall effect of the parade was extremely impressive, the contrast of uniforms and colours, the sheer presence of six thousand cavalrymen and dozens of cannon in superb condition was awesome, Blucher could not help but be impressed!

At two o' clock, the Duke of Wellington and Marshal Blucher arrived, followed by a great mass of senior officers and orderlies. Ten cannon roared their salute as they entered the field.

The Duke was, unusually for him, dressed in full uniform, scarlet jacket adorned with medals, white breeches and black bicorn tipped with feathers. Blucher appeared in the sombre, deep blue jacket of the Prussian army with little adornment, he would have been difficult to recognise but for the stars and medals that adorned his jacket. His grey hair and long white moustachio softened his worn, hard features and dark piercing eyes. 'Marshal Forwards' as his troops affectionately knew him, was every inch the old warrior, the men wanted to impress him with their bearing and sat awaiting inspection firmly at attention. The generals took an age inspecting each cavalryman in minute detail and it seemed to be an interminable length of time before they reached G troop. Blucher immediately showed his delight at the superb display of horses and equipment.

"Mein Gott, dere iss not von 'orse in dis battery which is not goot enough for a Veldt Marshal!" he exclaimed.

Wellington and his staff roared with laughter and were clearly delighted with his reaction. Alexander permitted himself a smile, but quickly stopped when he caught sight of the scowl appearing on the Duke's face. The Marshal inspected the troop in great detail asking Alexander a mass of questions about their capabilities. Alexander was extremely gratified by the obvious interest he displayed. After a full inspection, Blucher turned to Wellington.

"I vish dat vee may see dis vonderful battery in battle, vot a sight."

They moved off to review the others and Alexander had plenty of time to contemplate the compliments of the old warhorse. It was in stark contrast with the Duke, who had not uttered a word, just that scowl. Nobody expected anything more from his Lordship; it was his way. He had very high standards and you knew that if he didn't like what he saw, then you wouldn't have to wait long to learn of his displeasure. The review ended with a march past in salute to the two generals.

Following the inspection, the troop was ordered back to the chateau in the charge of Henry Leathes. Alexander joined the senior officers on a ride to Ninove for the banquet that was to further welcome their Prussian guests. At the formal meal Alexander was seated between Colonel Arentschild the famous German Legion light cavalryman and Strenewitz hero of the Prussian hussars. Conversation was lively as these two great cavalry leaders reminisced over their exploits.

Following an extravagant meal of eight courses and

unlimited wines, coffee was served. Alexander was stood in the great drawing room of the chateau, discussing the day with Arentschild, when the Duke approached. Ignoring Alexander, Wellington conversed with Arentschild for nearly half an hour regarding the situation on the frontier. Alexander had no retreat as he stood in a bay window; he was forced to stand in silence whilst the two conversed across him. Initially the conversation was interesting, he listened avidly to the latest reports and understood that presently all was quiet and that the armies would invade France early in July as previously agreed with Blucher. Alexander smiled when he heard Wellington refer to Bonaparte as 'Jonathan Wild the Great', a reference to Napoleon's regime. Wild had been a notorious criminal, an organiser of robberies and receiver of stolen property; he had been hanged at Tyburn in 1725. Alexander smiled at the subtle dig at the French Emperor and his nefarious ways of financing his army. Finally, his Lordship stepped away and Alexander could move freely again, he had not even indicated that he was aware of Alexander's presence, a fine return for the success of his inspection that morning!

Returning to Strytem the following day, the tedious routine resumed, they had now been there seven weeks and there was no sign of a change. Alexander mused over the problem of keeping the men away from the local lasses and more importantly, the Geneva Gin! The men frequented the hostelry alongside the church in the village on mass after stabling the horses each night; it was usually also crowded with locals. Luckily there had been no major disturbances, just some minor fracas that 'Petit Jean' had managed to quieten down; he was proving an extremely helpful ally.

That evening, whilst walking with Bal enjoying a cigar in the lanes near the chateau, Alexander neared farmer

Walsdragen's residence. He spotted the gamekeeper that was always scouting the woods around the farm, but mysteriously never caught any rabbits! The sight of a half dressed wench and a shriek of laughter told him why; Walsdragen's daughters were the game!

Passing the farm, a loud scream harshly rent the silence; it was a cry of extreme pain and was followed rapidly by loud groans and wailing.

Alexander was at a loss as to what could have happened, but it could not be good, he instinctively ran towards the farm. As he reached the farm door, it opened and Walsdragen emerged, tears rolling down his cheeks. He stepped forward seemingly unaware of Alexander, then sank to his knees groaning loudly, tearing at his hair in a frenzy. Soon other members of the family emerged, clearly upset, some of the women moved to console Walsdragen. Two men carrying a shovel stepped aside and cut a clod of earth, taking the sod back into the house they proceeded upstairs; Alexander was drawn after them in his desire to discover what had happened. Reaching the master bedroom Alexander stared at the dreadful sight of Walsdragen's wife lying on the bed ashen faced, the sheets sodden with her blood; she had clearly died in childbirth. Alexander strained his hearing for the sound of a baby, but the sight of a woman placing a blood stained rag enclosing an immature foetus on the corpse's chest told him that there was no hope. He watched as the farmers gently placed the clod of earth beneath her head for a pillow, as local custom required, then retired discreetly. Alexander felt sorry for Walsdragen despite his previous confrontations; no man deserved such sadness in his life. Passing the distraught farmer he could think of nothing to say that would console the wretched man, he simply placed his hand on his shoulder and squeezed hard as a sign of comfort, and then walked on, the message would be understood.

The following evening a loud rapping at the main door of the chateau foretelling visitors found John Bretton sat at dinner with Alexander. The servants opened the door to Sergeant John Nisbitt, the sergeant of the division at Yssingen village. He reported that a gentleman in a dark blue tunic had arrived at his post and demanded in a very imperious manner that the accommodation at the chateau and village be prepared for Lord Uxbridge and two hundred cavalry that would arrive within the hour. When told that there was no room, he required to know which units were stationed there. The sergeant had told him of the division of the troop in residence there, when the gentleman had ridden off to report this to Lord Uxbridge and to gain further orders. The officer had strangely ridden off just as Lieutenant Henry Leathes had reappeared from his ride. The sergeant had then been ordered by Henry to report the incident and he had immediately ridden to the chateau.

John Bretton looked pleased "Lord Uxbridge here tonight, it will be a jolly evening."

Alexander laughed "Do you not see Henry, Uxbridge has no business here; he is in Brussels as second in command to the Duke. Our clever fellow must have been a spy, you will not see him again as he has gleaned all the information he wanted."

Sergeant Nisbitt looked aghast.

"Do not fret Nisbitt, you were not to know, return to your unit, he will be well gone by now."

The following morning, the sun arose into a sky uncluttered by even a wisp of cloud, promising another bright summer's day. Around mid morning Alexander saw the other officers off on the road to Brussels. They were invited to attend the Ball being arranged by the Duchess of Richmond that evening. Alexander would stay to command the troop as he had little liking for formal dances. It was a lonely evening on his own, but he settled with a copy of Homer's 'Iliad' from the library and eventually drifted off to sleep in a chair. Nearly eight weeks here had made him relax; he had no worries of anything happening whilst the other officers were away. It was the night of the 15th June 1815, a date that he was never to forget!

THE WAIT

The month the Rifles had resided in Brussels was one of the best times they had ever known. The people had made them thoroughly welcome, food and beer were plentiful and cheap, and the girls were not only very beautiful but also very friendly! Many a romance started to blossom for those whose wives hadn't followed, the lads relaxed, indeed the threat of war seemed a million miles away; but all knew that Napoleon and his armies were preparing for the contest and rumours abounded that he was going to attack Belgium first. If he could take the capital city of Belgium and drive the British into the sea and the Prussians back to Germany, he would be on the road to continental supremacy once again.

Lord Wellington would not allow his men to become jaded and out of practice. Three times weekly the battalion must manoeuvre using battlefield tactics, live firing was used to accustom the new men to the noise of their rifle and the hefty kick it made into the shoulder when fired. Captain Jonathan Leach and Sergeant Robert Fairfoot put the Rifles through their paces, he ensured that the men had their pairs, each experienced peninsula man with a rookie. They would rely upon each other completely in battle, the pairs worked together in harmony, one firing, the second reserving his fire whilst the first reloaded, then vice versa. You were at your most vulnerable when loading, your partner covered you and with one up the spout of his rifle he could fire on any real danger threatening you. They worked hard to build this rapport and total understanding of each other; complete trust was the only way to survive.

The Baker rifle was their weapon and a damn good one it was. Most of the army was issued with muskets, the good old 'Brown Bess' as everybody called it affectionately. Couldn't hit a barn door at 100 yards! That's why the 'lobsters', as they called the red tunic'd infantry, fired on mass, if three hundred fired together some would hit the target. As the French attacked in huge 'columns', solid blocks of men, designed to overwhelm the opposition by sheer weight of numbers; the musket had a much greater chance of hitting someone when fired at such a mass of humanity. When you loosed off three rounds per minute as well trained infantry could, then they caused a lot of casualties. The large lead balls produced horrendous injuries, they flattened on impact tearing gaping holes in flesh and organs, splintering bone into hundreds of shards and often slowed enough to come to rest deep in muscle where it could cause discomfort but more dangerously, infection and gangrene. A couple of rolling volleys immediately followed up by a bayonet charge and the French would run away, at least they always had in Spain; they had never been keen on cold steel!

The Rifle troops had a very different role and Sergeant Fairfoot checked his men's understanding. The recruits had trained thoroughly but they hadn't used the tactics for real, it needed to be second nature, automatic, if you stopped to think you were dead.

He watched the pairs working together, advancing

against an imaginary foe along the hedge lined country lanes in the rolling countryside bordering the City of Brussels. They darted from one point of cover to another, taking up firing positions to cover the others movement; it was like watching an army of ants darting about in all directions with no obvious aim but actually all working to one overall objective.

Robert Fairfoot watched their progress with an eagle eye.

"Murphy get your fat head down, do you want it shot off?"

"Costello, if you don't run faster than that, you'll be on latrine duty for a week!"

"Maher, who are you covering?"

"Treacy, Sergeant" was the reply.

"Well Treacy I'd be bloody worried if I was you, Maher's dreaming. Wake up Maher; did the Froggies take your brain out in prison?"

This went on every other day for a few weeks, then the men started to work well together, their trust and understanding was now instinctive and eventually Sergeant Fairfoot was satisfied.

Target practice was another exercise that was regularly practised to maintain their proficiency. The Baker rifle was a much more accurate weapon than the musket; any half decent shot could hit a man at two hundred yards. The problem was that it was a nightmare to load, the quarter turn rifling on the barrel which made it much more accurate than the smooth bore muskets, also made it much tougher to drive the firing charge and ball down the muzzle. Sometimes the fit was so tight that a small wooden mallet was needed to drive it down to the bottom of the barrel. Even experienced riflemen needed at least a minute to load and fire. This was why most troops didn't use the rifle; it was too slow to stop a determined massed enemy force. Even infantry could cover the two hundred yards of its range in a few minutes, closer than one hundred yards the troops with muskets were just as accurate and could fire three times as fast! No, that was a fight they couldn't hope to win.

Riflemen had a different role; they were to counter the French tactic of sending out clouds of 'skirmishers'. These light infantry spread out up to a hundred yards ahead of the main force, taking cover and firing to upset the formed ranks of the opposing troops, whilst the columns closed, screened from attack until close in ready to break through. All armies used skirmishers to protect their formed infantry in varying degrees, but most still supplied them with muskets; even many British light infantry units had muskets. The opposing skirmishers fought against their counterparts for supremacy, which would then allow them to damage the massed ranks behind. The Ninety Fifth were designed to counter the clouds of French voltigeurs and were one of the few units in any army supplied with rifles. This gave them a great advantage at distance and five years of fighting had given them a psychological supremacy over the French.

Sergeant Fairfoot checked their understanding of the tactics; he picked out Private Palmer, known as the 'Bomb proof man', having survived a shell exploding next to him back at Badajoz in 1812. He was a bleeding miracle man, didn't even get a scratch!

"Palmer, list your targets"

"Officers Sergeant, on horses first as they are usually senior officers and the fancier dressed the better. Rich pickings if you can get to the body later!"

The men laughed.

Robert Fairfoot did not smile "Steady lads, who else Palmer?"

"Junior Officers, Standard bearers, drummers and buglers... and any one looking like they are giving the rest the courage to keep advancing;.....oh! and Sergeants, Sarge" he beamed.

The men laughed again.

"All right Palmer" Robert admonished. Then an evil thought flashed through his mind.

"Now let's see how your shooting is men. Plunket step forward and show them how to shoot, Palmer you hold the target."

"But Sarge" blurted Palmer.

"What's wrong Palmer, don't you trust Plunket? Get going, measure out two hundred paces and hold the target up."

Palmer looked worried and ambled disconcertedly out to the distance set.

"Get a move on Palmer" Fairfoot chivvied him.

Eventually he reached the correct distance; he reluctantly stood holding the raffia disc measuring twelve inches in diameter, high above his head whilst Plunket took aim.

Plunket was the best shot in the regiment, possibly the best in the army. He actually served with the second battalion of the Ninety Fifth, which had been in Belgium a month before the first battalion. He had been requested to come over for a few days to improve the shooting skills of the newer Riflemen. Tom was famous for hanging back on the retreat to Corunna to pick off General Colbert leading the French advance. He had taken his time, despite the French cavalrymen closing rapidly and his one shot struck the General, killing him outright. He then bolted for the cover of his colleagues, just reaching safety before the swords of the pursuing horsemen pricked his back. Tom was another Irishman, of middle height, brown hair and piercing grey eyes, he had become famous in the newspapers at home and he had risen to Sergeant. But, Tom liked the bottle a little too much; he was often to be seen dancing the hornpipe on a hogshead barrel or quarrelling with the locals when three sheets to the wind. He had actually tried to shoot his company officer Lieutenant Stewart one day when very drunk; luckily the guard having been alerted by his loud threats caught him and locked him up before he had found Stewart. They would normally have shot him for such a very serious offence, but he was only broken back to Private. His fame at home had saved him, the army not wanting any public embarrassment over its most famous ranker. That had been back in 1809 and he had stayed at Private ever since. To be fair to Lieutenant Archibald Stewart, he had never mentioned the incident again nor held a grudge against him.

Now, to take aim Tom chose to lie on his back, feet facing towards the target, just as he had with the shot that had General Colbert's name on it. He lifted his head to look down the line of the barrel which rested between his feet, he judged the initial rise of the ball as it left the barrel and the amount the ball would drop over two hundred paces, allowed a little for the light wind blowing on his right cheek and set his breathing into a slow deep pattern as he waited for the perfect moment.

Tom drew his breath and gently held it as he settled for the shot, his finger squeezing the trigger smoothly without snatching, to maintain his aim.

God, he wished he hadn't had so much rum last night! He thought.

The rifle suddenly exploded into life, flame spewed from the barrel.

"Jesus" Palmer exclaimed as the target was torn from his hands.

The lads all cheered as Palmer bent down to recover the target and pushed his finger into the hole where the ball had passed through, a bull's eye!

Tom smiled, "Thank God for that" he inwardly thought, "Easy" he stated nonchalantly.

Sergeant Fairfoot looked at Palmer, "You won't be so cocky next time, will you?"

"No Sergeant" he murmured apologetically.

Turning around to the rest, he bellowed "Ten rounds each lads, set up targets on those stands at one hundred and fifty paces", no one volunteered to hold the targets!

The training continued regularly and eventually Robert Fairfoot felt confident in reporting the men ready for action to Captain Leach. As he walked towards the billet of Lieutenant Simmons at Monsieur Overmar's house, a local merchant, Robert bumped into an old colleague from the second battalion of the Rifles; he had heard vague rumours about his friend and raised the subject that had intrigued him for weeks.

"How's Mary then Mark?"

"You telling me you ain't heard?" he asked incredulously.

"Well I've 'eard stories, but what's the truth then?"

"When I goes home after the War, I finds Mary wiv anover guy, living in a little 'ouse down Walfamstow way wiv faav kids, she had two when I left!"

"What did you do?" Robert probed incredulously.

"Got hold o' geezer's scrawny neck, but Mary screams, army says oi'd snuffed it back at Badajoz so what was she to do? So I says give us sixpunse for 'er. He gives us the money and I waarks."

"That all?" Robert enquired.

"Wull, Ned Costello was wiv me, so we goes to Black 'Orse an' drinks 'er 'elf, wot else? Devil takes 'em I says!"

They arrived outside Monsieur Overmars; Mark Sugden bid his fellow Sergeant adieu and sauntered on. Mr Overmar's house was a fine three-storey residence in the merchant quarter; he was ushered through to the garden. There in the summerhouse were the officers, entertaining a number of the local ladies of polite society.

Lieutenant George Simmons had fallen on his feet with his billet, he had wonderful rooms overlooking the gardens, and the others had helped him acquire a servant and cook, then set his rooms up as the battalion mess. Good food and wine with handsome, rugged young officers had attracted the local ladies to their dinners.

Robert Fairfoot knew that he would find Captain Leach here; indeed there he was supping a glass of claret in the evening sunlight.

Jonathan Leach saw Robert approaching.

"Sergeant Fairfoot, good evening, how goes training?"

Robert replied, "The men's ready Sir" then paused, finally asking the question on his lips, "Sir is it true that Boney's on his way?"

Jonathan looked intently then replied thoughtfully, "We have heard the rumours ourselves, but nothing official is happening here, so we don't rightly know what to believe. However it would be wise to maintain our readiness."

Robert nodded, "Aye Sir", he saluted and strode away purposefully.

George Simmons enquired, "Do you really know anything Jonathan?"

"Do you really think they would tell me George?" he replied. "There are no orders from headquarters, I doubt Napoleon would be mad enough to invade."

Edward Chawner broke the contemplative mood, calling

out, "Whenever the call comes lads, there'll be plenty of balls flying and that's the quickest way to promotion!"

They all creased with laughter, soldiers humour, the death of a senior meant promotion up the ladder for all.

"A toast... to warm work!"

Just as they finished the toast George cried out in delight, "Hey look its Harry".

They all rushed over to greet their old comrade. Captain Harry Smith was originally from the first battalion Ninety Fifth and had shared all their trials and tribulations in Spain. Since then, he had been put on the staff of Sir John Lambert and had gone to America with him, whilst the others had returned home from France.

"How are you Harry, what are you doing here?"

"I'm here with Sir John Lambert who commands the Tenth Brigade, I continue as his Brigade Major." Then turning to the young man who had arrived with him, he announced. "This gentlemen is my brother Charles, who joins you as a Volunteer, actively looking for one of your berths!"

They roared with laughter again, Volunteers were gentlemen who could not afford to purchase a commission as an officer. They hoped to prove themselves worthy in battle and gain a commission without charge when a vacancy occurred, usually by the death of an officer. He would mess with them but would fight with a rifle as a common soldier, an odd situation, but there was no shame in it.

"And where pray is the beautiful Juana?" Jonathan enquired.

"I am here my friends," Juanna purred softly in her delightfully thick Spanish accent as she stepped out of the shadows.

They were overjoyed to see her again; she had been with

them in Spain from the time of the storming of Badajoz. That terrible night was seared into their memories; after suffering horrendous losses the troops had gone on an orgy of murder and rape throughout the fallen town. Harry had taken her out of the town to safety, she was then a young girl of fourteen but she had stayed with him ever since. Everyone loved Juana, with her long straight black hair falling down her back, dusky complexion and beautiful white teeth, she was a great beauty and Harry was a very lucky man. Indeed they were all very jealous of him.

The evening swept on, the wine flowed freely and the party was enlivened by animated conversation of the old days, the good and bad times. They were carefree and life was good, indeed many were looking forward to the Duchess of Richmond's Ball the following evening as it promised to be quite a social event.

George Simmons relaxed on a chaise longue quietly enjoying his cigar and glass of port, the mellow smoke rising slowly in the still night air. He observed the numerous officers of the 'mess' enjoying the occasion into the early hours, but he couldn't help thinking that this good life could not last, rumours abounded of a French advance.

George watched them intently; for young men they all moved stiffly, some even needed a cane for support. They had all received numerous wounds throughout Spain and Southern France, which had aged their young frames prematurely. There was Major Alexander Cameron with a stiff left arm and weak side from a severe wound in Egypt some fifteen years ago and a limp from a ball through his thigh at Vitoria; Willie Johnstone, the first man into Ciudad Rodrigo, had a stiff left elbow ever since it had been shattered by a 'grape shot' at Badajoz, he hadn't been able to play his favourite fiddle ever since; Johnny Kincaid still got severe headaches from the musket ball that had dug a trench across the top of his head at Foz de Aronce; William Haggup held his stomach when standing, a stance he had maintained continuously since a ball ripped across his stomach at Nivelles, he'd nearly spilt his guts that day!

George rubbed his own thigh, which still throbbed occasionally. He still remembered the pain of the ball tearing into his right thigh. What wounds would the future bring them? He mused.

Johnny Kincaid sidled up close, "What will you get your young lady when we reach Paris, George?"

"Some fine lace I suppose, but I have promised her a lock of Bonaparte's hair, that's what she really wants!"

Johnny guffawed "No tall order from your Mary then!"

George smiled faintly, reflecting on his betrothed brought solemn thoughts of his future flooding forth.

Johnny Kincaid caught his mood and summed it up very succinctly "Wonder how many of us will live to see Paris, eh?"

Neither spoke again, they sat and drank in solemn contemplation of home and family until exhaustion drove them to their beds.

"Sergeant, Sergeant, you must wake up!" The words accompanied by a rough shaking of his shoulder wrenched Robert Fairfoot from his slumbers.

He opened his bleary eyes and peered into the featureless face of whoever was waking him so harshly. There was so little light from the poor candle flickering at the doorway that he could not make out his assailant. However, the unusual, clipped accent gave him away.

"What the bloody hell is going on, Casima?"

It had to be Casima; he was the only one with that shear quick speech and unmistakable pigeon English. Casima Casima was a short lad with jet-black hair and the dusky skin of the orient. He was originally from the East Indies and had travelled to England as a sailor on one of the Honourable East India Company's ships, merchant ships carrying the riches of the Far East to Europe, but armed like minor war vessels because of the threat of pirates and French frigates. Somehow Casima had volunteered into the Rifles in England but he seemed a round peg in a square hole.

"It is Maher Sergeant, he gone mad, he murdered man! They arrest him. You must see him."

As Duty Sergeant, Robert had to sort the matter out; he rose and dressed quickly, taking two men from the Guard with him, he proceeded with all haste to the Magistrates. He had the duty magistrate awoken by the court clerk and he eventually met Robert in his chambers. He was far from pleased at being woken in the middle of the night and did not hide his annoyance. However, following discussions with a police sergeant who had been summoned, he informed Robert that Private Maher had lost control when drunk; he had quarrelled with a local man outside a public house and as he had his musket with him, had shot him dead. He claimed self-defence and there was some evidence to support this, but he would be held until enquiries were complete and the Magistrate decided whether there was to be a trial or not.

Robert could do no more, he reported to Edward Chawner the Duty Officer, and returned to bed.

He had long expected Maher would eventually lose it one day. Since his harsh imprisonment by the French, he had developed a dark brooding nature, which had warned of something sinister lurking inside him and now it had finally broken out. Well he would have to sweat it out in gaol for a very long time before trial, he could hang for this.

The following morning, the 15th of June, Ned Costello

and a number of his company strolled through the bright streets of Brussels, their mongrels happily trotting alongside, eyeing the girls and enjoying the local beer at the many bars.

They sat outside a bar enjoying the warm sunlight of early summer and viewing the passing world, as it was a 'rest and recreation day'.

Palmer suddenly sat bolt upright, "Look lads, the 'death's heads', keep your dogs safe!"

The lads laughed, he'd seen some of the Black Brunswickers, German troops led by the Duke of Brunswick himself. They were always dressed completely in black apart from light blue collars and cuffs, a silver skull and cross bones on their caps completing their macabre appearance. They had worn those colours ever since the last Duke had died fighting at their head in Prussia in 1806. His son, the present Duke, had sworn vengeance on the French and had formed a force of infantry, cavalry and artillery from the mass of his subjects who had fled to England to escape the French occupation of his homeland.

The infantry had fought alongside the Rifles in Spain as skirmishers; early on they had been good troops, being all patriotic Germans. But as the war had dragged on and with the homeland no longer available as a recruiting ground, they were forced to recruit the scum of the earth including French, German and Italian prisoners of war who had been coerced to defect. These often joined simply to await an opportunity to escape back to their own side, which they succeeded in doing in terrific numbers. Lord Wellington would no longer allow them to go on picket duty for the army, to stop them running away so easily.

That's when they had got their reputation for stealing anything, including the dogs around the camp for food! Some officers had guards mounted on their packs of hunting hounds, used for recreation when in camp, just to keep them safe. Lord Wellington used to join the foxhunts; he liked nothing better than to chase the hounds across the barren plains of Spain.

The Brunswickers were much improved now, as during the peace the rubbish had been weeded out. The Duke was able to recruit in his homeland again, now that it was free of French domination and he had rapidly filled his ranks with loyal subjects. The Brunswick Corps was also billeted in Brussels alongside the Fifth Division.

Later, whilst walking the town the lads crossed paths with a group of surgeons, 'Sawbones'.

"Good day to you Mr Burke and Mr Robson" Ned called out in recognition.

Mr Burke was the battalion Surgeon and Robson his Assistant Surgeon; they had seen them safely through Spain, now they were checking their equipment in case of need again.

"Good day lads......ah Rifleman Jones, how are your piles?" Joseph Burke enquired maliciously.

"Look you they're fine Sir" he replied sheepishly in his lilting Welsh accent. The others laughed heartily, he had walked funny ever since he had run the gauntlet of French fire at Arcangues, they'd shot him in the rump!

"Ned your leg okay?"

"Aye no complaints Soir"

"Let me cut it out Ned"

"It don't bother Soir, I begs you leave it be!"

Ned instinctively felt his left thigh; the ball was still there under the skin after three years, he ran his fingers over the hard lump in the fatty flesh.

They had retreated fast at the Coa, thanks to a mess up by old General Craufurd. Climbing a wall, Ned had been hit in the leg just below the right knee and fallen. Good job

John Little had carried him back until he also copped a ball in the arm and dropped Ned like a ton of bricks onto the hard unforgiving earth. As he fell, Ned felt another ball enter his left thigh and was only saved by his mate William Green, who had carried him over the bridge to safety at the church where Mr Burke was tending the sick. Poor William had copped his home ticket at Badajoz later and was safe back in England, lucky sod!

Surgeon Burke had checked Ned over, the first ball had gone straight through without any serious damage, the second in the thigh lay near the artery, it was dangerous to probe for and thank God that Mr Burke was not like a lot of surgeons who amputated first, then thought later. Ned had recovered well and only remembered the ball when it became agony in the cold weather. It had slowly worked itself near the skin but he still had no intention of having it cut out.

Mr Burke then turned on Tom with a wry smile, "Aah, Crawley, how goes the hand?"

"It's foin Sir, oi must be off!" Tom darted away looking very uncomfortable.

They all roared with laughter, his hand had been injured slightly at the Nivelle last year, but they knew why Tom ran.

Tom had a real fear of medics ever since he was taken violently ill back in 1811. He had screamed and writhed in agony from the excruciating pains in his stomach. After two days, the lads had forced him to see Mr Burke who had proscribed an emetic to cleanse his system of whatever was upsetting his gut. The cramps were awful and Tom swore that he had been poisoned and became delirious. Eventually the emetic had worked, a major evacuation relieved his pain, and he was saved. Mr Burke had checked the faeces and was amazed to find that the cause of his problem had been a three-inch lizard!

"Here he is lads", Mr Burke shouted proudly, whilst holding up a jar of alcohol in which he had preserved the offending lizard. No wonder Tom had left!

They bid the surgeons farewell, hoping not to need their services for a very long time.

As they were leaving, Mr Robson called "Have you heard lads, Sir Thomas Picton has just arrived, he wants the Division to muster tomorrow."

They groaned openly, that tough Welsh bastard would ruin the good life they had been enjoying; he'd work them till they dropped.

"He may be a brother Welshman, but he is a rum fellow!" declared Jones.

"Aye he will run us bully ragged" added Ned.

"Let's have a bloody good time while we can" added William Mc Nabb helpfully, they agreed and promptly set off on a tour of the bars of the City to embark on an almighty drinking session.

Meeting up with Robert Fairfoot, they all piled into a bar near the Grand Place. After numerous rounds of drinks, their stamina waned and Robert Fairfoot started to fall asleep in his chair. He was brought sharply out of this stupor by the deep voice of Captain Leach, "Sergeant Fairfoot, are you drunk on duty?"

"No Sir" he blustered as he sat bolt upright and rapidly sought to clear his mind.

The bar full of men just roared with laughter!

Robert raised his heavy head and there was instant recognition.

"Hetherington you bloody nuisance!"

Josh Hetherington smiled and feigned complete innocence, Robert sat back and relaxed with an inward smile, not for the public, he had to maintain his status. He could see the joke, but he couldn't show that he enjoyed it or they may think it all right to hoodwink him again. Josh was a light infantryman and had fought alongside the Rifles at many a battle and shared many a bivouac. He was a fine figure in his red jacket, grey trousers and tall black shako, a real lady killer, the Belgian ladies seemed to have a thing for the 'lobsters'. Josh was a great joker, a boon to have around the camp fires on cold wet nights to perk the spirits. Ned Costello and Josh were bosom pals, Ned was quick to stand, shaking his hand in warm welcome and hugging him with real joy at such a happy reunion.

Robert stared at Josh; the happy go lucky cockney, who had developed a great ability for mimicking and ventriloquism. He still remembered the funeral for a soldier in Spain back in 1810. As the procession for the old sot of a hospital attendant at Elvas passed through the town on route to the cemetery, the pallbearers had heard knocking and cries of "O Jesus wept, where the hell am I? O God no! For pity's sake let me out!" The bearers had immediately lain the coffin down and used their bayonets to prise the lid off the wooden box. They were met by the nauseous whiff of putrefying flesh; it was obvious that the old soak was well and truly dead! They were all bemused, but Robert and Ned had spotted Josh quietly mingling into the great crowd that had formed. The sod! It had been him.

They had quietly forced their way out of the crowd maintaining an air of dignity until they had turned the corner of the street, when they had fallen to their knees in convulsions of laughter. It was fully an hour before they could compose themselves, for passing locals looked at them with pity, their expressions of sympathy toward the English soldiers whose minds had obviously been turned by the unrelenting midday sun, simply rekindled their fits of untrammelled laughter.

With Josh in town, it would surely be a night to remember!

Whilst the majority of the officers lounged at George Simmon's mess that warm evening, Johnny Kincaid preferred to spend some time alone. He could not shake off a feeling of melancholy and despair, which he had felt since the day before and could not explain. He just knew that something awful was going to happen soon. Was this a premonition of his impending death? He remembered numerous stories in Spain of brave men who on the night before a battle had felt such depression and pronounced their impending demise to their friends. They were invariably right and for such superstitious men as soldiers are; the omens for his future were decidedly poor. He had always wondered whether these thoughts had made them less careful, often taking the lead in the battle as they were sure of their imminent demise therefore ensuring their own deaths, or whether it truly was a premonition warning them to prepare to meet their maker. He pondered his own situation, he thought longingly of home and family in Scotland, his comrades and his own relative youth, he had hoped that God would allow him a little longer in this realm. But there had been no battle on the morrow, all was quiet, he eventually concluded that he was simply having an off day, a little home sick and had allowed his paranoia to take over. He strolled along the pathways through the formal gardens of the parc de Bruxelles, watching the traffic passing along the wide boulevards that bordered the park. They included numberless officers of the various nations forming the Allied army, entering and leaving Lord Wellington's Headquarters. It seemed quite busy, much more movement than on other days that he had been here, but there seemed to be little haste which would indicate impending trouble.

He wasn't going to the Ball that evening which the Duchess of Richmond was hosting in some shed prettied up for the occasion, neither were any of his chums, only Harry was going with Juana as he was on the Staff. They weren't man and wife but Georgian society worried little about such niceties.

He suddenly observed Major The Honourable Henry Percy of the Fourteenth Light Dragoons, whom he knew slightly as an Aide de Camp of Lord Wellington himself, one of his 'family', as he called his team.

Percy looked pensive and deep in thought as he strolled through the park.

"What ho Henry, any news?"

"Hello Johnny. That I cannot say, but are your saddle packs all ready to move instantly?"

"Nearly so" Johnny replied nonchalantly "At all events I don't suppose they need to be ready before tomorrow."

Henry replied earnestly "If you have any preparations to make, I would recommend that you do not wait so long!"

The reply sent a spark of electricity through him.

It was 9 p.m. and the searing summer sun was setting slowly, Johnny quickly returned to his friends to spread the word. Everyone arranged their belongings, packed everything they might need and retired to their beds at an early hour to gain some rest.

For who knew what tomorrow's sun would rise upon?

THE MARCH

The sultry still night air was harshly fractured by the call of a solitary bugle, this was quickly picked up by others and soon every bugle and drum in the army had taken up the call as it rapidly spread across the City; they all played 'The Assembly'.

The men were roused from their slumbers by the melodious call or were brutally kicked awake by colleagues; in stark contrast, the officer's servants politely awoke their charges.

"Sir, they are playing the Assembly, you must arise immediately".

The words whispered by his bâtman brought Johnny Kincaid out of his somnolent dreams with a start.

"What hour is it?" he enquired, his room was pitch black; he felt as though he had only been asleep for a few minutes.

"'Tis Eleven o'clock Sir" was the reply that confirmed he had managed only one hour's sleep!

He arose gingerly, stumbling in the utter darkness that was hardly pierced by the faint glow of the solitary candle held by his servant. He splashed his face with the ice-cold water from his shaving bowl, quickly donned his uniform and emerged from his billet into the cool night air. He noted that it was a cloudless night and the stars shone clear and bright. His servant was stood waiting for him, he had already prepared his horse, his saddle packs were already full following the warning he had received that afternoon. He mounted and rode out into the streets of Brussels on route to the assembly point in the Place Royale and the streets bordering the Parc de Bruxelles. The roads were rapidly filling with soldiers as they tumbled out of the houses; many half dressed still donning jackets as they stumbled along. Most were still groggy from the little sleep they had snatched and the beer that they had been revelling in hours before. As this tide of humanity neared the City centre, many more emerged directly from the bars to increase the crush once they had quickly finished their libations. They crowded together and soon the streets were a seething mass of uniforms all moving on the square. Wagons loaded with ammunition and horse teams dragging cannon also moving in the same direction caused bedlam.

Eventually as the troops filtered into the great square they picked out their regimental colours held high as a rallying point by the bright light shed from the immense rush torches lit for the purpose. Some semblance of order began to be established as each battalion drew together to muster. Within an hour the Rifle battalion was complete, the muster rolls had been checked and nobody was found missing. Many regiments had men billeted in the far suburbs and soldiers continued to slowly filter in, indeed it took over four hours for the last to arrive.

As the men gathered in their companies and awaited orders they became aware of the floating notes of dance music and laughter emanating from a large house nearby. Of course, it had to be the Duchess of Richmond's Ball, the rich and great of Brussels and many senior army officers were present including the Duke of Wellington as guest of honour. Had they not heard the Assembly?

However, a message was soon passed around.

"All officers obliged to chaperone a lady to the Ball are to continue to do so, maintain an air of normality to the populace. Officers are to report to their regiments before dawn."

Harry Smith and his lady continued to weave their way through the throng of soldiers, determined to enjoy the Ball. Juana was dressed in the finest full length white silk gown with puffed upper sleeves in the latest style and a square cut décolletage, cut low on her ample bosom. The ivory white dress contrasted beautifully with her dusky skin, deep black hair tied up for the occasion and her dark piercing eyes. The ensemble was completed by long white gloves; a red cashmere shawl draped fashionably over her head and flat dancing pumps to enable her to enjoy performing the latest waltzes. Harry looked dashing in his scarlet jacket with long tails, skin-tight white breeches and dancing pumps. They stood out as one of the most beautiful couples at the Ball and they were determined to enjoy it to the full, this was likely to be one of their last nights before he went to war. The Duke's presence at the dance and his affable demeanour proved that there was little worrying him that night; they all concluded that the alarm must have been a mere precautionary act and nothing to worry about, exactly the Duke's intention.

The battalions once mustered were told to stay in their ranks but to get what rest they could until orders were received. Some sat, many lay down on the wide cobbled roadways and pavements to snatch some sleep.

Johnny Kincaid and George Simmons curled up in a ball in a shop doorway to keep warm and tried to rest. However, they were constantly interrupted by passing locals shaking them violently, craving for news, they were ashen faced and their eyes betrayed their fear. But they had no news to give them and answered them gruffly. Eventually the pair renounced all efforts at sleep and discussed their predicament.

"I haven't been so cold since camping on the Pyrenees the other winter" groaned Johnny.

George rose slowly from his recumbent position on the marble doorstep and asked, "What do you think the alarm was for Johnny? Nobody seems to know what's going on."

Johnny nodded slowly, "Perhaps it is a false alarm or the Duke has simply called us out ready for the invasion."

"There are rumours that Napoleon has attacked" George added.

Johnny was aware of the rumours and the warning he had received to be ready to move. It all smacked of a planned movement perhaps over zealously instigated. "If he had attacked we would not be sat here now, I rather think that we would be marching south already if that was the case." He replied.

Like everyone else, they would have to wait for orders to clarify the situation.

"I think you will have to wait a while yet before you can get the lock of Bonaparte's hair for your Mary!" Johnny added playfully.

George smiled weakly as he settled back in the doorway; he might as well try to sleep again, as he wasn't missing anything.

After what seemed an age in this uncomfortable setting, they were interrupted again, this time by the nobs as they poured out of the Ball in the early hours. Many had drunk far too much and found negotiating the sleeping bodies of the Riflemen very difficult, many stumbling in the dark and falling upon some unsuspecting warrior. The shouting and swearing of disgruntled soldiers ruptured the air; the accompanying ladies attempted to blot out the foul language by covering their delicate ears. The whimpering apologies of these dignitaries did little to calm the situation, Johnny, George and their fellow officers had to get up often to calm their men down before they slit someone's throat!

They also suffered the loud drunks who assaulted them verbally, particularly picking on the officers as their ornate uniforms showed them as someone in authority.

"Get up all of you, how can you defend us lying down?"

"What is happening? Why haven't you gone to fight the French?"

"Are you going to just lay there whilst Napoleon comes to gobble us all up?"

They fended off these attacks brusquely, Johnny occasionally resorting to ordering the men to escort some extremely abusive gentlemen out of earshot. These nearly flew down the cobbled streets, escorted by a Rifleman holding each arm lifting them bodily from the ground and many a toff certainly retreated to bed with a kick on their derriere that night!

Eventually the Ball petered out and all went reasonably quiet, everyone grasped a few moments of sleep where they could.

They were harshly awoken again when the bugles blew hard to fall in as the new sun was rising; everyone assumed that they would soon depart, who knew where.

Ned Costello was detailed as his company's non-commissioned orderly officer to collect the rations for the company. The Commissariat staff issued Ned and his squad with their rations from a long convoy of carts lining the sides of the broad roads a block or two from the great square. He was issued with three days rations for each man against the muster list, which he then proceeded to hand out to the individuals. The young lads didn't know campaigning and had never gone without food since joining the Army; many chose to decline much of their issue, as they didn't like to carry the weight and they were sure that they would be fed regularly just as they had on the march to Brussels.

"Take 'em youze ijots, youze never know when rations will catch us up again!" shouted a frustrated Ned.

Some listened to their wiser comrades, many did not; the old heads knew they would rue this moment later when it was too late. On campaign, food in your hand was better than gold. Sometimes there was literally nothing to buy at any price and you can't eat gold! Costello gave the remainder to the other veterans as extra rations.

As soon as the sun rose above the horizon and they could proceed without stumbling in the dim grey light, orders were given to march. The battalions fell in and marched off with the bands playing in the intervals between the regiments, they played 'The Downfall of Paris' and other popular tunes. They were marching south toward the French border area, where either Bonaparte would attack or they would launch their invasion of France. It would be a leisurely and pleasant march with the clear skies denoting a warm sunny day to come. They wouldn't have to fight for a day or two yet, so they could just enjoy their time.

They marched out on the road to Namur passing through the Port de Namur, a great stone gateway, a remnant of those distant days when Brussels had a surrounding wall for defence. Soon, having passed through the outer suburbs of the City, the battalion proceeded along a wide chausee passing through an extensive wood, the Bois de Soignies someone said the locals called it. The woodland extended for some miles; it was full of large trees that had formed a dense canopy of leaves, which denied any of the sunlight to the ground beneath. This meant that there was little undergrowth and they noted that although from afar it had all the appearance of an impenetrable wood, in fact it was open enough that you could march an army through it. The shade was welcome, for the morning sun was already warming the air and the body heat generated within their tight, fully fitted uniforms had already led them to feel hot and sticky. Despite their burden of a very heavy pack they laughed and joked as they strode on, the day was delightful in every sense. They had no cares in the world as they marched slowly toward the forward staging area.

The gruff bellow of Staff Sergeant John Hall, who was standing alongside his bed in the pitch-black room, brought Alexander to his senses with a jolt. He had trouble shaking himself out of his deep slumber, it was obviously near midnight and he could have only been asleep for an hour or so. What could be so urgent at this time?

"A message Sir" whispered Hall, holding out the paper. "The dispatch rider said nothing and rode straight off, but at such a late hour I thought it must be important Sir".

Alexander grasped it and broke the wax seal with his fingers, spreading the sheet of paper wide. He strained to read the message in the dim flickering light from the candle held by Hall.

It read, "Captain Mercer's troop will proceed with utmost diligence to Enghien, where he will meet Lieutenant Colonel Macdonald who will point out the ground on which it is to bivouac tonight."

Alexander sprang from his bed. He had at first thought little of the order, just another simple movement order over eagerly delivered in the middle of the night. But something had told him that this time it was somehow different. Call it intuition, but he just knew.

"Sergeant muster the troop; have Bugler Bowen sound 'Boot and Saddle', also send a message to Mr Leathes at Ysingen to bring his division forthwith."

Dressing rapidly, Alexander thought.

"This is it!"

Joshua Coates burst in to Alexander's room; he was wearing only his trousers and continued dressing as he entered. He had heard the confusion in the passageway and had surmised the reason. "What, are we off Sir?"

"Yes, without delay. You must collect your wagons as quickly as possible", Alexander replied.

Coates looked worried, "I fear Captain Mercer that it will take some time, as farmer St Cyr's wagons are gone to Ninove."

The words shook Alexander to the core, his wagons were not ready and it was entirely his own fault. He began to fret over the consequences of his earlier decisions, which were now coming back to haunt him.

His problems were numerous; the officers were all away in Brussels at the Ball, the division at Ysingen with their two horse teams and cannon would take some time to arrive and here was Mr Coates reporting that the carts of provisions were not going to be available for some hours. They really had been caught on the hop, Alexander regretted allowing the troop to be broken up like this, but the seven weeks of waiting had led to a general relaxation of readiness and he had to admit to himself that he had been guilty in allowing complacency to set in.

"Just do your best and if you cannot be ready by eight, you must follow us," he answered quietly.

Within half an hour the welcome sound of horse's

hooves clattering on the cobbled driveway, clinking scabbards and the deep rumble of cannon on the move seeped through the mists covering the lawns. Suddenly dark masses could be discerned in the hazy distance, it was the division of Henry Leathes from Ysingen. At least Alexander now had the entire troop mustered and most importantly all of the guns. Things improved even further as shortly after the officers rode into the chateau grounds having returned at speed from Brussels. Their horses looked tired and blown.

"Thank goodness we found you Alexander, we thought that you may have left already" shouted John Bretton.

"Indeed we should have gone some time ago, but the troop has taken time to muster, Mr Coates will be a while yet with provisions. How did you come to know of our move?"

Henry Leathes joined the discussion "Whilst at the Ball, a message was passed for officers without partners to return to their units immediately, we have ridden all night. Indeed as we passed through Brussels, we observed the Fifth and Brunswick Divisions forming to march south. What are our orders?"

Alexander explained, "We must proceed to Enghien with all haste. We will give Mr Coates thirty more minutes, and then we will proceed with or without him. I have already ordered a large breakfast from the kitchen staff; I suggest we all partake of a hearty meal, for I know not when we will eat again!"

Everyone ate ravenously of a fine cooked breakfast and prepared to move out. Alexander was unable to relax over his meal; he worried over the carts and the consequent lack of supplies. Raising his eyes from toying with his food, he became aware of the smirk of self-satisfaction painted across the face of Robert Newland. He had been proven right and he was enjoying every minute of Alexander's discomfort. Everyone else knew of his embarrassment and they pointedly avoided eye contact.

At eight o'clock Alexander finally ordered the troop to march out on the road to Enghien. Mr Coates had not arrived and orders were left for him to follow as closely as possible. Alexander ordered a detachment led by Bombardier James Downie consisting of twenty-one drivers to remain to man the wagons for Mr Coates. Alexander could not delay any longer, how he lamented his decision to overrule Coates.

The Rifles approached a wide clearing in the woods; they noted a village formed of two rows of low houses hugging the road and to the right a large church, catering for the spiritual needs of this small community. The church was of a hybrid design, it sported a Romanesque columned portico at its northern end; this led into a tall, near circular red-bricked tower, capped with a copper dome encased in verdigris. A tall circular Byzantine style tower topped the dome, glazed panels encompassing it to two thirds of its height and at its apogee a cross. The main body of the church was conventional enough, but a square tower at its Southern end topped with an extremely pointed spire completed it. The overall effect was that of a curious monstrosity.

They received the welcome order to halt and cook breakfast. Filing off into a field, which formed a sort of green alongside the church, they immediately set off to gather wood, so that their ration pound of beef could be cooked. Other fires were set to boil iron kettles of water to which were added tea leaves, milk and sugar; everyone had to drink tea white and sweet. George, Johnny, Archibald and the other officers quickly identified an old dilapidated inn in the village. The white washed two-storey building was punctured by rows of large glazed windows to ensure that the interior was light and airy. It was 9 a.m.; the landlord was awake and happy to provide excellent fare for the gentlemen's breakfast in the small front room. In discussion with the patron they discovered that this was the village of Waterloo and that a messenger riding through last night had warned that Napoleon was coming soon. They smiled, there were no orders to proceed, no urgency, and these Belgies were apt to exaggerate, for they had a downright fear of Napoleon's return. How could there be a French attack without any warning?

Indeed shortly after nine, whilst they waited for their breakfast, Lord Wellington and his large entourage had ridden past. His 'family' were dressed in the colours of the rainbow, not only the scarlet and navy of the British contingent, but also Prussian blue, Austrian and Spanish white and Russian green. There were no signs of apprehension from them; they had ridden straight through without stopping, jesting light heartedly amongst themselves. Lord Wellington had looked relaxed and cheerful; they had left no orders, so all continued to enjoy their steaming food as it arrived from the kitchens.

After an hour or so, the officer's hunger sated and feeling refreshed, they sauntered out into the intense sunlight. The battalion was spread across the field, the old hands cooking all their beef for three days, for who knew when they would next be able to kindle a fire to cook the raw meat and the heat of the day was already making it smell rancid. The younger lads had little to cook and consumed their all for breakfast. They lay down and slept in the glorious sunshine, laughing openly at the silly old sods worrying about food, the Commissariat would catch up soon to issue more.

About 11 o'clock the Black Brunswickers marched into

the village and set down near the Rifles to cook. The Duke of Brunswick and his senior officers contrasted with their men dressed all in black, as their uniforms were adorned with silver lace and great white plumes surmounted their cocked hats.

The Duke and his staff selected the trunk of a fallen tree as a seat alongside the road where servants served them food. The Rifles watched with interest as he conversed with his entourage sat alongside him. Eventually his Aide de Camp sitting next to him stood to stretch his legs. As he sauntered away, a very dirty and flea bitten tramp, dragged his aching body towards his habitual perch. It was busy for a change but there was a space and unmoved he pushed his way through to sit down. As he sat, some of the officers went to remonstrate but the Duke raised his hand to stop them and continued as if nothing had happened. The Duke sat alongside the poor tramp for some fifteen minutes appearing totally indifferent to the foul smell and threat of fleas; however he had refrained from eating anything else!

The Rifles had sat mesmerised by the scene unfolding in front of them, when the order "Fall in" caused them to move away. The Duke and the Brunswickers rose as well and fell in behind the Rifles; they were all obviously required to proceed on a little further today.

Setting off once again, they soon cleared the southern end of the woods, emerging onto a rolling landscape of luscious farmland with head high wheat awaiting the scythe greatly obscuring the views. Large square farm complexes stood fortress like in the midst of the wheat fields and small clumps of trees and orchards were dotted randomly, it was a truly magnificent vista in the bright sunlight. They marched on through this undulating land without a care in the world, the birds singing, crickets chirruping, accompanied by the rhythmic clumping of the men's boots upon the roadway. They walked zombie like, marching to the rhythm of their feet crashing down whilst their thoughts drifted, they just kept in step mechanically. They had marched some three miles from the village of Waterloo and now marched through a cutting in a low rise, then immediately passed another enclosed farmhouse, which the owner, who nonchalantly watched them pass as he puffed on his pipe, called 'La Haye Sainte'. The officers noted with a professional eye that this ground was a good defensive position and wrote it in their notepads for possible use in the future. Any good officer always noted the lie of the land and particularly useful positions that could be of advantage later during any fighting in the area.

On they marched in the heat of the day, the sun glaring down, canteens were already empty of liquid refreshment, and the packs became a terrible burden.

Someone stumbled.

"Hold Charity up Mc Nabb" bellowed Sergeant Fairfoot.

Mc Nabb held the arm of Thomas Charity as he started to sag from heat exhaustion. Thomas was a tall gangly individual, one of the older survivors of Spain being all of thirty two, a ripe age for a soldier on campaign, but it had taken its toll on his constitution and he was often weak now. William Mc Nabb helped him to the side of the road and he sat down on the grass verge to recuperate.

"I'll catch up soon Sergeant," he cried weakly.

"E'ell be all right, Sarge, Oi'll stay wid 'im" piped up Mc Nabb.

"Not on your nelly Mc Nabb, fall back in; Thomas can get on by himself. I'm not letting youze out of moi soight!" Robert knew McNabb of old, a skiver, always looking for an easy life and apt to disappear whenever there was any fighting to be done! Well he wasn't disappearing this time.

The battalion hadn't stopped and they had to move swiftly to catch up.

Again they marched on, footstep following interminable footstep, would it never end?

Suddenly, there was a very distant low rumble.

"Thunder" said Jem Connor.

"Cannon Foir" corrected Ned Costello.

"Frenchy twelve pounders I tink, oi'd recognise dem bastards anywheres" he continued.

The air was suddenly electric as his words spread through the battalion; some serious fighting was going on somewhere up ahead, they thought. The battalion almost instinctively increased its pace of march, there was a renewed spring in the step, weary legs took on new powers, drooping heads rose, nostrils flared, the brain switched on and concentrated again, no longer worn by the mindless monotonous drudgery. Soon even Thomas Charity appeared back in the ranks, all strained their hearing for more sounds to confirm that they hadn't miss heard, but nothing, absolutely nothing.

Perhaps they were mistaken; maybe it was only practise firing or indeed thunder after all.

URGENCY

Alexander had failed to procure a local guide that could show G troop their way to Enghien, for none of the locals seemed to have been that far in their lives. He struggled valiantly with the poor map that he had purloined, which showed few of the roads or villages that they encountered and soon was quite lost in the maze of side roads. Alexander drove them on; he was acutely aware of their slow progress because of the delayed start and the maximum speed of the ammunition wagons, which held them back. Finally he decided to press on at a greater speed with the cannon and their limited ammunition supplies in the limbers. The ammunition wagons commanded by Quartermaster John Hall were ordered to follow at the best speed they could. It was a calculated risk, he realised that his guns might make the difference in any engagement and that he may already be expected. Hopefully the ammunition would catch up before it was needed to replenish the limber stock.

The order was given, but Alexander worried over this division of his unit, he had now effectively split into three columns and his guns could only have a partial effectiveness without the reserve ammunition.

Robert Newland had highlighted the weakness of course; "Captain Mercer, I must protest strongly against this decision and beg you to reconsider. We have already seen the effect of your over ruling Mr Coates for we have no supplies. It is sheer madness to separate the guns from most of the ammunition. It could lead to severe embarrassment in front of the enemy."

Alexander knew that it was a massive gamble and he prayed that it would not lead to their downfall, but he felt it was the right thing to do in the circumstances. He was aware that the others' silence spoke of their agreement with Robert, but he dug his heels in.

"Do as I bid Mr Newland" he answered curtly.

Newland ordered the Quartermaster to follow at their best pace and fell back into the column. He was not about to jeopardise his whole career by disobeying a direct order, that would be playing into Alexander's hands, no he would continue to gather evidence against him for the inevitable court martial if he continued making such high handed and dangerous decisions.

They pressed onward with the guns now rolling at a full trot until eventually meeting a group of farmers who were able to give confident directions to Enghien; they must therefore be nearing their goal.

A lone dragoon officer dashed past, his stallion lathering heavily, Alexander recognised him and called out.

"Charles, where do you rush?"

Charles Dance was a Captain in the 23rd Light dragoons; he recognised his old friend and reined in abruptly. Having regained his breath a little, he explained.

"I have ridden non stop, for my regiment has already moved to Enghien. The Prussians fought yesterday and good old Blucher won, so they say at Brussels. I hope that he has left some French for us! I am endeavouring to catch my regiment before they engage, I must retain my honour!"

Alexander understood, any officer absent from the fighting without good reason would be liable to have his honour impugned and would become a social outcast.

"Take care Charles, we will be up with you presently." He shouted as Dance spurred his horse forward again.

Charles sped on, seemingly oblivious to the discomfort his horse was showing at the long gallop he had performed, he simply drove him harder and was soon out of sight.

The road wound down a steep declivity as it entered a river valley, near the river the track was a perfect bog and the horses sank to their shoulders. With a supreme effort, each team led by their drivers on foot slowly dragged themselves through the quagmire and reached the hardened road again. Each team made the way more difficult for those that followed, the muddy banks became slippery and each successive cannon seemed to sink deeper into the mire despite bales of cut reed being thrown under the wheels to aid their passage. The final teams required the aid of those already safely through onto firmer ground to drag them through. Eventually all were through but everyone was now wet, cold and muddy, not a particularly pleasant feeling on a long ride. Having gained the firmer ground, Alexander ordered pales of clean water to be drawn from the river to douse everything, to remove the black mud; the warming sun, which had now broken through the early mists of dawn, could then do its work.

This was their final trial before arriving in view of the great park belonging to the chateau at Enghien, their rendezvous point. A number of cavalry units were already in residence in the park; they were relaxing and feeding their horses and themselves at numerous welcoming fires. Alexander halted the guns and sought out Lieutenant

Colonel Macdonald, but he was not to be found and on enquiry nobody had seen him or knew of his whereabouts.

Alexander did not order the horses to be fed, as they confidently expected to be ordered into bivouac here, when they would have ample time to feed them. He felt more relaxed, especially as this halt would allow the provisions carts to catch them up. A regiment of dragoons were resting nearby and Alexander sought out their Commander for any news or advice on which to base his further actions, as he did not feel he could turn to Newland. The officer was curt and ill mannered; he had no time for such idiotic interruptions.

"I know nothing of you Sir" was the only answer Alexander could obtain.

Other regiments of cavalry were constantly passing in a long procession; they were taking the road to a village marked Braine le Comte on Alexander's map. However on enquiry of those passing, he discovered that no one had received any orders beyond Enghien and seemed to be marching on in the simple hope of meeting somebody that could enlighten them. Most were unaware of where the road led; they simply continued to follow the previous regiment rather than do nothing. Alexander was amazed, so this was what it was like on campaign, utter confusion!

Alexander espied the approach of Sir Hussey Vivian and his Brigade consisting of three hussar regiments. Following them closely was his friend Major Robert Bull and his entire horse artillery troop, which unusually consisted of six howitzers.

Bull called out to Alexander.

"Alex, do you know what is going on?"

Alexander shook his head, "We have no orders beyond meeting Macdonald here, but I cannot find him. Do you know anything?"

Robert was just as puzzled, "Sir Vivian does not know, but is marching on and as I am attached to his Brigade, I go too. I would recommend you would do well to follow on with us."

Alexander decided to bite the bullet and took a moment to discuss the situation with Robert Newland; as usual they disagreed.

Alexander argued, "We must follow the others as we will achieve little here."

Robert was vociferous in countering this, "We must not proceed beyond where we are ordered; do not forget Norman Ramsay! Do you wish us all arrested on Lord Wellington's orders? If Macdonald comes here for us and does not find us that is what will happen!"

Alexander understood Robert's argument but once again decided to overrule him; this was becoming a dangerous habit. The next brigade approaching in the convoy were the Household cavalry, huge men on their beautiful horses, they appeared to be preparing to halt for a rest. Thus, a gap appeared in the column of cavalry and Alexander ordered the gun teams to fill the void and march on.

As the sun climbed toward its zenith the march became tougher still. The heat became oppressive and the glaring light exhausted their eyes. They boiled alive in their tight fitting tunics made worse by their heads sweltering inside the heavy cumbersome helmets. Mouths were parched crying out for refreshment, but canteens had been emptied hours ago. Stomachs were empty and rumbled loudly in protest at the enforced famine. The horses visibly deteriorated as the heat bore down on them and their energy waned through lack of nourishment. Still they plodded on; through mile after mile of hedge-lined roads in the vain hope of finding somebody that knew what was happening.

Eventually the village of Braine le Comte came into view; it was little more than a small collection of low houses lining the roadside. Richard Hichens rode into the village as the troop rode around it to avoid the bottleneck of the narrow streets. He returned shortly with three bottles of fine claret. Without a corkscrew a sabre did the trick, the neck of each bottle was removed with a sharp blow of the blade. The contents were eagerly consumed by the officers straight from the bottle; they held the jagged glass to their mouths and poured the liquid, despite the obvious danger on a moving horse it was a welcome relief to their suffering.

The hussars who had led them here had stopped to rest on a common, Alexander did not need to be told twice, the moment that they halted, he ordered the horses watered from the welcoming stream that gurgled along a shallow culvert nearby and fed with the supply of corn that they had brought with them. The nosebags had been filled that morning and at last once placed over their muzzles; the horses could flick the sacks skyward to enjoy their contents. The gunners collected all the canteens, and then proceeded to fill them at another stream that flowed through the nearby village; this source was cleaner than the waters of the culvert, which were now heavily muddied by the horses' hooves. Cossack greedily lapped up the water from the stream, Bal and the other dogs squeezed between the horses to gain a space to sate their own burning thirst. The men could have their fill of water but food was non-existent and would be so until Mr Coates and the carts caught up.

It was now four o'clock and the sun continued to beat down upon them mercilessly, surely they would be ordered to halt for the day now, thought Alexander. Minutes later the hussars were ordered to fall in and they resumed their march along the road; the march was not to end yet.

The troop had to keep in touch with the hussars and the

march was continued before the horses had finished their feed. The nosebags were pulled away; much to the displeasure of the horses, some jostled and kicked out, and others bared teeth and attempted to bite the drivers. It took some coaxing and whipping to drive the horses on again, but once under way they maintained a good steady walk behind the hussars.

A small cluster of houses, a poor excuse for a village even by Belgian standards, announced their arrival at a point where the road rose steadily to cross a major height, at least high enough to be thought as such in this region of flattish land. At the foot of the hill, the street was completely blocked by the carriages and baggage wagons of some Hanoverian corps. They were thouroughly jumbled and tempers were already frayed long before Alexander's guns arrived and attempted to force its way through. This was obviously more than some could bear, a few turned and glared or offered profanities in German; others less friendly cocked their muskets and pointed them at Alexander and his troop. The message was clearly understood and Alexander ordered his team to halt whilst the Hanoverians slowly sorted the mess out, which would allow the troop to proceed. The hussars had avoided this problem detouring through the gardens of the houses lining the road, bypassing the congestion. Alexander watched them in frustration at the impossibility of following their route with the cannon, as they rejoined the road beyond the constriction and proceeded up and over the hill.

Eventually the Hanoverians cleared the way, allowing G troop to move on. The hill was extremely steep and the road wound in a tight zigzag to its summit. Despite the reduced inclination of the road's engineering, it proved extremely difficult for the horse teams to haul the guns up. Alexander was forced to double the teams on each gun and carriage, leaving the other half of the equipment at the village. Following great exertion, these enlarged teams successfully reached the summit. The teams then unhitched and returned to the base of the hill to raise the other half of the guns and wagons. The descent back to the village proved even more hazardous, the horses being pulled back hard by the drivers to avoid them increasing their speed and losing all control.

Finally, having hauled the remaining wagons to the top of the rise, the teams were reallocated to their carriages before Alexander called a halt so that the horses could regain their strength. He noted with pleasure that the road ahead appeared to run across a gently undulating plain, the climbing seemed to be at an end.

Everybody was glad of the rest, such exertion on such a hot, sunny day sapped the strength, men and horses gasped to regain their breath and sought water to relieve their uncontrollable thirst, but it was not to be had so easily, for the canteens had been drained during the Herculean effort of climbing the hill.

Bombardier Thomas Masterton looked back down the steep descent they had just climbed then turned to John Hincks.

"That hill reminds me of Busacco Sir, bloody steep it were, one battery lost control of a six pounder as they rolled it to the edge to fire down on Johnny. Bloody great thing rolled over the edge, nearly took two gunners with it, crashed all way down to the bottom and landed in't woods, total mess it were!"

"For certain, I am glad that we have passed it," replied John casually.

"We must get on, Sir Vivian and the hussars are already out of sight" ordered Alexander, as he peered through his small spyglass for any sign as to where they had gone.

The road soon entered a great wood, the trees packed tightly with an abundance of dense foliage, which completely obscured the harsh rays of the unforgiving sun. The road passing through this woodland area brought a welcome respite, easing their sufferings. The stifling heat in their heavy, constricting uniforms was a nightmare; it felt like they would literally explode from the build up of heat within. Soon the cool shade of the woods refreshed them; the horses also showed their appreciation for this welcome shelter from the glare of the sun and became less fractious. The woods stretched for over a mile but eventually the troop re-emerged into the harsh sunlight, causing them to shade their eyes from the sudden glare, it was most unwelcome.

A low rumble became audible; Alexander looked puzzled, "Thunder on such a fine day?"

Robert Newland looked stern and pointed up the road, "That is not thunder, it is the roar of cannon, it comes from beyond that wood ahead, observe the smoke."

Alexander could see a plume of grey-black smoke drifting just above the trees of a large wood a few miles away; the road appeared to be running in that direction.

The atmosphere within the troop changed dramatically, everyone suddenly became very serious, the laughing and joking, the gaiety and singing, the light heartedness stopped abruptly. All clearly understood that they were soon to enter upon a battlefield where life turned to death with little warning, a few genuflected as they whispered prayers for their own deliverance. Every ear strained for further sounds that would indicate what was occurring beyond the woods. Only the sound of cannon fire could be heard, it grew in volume very slowly almost imperceptibly as they approached, but it remained stationary, which indicated to the old hands that the forces fighting were struggling for supremacy, neither side seemingly able to drive the other away.

Suddenly from nowhere a lone rider appeared riding across a field to their left, as he approached Alexander recognised the elusive Macdonald, the very same that he had been seeking for orders since early that morning.

Lieutenant Colonel Macdonald was breathless from his rapid ride and barked his order "Mercer, G troop is to attach itself to Lord Edward Somerset's Household Brigade, which consists of the Lifeguards, Horse guards and the King's Own."

Alexander could not believe that was all he ordered, "Do you know of their present whereabouts so that I may join them? What of the fighting ahead?" he asked incredulously

Macdonald was clearly angered by the questioning and answered abruptly, "I am not acquainted with their present location, but they are ordered to join Lord Wellington at the cross roads four miles ahead of you called Quatre Bras, find them there. Your orders are to join them, not to join the fighting!"

Instantly, Macdonald flicked his whip across the rump of his horse and sped off, back towards the noise of battle.

Henry Leathes looked perplexed, "Alexander, you knew that the Household Brigade was behind us, yet you said nothing!"

Alexander stared at Henry with fire in his eyes, "The battle is clearly in front of us, do you wish us to retire in such circumstances?"

Henry demurred.

Alexander bellowed a rallying call for all to hear, "We will proceed toward the sound of the guns; Lord Edward Somerset can join us! March on."

Alexander caught sight of Robert Newland's

disapproving look, well he was still in charge and he would do what he felt was right and hang the consequences!

As they began to trot on, a cabriolet dashed along the road from behind them, passing the troop at the gallop. Bal and the other troop dogs chased after it barking and nipping at the wheels until they were called off. Sitting inside was an officer of the Guards, obviously in a rush to join his regiment at the fighting. He was dressed immaculately in the finery of his regimentals sitting back in his carriage taking snuff with a nonchalant air whilst the manic driver lashed the horses constantly with a long whip. Alexander felt mixed emotions at the sight, here was a gay fop, and he'd probably been bought a commission in the Guards as a child by his papa and had probably never seen action before. His contempt for his lack of professional knowledge was tinged with pride and awe. How one so young, no more than eighteen, could dash on to death and destruction with such nonchalance simply to maintain his honour and family tradition for military prowess. However much you despised this breed of overbearing, pompous sons of lords, Alexander had to concede that they instinctively knew how to fight and die as gentlemen.

By now the noise of battle was becoming very loud indeed; it seemed that they would soon taste their first action of the campaign.

On the road ahead of the Rifles a great lolloping carthorse drew into view pulling a battered old farm wagon. It creaked and screeched along the rough roadway, the axles not having any grease applied since originally built some ten years hence. But, the noise that captured their attention was the soulful groaning emanating from the straw bundle on the back of the cart.

As they neared, it became clear that the cries of pain and

anguish were originating from a dozen wounded men lying on the straw, each a vision of agony. Ashen faced, many half naked, besmirched with grime and blood, they implored water as the troops passed. A few had remnants of uniform indicating that they were Belgians; on enquiry they told of a terrible battle raging ahead where they had been holding a crossroads against incessant French attacks since early morning. Surgeon Burke mounted the cart and inspected their various wounds, two were already dead, and no sooner than he had pronounced this than their corpses were unceremoniously dumped into the roadside culvert to rot. The others had terrible wounds, one man had taken a glancing blow from a cannonball, it had ripped his side open and smashed the ribs, through the gore his lungs could be seen rising and falling with each painful breath, he was in agony and would not last long. Some had injuries from musket balls, others with flaps of skin hanging from heads or limbs where swords had slashed them. The younger men felt queasy at the sights and a few were violently ill, this was their first real vision of the horrors of war but it would be far from their last.

They marched past rapidly.

"Christ I hope that doesn't happen to me, oi'd rather doi quick than linger for days in such pain" one of them whispered to his mate.

Ned Costello turned to face them, "Lissen lads, the ball wid your name on wull get youze wherever youze goes and whenever it loiks. Sometimes the same ball can even have two names on it. At Arcangues in '14, the same ball went through the heads of Lieutenant Hopwood and Sergeant Broverton together, it killed dem both stone dead it did to be sure!"

The march continued with renewed vigour as the occasional deep-throated roar of cannon could now be heard a little clearer. They passed through a large village and filed over the narrow bridge at its southern end. As they progressed nearer to the fighting, they encountered more flotsam from the struggle, wounded crawling or helped by fellow soldiers, carts of more wounded and supplies, local villagers fleeing the scene in terror, mothers dragging along screaming children, fathers pulling their prized cow or horse, or a cart of their meagre possessions saved from the ravages of war, it was becoming a living nightmare.

Still they forced their way forward through this mass of jetsam, the sound of cannon fire and even volleys of musketry were heard much closer and more regularly. By two o'clock in the afternoon a small group of houses and farm buildings clustered around a crossroads came clearly into sight. Beyond lay a plain rising slightly into the distance with a substantial wood bordering the plain on the right hand side. They could see the Belgians in ranks near the houses still desperately holding the crossroads.

In the open country beyond could be seen dark masses of men in motion directly towards the crossroads.

The French!

QUATRE BRAS

As the First battalion of the Rifles marched rapidly up to the crossroads area, the men became aware of a group of senior officers on horseback huddled together in conversation nearby.

"Aye up 'tis the Duke himself, we're sure of a foight then" shouted Tom Crawley.

The Duke of Wellington was conversing with their commander Sir Thomas Picton, the Prince of Orange and their Aides de Camp. The French had obviously spotted this group and cannonballs regularly bounded past them at no great distance, making their horses stir nervously. The officers seemed oblivious to the iron balls of death raining down upon them; occasionally spattering them with mud as they passed so close. They instinctively controlled their horses with their legs; nothing distracted them from listening to the orders of the Duke as he pointed out their various positions. Having received the movement orders for the troops, the aides turned their steeds and sped in all directions with great celerity to deliver their orders to the units arriving along the road. These young officers of such noble birth took pride in delivering orders as rapidly as humanly possible; they raced on their thoroughbreds along the roads and lanes at break neck speed. It was a point of honour to deliver a message to a unit four miles away within fifteen minutes. One aide hastened the short distance towards the Ninety Fifth, Colonel Barnard and Johnny Kincaid rode out to meet him.

As he approached, Sir Andrew called out in recognition "Edward, what orders do you carry from my Lord?"

Lord Fitzroy Somerset, Wellington's senior aide de camp and right hand man pulled his horse up as they met.

"Andrew take your battalion to the left of the plain, take that village you see which is named Thyle on the maps and hold it at all costs. If you cannot capture it then take control of the copse you can see this side of the village. This will allow us to use the road running east from this cross roads to communicate with our Prussian allies. It is imperative that the Duke can receive reports from them at all times."

Sir Andrew turned to Johnny, "Order the battalion forward at the double."

The men didn't need to hear the order twice, this was it, they would show those frogs what they were made of.

Somebody shouted from one of the British line regiments stationed nearby "Away the Sweeps", they smiled, for they knew it was the nickname of the Rifles because of their dark green uniforms.

Somerset continued to explain the situation to Barnard and Kincaid.

"It seems that Bonaparte has launched an attack at the junction of our two armies. He has caught us unprepared; indeed his Lordship says he's humbugged him! My Lord has met Blucher today as he prepares to face a sizeable French force near Ligny and Sombreffe eight miles from here. He saw the French and says there were at least forty thousand of them there. The Beau says that the Prussians were ill posted and thinks they will be beat. We are forming our army here; the road to the left is our link with the Prussians, which you must hold. We are unsure of the enemy numbers in our front but they are very numerous."

"Where is Napoleon?" enquired Sir Andrew.

"We don't know" Somerset replied, then spurred his horse with a parting "I must away."

Johnny understood the reasoning for the question. Napoleon had managed to gather his army between the two allies before they had had time to gather their own forces. This would allow him to detach a small force to occupy the one whilst he led the bulk of his army to destroy the other, wherever he was would indicate the main attack. A classic example of 'divide and conquer', Napoleon was certainly proving how brilliant a tactician he still was.

They marched across the crossroads and then filed into the head high wheat in the fields beyond, the officers on horseback guiding their direction as the men had lost all visibility beyond the wheat directly to their fore. Halfway, Johnny noticed that a French regiment of infantry was marching towards the same village from the opposite direction, "Run lads" he shouted, "or the French will get the village first".-

They broke into a trot, but it was impossible, as they tried to push through the wall of wheat unsure of their direction and weighed down by their packs they stumbled and staggered over the uneven ground, the wheat tripping them at every step. The sun beat down mercilessly and they quickly became exhausted and overheated within their tight tunics. It was no use, the French had a head start and an easier passage along a track, Johnny could see them reach the houses and take cover in the buildings.

Sir Andrew bellowed, "To the woods lads, take the woods."

Johnny inclined his horse to the left and led his men

toward the trees. He could see that a detachment of the French was now also racing forward for the woods. This time the Rifles would win the race; the leading files suddenly cleared the wheat and came directly upon the edge of the copse. Johnny dismounted and handed the reins to one of the men to hold. He led the others to the far side of the woodland, where they arrived to see the French no more than twenty yards away. The men didn't need telling what to do; they automatically dropped to the ground, took aim and let loose a devastating volley. The French officer and twelve of his men fell, the rest turned and fled back to the safety of the houses. The lads cheered and hugged each other, first round to them, that would make the French think again! Some of the raw recruits stood contemplating the novel scene, yes there was jubilation but there was also horror. Some of the French lay wounded screaming in agony and crying piteously for help.

The dead officer lay very near to them, he was a youth of no more than eighteen years, the top of his head had been shot away and the spongy material within spattered the grass. His piercing blue eyes stared accusingly at them in death; it caused their celebrations to become muted.

Tom Crawley stepped forward and kicked the head so that it turned away. "Can't aboid it when they eyeballs you."

The remainder of the battalion moved up through the wood and spread out as the companies settled down to defend this natural boundary.

Suddenly there was a strange strangled cry from the rear.

"Sergeant Fairfoot, it's Will Smith, 'ees gone mad!"

Robert turned to see Smith dropping to the floor, he curled into a foetal position for a moment and then seemed to be convulsed by spasms, which caused his legs to straighten again and become rigid. It lasted no more than a minute then stopped, he lay still, and they knew instinctively that he was dead. Robert simply shrugged; he had seen it happen all too often before. Sheer exhaustion and excessive heat had killed many in Spain just like that. They unceremoniously pushed the corpse to the edge of the wood and Tom Crawley lay behind him, using the body as protection and as a rest for his rifle; which helped steady his aim. Will wouldn't care now!

The shout went up "Here comes Old Trousers", the nickname they gave the French, named after their drum roll for attack. The French approached in column behind a cloud of skirmishers, peppering the woods with their musket shots, trying to drive the defenders out.

The Rifles had the advantage of superior weaponry and the cover of trees to protect them, but the work became very warm. They took careful aim and dropped many officers and sergeants in an effort to disrupt the attack, but soon the French were close enough to use their muskets accurately and they poured in a storm of lead balls in a strong reply.

Ned had rarely seen them fight so hard, he found a tree wide enough to cover his body from which he emerged to fire, and then retired into cover again to reload. It was a good job that he had used the tree, he thought, as he heard two solid thuds as balls struck the trunk at his back. When it was this dangerous he had to steel himself to be brave enough simply to step out and fire again.

As he reloaded, he spotted Moses Blythero who was a great ox of a man and Joshua Mc Bain, they were two of the new lads; they were standing away from cover and rooted to the spot like statues.

"Fur Chris' sake, get down lads" he called.

They couldn't hear him, they were rigid with fear and the balls whizzed around them. Inevitably, Moses was hit in the stomach and screamed in agony as he fell, Joshua just looked at him but didn't move, suddenly Joshua's head exploded as a ball struck and his body slumped to the floor.

"What a bloody waste", Ned thought, but this was no time for maudlin, he stepped out to fire and struck the bastard who had done for Joshua. The Frenchman was hit in the groin and dropped clutching his crutch.

"That's for Mc Bain," he hissed.

Within a few minutes Ned had forgotten that Joshua had ever existed, the living were all that mattered.

The French finally gave in and returned to the village, leaving the field dotted with their dead, many others lying horribly wounded implored help, but no aid would come to them today.

Robert Fairfoot, as all the Sergeants did, stepped out from cover and checked for wounded and dead. Stepping over the bodies of Moses Blythero and Joshua Mc Bain, he discovered another corpse sitting against a tree. The head of the corpse was a bloody mess; the ball had struck square between the eyes. Robert cupped his hand under the chin and raised the head to look carefully into the face. It was difficult to make out the visage; there was so much congealed blood that recognition was nigh impossible.

Then he twigged, it was Battersby. Well he wouldn't be able to run away this time!

Robert remembered that back in Spain, Battersby had met up with a very beautiful young girl, he couldn't remember her name. Well, she had an old suitor, a dragoon, who wouldn't believe that it was all over between them. One day the dragoon caught them together and threatened Battersby and the girl. She told him they were finished, so drawing his knife he stabbed her numberless times then turned for him. Battersby had run like the wind back to camp, the fiend on his tail. The camp guard had captured the dragoon and he had been duly hanged for murder. The girl had been the prettiest in the whole camp and pregnant to boot! Battersby had never got over the tragedy; well he was at peace now.

Robert heard a whispered "Sergeant Fairfoot, here", Robert turned to see Lieutenant William Lister lying in the undergrowth, he knelt by his side and observed a large red stain on his tunic, he had been shot in the chest and coughed blood.

"Four men here now" Robert bellowed.

Casima, Castles, Connor and Kitchen stepped up.

"Carry Mister Lister back to the farm at the cross roads, Mister Burke'll take care of him."

They lay a blanket on the earth and lifted Lister gently onto it; they carried him by hauling the blanket up by the four corners. They tramped back to the farmstead at the crossroads through the fields of flattened wheat, Lister moaned in agony as he bumped along. Eventually they arrived at the farmhouse, which was set up as a hospital; they found Mr Burke who ordered them to lay Lister on the kitchen table. Joseph Burke then quickly assessed the injury, one lung was collapsed and he feared that the ball might have clipped an artery.

"We'll soon have you mended William" he stated confidently, and then turning away he led the men back to the doorway.

"Tell Major Cameron that Mister Lister will not make the night."

What a waste Joseph Burke thought, William was only twenty-five.

There was a lull in the fighting at the woods and Johnny Kincaid watched as the rest of the Fifth Division deployed in line along the road between this copse and the cross roads, then advanced into the wheat fields.

To his left he could see a single French Cuirassier with

his great iron breastplate glistening in the sunlight. He was spotting for his regiment and the troops in line obviously couldn't see him over the tall wheat.

Johnny shouted to Daniel Kelly, "Take that man down".

Daniel took very careful aim and fired, the Cuirassier's beautiful chestnut horse snorted, then dropped like a stone. The Cuirassier fell to the ground with his charger and struggled to pull his trapped leg from under the animal's body. Eventually he managed to extricate himself, he was furious and as he stood up he drew his sword and waved it at the Rifles, shouting defiance. The words "Coquin" and "Merde" hung on the breeze.

Finally Daniels grew bored of listening to the insults, he took aim again and this time the Cuirassier fell stone dead across the body of his horse.

"Wull that's foinally shut him up," he snorted.

Despite the loss of their spotter, the French cavalry regiment arrayed in column started moving towards the thin red line of British infantry. They advanced at a steady walk. The tall wheat concealed each protagonist, they closed rapidly, completely unaware of the close proximity of the other.

The Rifles from their vantage point could clearly see the danger to their comrades and they attempted to warn them. Some waved their arms and shouted others fired at the cavalry to put them off. But the cavalry were not so easily deterred and the infantry could not hear their shouts.

Suddenly the cavalry discovered them and immediately broke into a charge; infantry in line were too good a target to miss. Some infantry units spotted them as they approached and hurried orders to "Form Square" were heard and instantly obeyed. It was the only chance of survival for the infantry; any delay would almost certainly be fatal. The Cuirassiers passed by these ragged squares so hastily formed, receiving their erratic fire with nonchalance, for they had turned the line and had spotted one regiment that had not realised the danger and was caught still in line. Johnny groaned inwardly and watched helplessly as the Cuirassiers speared the infantry on their straight swords. Infantry have always found defending against the height and long reach of horsed assailants difficult to contend with when massed, alone it was impossible. This time was no exception; it was all over in seconds, a hundred or more dead and dying, a massacre.

The Cuirassiers' blood was now up and they sought to emulate this against a highland regiment, easily recognised by their kilts and feather bonnets, which stood next in front of them. These hardy Scots did not run or attempt to form square, they realised that they were too late for that. Instead, they stood in line and met them with a hail of lead balls, which spattered against their breastplates like rain on an iron roof. The breastplates were supposedly ball proof, but the number of Cuirassiers that fell proved that they certainly were not. The Cuirassiers had seen enough; they broke and fled back towards their own lines in little groups. Many horses had been struck and had fallen, dashing their riders to the ground. Those who had lost their steeds sought their way back nervously across the fields of trampled wheat on foot. They had to pass the infantry in squares again, which sent them packing with a few shots. They no longer had any thought of attacking anyone.

Johnny's men took a few shots at long range to help them on their way.

A battalion of Brunswick infantry had been sent to bolster the defence of the wood and with this sizeable reinforcement Sir Andrew Barnard decided that they were now strong enough to go on the offensive. He ordered that the few houses forming the village of Thyle were to be taken.

Captain Edward Chawner, Lieutenant John Gardiner and Lieutenant John Fitzmaurice were ordered to advance with two companies of ninety men each, one of whom was Ned Costello. John Fitzmaurice commanded Jonathan Leach's company whilst he was away on staff duty.

Discarding their packs for speed, they ran frantically towards the stone buildings, the air was suddenly thick with musket balls whistling around them like a swarm of bees.

James Burke was running next to Ned when he suddenly clutched his stomach and fell.

"Ned oim done fer" he cried.

Ned stopped and grasping James' collar dragged him the final few yards to the nearest building. The wooden door was bolted but didn't stand up to a 'Rifleman's key', a ball through the lock and a shoulder charge. Ned fell through the door as it gave to his shoulder and he landed on the cold hard slabs of stone that formed the kitchen floor. Others trampled over his body with little ceremony to take covering positions at the windows. He winced as each booted foot dug deep into his back and rump as his colleagues passed him. He had never realised before how bloody heavy his mates were! Finally, they had all passed and Ned slowly raised his head to be met with the angelic vision of a young girl of fifteen sitting next to him offering him a glass of water. He shook his head to rid himself of the hallucination, but on looking again she was still there.

"Wot the hell are youze dooing here?" he asked incredulously.

The girl smiled and in very softly spoken broken English replied.

"I am eere for my father gone to Brussels; I look after 'ouse".

"Well you'll be lucky if this house is standing soon" Ned replied.

She appeared unconcerned, and held out the water again, "My naama if Marie"

"Oi'm Ned, now get yousell over dere out of harms way".

Suddenly there was an almighty crash, a thick cloud of dust and brick showered everything.

"Blood and sands, Froggie artillery!" Ned exclaimed.

Marie was still there seemingly unperturbed by the cannonball smashing through the upper floor of the house. She moved to help James who was lying by the door; Ned rose gingerly as he held his aching back and straightened himself. Together they sat James upright in the corner of the room. He was extremely pale, clearly in great pain but thankful for the water Marie offered. The wounded and dying always had a tremendous thirst and they took great comfort from the relief of a mouthful of water. Ned took a good look at his friend's wound and immediately knew that it would prove fatal, but James would probably endure weeks of lingering agony before finally dying.

They were the worst of injuries; everyone wanted a quick death, no slow agonising demise. Ned did not offer James comforting words, he knew that he had realised the score already.

No more cannonballs came; it must have been a stray shot. From a small window Ned observed the road, which they were tasked to keep open for communications with the Prussians. It was a veritable hail of bullets, nobody could possibly live through it, the road was deserted except for a few corpses. Eventually the firing eased and a desultory fire at opportunistic targets took over, both sides simply clung to what ground they held.

Johnny had settled into a stupor in the wood, it had been a long, fatiguing day and now that it had quietened, weariness overwhelmed him. He looked at his pocket watch, four o'clock.

The cry went up "Mister Kincaid Sir."

He strode towards the source over on the left side of the copse where it skirted the road. As he approached the highway Johnny was amazed to see horses through the undergrowth, where had they come from? As he emerged from the trees his face came directly up against the great head of a jet-black horse, it was unkempt, dishevelled and its eyes shouted fatigue. As he altered his sight upwards he stared into the similarly exhausted eyes of a cavalry officer. Twenty men accompanied him, all were dressed in dark green uniforms, with oilskin covers over their helmets, they were Prussians. Their small horses were in terrible condition; indeed in England horses in such poor fettle were usually shot for humane reasons.

Their Captain spoke in broken English.

"Vee comm to see that Vellington's army fight"

"Lord Wellington will hold here, is your army joining us?" Johnny enquired.

"Nein vee are fighting Napoleon himself at Ligny, Marshal Blucher 'opes Vellington vill 'elp us soon".

Both quickly realised that they had their own battles to win before there would be any help from the other.

The Prussian Officer had noted that there were few troops at the cross roads and that much of Wellington's army still had to arrive, they would not be able to join Blucher today.

The cavalryman bade farewell and the Prussians dashed back down the road towards their own army, seemingly impervious to the hail of shot that they enticed. They seemed to bear charmed lives as no one was struck and they soon disappeared from sight.

Lord Wellington sent a further reinforcement of a

Hanoverian regiment to help hold the wood. They were young and ashen faced, the stray shots and noise of battle clearly discomforted them. They fired erratically at anything that moved and soon frantic messages were coming back from the Rifle skirmishers to the front, 'to kindly not fire upon them'!

Johnny tried to make the Hanoverians understand that they were firing on his men, but they did not comprehend. Eventually after three messages, each one more irate than the previous, Johnny decided to stop them firing at all. He managed to get their officers to move them back into the core of the wood for everybody's safety, where they couldn't cause any more harm! There they stood quietly, unable to see any targets to shoot at and feeling fully protected in the centre of the copse. They now stood bravely awaiting orders; they were not terrible troops just inexperienced Johnny thought.

Slowly but surely over the last few hours more troops had been arriving and Lord Wellington now felt able to take the offensive. From their position, the Rifles could hear heavy firing emanating from the great wood on the opposite side of the plain. The sounds slowly moved to their left through the trees, towards the French line, obviously whoever it was in there were winning the woodland for Wellington. Eventually this battle eased as the French were expelled from the woods completely. Orders arrived for the centre and left of the army to advance and push the French back.

The men prepared their weapons ready for the advance, the French were no fools, they would have sensed the preparations for an attack. The Rifles emerged from the copse and the houses, scampering forward always seeking their next cover, pushing the unit bodily forward.

The Hanoverians emerged behind them and formed into

line as ordered, they would form the reserve to protect them. These raw soldiers were much more confident now. The musket ball's whistle had lost its mystery and advancing always raised the spirits, it was always much better than standing taking punishment from the enemy. They were becoming useful soldiers at last.

The French scampered away before the attack; however, they regularly turned to fire as they fell back. As the Rifles overran the village, they met the French reserves and the volume of lead in the air steadily grew greater until it got to such a level that they were afraid of raising their arms for fear of having them shot off. This was worse than being in the woods, with little cover to protect them they just kept moving forward, hoping the French would break and run before they had to taste cold steel.

"Bugger" Lieutenant John Gardiner exclaimed as he fell just in front of Ned Costello. He sat on the ground and held the calf of his left leg, a ball had passed straight through the muscle, and it hurt like hell. The good news was that it had missed the bone and hopefully hadn't hit any arteries. He sat and watched the lads go forward.

"Well done the Ninety Fifth, keep them running" he cried.

After a few minutes all that remained around were the dead and wounded and John forced himself to his feet. Picking up a discarded musket, he turned it face down to use the butt end as a crutch. He proceeded to hobble back towards the cross roads to get a dressing put on his leg by Joseph Burke.

A few yards further on Ned Costello spotted a Frenchman levelling his musket and taking deliberate aim at Johnny Castles, he couldn't miss that great tub of lard. Ned raised his rifle and took very quick aim at the Frenchie and squeezed the trigger.

"Jesus Chris" Ned roared, as the rifle flew from his hands, his fingers were suddenly in agony. Ned surveyed his right hand, it was a mass of fresh blood, and it stung like hell. Looking closely, afraid of what he would see, Ned realised that two fingers had been hit by a musket ball and were shattered. One of the fingers was hanging on by a thread of skin; that had been his trigger finger. Whilst he stood there, a second ball hit the mess tin strapped on to his backpack making a great clanging noise; it was too hot to hang around here.

"No bloody use staying 'ere now" he growled.

He felt a little faint and shocked, the pain seared through his arm; with his good left hand he pulled out a large pocket-handkerchief stained grey, it had seen better days. He wound it around his hand and formed a knot by holding one end in his teeth; he tightened it as much as he could bear to stop the flow of blood. He needed to go to the rear, as he couldn't fight anymore. He wearily trudged back towards the cross roads, occasionally looking over his shoulder to see how the lads fared. They seemed to be steadily advancing, but they were taking casualties.

Ned walked past the farmhouse again; looking up at the building he spied Marie standing at an upstairs window watching the battle. Marie saw him and waved; she was obviously all right and wasn't going to leave. Ned waved back and blew a kiss, he wished her well.

Robert Fairfoot led his men forward until the French retired out of range.

"Our work is near done", he exclaimed to Castles who was bent double gasping for breath.

His arm suddenly hurt like mad, so much that he dropped his rifle. A ball had entered his right arm and broken the bone, it was sheer agony. He picked up his rifle with his left hand; he saw a Frenchman and wanted to fire.

Seeing Captain Henry Lee he walked over to him and explained.

"By all means use me as a rest and fire away at Johnny Frenchman" he replied.

Robert continued firing until the French had retired out of range Henry lees helping him reload. Only then did Robert think about the pain in his arm, he had lost a fair drop of blood, which made him feel faint. Henry Lees bound his wound and used his handkerchief as a sling.

The advance was over; the men returned jubilant, the officers and sergeants reformed the unit and many with a story of daring do or of lucky escapes recounted their exploits. It was dusk, fighting was likely to finish for the night; the muster needed to be taken and wounded cared for. The roll call soon told its own story, the battalion of six hundred men had lost sixty killed or wounded.

General Alten brought forward his fresh Hanoverian troops to relieve the Rifles, they were to fall back and rest at the crossroads.

They trudged wearily back, carrying or helping along the wounded, there was no time to do anything for the dead.

Suddenly a huge explosion near the cross roads made everyone start, an ammunition cart must have exploded, probably caused by a stray spark.

It was well away from them and no concern of theirs so they just trudged on.

LATE

Alexander observed another officer riding rapidly towards the troop. He rode at a gallop directly at him and brought his horse up hard, just feet away before colliding with Cossack. It proved to be an Aide de Camp of Sir Hussey Vivian.

"Whom do you belong to?" he enquired.

"The Household Brigade, Lord Somerset" Alexander answered.

"Well never mind, there is something serious going on to judge from the heavy firing ahead and artillery must be wanted. Therefore, bring up your guns as fast as you can and join us Hussars. Can you keep up?"

Alexander smiled, "I think so Sir"

"Well come along without delay, we must move swiftly".

The troop was ordered to march immediately; they broke into a canter to catch up with the Hussars now visible beyond a small rise. Alexander was a worried man, they were likely to be in action very shortly and he had no idea where his ammunition wagons were. That meant that he had no more then fifty balls per gun on the gun limbers, it wouldn't last long in a serious action.

They approached a small town, its houses clustered

around the road; Alexander identified it as Nivelle on his map. The intensity of the cannonade and the pall of thick black smoke billowing into the blue sky led him to think that the fighting was just the other side of the town. The inhabitants were stood in the street looking in the general direction of the firing, not knowing either what was happening or what to do. They watched the maimed blood bespattered wounded that had struggled this far from the fighting often with the aid of a colleague or two for support, with a mixture of compassion and revulsion. The remnants of uniform told Alexander that these were Dutch and Belgian troops, many were pleading for help, which the inhabitants seemed happy to proffer, but more alarmingly they cried out that all was lost, Napoleon was coming!

The troop hurried on up the main street of Nivelle to cheers and the heartening cries of "Vivent les Anglaise" as they passed. Some held out their hands to stroke or pat the horses and to shake hands with the riders in a show of support and solidarity as they sped past. Young maidens threw kisses to "Mon Braves", the men raised their hats in salute, the support of the population encouraged them greatly.

Henry Leathes called to Alexander, "they will celebrate just as much if Napoleon comes here tomorrow, I wager!"

Alexander smiled, the villager's loyalties were mixed, they had been under Napoleon's rule for twenty years suffering from his excessive demands for men and money to feed his ambitions; they had craved independence, but the Allies had failed them by linking them with the hated Dutch as a joint Kingdom at the end of the war. That was nothing less than a betrayal for many Belgians. Since then the clamour for Napoleon's return with his false promises of Belgian independence, within the benign and supportive French Empire had found many supporters. The Allies were operating in nominally friendly territory, but few doubted that their support would last only as long as they were in the supremacy.

As they cleared the town, the road formed a slowly ascending chaussee wide enough for four carriages to travel abreast, lined with great elm trees. The intensity of the firing was so great that they felt that the battle must be just over the brow of the next hill and they pushed their teams on as hard as they could. The crimson skies of sunset were truly beautiful; however the red orb slowly descending below the horizon marking the end of such a glorious day meant that new and greater fears arose. They would shortly be entering the field of conflict in at best half light, when friend and foe would be difficult to distinguish until it was too late, apprehension started to gnaw at them.

The road was becoming heavily congested with the flotsam of war, there were numerous Dutch, British and particularly Belgian casualties, but even more plentiful were their helpers; some wounded had up to ten men each aiding them to retire to safety. This did not bode well, for when men found such poor excuses to retire in such numbers, then their units are no longer capable of offering meaningful resistance. They all cried warnings of the French, of their success in defeating the Allied armies and their imminent arrival on the scene.

Amongst the steady stream of casualties hobbling along the road was a solitary Scotsman in his kilt and black feather bonnet using his broken musket as a crutch. He called out to the troop as they struggled up the slope.

"Ha ye any rum to ease the pain, lads?" the Scotsman enquired.

Alexander stopped the troop to enquire whether the French were winning.

"Na, na Sir, it's aww a damn lie, they was fetchin' yet

wun I left 'em, but it's a bluddy business aww reet and thars na sayin what may be end o' it. Oor regiment was nigh clean swept off and oor Colonel kilt jist as I cum awaa." He replied assertively.

Richard Hichens, the Surgeon, dismounted to examine the brave Caledonian's wound. He discovered that the infantryman had received a French musket ball in the knee joint, Richard felt all around the wound squeezing the flesh firmly.

"There is no exit wound, so the ball must still be in the leg. I will need to get it out or the leg will become gangrenous. Hand me my medical case."

Alexander ordered the troop to march on and wished them luck with the operation; Richard could catch up when it was completed.

The case opened to reveal a ghastly array of tools, saws, gouges, and files all forming a collection better than many self-respecting carpenters would own!

The Scotsman sat on the grass verge with his damaged knee raised. Richard took a scalpel in his delicate hands and immediately set to work. Initially he removed any damaged tissue from around the wound to allow the good flesh to heal unhindered by decaying matter, which could otherwise become fatally infected. The Highlander was lucky, as his uniform formed of a kilt and long woollen socks left his knee uncovered. This meant that there was little fear of fragments of uniform being driven deep into the wound with the ball. That was the main fear when wounded by a lead shot, as it was universally believed by all military and medical men that the cause of gangrene and septicaemia was not the lead ball itself but the fragments of dirty material dragged into the wound along with it. That was the main reason why so many sailors stripped almost naked during the great sea battles when manning the guns between decks on those great oak leviathans. In most cases where the ball was lodged deeply in the flesh with little practical possibility of extraction without killing the patient, it was standard practice to leave well alone, letting the wound heal, sealing the ball away, where it would hopefully not infect and give little more than irregular twinges. Often, many years later the ball would work a route to just below the surface of the skin of its own accord and then could be removed with ease by simply piercing the dermas to allow it to pop out. In this case, as the ball was near the knee joint, which would leave the man with a stiff unbending leg, Richard proceeded to extract it.

He could feel a lump deep below the surface when squeezing the flesh. He cut across the entry wound widening it to allow his fingers to probe deep into the leg without tearing the skin apart. He pushed hard and his finger slowly disappeared into the flesh and gore up to the second joint of his digit. There his finger became aware of a solid object; feeling around it confirmed that it was the blighter. With great force, he managed to prise his instruments into the wound and eventually grasped the ball and removed it.

"Got it," he exclaimed ecstatically.

Extracting the ball gently, he then bound the knee with a lint bandage.

The Scotsman had not grimaced once nor let forth a word of complaint or cry of pain; once it was over he hauled himself back onto his feet and thanking Hichens, simply turned and continued on his way, hobbling along with the aid of his makeshift crutch.

Richard watched him go, that was a truly brave man he thought. Packing his equipment away in his leather holdall, he raised himself up onto his fine horse and trotted on to find the troop again.

The last vestiges of daylight were fading fast as the troop crested the rise and finally passed the great wood which they had been approaching for an age; the noise of battle was now overwhelming, indeed the jarring screech and feint glow of the burning fuses of occasional shells passing overhead and landing beyond told them that they were now in the battle zone. Unseen explosions, bugle calls, musketry and cries of pain and suffering focused the mind; they could see little in the fading light, this tended to cause their imaginations to exaggerate the awfulness around them. All were deathly quiet straining to catch every sound, afraid of what would suddenly appear before them.

They passed a tavern, which was obviously open for business; it seemed to be slightly incongruous in this wilderness. The light from its windows showed a crowd of soldiers revelling at this watering hole, whilst obviously discussing their adventures of so recent past. Uniforms of all the Allied nations could be seen within, cavalry, infantry and artillery all carousing as if they did not have a care in the world, yet the fighting was only slowly spluttering to an enforced close with the termination of daylight a few hundred yards away. Numerous horses were tethered outside; all looked worn and dishevelled from the hard riding they had obviously endured. The sounds of raucous laughter wafted on the breeze, which struck Alexander as completely remiss.

"This is a strange time and place for laughter," He stated gruffly.

But as Henry Leathes replied, "Sometimes the sights of the battle mean that men cannot sleep without strong liquor to deaden their senses, the laughter is simply a manic reaction to the build up of tension and the horror of what they have endured. Do not condemn them too harshly, for we know not what they have suffered."

The road skirted the trees, as they travelled along the road bodies of troops occasionally came into view resting at their arms in the adjoining fields, they displayed the blackened faces of men that had been in heavy fighting, their eyes glaring starkly white in the fires reflection. Wounded men were passing continuously, more sat or lay by the roadside unable to proceed any further, some begging for help or the Lord's mercy, a few sobbed from the sheer pain, others lay silent awaiting their maker's final call with dignity. Death had already called for many to cross the Styx with him, the corpses lay scattered across the road and in the hedges, and many more must surely lie unseen within the woods. Alexander wondered that they were all naked as the day they were born, but the vultures, fellow soldiers or local villagers had robbed them of everything often before the body was cold.

The troop trotted wearily on through this vision of hell, the horses were completely worn down and the men drooped with exhaustion despite the scenes and dangers around them. Nobody dared halt the horses for fear they would not restart their march and the men were also far too tired to make the effort, so any bodies stretched across the roadway were simply ridden over. The sickening cracking of bone and the squelch of tissue were listened to with horror by all, but everyone chose to pretend it wasn't happening and tried to blot the sickening images from their minds. The unmistakable splintering of skull and flattening of brain tissue was particularly gruesome, but still no one stopped.

Finally they came to a cross roads encircled by a cluster of houses and farmsteads. It was clear from the number of fires lighting up the darkness of a starless night that a large part of the army was encamped here. The sounds of fighting had petered out, and the only sound was restricted to the occasional pop of musketry between the opposing pickets as the armies set down the boundaries of their respective territories for the night.

As the Rifles retraced their steps toward the crossroads they came across the scene of devastation left by the blast of the ammunition wagon. Among a number of bodies scattered about the road one particularly stood out. Lying face down in the mud was a figure in a floral dress.

Tom Plunket suddenly appeared to welcome them, as the Second battalion had just arrived having marched all day, entering the battlefield from the Nivelles road.

Tom called out, "Hey lads! Have youze seen my Mary?"

Mary was a camp follower that Tom had feelings for; indeed he was talking of marriage to legitimise her position. She was a homely woman of mid height, stockily built, with a rugged face. She had followed them in Spain and had stayed with them through thick and thin. Her previous man had been killed at Arcangues. Camp followers were a Godsend; they were there to provide food and drink after hard marches, for a price of course, to tend lovingly when sick or hurt and to provide womanly company as well. It was fully understood that once the husband was dead the women would latch onto someone else before they were even cold, as without a protector she would receive no rations and could not survive. Tom was her latest partner; there was little love, more mutual support to survive. Mary would keep his spare food for her man and his friends; she would stay closer to them than the commissariat. When they ordered baggage away, they all went far to the rear, not to be seen again for days. Mary however always contrived to stay near the front; she was under nobody's orders!

Tom suddenly spotted the body in the roadway and recognised the dress instantly.

"Mary? Jesus No!" he exclaimed.

Running up to the body, he spotted some movement of the arms and called back "She's aloive tank God". Tom took hold of her shoulder and pulled her over onto her back.

"Christ" Tom started. Her face was missing!

The explosion had seared the flesh from her face even her nose had disappeared! Her face was now just a pool of gore. They lifted Mary and carried her to Mr Burke at the farmhouse, who held little hope of recovery.

As they dragged themselves back to the farm, the wounded were taken in for the surgeons to treat. The unwounded survivors collapsed on the ground to get rest, many falling asleep as soon as their heads hit their earthen pillow.

"You not dead yet Moore?" shouted Robert Fairfoot.

They all laughed loudly.

It had worked; he had broken their stupor and breathed new life into the men. Back in Spain, John Moore had caught fever and been pronounced dead. He'd come round in the chapel of rest at midnight whilst his body awaited burial the next morning; he'd never taken jokes about his death well after that!

One of the men fell to the ground and started to convulse, in the darkness no one knew who it was.

"Woss wrong, sumun hit?" someone cried out.

Robert Fairfoot walked over to check.

"John give us your strap" he screamed.

Robert forced the man's mouth open and put the leather strap between his teeth for him to bite on.

It was 'Long Tom of Lincoln', as the lads called him. Tom was one of the older men of the battalion at forty-two, a six-footer, lanky and awkward. He had fits, Mr Burke called them epileptic seizures or something, he'd always had them, but it never stopped him being a good soldier though. The fit passed and the lads quickly settled down to sleep without cover under a starless sky, after the day's exertions they would sleep anywhere.

The officers sat together around a warming fire and discussed the day; some dressed minor wounds themselves, so that they could remain with the battalion when the fighting continued the next day as it surely would. Major Alexander Cameron had a small contusion on his side; Captain William Johnston had a flesh wound, as did Lieutenant Orlando Felix.

Even the officers had nothing to cover themselves with, as the baggage was miles away to the rear. George Simmons had recently gone back into the fields with three men to bring in one of the men who had suffered both legs being broken by a cannonball. He was now better off than the other officers, having taken a large cloak off a dead Cuirassier as his reward on the walk back. Those like Johnny Kincaid who had food, grabbed something from their pack to share with their colleagues, the rest suffered hunger pangs in silence. Soon, however, sleep took them all, it was near eleven o'clock.

It had been a long and eventful day.

As G troop arrived at the crossroads, the apparition reappeared; Macdonald suddenly emerged from the blackness like a spirit and swiftly approached them.

"Ah Mercer, you have made it, the army has endured a very hard fought battle here at Quatre Bras and has been victorious. Have your troop bivouac in the field here for the night; I will bring orders in the morning."

The troop wearily pulled off the road into a field adjoining a farmhouse. The limbers and cannon were parked and the horses unharnessed. Despite their utter fatigue, the men automatically followed their training and sought to settle the horses. The limited hay supply they carried with them was to be preserved, as there was no sign of Mr Coates and the carts. Therefore half the men set out with sickles to cut down the tall wheat standing in the fields beyond. The remainder sought out water for the poor beasts. It transpired that the only water supply nearby was a deep well in the courtyard of the farmhouse and it took no less than two hours for the men to draw enough water to refresh all their steeds. The clamour for water at the well continued all night long as a continuous stream of soldiers made their way to raise the bucket to quench thirsts.

The horses being satisfied, the men now thought about themselves, the Peninsula hands searched out their meagre supply of cooked morsels from their haversacks, which they had saved for such an occasion, the lesson was hard learnt by the inexperienced who had kept nothing. The officers had nothing either, their sumptuous breakfast was now a dim memory and their stomachs voiced disapproval. Richard Hichens the Surgeon had rejoined and his servant beamed proudly as he carefully removed a large gingham cloth from his saddlebag, it contained the remains of the large game pie they had enjoyed at the breakfast table at Strytem that very morning. It was joyfully accepted and portioned out amongst the officers, but the morsel each received barely touched the stomach cramps they endured. Alexander passed around his cigars and they all lit up and puffed away as a release from the gnawing in the pit of their stomachs.

There was nothing for it, they lay down around the fire pulling their coats and blankets close up to protect them against the cold whilst attempting to ignore the hunger pangs and noise at the well, they eventually settled into a fitful sleep.

THE RETREAT

The frequent pop of musketry woke the Rifles, it was still dark but they rose instinctively and formed up, was it a French attack? George Simmons as commander of the picket line went out to discover the cause of the firing; he could just make out the sentinels in the darkness. He approached them as they fired sporadically into the night.

"What's happening, are they attacking?" George whispered.

"Blessed if I knows Sir, they started firing to the roight of us and we just joined in."

George realised that it was probably a false alarm; everyone had the jitters at night and if one fired then they all did, firing at shadows.

"Cease firing," he ordered, "Stand to and strain your eyes and ears, let's see if they really are advancing"

Slowly the firing eased and indeed it soon became clear that there was no sound of movement, confirming that the French were not attacking.

Leaving the pickets in more relaxed mood, George returned to the battalion and they stood down. The men lay down again and attempted to sleep, but their efforts were largely in vain. Still occasional musket shots were heard as some sentry thought that they had seen movement in the shadows; it kept everybody on the alert.

Some finally relaxed and started to drift off to sleep when they were rudely awoken by the bugle call for 'stand to' again. It was fast approaching daylight and as they had always done in Spain, they were formed ready to fight one hour before dawn. They stood for over half an hour in the darkness until the grey light of dawn slowly but surely started to bring the ground around them clearly into view. They stood until a white horse could be seen at a mile, which was the traditional benchmark. The hour for surprise attacks was then over, clear visibility confirmed that the enemy were not attacking and the bugle call for 'Stand down' was gratefully heard.

Now the men could light fires to warm themselves and brew tea and cook food if they had any left. The young lads now realised why the veterans had taken their full rations at Brussels, where the hell was the commissariat with their victuals? The old hands knew.

"Victuals won't come t'day. We left Broosels too quick; wagons will still be there. If we goes for'ard today you'll not see them tomorrow neither!" Tom Crawley mused.

Some cadged food from their friends, others scoured the abandoned farm buildings and cottages for a morsel, but many others had already tried there in vain. A few went into the fields to harvest some wheat to bolster a scrap of meat they had boiling in a pot to bulk it out into a soup. Most simply sat and warmed themselves at the fires desperately trying to forget the gripes and rumbles in their empty bellies.

The weather was much cooler today; they shivered in the chill morning air, aching in every joint, for the damp and cold had gnawed deep into their very bones during the night. A few like George had found a cloak or coat from a dead man, French or British, they didn't need them anymore. Nobody had wanted to carry their greatcoats yesterday, then it had been glorious sunshine and the coats were so heavy, they had all been put on the carts. What they wouldn't give now for a greatcoat and food; they had learnt a valuable lesson for the future, but that was no comfort now.

As they rested near the farmhouse they ensured that their weapons were clean and ready for use; they used brushes and oiled cloths to remove the black powder residue from the barrel after yesterday's firing. A clean weapon could mean the difference between life and death, dirty weapons were apt to clog and misfire.

They talked and joked over the previous day's exploits, the close shaves and their moments of individual glory. Dead colleagues were mentioned in passing but most were lucky to get a moments thought; they considered the present only; there was nothing they could do about what had already passed.

"Hey Tom 'ow comes Johnny Frenchy ain't attacked yet?"

"Dunno" Tom Crawley replied, "Maybe Prussians beat them good an' they've gone."

"Nah, the Froggie pickets are still there, mark my words boys they'll come" Robert Fairfoot piped up.

Johnny Castles dashed up to the group, he breathed heavily from the exertion, "Hey lads, hussars just come back from the Proosians, they've been beat bad by Napoleon. Reckons they's coming fur us next".

Robert looked stern "If it's true, we'll have to retreat, this ain't no ground to foight Napoleon on."

The lads quietened, they still talked, but the spirit had gone out of their discussion. Nobody dared say it, but everyone was concerned; without the Prussians help retreat was inevitable and retiring with French cavalry on your shoulder was no joke. They knew that they would probably be ordered to hold the rear, so they would certainly take the brunt of any attack. Yesterday might look like a picnic by the end of this day!

Remarkably all was still quiet, it was gone nine o'clock before the order was passed for the walking wounded to set off for Brussels along the high road; the order confirmed a retreat.

Ned Costello pulled himself upright and began to walk along the road to Brussels. His comrades said nothing to him, he was alone now, useless and weak, the others had more important matters to attend to, and Ned understood that, he had done just the same to others before.

Tom Plunket sauntered into the farmhouse building housing the hospital to enquire after Mary.

Surgeon Burke took him aside, "Tom we'll put her in a cart with the others."

"Will she live?" Tom asked plaintively.

Joseph Burke was solemn, "I didn't think she would see this morning Tom, but she is resting well. If Mary can survive the journey to Brussels she might live, but I hold out no real hope, her wounds are very severe."

Tom released Mary's hand and wiped a single tear from his cheek, then strode back outside into the cool morning air, there was nothing he could do for her, it was up to the Good Lord now.

George Simmons and Johnny Kincaid were also in the farmhouse looking down on the lifeless body of young William Lister. His form was pale and still, Joseph Burke held a looking glass to the lips, there was no breath, and no pulse confirmed his demise. The poor lad had lain in agony all night; it was a blessed relief for him, as he had no hope of surviving his wounds. The burial, party approached silently; wrapping the body in his own blanket they carried him to a freshly dug hole and laid him to rest. A layer of earth and a few stones marked the shallow grave, Padre Williams spoke a few words and it was all over. Opportunities for advancement were already appearing for the volunteers!

Ned's hand ached like hell, he bore the pain with stolid forbearance as a soldier was expected to do, but it gnawed at him constantly; he wished that there was something he could take to numb the ache of his throbbing fingers, but he had no rum. He forced himself to walk on, pushing his tired body to make each further step. The road was already very congested; the followers of the army with their wagons and animals were aware of the retreat and were determined to be gone well before the French arrived.

Faintly at first, above the cacophony of sound from the throng he heard the cries of a child, as he walked it became louder. Ned found himself getting closer to the cries, they were now to his right in the hedge and he decided to investigate. Crossing through the thorny hedge with some difficulty Ned entered a large open field; he peered into the slight morning mist lying like a blanket on the damp fields. There! He could just see a small boy sitting on the grass crying his eyes out whilst holding the head of a young woman who lay beside him. One look at the cold pallid features of the pretty lass showed that death had already been to claim her soul. A large red stain on her temple showed where a stray musket ball must have struck her last evening. Ned crossed himself and blessed this innocent, then looked to the boy. He appeared to be about three years old, he was soaked through and shivering and could not understand why his mother would not wake up. With great difficulty, Ned lifted the boy onto his shoulders, he had no pack or rifle now but this was still a heavy load for an injured man and lifting him hurt his hand like billy'o. He got back onto the road and trudged even more wearily towards Brussels, pushing his feet forward mechanically, not allowing his brain to dwell upon the pain and burden nor the long distance to go.

The battalion stood to arms yet again and patiently watched the rest of the army slowly march away down the road to Brussels. Eventually the fields around them emptied of men and then all that could be seen were a few cavalry pickets to the front. They knew they were the rearguard but they hoped that they hadn't been forgotten!

The scene became somewhat unreal and eerie, little now indicated the proximity of the enemy in vast numbers and only a few cadavers lying near the crossroads, the hair on their heads stirring in the breeze mimicking life, told of the severe fighting there the previous day.

That morning at Quatre Bras, the sounds of the brisk fire of musketry had also awoken Alexander. It was not fully daylight yet and he was so tired that he simply rolled on his side and fell back into a deep sleep. He was unconsciously aware of the noise and its association with danger, but fatigue simply overwhelmed him.

John Bretton sat up abruptly from his earthen mattress and asked nonchalantly "I wonder what all that firing means?"

The words sparked through Alexander's head like a bolt of lightning, suddenly he was wide-awake and on his feet to assess the situation.

The immediate good news was the sight of Quartermaster John Hall and the ammunition wagons, they must have arrived in the night whilst he slept and they had somehow found them in amongst all the other units. At least he now had a unit able to sustain itself in action for a reasonable period; his only remaining embarrassment was the lack of food supplies as there was still no news of Mr Coates and the wagons.

Alexander quickly scanned the fields to discover an explanation for the heavy firing but could see nothing in the half-light. It seemed that either the skirmishers of each army were out sparring early or the men were simply clearing their muskets of the overnight damp.

The troop had unknowingly lain near the Ninety Fifth Rifles overnight and Mercer watched them perform their roll of skirmishing for the army, ensuring that the French did not encroach upon the cross roads. Alexander watched an officer of the Rifles tour his pickets which were strung across the plain, he couldn't know that he was watching George Simmons at his work.

There was little interest by the rest of the troop in the brisk firing; indeed many individuals still lay sound asleep. They hugged the ground almost hidden by the grey morning mist; indeed they appeared like so many rounded rocks just peeping above the surface of the sea.

All of a sudden Macdonald was stood at Alexander's shoulder; he had an unnerving knack of appearing as if from the ether itself. Tapping Alexander on the back, he proceeded to relay orders for G troop.

"The Fifth Division are marching back along the Brussels road, you will follow them in the retreat."

"Retreat".

The word seared through Alexander as effectively as if a dagger had been plunged into his breast. The talk last night was that they had snatched a victory from Napoleon's grasp and everyone was expecting orders for an advance to complete their success. Alexander was shocked at the order to retire; he was simply mentally unprepared for the bombshell. The men nearby had caught the gist of the conversation and a low murmur of discontent spread rapidly. An air of depression soon settled on the troop as they sat in the chill dank atmosphere of the morning.

Macdonald remained oblivious to the reaction and continued.

"Major Ramsay's troop will remain in the rear with the cavalry to cover the retreat."

He paused unsure whether to continue, then steeled himself and said, "I will not conceal from you that it actually falls to you to carry out this duty".

Alexander felt incensed; Macdonald was offering him a way out of rearguard duty because of his inexperience. He stared at the Lieutenant Colonel struggling hard to contain his rage; he so wanted to strike out.

"I beg you give the devil his due and me mine!" he snapped.

Macdonald acquiesced in his demand for the place of honour in the rearguard and stepped away smiling inwardly, Mercer had been offered an honourable way out but he had chosen to prove that he could equal the great Ramsay, just as Macdonald had hoped.

A great outcry emanating from the farmhouse caused everyone to look, was it the French? All eyes scanned the horizon for the cause of the commotion with little success. Suddenly, a confused mass of soldiers of all the allied nations emerged from the farmyard firing so erratically, that some observers actually jumped up fearing a cavalry surprise. Then from between a mass of flailing arms and legs, a large sow emerged squealing expressively, imploring mercy from its pursuers as it ran for its life. The onlookers laughed and cheered, encouraging the chasing pack. Bayonets and swords hacked at the pig in rapid succession and soon it succumbed to the blows. Within seconds of collapsing on the ground, a few hard blows from musket butts smashed its skull and dashed the brains out. The swords and axes fell on the still pulsating body to dismember it. The crowd then fought frantically for a morsel of the still warm flesh and turned away in triumph brandishing their bloody treasure. The carcass was stripped completely clean in less than a few minutes; entrails and all, starving men are never particular about offal. The dreadful execution and dismemberment played out before Alexander's eyes would have normally provoked feelings of utter revulsion in him, now he, like his fellow hungry men just saw an act of necessity which provoked little emotion from him. The excitement over, everyone resumed their own space on the ground and awaited the order to move.

Thoughts of food crowded their minds, particularly those who had missed out on a share of the pork. There was still no sign of Coates or the supplies and their stomachs protested loudly but there was little hope of relief. It was some twenty-four hours since they had received anything substantial to eat. The officers sat and smoked cigars, some men preferred their pipes, the tobacco helping to quell the hunger pangs and making their privations a little more bearable. Alexander reproached himself for his poor decision, allowing the farmers to utilise their carts until the moment that they were required. He had made a number of mistakes to date through his lack of experience, which Robert Newland was always so quick to point out. So far, he had not been completely ruined by any of them, but he worried that with the French at hand any more errors might lead to a terrible disaster.

Each corps moved in turn from the left and proceeded along the wide Brussels chausee; looks of concern and dejection told on every face.

The elation following yesterday's victory, when a mere handful of infantry without cavalry or artillery support had stopped the French advance, was harshly deflated by the order to retreat. The army having finally been brought together and therefore being much stronger, led them to confidently predict an advance; retreat was incomprehensible to them.

British armies were never good at retreating, it always brought the worst out of the men, they would always prefer to stand and fight even with little chance of success, a real back to the wall mentality.

Alexander and his troop sat leisurely on the ground watching the various regiments march off; the warming sun made the wait pleasant and they enjoyed being able to relax.

"Hello Alexander, what goes?" brought him instantly out of his daydreams.

Looking up, Alexander registered the uniform of a fellow horse artillery officer, dusty and grimy from hard riding, he realised that the long features and dark hair were familiar, then it struck him, it was Alexander Dickson, rightful commander of the troop!

"The troop appears in fine shape Alexander, look after them well for me."

Alexander found his voice "It is good to see you again Sir, I hear that you are attached to the siege artillery."

Dickson looked pained, "I dare say Lord Wellington needs me for the post, but I wish I were with you in the battles to come, there seems little chance of any siege work at present."

Alexander looked at his dusty uniform and worn horse, "You have travelled hard!"

"I am just returned from that debacle at New Orleans, it was sheer bloody murder. Attacking the American's prepared defences head on was madness, two thousand peninsula veterans killed and wounded for nothing. The

Duke would have taken more care of his men, General Packenham may well have been his brother in law, but had he survived, his Lordship would have seen him court martialled."

Alexander pointed to the French who now started to appear on the far hills, "They will be here soon, the army retreats to Brussels."

"Then there must I go," answered Dickson, and bidding his troop adieu and good luck, rode off.

At twelve o'clock with the sun at its zenith one of those dandies of Wellington's 'family' rode up at frightening speed and reported to Sir Andrew Barnard.

"Sir Andrew, Lord Wellington now deems the army to have retired beyond immediate danger. You must retire with the Ninety Fifth now, along the Brussels road. The Earl of Uxbridge with his cavalry shall shield your retrograde movements. My Lord urges haste but caution as the French will not be far behind."

"Enough Sir!" Sir Andrew snapped, "I know what is to be done, you have carried your orders, now be gone Sir." He did not relish being told his job by some young whipper-snapper.

The battalion formed up in column formation and commenced their retreat. The cavalry formed between them and the French to screen them. This did not stop the officers regularly casting a nervous glance over their shoulders to ensure the French did not break through. British cavalry were excellent fighters but were apt to be very gung ho; they would forget their task of protecting the battalion if a good opportunity to attack the French arose. The road was clear of impedimenta, the rest of the army were already gone and they were able to march at a good pace.

Ned Costello was a few miles ahead of the battalion and here the road was heavily congested slowing everything. The army had marched past and Ned had been forced to step aside for them; it had made him feel dejected that he might be left behind. He spurred himself on, he must keep going and avoid stumbling, as the wagons would crush a man with their heavy wooden wheels. The congestion grew and finally the traffic came to a virtual halt. A narrow bridge over a river constricted the road and a mass of wagons and gun carriages waited their turn to cross. This was dangerous thought Ned, if the French arrived now there would be panic. There was no way past, so he sank to the ground on the roadside and chewed on the remaining meat in his pack, sharing his food with the boy. He looked on as Staff officers arrived and organised the crossing, shouting, gesticulating and striking both horses and drivers with the flat of their swords to make them listen and obey. Soon the mess was unscrambled and the bridge slowly cleared.

As one of the wagons passed, a woman called out.

"Ere that's young Meg's boy, Tom."

Ned jumped up "Youze know 'im?"

"Aye Meg's boy, come 'ere Tom, 'er man's in't Royals. Where's Meg?"

Ned shook his head, "Took a ball, no chance."

"Oi'll take care of the little bugger till I can get him to 'is dad," she offered.

Ned was pleased to be relieved of the burden and happily handed Tom up to the woman, he would have a much better chance with her. Ned watched the wagons cross the bridge and then followed them, as he did so he looked back to see the Rifles coming up the road closing with him rapidly. Beyond them he could see a few cavalry units but further beyond them on the rising ground in the distance, numerous dark masses were visible, more appearing with each minute. Napoleon and his army were finally on their way. Fortune had smiled on Wellington, whilst they had commenced retreating the French had rested and reorganised, Napoleon had missed a massive chance to destroy them. The army would take some catching now, with this thought Ned turned and followed the army; he wasn't going to be left behind.

LAST OUT

At noon, even the Rifles had moved out along the Brussels road and all that Alexander could now see in advance were a few cavalry videttes dotted across the fields. The scene was now a very melancholy one, the fields were littered with corpses which were in especially large numbers around the cross roads, the carnage here had been tremendous. Here the highlanders had been slaughtered in great numbers and an abundance of red-coated bodies could be seen, black feather bonnets and kilts stirring gently in the mild breeze. Intermixed with them were numerous mangled horses and French Cuirassiers, they had all sold life dearly.

Looking to the rear of the troop, Alexander could see an impressive line of light dragoons, the brigade of Sir Ormsby Vandeleur, all dressed in their smart blue jackets, the three regiments simply identified by different coloured facings, buff, yellow and scarlet. They stood in a long line two horses deep, some three hundred yards to his rear near some houses. Their imposing presence gave the troop great confidence in such an exposed and advanced position.

Still no orders came to move, there was little sign of movement from the French and Alexander became curious.

Mounting Cossack he rode slowly forward far beyond the cross roads, but still he could see little save the cavalry pickets off to his left. Coming upon a thicket, Alexander egged Cossack forward to push on through, but the horse suddenly halted and refused to proceed, Bal growled and barked at something he did not like. Alexander peered cautiously into the bush to identify the cause of their discomfiture. Hidden beneath the foliage was the naked corpse of a young man, he had been a handsome youth, an embryo moustache had just started to sprout on his upper lip and his demeanour in death was serene and peaceful. There was no wound or gore to indicate a cause of death. The sight of such waste brought on a feeling of sadness within Alexander, in stark contrast to the sights of the cross roads, which had failed to stir any emotion at all. The youth's horse lay dead alongside; they would both soon form ample meals for the carrion crows and wolves. Alexander rode slowly back to the troop, no wiser for his reconnaissance.

On his return, he discovered that Sir Augustus Frazer had ordered the troop's ammunition wagons to withdraw so as not to impede any retreat, especially if it became necessary to retire in haste. This left the troop with only their fifty rounds per gun in the limbers again; Alexander hoped that this would not cause a problem.

One o'clock came with no change, the troop stood ready to move as they had for the last few hours.

Lord Uxbridge and his Aide de Camp appeared from the rear and rode beyond the troop where they halted, tethered their steeds and sat down on the ground whilst they surveyed the front with their small spyglasses.

A large body of cavalry in dark uniforms appeared approaching them slowly; Lord Uxbridge seemed unperturbed and continued scanning the fields to his front.

Alexander assumed that they must be Prussians, as the videttes also showed no sign of alarm.

Suddenly all changed, the videttes must have suddenly recognised them as French and they all galloped back frantically to the safety of their regiments. Alexander was uneasy for Uxbrige's safety, as he still sat scanning the front seemingly oblivious to the commotion all around. He was even more concerned for the troop as no orders appeared, how long was he to stay there so exposed?

Alexander was aware that he was much too far in front of the dragoons for safety and decided to retire on his own authority.

Immediately Robert Newland voiced his disapproval, "You must wait for orders; the Duke will have you arrested if you command a movement without his instruction."

Alexander ignored him and ordered the troop to gallop back toward the light dragoons, then halted them again some fifty yards in their front. The men proceeded to unlimber the guns ready to fire, Alexander planned to give the French one salvo then retire behind the dragoons.

As his troop aimed the already loaded guns, Sir Ormsby Vandeleur appeared at Alexander's side, he was quite obviously furious.

"What are you doing here, Sir? You encumber my front and we shall not be able to charge. Take your guns away immediately, Sir!"

Alexander attempted to explain his intentions, but Sir Ormsby would not listen.

"Instantly I say take them away" he insisted.

Alexander tried again, but only succeeded in irritating Vandeleur further.

"No, no, take them out of my way Sir!" he ordered.

Alexander saw that further discussion was futile and drew breath to bellow the order to limber up.

Before he could utter the words, Lord Uxbridge galloped up and asked, "Captain Mercer, are you loaded?"

Alexander nodded. "Indeed Sir".

"Then give them a round as they rise over the hill and retire as quickly as possible to allow the dragoons to charge," he ordered. Uxbridge then retired to the Dragoons to wait for the right moment.

Alexander gratefully continued preparations to welcome the French with a six-gun salute.

Uxbridge called across, "They are coming up the hill", and then betraying his own anxieties, added, "Do you think you can retire quickly enough afterwards?"

Alexander replied with a confidence that belied his inner fears "I am sure of it my lord."

Uxbridge smiled at his assurance, "Very well then, keep a good lookout and point your guns well."

The dark grey skies above them contrasted vividly with the bright sunlight reflecting off the hills on the horizon. A lone horseman crested the rise; he was silhouetted majestically against the golden sunlight, the squat shape and large bicorn spoke only one name, Napoleon!

The guns remained silent, the thought of destroying the 'Ogre' did not even cross their minds, war was still a gentlemanly pursuit, and one did not fire deliberately at opposing Generals. A few horsemen rode up and joined him on the crest, probably a few of his Staff, the legendary French Marshal's such as Ney and Soult, Alexander pondered.

Still he waited until formed squadrons of cavalry finally appeared in sufficient numbers so that they started to obscure the horizon.

Alexander drew a deep breath and thundered out the order "Fire".

The six cannon roared, kicking backwards furiously, the

nine-pound iron spheres being propelled forward to smash everything in their path.

Alexander did not pause to view the course of the shots or the damage caused.

"Left limber up" he bellowed, the horse teams galloped back to their cannon, the guns were hitched up and the gunners mounted in an instant. They worked perfectly in harmony as they had practised so often. Alexander was proud of his troop, all had performed to perfection and they were galloping to the rear in a moment.

The roar of the cannon seemed to reverberate throughout the heavens above. The black clouds suddenly opened to release an almighty deluge that was accompanied by harsh flashes of lightning and crashes of thunder so loud that all mortal sounds of war were completely drowned out. It seemed that God wanted to show the futility of man's weapons in comparison with the frightening power of the elements.

As G troop rapidly rode to the rear of the dragoons, the French blazed a few cannonballs from their horse artillery, the balls bouncing across the plain, splashing muddy water with each bound but striking little.

Captain Edward Whinyates' Rocket troop stood just to the rear of the dragoons contrary to his orders to retreat with the army, in the hope of finding an opportunity to prove the value of rockets. His troop suffered the only casualty from the French fire, a cannonball striking a carriage and driving a large wooden splinter hard into Whinyates' servant's leg. The splinter was about a foot long and the point had driven right through his leg. The poor man screamed in agony as he grasped his thigh and fell into the mud writhing in pain. Two colleagues raised him back on to the carriage; they harshly yanked the splinter out and bound his leg. He was lucky, it hadn't hit an artery and hopefully he would survive, if the wood was all out, his leg shouldn't become gangrenous.

Alexander heard Lord Uxbridge command the dragoons to retire; the French were obviously in too great a number for his small force to stop them. In fact they were in grave danger of being overwhelmed, and the ordered trot of a slow deliberate retreat started to quicken as the pressure grew. G troop was soon galloping to keep up with the dragoons; it was becoming a veritable race. Above the noise of incessant heavy rain, thunder and hooves splashing in pools of water, came the frightening howls and yells of the French cavalry as they pursued them menacingly. Their blood was up, this was their opportunity to destroy the English cavalry before the very eyes of their Emperor and gain revenge for yesterday's failure.

The Rifles approached the river and the town of Genappe beyond; there they had to slow down to file across the narrow bridge. As they waited to cross, the skies that had been growing darker and more brooding by the minute, finally unleashed their burden. A horrendous crash of thunder presaged an extremely violent storm. The rain fell, it was torrential, some old hands remembered the monsoons out east, this was just as heavy, but here it was freezing cold rain and didn't just last a few minutes. It was unrelenting, soon everyone was soaked through, the roads became awash with streams of water and more importantly wet their rifles, dampening the powder and making them useless. Infantry in the rain had little protection from cavalry except their bayonets, but the Baker rifle was short and the sword bayonet was not particularly good, being long and cumbersome. The men felt vulnerable and they pushed on over the bridge a little more hurriedly.

As they crossed, Johnny Kincaid bellowed "Into the houses lads."

The town consisted of a few dozen cottages hugging the road on the north side of the bridge. They could shelter from the rain here and rest, as there was no immediate threat.

They piled into the houses and took up positions to control the approaches to the bridge, glad to be under cover. Again they rued their decision to leave their greatcoats in Brussels for they were completely drenched, and they had little prospect of drying their clothes out.

A frightening flash of fork lightning lit up the whole sky, closely followed by a clap of thunder far louder than anything anyone could remember.

"Bloody hell, that was a big 'un", Johnny Castles exclaimed.

Daniel Kelly nodded agreement, "that was bigger than the one a couple of nights after Vitoria, remember?"

"That one struck Lieutenant Masterman of the 34th on his horse didn't it?" chipped in Jem Connor.

"Aye" agreed Kelly, "they were burnt to a cinder both of them, poor buggers!"

Suddenly Johnny Kincaid could be heard again, "Out, out, form up!"

The men obeyed immediately, something was up, and they reformed the column in seconds, despite the sustained downpour. The British cavalry were retiring in haste; French cavalry were very close behind them. The march had to be continued; they trudged along the road, which now resembled a swamp, mud and deep pools of water everywhere. They slipped and slid along, the mud grasping at their footwear tearing them from their feet, boots disappearing into the quagmire never to be seen again.

G troop galloped hard toward the bridge over the river, with the town of Genappe in view just beyond. Alexander became aware that the dragoons were also converging on this passage across the river and he feared the French might catch the troop in the inevitable congestion. He peered through the gloom and heavy rain vainly trying to identify another passage over the river. There appeared to be no alternative and he continually urged the troop to dash for the bridge. The rain was so heavy that visibility was reduced to a few feet at times and the port fires keeping the slow matches burning were extinguished. They rushed on for the protection of the town helter skelter.

Lord Uxbridge galloped past, shouting a warning.

"Make haste, make haste for God's sake, or you will be taken!"

The troop needed no warning; they were driving at breakneck speed, the horses straining on their bits, seemingly unconscious of the driving rain in their faces. The drivers bent forward against the deluge, applying their leather straps to the horse's flanks, whipping them frantically, and demanding an even greater effort. With their spare hands they desperately held on to their cumbersome helmets, it might be a pain to wear, but it did afford some protection from the downpour. The gunners sat on the limbers holding on tightly to the bars of the carriages as they bucked wildly over the roads.

After what seemed an eternity, the hooves of the lead horses clattered onto the cobble stone bridge and in seconds without any easing of the pace, the troop dashed over the river and into the main street of the town. The town was drab and barren, deserted of all outward signs of human habitation, the locals having either fled or locked themselves in their cellars, praying that the soldiers of both armies would leave them in peace, a vain hope. The dragoons had entered the river to left and right of the bridge and waded across; by a miracle they had evaded capture. There was a palpable feeling of relief and Alexander shouted to Henry Leathes as they cleared the bridge.

"That was too close Henry, I thought we were lost." Alexander beamed.

Henry smiled back, but suddenly his face changed to one of horror as he pointed ahead.

"The road.... It's blocked by troops!"

Alexander looked up to see that a regiment of British Hussars slowly filing through the town completely blocked the narrow street.

Alexander bellowed out the order to halt. The drivers strained to rein back their horse teams and they managed to stop just before they crashed into the rear of the hussars. What were they to do now? The houses to each side restricted the horse team's movement, they would have to wait for the hussars to clear the village, but would they have enough time before the French caught up?

Alexander could see the other dragoon regiments passing through the gardens of the houses to both sides, the French would soon be doing the same and they would be trapped!

Lord Uxbridge suddenly appeared again.

"Here, follow me with two of your guns."

Alexander called to Henry Leathes to follow with his division of two guns that was leading the troop. Lord Uxbridge led them into a straight and very narrow lane leading off to the left, bordered on each side by high earthen banks. Presumably they were to clear the village and deploy to prevent the French advancing on that flank.

However there was no opportunity for Alexander to discover Uxbridge's real intentions. The lane stretched for some two hundred yards but having traversed half its length, Alexander suddenly became aware of a troop of French Chasseurs sitting astride their horses simply waiting for them at the end of the track!

"Oh my God, what do we do now?" Alexander cried out.

Not only were Alexander and his two guns in grave danger, but he also could not believe that Lord Uxbridge, the Commander in Chief of the allied cavalry, had exposed himself to such danger, with no escort for protection.

"By God, we are all prisoners!" shouted Uxbridge, dashing his horse at the steep bank to the right, which his great charger mounted with aplomb and he promptly disappeared!

Alexander now felt very exposed and vulnerable; the distance to the French was now little more than fifty yards. He could not believe it, but the Frenchmen merely stood there and waited for them.

There was nothing for it but to order the teams to reverse direction.

"Reverse by Unlimbering" he ordered.

No sooner had he shouted the order, than the drivers hauled back on the reins and brought the teams to a halt.

The cannon were unlimbered and pushed to the side of the lane. The horse teams were led round to face the opposite direction and walked back past the guns. The cannon were then rolled back out and reattached to the limbers.

Alexander admired the calm and organised way his men rapidly carried out the manoeuvre in such circumstances. His amazement was reserved however for the Frenchmen, who remained impassive and unmoving, simply watching the troop alter formation.

The guns moved off back down the lane with no

interference from the French, they trotted slowly in a slight show of defiance, now that the threat was much reduced.

A low rumble to their left caused Alexander to fear that he was now surrounded, but all of a sudden, British hussars lined the bank of the lane accompanied by Lord Uxbridge. He had obviously brought them up to save the guns; perhaps their approach was the reason the French had not overwhelmed them.

Once back on the main street they discovered that the hussars and the troop had already passed out of the town. Clearing the last of the houses, Alexander found Robert and the rest of the troop and having reformed they moved on rapidly together.

Beyond the town the cavalry were ranged in two long lines right across the road as they had now caught up with the army's rearguard and they needed to gain more time so that they could get clear again.

G troop was ordered by an Aide of Lord Uxbridge to return towards the French and support the advanced picket of hussars. As soon as the troop moved forward and came into the view of the French, their cannon made them a particular target. Their cannonballs bounded past regularly, but remarkably failed to hit them at all, even though they were little more than two hundred yards away.

Alexander halted the troop and waited for the inevitable attack.

TURN & FIGHT

The Rifles could now see cavalry units on either flank, they must have crossed at fords on the river but they were British thank God! Behind the town of Genappe, they were ordered to halt and form line facing the enemy. French cavalry were now to be seen moving along the narrow road through the town.

The order rang out "Form Square!"

The men ran to their positions, the square had to be formed perfectly before the cavalry could charge them or they would be slaughtered. They were getting very close and not a single bloody rifle would be able to fire for the rain! The leading French horsemen were lancers. They could outreach the rifle and bayonet and pick them off with their outstretched lances, as they stood in square unable to fight back. Their hearts sank, they couldn't win this fight, and this surely was the end!

As the French lancers began to clear the houses and reform for their advance, a British hussar regiment gallantly charged them. They met bravely, the lancers impaled some of the hussars but others dodged the lance thrust and struck them aside enabling them to close with their opponents. The hussars now had the advantage close in where they could use their curved swords to slash away, causing horrendous flesh injuries. The French cavalry were too numerous however and despite hard fighting the hussars were eventually beaten back.

A great cheer arose from the French cavalry as they brushed this opposition aside, the hussars had fought bravely but were light cavalry, small men on small horses, they were no match for the French cavalrymen who completely outnumbered them.

Lord Uxbridge smiled; the hussars had done their job of delaying the lancers well. Whilst their attack had foundered, he had formed up his elite heavy cavalry, the Lifeguards. These huge men on towering horses watched impassively as the hussars were eventually brushed aside. They hungered to redress the balance; their horses snorted with flared nostrils whilst champing on their bits, they awaited the charge impatiently. The men strained their ears eagerly awaiting the order to advance.

The command finally arrived, they trotted forward but it was hard work for the horses to pick their feet out of the sodden ground. With seventy yards to go they broke into a canter, the horses straining to break into a gallop had to be held firmly in check to maintain formation and to conserve their energy.

The French lancers had been too busy celebrating their recent success to take notice of this new threat. Suddenly they realised the danger, some called out warnings, others tried to reform the wall of lances, a few tried to turn their horses in an effort to flee, but the crush behind was so immense that they were being pushed bodily to advance.

Surprise had destroyed the French morale, before a weapon had crossed, they were already half defeated. The Lifeguards crashed home, horse colliding with horse, some lances impaling a Life guardsman but many more were irresolutely held allowing a deft sword stroke to brush them aside.

Their heavy swords crashed down on heads, shoulders and arms rarely severing completely, but carving great gouges in the flesh, their helmets providing little protection. The screams and cries were awful to hear, those that fell to ground being trampled horribly under horses hooves. The Lifeguards scythed through the front ranks and slashed left and right as they drove deeper and deeper into the column of French horsemen still crowded in the town's main street. The lancers had seen enough being constricted by the surrounding houses and unable to deploy, panic set in. This caused the rear units to turn and fly back across the bridge eventually allowing the crush in the town to ease and the surviving lancers to flee.

The Rifles watched the struggle, anxious for success and cheered the Lifeguards until they were hoarse.

Tom Crawley watched in admiration, but had spotted numbers of Life guardsmen returning from the struggle on foot leading their horses, but neither man nor beast showed any sign of injury.

He called out to one passing. "Where's you going? yer ain't cut!"

The Lifeguard looked straight at Tom and answered indignantly, "Oi'm forced to retoir as I 'as fallen. Sergeant says we must retoir if'n our huniform is dirty!"

Tom and the lads roared with laughter "These 'eroes tink theys at Orseguards not foighting Boney!"

Palmer joined in "You knows wot they sez. The uglier and dirtier, the better the soljer!"

"Wull you must be a bloody foin soldier, cos youze damn ugly!" the Lifeguard retorted.

Everyone looked at Palmer and waited for his violent

temper to explode but he just stared for a moment, and then roared with laughter.

"Good answer lad, 'ere share moi rum!"

The Lifeguard smiled, drank a good half of Palmer's canteen of rum off in one go and bid him farewell.

The French followed cautiously after that, the Rifles and cavalry retired slowly but steadily, the squadrons of cavalry each standing ready to fight as the adjoining squadron retired, then retreating themselves as the others took their turn to cover them. This led to a checkerboard effect across the fields, which the Rifles could view and admire as they marched, a textbook retreat.

The rains had now eased a great deal and the slow matches were re lit. Alexander ordered G troop to deploy and return fire on the French batteries. As they unlimbered the cannon and loaded with spherical case, Macdonald mysteriously appeared again at his shoulder. He showed a professional interest in the length of fuse applied for the shrapnel to burst directly above the French artillery.

"Mercer, which fuse have you ordered, A or B?"

"A Sir" Alexander replied in a tone that barely concealed his irritation.

"Are you sure that's not too short?"

"No Sir, I believe it will be just right"

"Personally I would have chosen B, but it's your battery."

Alexander said nothing; his nit picking was driving him to distraction. However the first discharge from the right hand gun proved his point, the shell exploded perfectly just above the enemy guns and a number of their gunners fell, others ran, it was a perfect shot.

Alexander turned in triumph to confront Macdonald, but he had vanished once again.

The troop fired slowly taking deliberate aim, Alexander

was acutely aware of the shortage of ammunition as the wagons were ordered well to the rear for safety. He sent Staff Sergeant Henry Parson to recall Quartermaster Hall's wagons, as he could not fire much longer without replacement ammunition.

He was intrigued to watch the hussars skirmish with their French opponents. The horsemen trotted forward, took aim with their inaccurate short muskets known as carbines and fired before trotting back out of the firing line to reload. This little circular equine dance was being played out all along the line, with no perceivable benefit to either side. Alexander found the scene both amusing and a great waste of time for all, a mere futile charade.

This fascinating entertainment was interrupted by Major Macdonald's reappearance with a rocket troop; it was Captain Edward Whinyates' men. They had been ordered to join the retreat, but Alexander had noted all day that they were hanging just behind the rearguard in the hope that they could join in. Obviously Edward had persuaded Macdonald to let him have a go at the French.

Whinyates was lucky to be there as he had nearly drowned when his transport almost sank on route to Spain in 1810. He was an experienced peninsula man who had been mentioned in Lord Wellington's despatches, a major honour although Wellington was no lover of rockets.

The Rocket troop dismounted and unpacked some of their missiles. They marched forward as far as the picket line, and then set a small iron framed tripod on the ground. A rocket with a long wooden tail attached was placed on the tripod and pointed at a French cannon which was deployed on the road firing at the British cavalry. The slow match was applied and the rocket fuse fizzled into life, it sparked and juddered then with an almighty whoosh! It flew as straight as an arrow directly up the road, striking the cannon. The explosion destroyed the gun's carriage and its crew ran for cover like frightened whippets closely followed by the neighbouring gun teams who didn't fancy being next.

A great Hurrah! Arose.

Whinyates' men encouraged by this splendid success eagerly fired a number of further rockets, but they could not match this early success. Later rockets flew in all directions all but the one intended; eventually the French gunners gained renewed confidence and returned to their guns. The final rocket initially flew perpendicularly, then descended and turned towards the guns, the British guns! Alexander watched its flight with amazement, which quickly turned to horror as its trajectory altered directly toward him! He deliberated his courses of action for a split second then ran like hell! The adrenaline pumped profusely, he ran quicker than he ever thought he could. He was aware of the hissing rocket approaching at great speed, knowing that he couldn't outrun it. There, just ahead of him was a shallow culvert in the field, Alexander dived head first into the narrow ditch, which was filled with water from the rains, the rocket passing overhead harmlessly. Picking himself up from the muddy trough, sodden and cold, Alexander had lost all interest in the rockets!

The cavalry started to retire slowly as the infantry had marched clear again. The racing was over; an orderly retreat was now the way of things. Slowly and methodically, the line of cavalry retired by alternate squadrons. It was carried out as if on the parade ground with the King himself watching at Horse Guards. The French cavalry seemed to have lost their drive and meekly followed these movements without any threat to disrupt these beautiful evolutions.

Slowly they retired, G troop standing by to deploy, but

never needed. The gun teams trotted along the chaussee and eventually caught up with a battalion of Brunswick infantry, dressed all in black. At the sound of the horses in their rear, without even bothering to look to identify whether they were friend or foe, they simply broke and fled! This was not an auspicious sign from their German allies!

Evening crept up on the Rifles as they continued to march, the rain falling incessantly again, darkness came early with the black foreboding clouds threatening to engulf everything. The battalion trudged past the large farmhouse that they had passed only yesterday in such heart, called La Haye Sainte. They became aware of large numbers of regiments encamped in the fields around.

A messenger rode down the road calling out for the First Battalion Ninety Fifth. Colonel Barnard hailed him as he approached. The lads nearby eavesdropped on the discussion.

The messenger was one of Sir Thomas Picton's young lords. He called out "Sir Andrew, Sir Thomas requests that your battalion halt in the fields to the right just beyond the cross roads ahead for the night. Be aware Sir that the army is encamped to your right and left and that it is Lord Wellington's intention to offer Napoleon battle here tomorrow if he has the support of the Prussians. The General compliments you on your success in delaying the enemy today and advises that your unit is placed behind the front line tonight to allow all your men to rest. There will be no need for pickets."

"Thank Sir Thomas for his kindness; we will be ready for the fight tomorrow." Sir Andrew replied.

Eventually, G troop trotted past the large enclosed

farmhouse of La Haye Sainte on their left. As they passed on, the French advanced nearer and Alexander sought a spot on which to deploy. To his right was a sand pit, the troop turned into it and positioned their cannon on the roadway to warn the French that they were encroaching.

The French were some eight hundred yards away and Alexander ordered the guns to aim carefully not to waste their shot. The first gun fired and to everyone's amazement dozens of cannon roared into action just to their rear from atop a low ridge running to right and left. They had clearly caught up with the main army and they were serving notice of their intention to dispute this ground.

The French retorted in similar vein and a regular cannonade developed for a considerable length of time.

"Look Sir" cried gunner John Death, "It's the monster himself!"

Alexander peered through the gloom of sunset, on a low ridge he could discern the squat body and low bicorn of the Emperor himself for the second time. A large group of senior officers swarmed around him in deep conversation. They were obviously counting the flashes of the guns to judge whether Wellington had stopped retreating.

Lieutenant John Hincks took great care in laying one of his guns, taking very deliberate aim, finally loosing a cannonball that passed through the group, clearly causing great confusion and consternation.

"That will give them something to think about" Gunner Philip Hunt shouted.

The French took the hint that the army was not to be moved on that night and the cannonade slowly fizzled out on both sides, the French had clearly stopped driving them hard in their retreat.

A stubby little man, unshaven, wearing drab ill kempt clothing and a battered hat approached Alexander. In a deep, gruff voice with the hint of a Welsh accent, the stranger attempted to engage Alexander him in conversation.

"Damn Frenchies look as though they have had enough to day."

Alexander forced out an ill-tempered "Yes".

The stranger persisted "You form part of the rearguard?"

Alexander could not disguise his ill temper, he was tired and ravenous, and he had no time for Lords who fancied themselves as amateur Generals.

"I am very busy Sir, You must excuse me."

The stranger retired, with no sign of irritation at Alexander's off hand replies.

John Hall approached surreptitiously, talking quietly to avoid being overheard.

"You do know who that was, Sir?"

"I have no idea and I do not much care" Alexander replied caustically.

"If I am not much mistaken, that was General Picton, Sir".

Alexander's jaw dropped, the famous Picton, the foul-mouthed Welshman was the fear of every soldier. He was known as a hard-bitten General and one of Lord Wellington's most able lieutenants. A man of supreme grit and determination, Alexander had just treated him like a mere subaltern!

The Riflemen marched through a cutting and across the crossroads where they were relieved to hear the orders "Halt" and "Fall Out". The men found a patch of unoccupied ground and slumped to the ground. They lay with no protection from the heavy rain and cold evening temperatures, water flowing beneath them in tiny rivulets and bodily sinking into the soft muddy ground, but exhaustion allowed them to snatch some sleep.

George Simmons watched his men lie down without cover and thought how best to use his greatcoat to most advantage. George laid his coat on the ground and encased it in clumps of turf. Once the coat was completely covered in a thick protective layer of mud and grass, he slid beneath it and lay snug within for the night, his hat protecting his head from the beating rain.

Johnny Kincaid tethered Beth and sat beneath her for shelter, wrapped in his cloak for the night as protection. Eventually most fell into a fitful sleep occasionally disturbed by the water trickling over and under them and the gnawing cold.

An Aide de Camp approached G troop, carrying orders for them to retire a further mile, to form in a field and orchard near the farm at Mont St Jean.

The troop marched back until near the farm which formed a square of solid brick barns with high slate roofs. They turned into the field on the left of the road, where the wagons sank into the soggy turf; feet sank up to the ankles in the bog. The horses were tethered and corn supplied from the few sacks they had brought with them. Soon they were satisfied; the men however sat in sullen silence, the rain running down their bodies and the pain of acute hunger gnawing unmercilessly at the pit of their stomachs.

The men transferred the remaining ammunition from two of the wagons to the limbers and Bombardier Thomas Masterton was ordered to proceed to refill the wagons at the depot set up just beyond the village of Waterloo. He set off with his teams without complaint, despite the prospect of marching through the night to replenish the ammunition. He had no prospect of any sleep that night, but those he left behind had little more, work at least had the advantage of keeping his mind occupied and would help him forget his miseries.

They all sat huddled under the wagons, stretching the canvas covers out in a vain attempt to obtain protection from the renewed heavy rainfall. They were soaked through and they dare not move as that brought a colder portion of their wet clothing against their skin, which further increased their discomfiture. The officers set up a tent, but the water seeping through it and the wet soil beneath ensured a very uncomfortable night. They huddled close together in an effort to maintain some warmth but it was futile, little sleep was to be had.

In the lee of the wagons, poor excuses for fires were kindled which hissed and spat as the raindrops attempted to extinguish them. The warm thoughts inspired by these minuscule flames were infinitely more rewarding than the actual heat generated by the green wood, which smoked away. Robert Newland produced cigars and an umbrella to ward off the rain, Alexander eagerly accepted a share of both when proffered as enmities were put aside at such times of joint suffering. There they sat as miserable as sin enduring all in silence, as nobody wanted to be mocked by the old peninsula hands. They were always ready to chastise the new lads with their "Lord have mercy on your tender carcass!" or "Ho, my boy this is but child's play to what we saw in Spain!"

Robert Newland eventually broke the silence.

"I haven't seen rains like this since Burgos, now that was bad. Every day the rain filled the trenches, men had to stand up to their shoulders in water for up to four hours at a time."

Pausing for a few moments to recollect something, he continued. "Three eighteen pounders were all we had to take that bloody fortress of hell! Thunder, Lightning and

Nelson they were called, we were so short of ammunition that the men were paid nine pence for every cannonball recovered from those fired at us by Johnny Frenchman. On the retreat they were too heavy and were constantly sinking in the mud. One night we knocked them off their carriages and buried the barrels, I wonder if they're still there?"

Henry Leathes joined in, "That retreat back to Portugal was the worst we ever had. His lordship was very hard on the army, said we fell apart despite being well supplied. Well no one I knew got more than a handful of rice in five days!"

There was a great rustling in the bushes close at hand, then a Hanoverian infantryman crawled out of the undergrowth and sidled up to the fire. He was looking for his regiment but could not find them in the dark; he stayed by the fire for a while to recuperate, adding his smoke from his clay pipe. Eventually, moving on, he generously offered Alexander the scrawniest chicken he had ever seen, but at that moment it was the greatest thing he could have possessed. He thanked the German profusely, this was wonderful. Everyone cheered up; all the other officers suddenly appeared from their tent, they hadn't been sleeping that soundly! Water was boiled in the large kettle and the chicken tossed in, but ere it was half cooked, they could wait no longer. It was extracted from the boiling water and roughly portioned between the officers. They tucked in gratefully, but there was little more than a mouthful of half raw meat each. If anything it reawakened their hunger pangs and made things worse.

The only recourse was to sit silently under the umbrella smoking their cigars, it was their only comfort but they suffered patiently. Slowly, despite the cold rain and gnawing hunger, they succumbed to exhaustion and slept on the sodden ground.

Ned Costello dragged himself onwards and passed the ridge and cross roads where the army was encamping as it fell dark, he was directed to continue to the village of Waterloo for medical aid. He forced himself on, cold, wet and weak from his wound, he continued his weary way. He was brought abruptly out of his stupor by the sound of raucous laughter. Looking around he surmised that it had to emanate from a farm cart pulled by a worn old mare and followed by a group of women coming along the road behind him. Ned stepped over to the wagon and standing on tiptoes, peered over the edge of the open cart to see who was within. The cart was layered with straw for bedding and a dozen or more wounded soldiers lay atop.

"Wull bugger me! If it ain't old Ned Costello, jump aboard me old mate".

It was Josh Hetherington! With a helping hand up Ned managed to pull himself onto the cart and collapsed on the straw next to Josh.

"Wot the bleeding 'ell you been up to Josh?"

"Got shot in leg didn't oi, Sawbones put us on cart fur Brussels."

"Aye but what's all the laughter about?"

Josh's white teeth dazzled in the light of the cart lamp. "Wull these dear ladies we passes enquires for their men folk loik, wull not as to disappoint 'em, I pretends to be 'um see, cos they can't see me in't dark. Wull they gives me food n'drink and I don't loiks being rude so oi takes it an' shares it wiv lads. Wun we finished oi tells um they're mistaken; oi never said oi was their man, oi just sound loik 'em!"

"Bastard" Ned retorted but he didn't stop him when he did it again, the food was too welcome.

Soon the cart trundled into the village of Waterloo, which Ned could recognise, from the odd looking church.

They stopped for the night here and lay on the ground underneath the cart for protection from the rain. Ned noted the large numbers of people camping in the woods just beyond. They were the stragglers that travelled in the trail of every army, men who always found excuses not to be at the front when any fighting occurred. These and the camp followers were the scourge of any army, taking liberties with the locals and stealing everything whilst the army was busy. He was also aware of numerous messengers hurrying to and from the tavern; someone had told him that Lord Wellington was using this as his headquarters.

Within those very quarters at Waterloo Harry Smith grasped Juana close to him as if he would completely smother her, they kissed tenderly. As he kissed her neck slowly and softly, Juana let her head arch back. Despite the fears for the future, she would abandon herself to her love one more time. Slowly and methodically Harry unbuttoned the front of her dress exposing a glimpse of her bodice. Harry's lips now darted lightly across her heaving chest, occasionally brushing the tops of her constricted breasts, which thrilled her more. Their eyes met, the burning passion and desire for each other was overwhelming and they set upon each other with unbridled lust. Their bodies melted into one, their passion rising to a crescendo, they then lay curled in each others arms, both afraid ever to let go and end this special moment.

Their last night in rooms at Waterloo had been poignant, a time of tears, hugs and muted discussions of their future as they pretended to each other that nothing would change tomorrow.

PREPARATION

Ned Costello, Josh Hetherington and the other wounded awoke early that Sunday morning from the cold damp air, which seeped into their very bones as they lay underneath the cart. Before daylight there had been signs of movement in the village and it was not long before Lord Wellington and his staff were mounting their horses and riding off to organise the army. The only topic of discussion at every campfire was what did Wellington plan to do? Were they to continue retreating or stand and fight? Having won at Quatre Bras they had retreated because the Prussians had been forced to retire, what were the Prussians doing now?

Ned and the few others that could walk unaided clambered out painfully from underneath the wagon, which had served as their protection from the harsh elements, to collect kindling from the edges of the wood that skirted the village. With a bit of perseverance they managed to get a decent fire burning despite the damp wood. A few others had managed to obtain some food by begging from the few village folk that hadn't fled in terror; this was added to any remnants left in their haversacks. A tolerable breakfast was put together and a steaming mug of sweet tea, that 'National cure all' raised their spirits.

As the sun peeped over the horizon, shedding a meagre light from behind the dark clouds that covered the morning sky, the regiments of infantry and cavalry that had bivouacked near the village overnight rose and prepared for a move in whichever direction ordered.

Nobody seemed aware of what was going on, no one knew of any orders. Ned sat warming himself, vainly trying to dry out his sodden uniform from last night's heavy rain. Wet clothing had a terrible depressing effect on the spirits, if you sat still the areas of clothing in contact with your body warmed a little and became bearable, but any slight movement brought your skin in contact with freezing cold parts and it felt doubly uncomfortable.

At least the rains were gone, the cold misty morning didn't help however, what they wouldn't give for that summer sun to break through and warm the air.

Caught up in these feelings of depression and melancholy, Ned simply stared into the fire; even Josh wasn't his ebullient self. Eventually Ned started to warm a little with the help of the flickering flames and started to take notice of the scene around them again. All that could be seen were ammunition and sutler wagons and the other entrails of an army, parked haphazardly. The infantry and cavalry had all gone!

"Hey Josh, do you remember that Old Portuguese crone, with our pot of food?" Ned enquired.

Josh smiled, "Course I remember, you spotted her trying to nick our ham joint out of the pot whilst we were out of the room."

Ned laughed, "No, you throwing your voice into the pot scared her to death. She was sure it was a magic pot and we must be in league with the Devil himself!"

"I'll wager she never tried to steal from a British soldier again!" Josh laughed.

That brought their spirits up.

During the early hours of that fateful morning, the incessant heavy rain had eventually eased to a drizzle and stopped completely by dawn. There was little comfort for the Riflemen as they awoke with the early light of the new day. Tired, bitterly cold, with saturated clothing they rose from the damp ground and shook sleep off. Being protected by troops in their front, they were not called to arms at dawn but awoke automatically with the bugle calls and drums of those further forward and so had a little time to consider their situation. Reflection led to feelings of utter despair, hunger and cold sapped even the jolliest spirits. A few old hands forced themselves to their feet and strode off to gather twigs and branches, as a fire would help to rekindle their spirits.

Within half an hour a plentiful supply of wood had been collected and small fires dotted all along the front of the army helped to colour the dull grey morning. It was dry, but the sky was overcast, the cloud obliterating the warmth of the early morning sun and a thin mist lay upon the fields. Soon a hearty fire topped with a pot of water, sprinkled with tea leaves and a splash of milk and sugar started to lift their dismal feelings. Hands and feet were pressed close to the fire sending a warm glow through their bodies, the heat caused the men's uniforms to steam as they dried and the warming and nourishing effects of the hot sweet tea restored their flagging spirits.

The main fire was lit up against the wall of a small stone hut that Sir Andrew Barnard had used to sleep within to avoid the rains overnight.

"That was some bloody storm," commented Robert to break the silence.

"Aye Sergeant Fairfoot that it was, Wellington weather" added Tom Crawley.

"Good omen that," commented Johnny Castles, "Wellington always 'as a bloody big stormy night before a great victory. 'Appened at Salamanca an' Vitoria, bloody awful storms they wus an' all."

"Old Nosey'll see us frew, like ee always does" Palmer interjected.

"Bloody look out, 'tis Nosey 'imself" snapped Robert Fairfoot.

A dozen horsemen rode up to the fire, leading was the great chief himself Arthur Wellesley, Lord Wellington, an Irishman to boot. Wellington brought his chestnut mare Copenhagen to a halt and his 'family' stopped beside him.

"Sergeant is there enough tea for us?" he asked.

"Sure, your lordship, you're welcome to share our fare" Robert beamed.

Lord Wellington as always wore a simple garb, no bright red tunic scattered with gaudy bejewelled decorations for him. He sported a simple cocked hat worn fore and aft with an oilskin cover to protect it from the damp. He was dressed in a long blue frock coat, buttoned up high, pristine white buckskin pantaloons tight to his thighs, rounded off with black Hessian boots. A plain silver scabbard held his sword hanging at his side, not that he should ever have to defend himself, but Wellington was always at the point of most danger and often experienced close calls. A small portfolio for pen and paper had been designed to replace his pistol holster on his saddle. Wellington sat bolt upright on Copenhagen, a small telescope permanently held ready for use in his right hand. Despite his lack of finery, everything about him spoke of total command, a professional soldier.

Wellington had obviously already been out riding for some hours, his coat and pantaloons heavily speckled in splashes of mud.

He thanked Robert sincerely for his kindness and swiftly downing the hot sweet tea, he rode on to continue preparations for battle and his entourage galloped in pursuit.

George Simmons awoke feeling stiff and constrained by his self-made grave; he pulled himself out from his earthen tomb and was pleased to find that it had protected him well and that he was relatively dry.

He spied Johnny Kincaid sitting upright still wrapped in his cloak, his head resting on his chest fast asleep. He bent down and shook Johnny gently by the shoulder.

"Johnny, are you well?"

"Well? I'm bloody soaked through, aching in every bone and frozen to the core, what could be worse?"

George hesitated before delivering the coup de grace, "Where's your horse Johnny?"

"Blood and sands George, where's she gone? She was tethered to my pack and I was sleeping beneath her."

"She must have broken loose during last night," George explained.

"I'll have to find her" Johnny stated and rising slowly feeling like an old man with pronounced arthritis, Lieutenant Kincaid straightened himself and hobbled painfully away to find his steed.

As Johnny grumpily searched for Beth, he was able to see the general layout of the army. Initially he strode to the crossroads close in front of the Rifles. Just to the right he could see Lord Wellington and his generals discussing the dispositions of the troops and the plan of battle. Here the ground rose slightly, allowing one to see virtually the whole of the Allied front line.

The main road from Brussels ran forward into the distance towards the French campfires that he could clearly see on the horizon. The road passed through a cutting some ten feet deep at the point where Johnny stood.

The road crossing this cobbled highway was little more than a mud track and passed to left and right in a straight line across the battlefield, producing a natural line for the front of the army to form upon. Again near the crossroads this track formed a cutting well below the height of the raised ground he stood upon. Further away in both directions, the track ran along the crest of a low ridge, which would form Wellington's front line. Wellington would station his troops as he always did, just behind the ridge to hide his dispositions and to protect the units from the heavy artillery fire, which Napoleon was sure to use. They would only move forward to defend the rise when the French attack had neared.

Just in front of the crossroads stood the farm of La Haye Sainte, which Johnny had passed on route to and from Quatre Bras the previous days.

The La Haye Sainte complex consisted of a large house and two large barns that effectively formed a U shape, high walls linked the buildings to form a square fortified farmstead. In the wall bordering the road was a large pair of wooden gates surmounted by a small tiled dovecote. This enclosed farm formed a strong defensive position and Johnny was aware of darkly dressed allied troops preparing their defences within.

He studied the landscape in front of the allied line, which the French would have to traverse in their advance. From the Allied crest, the ground gently fell away into a shallow valley before rising slowly towards a similar but lower ridge where the initial French line would have to form. To the left of the Brussels road, a smaller rise was noticeable half way across the shallow valley, Johnny's trained eye spotted this hillock some eight hundred yards from where he stood and realised that it would form a good platform for the French artillery which would threaten this part of the line.

Having reconnoitred the battlefield, his thoughts returned to Beth and he stepped off to the left to continue the search for her. As he walked along the track cresting the ridge he looked around the camp of a Belgian regiment stationed on the front of the rise in full view of the French. He then stepped across the track and down the reverse slope of the ridge where he met Sir James Kempt and near at hand the Fifth Division, which the Rifles were attached to. In the fields behind, Johnny could see cavalry regiments awaiting orders.

"Good day Sir James, methinks Lord Wellington is happy the French delay attacking." Johnny observed.

Sir James smiled, "Good morning Johnny, My Lord Wellington will indeed be glad for every hour that Bonaparte wastes. His Lordship has been promised that the Prussians will join us from Wavre by early afternoon if he stands here." Looking to the left, he peered into the distance. "Let's pray that Blucher and his Prussians do come as promised."

Johnny probed further "Can we hold?"

Sir James looked thoughtful, "The Duke commands an army of some seventy thousand, and Napoleon we believe markedly more. My Lord is wary, as he commands a mixture of Dutch, Belgians and Germans, many with mixed emotions, as they fought for Napoleon only eighteen months ago! Even his British troops who are painfully few are generally inexperienced youngsters; this is not his Peninsula army by any means. Lord Wellington has cleverly brigaded a mix of nations together to strengthen the weaker ones. This is an infamous army and my Lord will have to work miracles to stop Napoleon." He finished ominously.

A plump officer dressed in dark blue with a great cocked hat and white plume rode off to the left with a small lancer escort. Sir James and Johnny watched them go.

"That's Von Muffling, the Prussian liaison officer to Lord Wellington, he'll be looking for signs of his countrymen, otherwise the Duke will have him hung!" he jested. "There's a rumour doing the rounds that Lord Wellington when in Brussels was surprised with news of Napoleon's attack because that great tub of lard took forever to deliver the report from Blucher, taking twelve hours to ride twelve miles. Scurrilous rubbish! Poor Muffling is livid, as a General officer he doesn't run messages, he doesn't know why the despatches took so long, but it wasn't his fault. Now if he can save the day with his countrymen, he'll squash that stupid rumour."

Sir James bid Johnny farewell and wished him luck finding his horse, he was going to be busy now deploying his brigade as ordered by Sir Thomas Picton including the Rifles moving forward, to occupy the sand pit opposite La Haye Sainte.

Johnny returned to the cross roads and passed to the right of the position, he found that artillery units were setting up along the track, infantry units filled the gaps between the batteries but were set slightly aback behind the crest of the ridge as he had predicted. To Johnny, the fresh-faced youths he encountered looked pale and frightened, his confidence rapidly drained away, how could they ever cope with Napoleon's veterans? The Dutch Belgian units were intermixed with British units all along the line to give mutual courage and support. As he progressed to the right he could see woods, orchards and a large chateau, it was clearly held by British troops, their distinctive red uniforms could be seen scurrying about as they prepared to defend its walls.

The cold had permeated through to Alexander's bones, the rain had continued relentlessly; it had been a truly miserable night. Alexander had suffered like all the others, drifting into a light sleep but reawakening with annoying regularity from the discomfort. The night hours seemed to pass exceptionally slowly but as the first hint of dawn's approach lightened the night sky almost imperceptibly, he cheered himself as he subconsciously registered that the rain was no longer falling. This small improvement in conditions made him relax a little and he fell into a deeper, more restful sleep.

It did not last long however, the neighing of horses and trundle of cartwheels announced the return of the two wagons sent to replenish ammunition. Alexander raised himself wearily from the sodden ground half dazed.

"I trust that you were successful, Bombardier?" he called out.

"Indeed Sir" came the cheerful reply, a lot more amiably than Alexander had expected from men who had spent the night on the road.

"There was much confusion on the road with carts blocking it every so often Sir, but it gave us the opportunity to obtain some supplies from the commissariat wagons on the way" the Bombardier continued.

Alexander looked up to see the white teeth of the men emblazoned in broad grins, reflected by the early dawn light, they were holding up food! Within moments the entire troop was around them, the prospect of sustenance was too much to bear.

They had managed to acquire by various nefarious means, beef, biscuit and oatmeal, which was quickly divided between all. Better still, they had discovered a hogshead of rum and had filled all their canteens to the brim! Not one of the men had partaken of it on the journey back; they were all perfectly sober and happy to simply take their fair portion of spirits with everyone else. Alexander was proud of these men; the army was infamous for its drunkards, many would have consumed all of the rum themselves and turned up blind drunk, if they had returned at all!

The men beavered away to collect brushwood and with a little difficulty managed to build up the fires despite the damp. Once the wood had lit properly and produced heat rather than pure smoke, the iron pots were hung above. Water mixed with the biscuit and oatmeal was mixed into a sludge called 'stir about', many were so ravenous that they drew off a mug of mix as their share before the pots were fully warmed through. The more patient added the scrappy pieces of beef to boil in the mixture, forming a decent soup.

Whilst engaged in producing this meagre ration, dawn stole up on them; in the dull half-light dark objects near at hand started to become visible. Soon the objects took on a clear shape, indeed some showed animation, moving around distant fires. Alexander could make out other artillery troops; he rose from his warm soggy patch of earth and strolled about to investigate. One troop which he hadn't noticed last night, was even sharing the same field. As Alexander approached their fires, he recognised the group of officers huddled around smoking cigars for comfort in the morning chill. It was Norman Ramsay's troop, there sat his friend Alexander Macdonald discussing their situation with the famous Norman.

"Alexander, are there any orders?" he enquired.

"Alex my dear fellow" came the welcoming reply, "Norman and I have no idea what is going on, probably continue yesterday's retreat back to Brussels I dare say".

Alexander was perplexed, so this was what campaigning was like then, hours of sheer tedium and starvation, mixed with periods of complete confusion and extreme excitement. No wonder everyone said their training in England could never prepare them for real campaigning.

He did not stop for long, but walked across the field to a low hedge, beyond which he could see numerous cavalry regiments, the horses tethered and grazing nonchalantly, whilst many of the men lay nearby still rolled in their grey blankets sound asleep. Another troop of horse artillery was parked amongst them; Alexander recognised them instantly and ran over to greet them.

It was D troop, Captain George Beane commanding, a peninsula veteran who had got to know Alexander well back in England after the last war. William Webber another old hand was there as well, they were extremely pleased to see him as he walked into their camp.

"Alexander, what a joy to see you, where is G troop?"

"We are just beyond the hedge with H troop alongside."

"We arrived last night, direct from England, what's brewing?" George Beane enquired.

Alexander shrugged, "No one seems to know the Duke's plans, we had a fine retreat yesterday, just like on a parade ground, with Boney himself watching!"

Alexander could feel their bitterness and jealousy at his words. For all their peninsula experience while Alexander had languished in England, he now had an experience they could not better. He had seen Napoleon himself! They hadn't faced the 'Ogre' in Spain, just his hench men.

"Perhaps we will see him today" William said hopefully, "we may even have him in our sights!"

Alexander looked doubtful, "All the talk is of retreat as the Prussians have been beaten heavily."

George Beane looked gravely serious for a moment, "His lordship will have picked some ground for us to stand upon soon, mark my words, as he will not sell Brussels so cheap!"

Alexander bid them adieu, with the hope that they would join him for dinner if his provisions caught up with him that day, they happily accepted and he strode back to the troop.

Still no Beth, Johnny Kincaid had been searching for the best part of an hour now, but there was no sign of urgency or fighting yet and he decided to continue his quest. He came down from the crest and walked to the rear of the front line. Here second line and reserve troops of all arms stretched for half a mile or more back on the road to the village of Waterloo. They all milled about within their units, preparing food and checking weapons, indeed all along the line could be heard the irregular popping of muskets being test fired after the punishing rains. Aides de Camp could be seen darting about relaying orders to units; other regiments could be seen marching through the mire to their positions squelching through the mud. Johnny arrived at a Horse Artillery battery well behind the front, the horses still unhitched from their carriages chewing the sodden grass, unconcerned with all that went on around. There, happily joining in the breakfast was Beth, Johnny was so relieved! He ran to her, caught her reins and caressed her head.

"I'd thought you'd gone for good Bess".

He'd given twenty guineas for her to a Guards officer in Brussels; he couldn't afford to lose her.

An unseen voice rang out, "Sir, do I take it that this is your horse? For it has upset my horses all morning with its excitable state."

Johnny turned angrily to face an officer of the Royal Horse Artillery in his dark blue hussar style jacket. The officer had obviously only feigned irritation and smiled broadly as he held out his right arm to shake hands in friendship.

"Captain Alexander Mercer, at your service, Sir."

Johnny took his hand and shook it, "Johnny Kincaid, First Ninety Fifth, thank you for your care of my horse, it bolted during last night's storm."

"A pleasure, she wandered in this morning, she is a fine looking animal."

Johnny looked about at the horses and equipment of the battery, "Your battery is a credit to you Sir, I warrant this must be the best artillery unit in the army."

Alexander was pleased at such an evaluation from an experienced officer. "Thank you, for your kind words, I hope that we have the opportunity to show that we can fight as well as we look and not remain in the reserve as at present."

Johnny looked Alexander straight in the eye, "Napoleon will ensure more than enough work for all of us I will wager. I hope we shall meet again after the battle." he held out his hand again, "Good luck Alexander, for I fear many will not see the sunset tonight."

Alexander looked surprised, "Are you certain we fight? For the rumours are of continued retreat."

Johnny Kincaid smiled wryly, I have walked the position our army takes up at present, and Lord Wellington will not retreat further unless forced to. Expect a clash of the Titans today!"

Alexander strode with Kincaid up the rise to the top of the field, from here he could see the Rifles taking up positions near the farmhouse just below them and he watched Johnny ride back down to his men.

Alexander soon lost interest in Johnny and he scanned the horizon in front. There were numerous dark masses and myriad fires to left and right about a mile or so away. It was the French army, quietly encamped on a low ridge the other side of the valley, who knew how many were there? Eighty or Ninety thousand? It was an imposing spectacle. There was little sign of early activity from the French and after observing them for a few minutes; Alexander turned to stroll back to the troop.

Nearing the bivouac again, he spied a number of Lifeguards digging in a plot adjacent to the farmhouse of Mont St Jean; he approached them to discover the cause, it was potatoes! The field was full of them.

Calling to the troop, Alexander thought little of his rank as he set to work with the men to haul the vegetables out from the sodden clay soil, for he was famished and they would make a very welcome addition to the 'stir about'. They stood in a sea of mud, their uniforms becoming ever more besmirched and grimy, but they cared little for their appearance. Hunger took over all other considerations. They busied themselves for a considerable time and succeeded in piling up a substantial number of young potatoes.

Gunner James Putten arched his aching back to straighten from the constant bending. As he surveyed the fields around him, he let out a cry of surprise. "Eh, everyone's gone except our troop, where the bloody 'ell have they all gone to?"

Johnny arrived at the crossroads to find the Rifles moving to their positions as ordered by Sir Thomas Picton. They had marched forward and passed the cross roads in the direction of La Haye Sainte, which now formed an outpost in front of the line on the ridge.

Sir Andrew Barnard had called the officers together and explained that they were to hold the left side of the crossroads area, forming the right wing of the Fifth division. They were also required to support the Second Light Battalion King's German Legion who were to defend the farm of La Haye Sainte, it was they whom Johnny had seen preparing the defences there earlier.

As they passed the crossroads, three companies were ordered to halt and form a reserve along the line of the track leading to the left. William Johnstone's company was to hold a small rise or knoll, some fifty yards to the front, this they did by lining a thick hedge at its base on the side facing the French. Jonathan Leach's and Edward Chawner's companies were ordered another fifty yards in front of this knoll, into an old pit formed by locals digging out the sand for building. The hole was oval in shape, measuring some fifty by one hundred feet and excavated to a depth of about twelve feet below the normal surface level. The men moved into position rapidly, they lined the rim of the pit, resting their rifles on the forward edge and waited for Johnny Frenchman. The pit was about sixty yards to the rear of the farmhouse of La Haye Sainte on the opposite side of the chausee.

Johnny arrived as they were taking up positions and sought his orders. Sir Andrew Barnard and Major Cameron would command from the cross roads, he was to stay with the two companies at the sand pit. As Adjutant Johnny remained in the saddle, giving him additional height to scan the horizon for a better view of threatened attacks.

"Well Gentlemen, there will be warm work today." Johnny proffered.

Edward Chawner smiled, "Let them come, they'll not take this spot from us easily."

"What about the road, it will give easy access for cavalry?" Johnny countered.

William Johnstone replied, "That's under way, we will construct two abattis of branches, one just in front near the farm, the other further back on the approach to the sunken part of the road at the cross roads. George Simmons is getting them organised right now."

George Simmons was indeed watching his detachment of men dragging logs, old farm implements and broken branches, anything to form an obstruction on the roadway to stop cavalry charging along it.

"Keep going lads, Crawley, Kelly, give Sergeant Fairfoot a hand with that old carriage there."

Soon they had completed an obstruction that would stop anything and they returned to the sand pit.

A few minutes later, a cavalry patrol of British dragoons approached the crossroads and moved forward at a canter along the chausee towards La Haye Sainte on a reconnaissance mission. George and his men stood in horror, open mouthed, as they approached the barricade and nonchalantly brushed it aside to ride on!

"So much for all that bloody work" Tom sighed.

"Well we will just have to build it again and stronger still" George added.

Half an hour later, the two abattis were completed again and no horse was going to charge through these ones!

Johnny noticed Joseph Burke the Surgeon, and his Assistant Surgeon Robert Heyt, setting up their equipment on the top of the knoll ready to deal with the wounded from the front line. Their trestles were set up under the canopy of leaves of a large beech tree and they were unpacking their vile instruments, their saws and the razor sharp amputation knives. As he watched them, the dull thud of a distant cannon firing registered in his head, a ranging shot or test firing from a French cannon in the distance.

The cannonball crossed his view as it bounded over the knoll, severing the canopy of branches from the tree stump, and he watched in awe as the whole mass of branches and leaves collapsed in a heap upon the heads of the said Surgeons! Within seconds the medics emerged, showing no ill effects but mortified by the roar of laughter from the battalions that witnessed it. Hurriedly, they repacked their equipment and retired to a safer location. It must have been a fluke; nobody could have aimed such a shot with any hope of succeeding. As they passed to the rear Joseph Burke informed Johnny that he would set up again at the farm half a mile back at Mont St Jean.

Looking back towards the cross roads, movement on the ridge to his left, on the opposite side of the Brussels road, caught Johnny's eye. A single young yew tree grew on the rise and near it he could make out Lord Wellington and his staff gesticulating as they discussed the troop dispositions. The movement that caught his eye however, was the arrival of a Horse Artillery battery, which promptly started to unhitch its guns and load them.

Johnny decided to investigate; it could turn out to be his new found friend Alexander Mercer. As he pressed his horse up the slope however, he was overjoyed in recognising very old friends.

"Well Ross, it's good to see you again, we can trust you to support us well, just as you always did in Spain."

"The Devil take me if it isn't Johnny Kincaid, how the devil are you old boy?"

Lieutenant Colonel Hew Ross was delighted to see Johnny again. Hew had commanded 'Chestnut Troop' Royal Horse Artillery, attached to the Light Division throughout the Spanish war, he knew the Rifles well.

Major John Parker and Lieutenant Phipps Onslow also approached and heartily shook his hand, he was a welcome sight.

Hew Ross explained, "We are to protect you and the Germans in the farm, I will place four of my nine pounders up here to dominate the ground and place John with his division down behind that abattis at the cross roads. Just don't get in John's way when the French come!" he warned playfully.

Johnny returned to his station at the sand pit to complete the preparations.

Eventually, as the early morning light flickered through the curtains, Juanna rose, dressed hurriedly and walked out to her horse with Harry. One final passionate embrace and she mounted her horse, turned away to hide her tears and headed out on the road to Brussels where Harry hoped that she would be safe. He watched her disappear into the woods, frantically trying to keep her in view for as long as possible, eventually she was gone and fighting back his fears for the future, he rode hurriedly to the front.

He arrived to discover his brigade in the reserve so he proceeded on to the crest of the ridge where he spotted the Rifles and rode down to join Johnny Kincaid.

"How does it appear Johnny?"

Johnny looked thoughtful, "They take a devilish time about attacking us."

As the words fell from his mouth, numberless cannon

roared into action far to the right, near the chateau Johnny thought.

He hooked out his fob watch by the gold chain, eleven thirty five and the wait was over!

BATTLE COMMENCES

The heavy cannon fire to their right grew to a crescendo; it was accompanied by the faint sounds of distant beating drums, blaring bugles and the pop of hundreds of muskets, creating a veritable cacophony of sound. The Rifles could see nothing of proceedings beyond the farmhouse of La Haye Sainte, except for a thick plume of light grey smoke rising high into the sky about a mile away.

Johnny Castles looked at the telltale signs of war, then turning to the lads around him shouted out "Well 'ere we go lads, we'll be next mark moi words. That there farm is a big proize fur Boney, he'll cum t'take it soon!"

Tom Crawley turned to George "Lefftenant Simmons, begging yur pardon Sir, but Johnny Frenchman's up to some ut, look there." He pointed toward the low ridge half way across the valley.

Just visible to the naked eye were numerous solid black objects appearing along its crest with small groups of men moving around them with purpose.

"Artillery" George muttered as he used his spyglass in an attempt to count the guns; he lost count at seventy.

"Shit!" he exclaimed.

Over seventy six and twelve pounders and howitzers, they were surely in for a severe pasting. George ordered Private John Palmer to pass the word to Lieutenant Kincaid and then to the reserve companies. Napoleon had started as a gunner and was still in love with his 'Children', his twelve pounder iron and brass guns; he would use this massive battery to demolish the units facing them, before his infantry and cavalry closed to smash through and deliver the coup de grace.

The battery was obviously taking some time to move into position and set up ready for action. The men watched as their preparations continued, they could do nothing; the guns were well beyond rifle range.

Johnny Kincaid approached George Simmons and Jonathan Leach.

"They must be sinking deep in this mud," suggested Johnny.

"An hour now since they started moving, I think they are near ready" Jonathan Leach replied.

"The firing to the right is still heavy and seems stationary," George observed.

Johnny agreed, "It must be an attack on the chateau I saw this morning and as the firing stays constant it must be holding firm."

Their conversation was interrupted abruptly when a dull thud was heard on the breeze. A small puff of smoke could be seen emanating from one of the French guns on the ridge. They could not see the cannonball's trajectory however; it must have passed to their left.

Major Cameron saw it coming though; flinching instinctively he felt its pressure wave as it passed close to his right. He looked over his shoulder at the line of Rifles formed as the reserve. There was movement and a shuffling amongst the men at the extreme right of the line.

"Stand still, Sergeant Morgan take charge there!"

Sergeant Morgan had already spotted the movement himself and had moved swiftly across to discover the cause. As he approached, the reason was abundantly clear. Summers, the tall right hand man of the company, lay flat on his back on the ground as if at attention, the corpse had no head. The solid iron cannonball had smashed Summer's head removing it completely! The men behind had recoiled in horror, partly at the sight, but mainly because they had been completely smothered with the pulped contents of Summer's head! Blood, brain tissue and fragments of skull still retaining his hair, bespattered them. Dooly was physically sick, Smith and James stood rigid being afraid to move, they looked to be in complete shock.

"What a baptism of fire" thought Thomas Morgan. He thoughtfully offered them his canteen of brandy to swill their mouths of the taste of Summers.

Having shown them sympathy they needed shocking out of their stupor.

"Get back in line, James take right hand man, dress off him." Despite their recent experience, complete obedience to orders made them fall back into line, to face death like men.

Johnny Kincaid watched the long line of guns with his spyglass and observed a number of small billows of smoke swiftly followed by the deep-throated roar of the guns as they finally came into action.

The ranging shot had obviously been observed and a similar range set on all the French guns, the balls could be tracked as they flew mostly to the left of the Rifles, aimed more towards the British Fifth and Belgian Divisions on the crest of the ridge. The French could not observe many units however and they had to guess the location of the defending forces.

Sir Thomas Picton had known what was coming and as instructed by Wellington, he had his troops retire behind the crest of the rise and lay down to reduce casualties to a minimum.

The Belgian units holding the crest in front of the Fifth division also retired, but one regiment stood unmoved near the crest, clearly visible to the French gunners. They paid dearly for this mistake; they stood awaiting orders to move, they were either forgotten or needed for a purpose they didn't know of. They stood and took the terrible punishment meted out, cannonball after cannonball smashing through their massed ranks, knocking numbers over with every strike. The wounded streamed back helped by uninjured colleagues, which rapidly depleted the regiment. They clung together like sheep clustering for protection and stood their ground, but they shouldn't have been left so terribly exposed, it was sheer murder.

Johnny Kincaid rode back to the reserve, he could see them standing protected largely from the artillery fire by the knoll in their front. To their left, Johnny could see the Belgian units with the Fifth division behind them; all were lying down to avoid casualties. Occasionally, a cannonball bounded over the crest, landing on some poor sod lying on the ground, they rarely let out a cry but succumbed to the reaper swiftly and silently. Some, who suffered smashed limbs, made up for them by screaming in agony and had to be carried back to the surgeons. Morale however was excellent, as Johnny passed behind the troops, he was amazed to hear them laughing and joking, Napoleon's tactics which were designed to destroy their spirit was clearly not working.

Every few seconds another solid iron sphere bounced across the fields smashing everything in its path. The wet ground swallowed up many a cannonball but some were only slowed each bound of the ball being much lower, but danger still remained. Johnny caught sight of a Rifleman stopping a cannonball with his foot that was simply rolling slowly down the knoll. The shouted warnings from colleagues to leave it be, were not heeded, which was followed by the inevitable scream of agony as the ball still had the power to tear his foot away.

Casualties mounted slowly but steadily with no ability to answer, how long would this go on for?

The British artillery batteries occasionally fired at the French guns to ease the bombardment but there was little visible lessening of the cannonade. As Johnny observed the guns, he could now see the movement of large bodies of troops beyond them; the French were finally going to launch their attack.

The cannonade had continued for half an hour or more and it was a relief of sorts to prepare for infantry and cavalry attacks, as at least the guns would have to stop to avoid killing their own men.

Throughout the allied forces, preparations began to receive the French attacks. Johnny returned to the sand pit to ensure that Jonathan Leach had prepared the advance companies. He arrived to see Jonathan and George Simmons viewing the French formations as they prepared to advance.

"How many do you make it Jonathan?"

Jonathan looked stern, "By our calculations up to eighteen thousand infantry formed in columns as Johnny Frenchman always attacks. A Cloud of skirmishers in front and Cavalry on both wings, light cavalry far side, Cuirassiers bordering the road our side. Classic all arms attack as you would expect from Mister Bonaparte."

Johnny Kincaid took another look with his spyglass and inwardly agreed with Jonathan's professional assessment.

"Ranged from the road in our front across to our left wing, but the columns are broader than normal, the French must be looking to increase their firepower, the Fifth Division will have their hands full!" Johnny looked at his pocket watch; it was now half past one.

"There, Look!" George shouted excitedly, pointing up the road. They all trained their glasses towards a party of French near the cobbled road, "I'm sure it is, yes, it's Bonaparte himself."

There he was, squat, plump in a grey coat with a large cocked hat lying crossways on his head, he sat astride a beautiful white horse. The French troops were clearly saluting him as they passed him on their advance; shouts of 'Vive la France' and 'Vive l'Empereur' could be heard faintly on the breeze.

"Look lively lads, 'ere cumms Ole trousers!" shouted Sergeant Fairfoot.

"Come on you bastards! Let's tank you proper loik fur the pasting we just 'ad" added Jem Connor.

"Aye, their turn to eat lead" George Kitchen concurred.

Rifle barrels were rested along the crest of the sand pit and careful aim taken, each man choosing their individual target as they waited for the range to close.

William Johnstone's company at the hedge on the knoll, received reinforcements, Lord Wellington who obviously had seen the build up of French troops had sent troops from Ompteda's Light Battalion of the King's German Legion.

The noise of battle now grew louder by the second; the allied artillery concentrated on the massive infantry targets, which they could hardly miss. They worked as fast as they could to pour their terribly destructive fire into the masses. The commotion from the French rose as they marched towards the crest, drums beating and bugles blaring, men shouting encouragement, all designed to bolster morale, the theory being that the greater the noise level the more confidence was maintained. The 'Pas de Charge' was the rhythm, which they beat, sounding something like 'the rum dum, the rum dum, the rumma dum dumma dum dum dum' played incessantly.

Despite these attempts to maintain their morale, the French started to become nervous as they climbed the slope. The British and Belgian units remained unseen and unheard behind the crest, which had a great dampening effect on their ardour as it had in Spain, old hands became worried by the reception they knew that Wellington and his army had waiting for them.

One column of Frenchmen headed directly towards the farm of La Haye Sainte, a second moved towards the Rifles on the knoll, they were obviously unaware of the sand pit and its defenders in their path. Further columns advanced toward the main crest to the left of the Rifles. The Cuirassiers could be seen to move over to the far side of the farmhouse and advance on that side.

The wait felt like an age, the Rifles holding their fire until the optimum moment.

Finally the French skirmishers were at a range of one hundred yards and the rifles roared into life. The aimed shots held so long were finally released, decimating the skirmishers. The shock was palpable, they had not suspected any resistance before the crest, and certainly not so deadly. The skirmishers reeled backwards, but the main column soon came up to them and marched on, they had been saved from this initial destruction and saw no reason to stop.

The rifles now concentrated all their fire on the head of the column; this was much the greater threat now. Every Rifleman poured in as great a volume of fire as he could, the company behind the hedge on the knoll contributing fully as well. The noise was deafening, soon the smoke from the rifles caused a thick smog, occasionally obscuring the column altogether. There was no need for taking careful aim now though, simply load and point, for the target was so large you had to hit something. They quickly became tired, it was really hard work ramming the cartridges of ball and powder home, the mouth dried with fear, tearing the cartridges with your teeth to prime the firing pan contributed as the gunpowder seared the throat.

Despite horrendous casualties, which increased with every moment, the column continued to advance steadily. The dead and wounded at the front of the formation were simply trampled on, the wall of men behind still marching forward stopping those that sought to turn back, there was no escape. Those troops further back in the mass were protected by the men in front from injury and did not feel the same fears, they simply strode forward.

For all the death and destruction they meted out, the Rifles could not stop the French advancing. The column just kept coming on, but it did veer a little to the Rifle's left, towards the main crest, which obviously appeared to offer a less hostile and painful route.

As the columns passed the sand pit the Rifles fired into their flank, forcing the columns to deploy more skirmishers to keep the rifle fire down.

The units that advanced on La Haye Sainte wrapped themselves around three of its sides as they endeavoured to break in to this ad hoc fortress. Skirmishers from this attack approached the gardens behind the farm and the abattis, firing through it at the more exposed side of the sand pit.

It was now getting too hot to handle, threatened on three sides, it was time to reconsider their options!

"Tis too bloody warm dis" shouted Mc Nabb "oim orff".

He hadn't moved two feet from his firing position before

he came face to face with Sergeant Robert Fairfoot, his loaded Baker Rifle in his good hand. He gently placed the muzzle under Mc Nabb's chin.

"Back in loin Mc Nabb or Johnny Frenchman won't get the chance to kill you, cause I'll do you moiself!"

Mc Nabb had little choice; he turned back to the firing line with a sulky look.

French infantry constantly encroached on their rear, attempting to envelop them completely. A few, a little more brave than the others moved forward, thrusting their bayonets towards the Rifles. George Kitchen sprang forward at one Frenchman; knocking his bayonet aside with his rifle he drove his sword bayonet, which he held in his left hand deep into the Frenchman's chest with such force that the point emerged from his back. The Frenchman fell with a slight groan; George put his foot on the body to increase leverage to extract his bayonet but as he did so he became vulnerable to attack. Another bayonet suddenly threatened him and he gulped hard as the point approached his stomach. He closed his eyes to the inevitable and braced himself for the searing pain to come.

There was a thickening thud, a loud cry and he was knocked over. George reopened his eyes to find the Frenchman lying dead across his legs, his skull smashed. He looked up into the grinning face of Palmer who held the remains of his rifle in his hand. The butt of the rifle was very useful as a club; he must have hit him hard as the wooden stock was broken and twisted. Palmer threw it away as useless.

"Bloody close that 'un" he said offering his hand to help George up.

George pulled himself upright patting Palmer on the shoulder, "You just earned my tot o'rum for a year, tanks mate."

The touching moment of comradeship was broken by the whiz of a musket ball narrowly missing Palmer's nose.

"Jeez dis is too hot" he exclaimed.

The welcome cry of "Fall Back" finally came loud and clear. Jonathan Leach as Senior Captain in the sand pit had held on as long as he dare, but any delay now would be sheer suicide. Discretion was now the greater part of valour, the companies were taking casualties quickly and were in danger of being completely overrun, so flee they must. They all ran towards the reserve companies, behind which they would reform. The company on the knoll joined this movement, two hundred or so men running a race for their lives.

The French did not delay, they swarmed into the sand pit and sent a tremendous fire after the fast retreating Rifles. Johnny Castles for all his bulk kept up with the front-runners, he'd learnt to be fast ever since Arcangues, Jones was just behind running with his free hand on his backside for protection, as he didn't fancy another ball there! Even Thomas Charity, weak as he was summoned up huge reserves of strength, it was amazing what the will to live did to a man!

The hundred yards felt like a mile. The balls whipped by, sounding like supersonic flies buzzing past. Some however struck their mark; Lieutenant Stilwell was hit in the back, falling forward stone dead. Lieutenants Molloy and Wright fell with shots in the legs; Lieutenant William Shenley was hit in the arm. Men were falling like ninepins. Eventually the relative safety of the reserve came in sight, but what was happening? They were retiring as well!

Johnny Kincaid could see this retrograde movement clearly from his horse and spurred Beth on.

"Hold your position" Johnny roared "What is the

meaning of this retreat? We must stand. Companies Halt, Face Front, Engage the enemy at will" he bellowed.

"I ordered the retirement Johnny."

Johnny looked to identify the speaker, it was Henry Lee.

"We were simply retiring to allow your units to form here; we could then act as your reserve again."

Johnny had no time to discuss the near disastrous error now; he had rectified the mistake and turned toward the front-runners from the sand pit and knoll, ordering them to form up behind the reserve.

As the battalion formed up rapidly again on the rising ground beside the roadway, every rifle was able to take revenge on the still advancing French columns. George Simmons and Jonathan Leach arrived last and stood gasping for breath.

Johnny Kincaid spurred Beth to the left flank of the battalion. Further to his left he could see the French masses marching on, seemingly impervious to the destruction from the artillery fire, now raking them with canister shot. The tins full of musket balls were fired by the cannon at very close ranges, the can split on firing peppering the target with the balls, causing much greater destruction than a single solid ball at one hundred yards and less.

The gunners fired incessantly, the sweat ran off them in rivulets as getting that extra shot in could be the breaking point for the columns at this stage. Dozens dropped with each discharge from the guns but they strode on undeterred.

The Belgian unit that had been under cannon fire for so long and had stood their ground heroically; had found that the firing had eased as the columns advanced, but now the French neared and nothing appeared capable of stopping them. A few more found wounded comrades to help to the rear, and then a small trickle started to retire without excuse, which rapidly turned into a flood. It was the final straw; they turned and ran over the crest and past the Fifth Division who were standing in second line. As they retreated, some of the British regiments booed and hissed them, some even struck out or called them "Cowards", but away they went. Many like Johnny sympathised with them, they had been left on the exposed crest and their morale destroyed by murderous cannon fire, few troops would stand after that punishment, not even British. They should be booing the bastard that had left them out there!

The French infantry gained renewed strength from the Belgians flight, nothing now stood before them, and the crest was theirs. A cheer went up; the drummers beat harder as victory was theirs for the taking. As they crested the rise, the British and Belgian units suddenly came into view; the front ranks of the French ceased celebrating as they stared down upon a sea of muskets pointed directly at them.

The order "Fire" rang out and two thousand flintlock muskets snapped shut almost simultaneously decimating the French ranks. Men who seconds before had been cheering, now fell screaming in agony. They were not to be stopped so easily however, those behind still pushed on; victory must be theirs. They burst upon the Belgians in the front line pushing them back upon the Fifth Division. Johnny watched as these British regiments resisted manfully, but the odds were four to one against them, numbers would surely win.

He watched the fight unfolding; he could still make out Sir Thomas Picton leading his Division and could see him lead them forward. Suddenly Picton's head went back, there was blood, his body slipped from his horse and lay crumpled in a heap on the ground, he was obviously dead. Still his troops battled undeterred by his death.

Johnny noticed a rider approaching fast it was Sir James Kempt.

He called directly to Johnny. "Do not quit that spot."

Johnny proudly replied "You can rely upon it."

It was enough, there was to be no retreat whilst a man stood alive. Johnny turned his horse and rode to the cross roads to view the fighting here. He knew the battalion would fight, but the crisis was upon them and the chances of success looked slim.

Johnny looked again towards the farmhouse of La Haye Sainte where fighting continued, the Germans still managing to hold out. Suddenly a frightened shout was heard.

"Cavalry, cavalry!"

He looked up to see a mass of Cuirassiers riding from the right of the farmhouse, across the road and directly towards him.

Johnny grasped the hilt of his sword to draw it in a desperate attempt to defend himself, as they galloped towards him swords held straight out in front of them, pointing directly towards his breast. Johnny pulled again at his sword to extract it from its protective scabbard, but nothing happened. Johnny's sword had rusted solid with all the rain, he sat still and closed his eyes to await death patiently and calmly as a gentleman officer should.

He uttered a short prayer as he waited.

"God.. Help me!"

IN RESERVE

Alexander hauled himself upright, his hands planted firmly on his hips to ease his aching back. He surveyed the scene around him from his spot in the middle of the muddy potato field. Putten was right, the other artillery troops and all the cavalry had simply disappeared! G troop stood in grand isolation.

Alexander suddenly became aware of the deep-throated roar of a heavy cannonade. What was happening?

They all made haste toward the troop, but having hurried back Robert Newland simply confirmed that no orders had arrived for G troop and that they were just waiting.

Even so, Alexander decided to be fully ready for the order when it finally came. "Put the horses to" he bellowed.

Instantly all was bustle, the horse teams were harnessed to the wagons, the men replaced their jackets ready for the off and fires were extinguished as all thought of food was forgotten in the excitement.

Alexander ordered the officer's kettle of soup, which he had slaved so diligently for in the potato field, to be hung under one of the carriages, where it could be retrieved to finish later. He watched in total horror however as William carried out his order and hung his pot under the carriage, but only after he had emptied the full contents, their only rations, onto the fire to extinguish it! Now where were they to get food from? There was still no sign of, nor word from Coates and the provision carts.

Alexander scanned the fields that had been filled with troops so recently; nothing was now to be seen of them at all except their tracks in the mud and the flotsam they had left behind. The only thing that confirmed their continued presence nearby was the unmistakable din of artillery fire and great plumes of dark smoke rising from just over the ridge that lay directly to their front.

Once everything was loaded and hitched up, the troop stood and waited with no idea of what to do next.

There they whiled away the minutes, but they waited for what seemed an eternity and Alexander looked to Robert and Henry for some guidance on what to do.

"Have we been forgotten?" he asked.

Robert looked grave, "Possibly, but unless directly ordered never move, for Lord Wellington will not forgive you if he sends orders and we are not where he expects."

Alexander considered the implications for himself, but decided that a slow move nearer to the front would still be advisable despite the warnings of the others. They would be closer to the fighting when finally called into action and could still be seen from here if any order did arrive, providing that they remained this side of the ridge.

As the troop moved slowly up the rear slope, an officer on a fine grey mare crested the ridge from the firing line. Surveying the scene quickly, his gaze fell upon G troop and he spurred his horse directly toward them. He approached at break neck speed and Alexander rode forward to converse with him, perhaps he brought orders. As the rider neared, Alexander could make out the uniform of a foot artillery officer but did not immediately recognise him.

The horseman drew up hard as he reached Alexander; he was breathless from exertion and could hardly speak as he gasped for air, the veins stood out on his forehead denoting his extreme agitation.

"Major William Lloyd" he blurted out, then gasped for another lung full of oxygen before continuing, "My battery is under intense pressure, we need urgent help!"

Alexander tried to calm him, "Where is your battery situated?" he asked in a strong controlled voice.

"Over on the right of the line, the French are attacking in immense hordes," he stammered almost incoherently. "Where are you going at present? Have you no orders? You must help us!" he continued to bluster.

Alexander sought to ease his hysteria, "We have no orders, none what so ever, I have not seen a soul."

Lloyd looked imploringly at Alexander, "Then for God's sake, come and assist me, or I shall be ruined. My brigade is cut to pieces, the ammunition is nearly expended and unless we are reinforced we shall be utterly destroyed!"

Alexander did not hesitate, "We shall come to your support immediately!"

Robert Newland shouted, "Alexander no, remember Ramsay, you must await orders!"

Alexander turned on Robert and answered sternly, "I cannot wait and see them slaughtered, when we could save them. We go, hang the consequences!"

Lloyd took Alexander's hand, "God bless you, I will ride back and hold out until you can support us." He turned his horse's head up the slope and galloped back over the ridge into the thick of battle.

"There goes a brave man, let us go and help him" Alexander bellowed.

Robert knew that further argument would not dissuade Alexander from his decision and like any good second in command, determined to carry out his chief's orders to the best of his ability. He had made his concerns known but had been overruled, now he must do his duty to his utmost for their lives would depend on it.

The troop cantered up the slope directly toward the sound of heavy cannonading and intense musketry fire. From their position, nothing could be seen but a thick cloud of acrid smoke billowing up from the inferno beyond the horizon. They urged the teams forward towards the crest but every stomach churned with the fear of death; no one knew what to expect of the different world they would enter as they descended the opposite side of the ridge. They were frightened, but they drove on, the bond of unity and of family within the troop gave them the inner strength to face the unknown together.

Their steeled determination was suddenly disturbed by the command "G troop, halt. Halt immediately I say."

The drivers instinctively hauled back hard on their reins and the horses slowed as quickly as they could and ground to a halt. What was wrong?

"Who gave the order?" Alexander enquired.

Alexander turned to see the inimitable Colonel Macdonald galloping up alongside him. How was it he just appeared from nowhere at such moments? Alexander wondered.

"Captain Mercer, where are you going? You have no orders to move!"

Alexander became agitated, "Major Lloyd has requested help to save his battery, and I have promised our aid."

Colonel Macdonald was clearly angry, "Mercer you have no orders from me, you are to remain in reserve as Lord Wellington demands until he sees fit to order you into action. You are not to move of your own volition!"

Alexander disagreed "We are wasted here, Lloyd needs help, I gave him my word!"

"Your word is not your own to give!" Macdonald sneered, "Remain here until you receive further orders."

Macdonald then spurred his horse on and disappeared over the ridge as quickly as he had come.

Alexander could hardly control his temper; Macdonald was becoming a real thorn in his side. He worried for Lloyd, how would he ever explain to him when they met again?

Robert looked on, he knew that something like this would happen, Macdonald was right, but he was not about to rub salt in Alexander's wounds.

"Shall I order the troop to dismount?" he enquired gently.

Alexander raised himself from his stupor, he recognised Robert's gesture with gratitude, he was still in command. "Order the troop to dismount Robert."

Cannonballs were occasionally bounding over the crest and landing near the troop. Some landed solidly in the sodden mud and buried themselves relatively harmlessly, showering all around with brown sludge; others striking rocky outcrops bounced just like cricket balls had on the cobbled streets when they were lads.

There they stood, waiting impatiently with not a living soul in sight. But for the sounds of conflict and dark ominous smoke, one could imagine oneself in an English park on exercise.

Driver Thomas Dibbin suddenly looked up and pointed, "What the bloody 'ell are they doing here?"

Everyone looked at once and were amazed to see a smartly dressed civilian gentleman on a beautiful stallion; two young lads also mounted on fine horses flanking him. They cantered slowly across the fields, the gentleman pointing in various directions; he was obviously explaining the battlefield to his tender companions. Finally they crested the ridge and descended into the battle beyond, quite unperturbed by the death and destruction all around.

Everyone sat silently, not believing that anyone would take such fine youths into death's lair if they didn't have to. There were plenty of kids in this battle including drummer boys of fourteen and fifteen, but they were in the army and had to carry out their duty; not one of them would be mad enough to enter this field of death and destruction as a civilian. Balls and cannonballs were no respecter of civilian credentials.

Henry Leathes announced, "That Gentlemen, was the Duke of Richmond and his two fine sons of Earls. I met him briefly at his wife's ball the other night, before we were hurried back. Some baptism of fire for his boys, eh!"

Another horseman came dashing through the mud, as he neared the bespattered uniform of an artilleryman became obvious. His steed was worn and dirty, for the horse had been used unsparingly throughout the last three days to rush orders and messages.

He proceeded directly to Captain Mercer.

Alexander greeted an old acquaintance, "William do you have orders?"

The messenger saluted and passed his message.

"Captain Mercer, you are to follow me. I am to indicate where you are to deploy."

Alexander was ecstatic, "Then pray lead on Bell, action at last!"

Virtually as quickly as the order to move was given, the whole troop was galloping after Lieutenant William Bell, the Staff Adjutant to Sir Augustus Frazer himself, everyone was desperate to join the action. As they rode across the fields, they suddenly became aware of masses of infantry in reserve, they had not been alone at all; the folds of the ground had simply hidden these nearby troops from view. They were lying down to reduce casualties, indeed some were sleeping soundly despite the firing just a few yards away.

They rode some distance, to the extreme right of the army, but still in the reserve second line. Finally Bell indicated their new position and the order was given to unlimber. The teams slowed, the gunners dismounted and prepared the guns for action; the drivers withdrew the teams and advanced the lead ammunition wagons to a position where a dip in the ground just behind the guns hid them from the enemy, hopefully out of danger of their shot, but close enough to provide ammunition to the cannon.

Alexander surveyed his position with William Bell; they were situated on a low ridge, which ran back almost perpendicularly from the crest on which the army's front line was deployed. It joined the main ridge just behind a large chateau and wooded area some one hundred yards away, which had obviously been the scene of much of the early fighting, as plumes of thick smoke billowed from the chateau's buildings. A Union Jack still fluttered from its walls, its brave defenders still held out, and good luck to them, whoever they were, he thought. This ridge was designated as part of the reserve, but the French ridge also curved round with it and the extreme left of their army obviously held the opposite heights, therefore they were now effectively on the wing of the front line. Between the opposing ridges stretched a shallow dip which was now the stage for numerous Allied and French skirmishers to take pot shots at one another and dart back and fore in the same merry dance that had amused Alexander so much before.

Bell pointed across the valley to the French heights, which were about eight hundred to a thousand yards away.

They could make out a line of lancers, the pennants on their lances fluttering in the breeze, formed on the opposite ridge watching them.

"You are merely to watch those cavalry, to deter them from making any attempt to attack at this point. You are specifically ordered not to engage unless attacked!"

Bell wheeled his horse and rode off again.

There they stood waiting again, amusing themselves by watching the skirmisher's antics as the front line ebbed and flowed across the floor of the valley with neither side seemingly able to gain the upper hand. They also watched the small puffs of smoke emanating from little French four pounder cannon attached to the lancers vainly attempting to reach them. Their balls fell harmlessly into the valley, as the range was well beyond these puny cannon, only the skirmishers felt any minor discomfort from their efforts.

Only fifty yards to his left front, Alexander could see Captain Samuel Bolton's foot artillery battery also deployed facing across the valley. He observed that they were busy firing at a target outside of Alexander's field of view and Bolton's battery was also under enemy artillery fire. Men and horses were occasionally hit but strangely Alexander could not see any assailant and G troop were not really under fire at all.

Samuel came across from his battery to converse on their adventures for a short while but he was hurriedly called back to his troop as they resumed firing, Alexander still could not see the cause.

The only slight annoyance to his battery came from a few unseen howitzers that lobbed occasional shells at them. These guns were obviously of large calibre as they could reach them comfortably. Their high trajectory could be traced as the metal spheres appeared whenever a wisp of smoke rose across the valley. The shell would climb steeply and then arc slowly, eventually plunging deeply into the sodden earth where they sat fizzing away until they finally exploded, sending a great plume of mud into the air. There was a fear of fragments causing injury, but the men were worried more by the potential threat than the real danger, as few actually suffered more than a spattering of mud!

A few stray balls bounded over the main ridge to their left and threatened more destruction than the French artillery fire to their front. One round shot bounced across the face of the troop and struck an ammunition truck; the ball smashed it's way through the thin wooden walls, but as it crashed out of the opposite side of the second box on the wagon, it ran out of strength and remained jammed, half revealed in the wall of the box. It caused a great deal of merriment in the troop despite its near fatal path through their ranks only seconds earlier.

Alexander trained his gaze upon the main ridge; the ball had made him aware that presently, this was the greatest threat to his unit. As he watched further balls bound over the crest and crash through the reserve infantry that were lying down to avoid its worst effects; he suddenly became aware of the infantry rising to their feet and forming hollow squares. Each face of the squares were four ranks deep, the rear ranks standing with muskets aimed ready to fire and front ranks kneeling, wedging the stock of their muskets against their boots and offering their bayonets outwards. The squares reminded him of so many hedgehogs with their prickly spines protruding for defence. As the infantry completed their square formations, the crest of the ridge became dark with the massed ranks of French cavalry!

The cavalry passed the squares, ineffectually prodding their swords and lances at the unperturbed infantry, then wheeled off out of view, probably arcing back towards the crest at a point out of sight from Alexander's viewpoint. Alexander was frustrated, they had now stood for hours in various positions without doing anything, yet the battle raged furiously just beyond them.

Despite his rules of engagement, Alexander finally lost patience and ordered his guns to open up on the French lancers on the horizon. The guns had been laid for the range since their arrival and they needed no further alignment, the right hand gun boomed out and he stood with his eyeglass to observe the fall of shot.

No sooner had his cannon opened fire than a previously unseen French battery was unmasked to the left of the cavalry; Alexander spotted the plumes of smoke as the guns discharged. A great whoosh of wind roared through the troop and beyond, the pressure waves of cannonballs passing close by, bloody big ones at that! A loud scream behind him forced Alexander to turn, it was Gunner Philip Hunt of John Bretton's division, a ball had shattered his left arm, it hung limp and mangled by his side as he sunk to his knees in agony. The profusion of blood, his screams of pain and deathly hue shocked Alexander, it was the first casualty in his troop and it was his fault! He turned away shame faced, unable to bear the guilt, but determined to show a brave unconcerned face to his men. He left it to John Bretton and his men to escort Hunt back to Surgeon Hichens who would undoubtedly have to amputate the remains of his arm. Those had been powerful shots; the French must have hidden a battery of twelve pounders at least! Alexander ordered the guns to cease firing, he could take the hint, his battery was no match for such huge brutes! Alexander rebuked himself mentally, he had been ordered not to fire and again his failure to keep to orders had caused suffering to others and nearly landed him in very hot water indeed!

All settled again, the enemy battery fell silent and the scene descended into a monotonous continuation of the darting circles of the skirmishers. To the left the cavalry had completely disappeared and the infantry had lain down again.

Alexander watched as a surgeon from one of the infantry regiments walked up to G troop to view the battle that still raged in the valley. A shower of heavy rain started, most just stood and attempted to ignore the water flowing down their faces and drenching their uniforms, but the surgeon promptly opened up a large black umbrella to ward off the deluge. He looked completely out of place, standing on the ridge holding up his umbrella whilst cannonballs whistled past; indeed he became a figure of novelty and the whole troop watched his perambulations. Obviously the French gunners had also found him a good mark, an aiming point! The massive cannonballs bounding over the ridge seemed to progressively close nearer to him, which alarmed him and persuaded him that this was not a healthy place for his meanderings. It seemed that the whole French artillery was seeking the prize for knocking this specimen off the ridge. The surgeon became aware of the unwanted attention he was attracting and decided that he should retire. His retreat however was not particularly dignified being rushed; indeed he dashed back down the slope out of view of the French. He continued to hold his umbrella up to protect himself from the rain as he ran hell for leather toward safety. Indeed, he was so wrapped up in his thoughts of escape that he did not take due care of his footing. He skated on the slimy mud recently rewetted and collapsed into the sludge, completely covering his fine uniform in thick mud. He continued to hold his umbrella aloft throughout, even now when the rain would have been welcome in removing some of the earth from his uniform.

All the men watching laughed raucously, this whilst death and destruction continued merely yards away. For one short moment they forgot the danger and enjoyed the farcical sight, indeed the relief of tension was immense, the laughter became almost uncontrollable. The surgeon became aware of the jesting at his expense and slunk to the rear, to a more appropriate station for a gentleman of his profession.

Some of the horse teams of Bolton's battery stood just to the left of Mercer's troop. A cannonball smashed through the horses causing the animals to move about nervously, their handlers having to fight hard to control them. They shied away from one horse in particular and as the horse turned toward the troop the drivers could be seen turning away in horror or shooing it away; the reason for their alarm became all too apparent. The horse stood impassively with no sign of injury until its face came into view. The cannonball had smashed into the horse's head and completely removed it's snout from just below the eyes. Its eyes appeared melancholy and it edged forward toward the troop as if imploring help from its masters. The men looked away from the awful sight, but for one man. Farrier Robert Price stepped up to the poor animal and patted the mare's withers whilst whispering calming words to ease its suffering. Unseen to the horse, Price drew back his arm, revealing his sword to the watching gunners, then with a swift thrust he plunged the blade deep into the soft under belly right up to the hilt, through to its heart. The surprise was complete; it collapsed immediately and expired within moments. Price placed his foot on the mare's stomach and withdrew the sword, which he wiped clean of blood with a rag from his pocket. He showed no sign of emotion, he had simply shown great mercy to the poor animal, it had not suffered for long, others less fortunate dotted all over the battlefield would suffer for many hours.

Suddenly there was an almighty explosion, which knocked some of the men completely off their feet. Dazed, they turned to see a great mushroom cloud of thick white smoke slowly forming above the fields. An ammunition wagon had received a direct hit; three men that had stood near by were completely gone, literally blown to pieces! A boot struck Butterworth's shoulder, picking it up he realised that a severed foot remained within, it must have belonged to one of those poor bastards, he just tossed it away with little thought.

Another mass of French cavalry appeared on the main ridge; as they advanced a squadron of Belgian cavalry moved to meet them. The two lines approached each other, the horses trotting calmly and the men pointing their swords towards their opponent's breasts. Alexander watched as the two lines closed and awaited the horrendous crash, which must surely follow. They neared, when without any word, the two lines opened a little, allowing the opposing horses to pass each other. The cavalrymen struck out with their swords, a few hit home and a handful of men sank from their saddles but most thrusts were parried. The lines had passed completely through each other following this short ineffectual clash. Alexander was amazed; it appeared choreographed as if it had been orchestrated in advance. The opposing cavalry then filed off and returned over the crest honours even.

Lieutenant Colonel Charles Gold, who commanded two-foot artillery batteries approached the troop, he was known slightly by Alexander, whom he obviously wished to engage in conversation.

He seemed worried, "I do not think our position looks good Alexander."

Alexander was shocked, "Do you not think we can hold the French?" he enquired.

"The front line is under extreme pressure and most of the troops are young and inexperienced. I fear these cavalry attacks will force a break through soon. Have you considered your retreat?"

Alexander immediately realised that he had no contingency plans worked out at all. If they were forced to retreat he had not given any thought to his course of action. Charles Gold was an experienced artillery officer and was right to consider all the possibilities, but Alexander found him too pessimistic for his liking.

"I have made no plans, but we could retreat on the roads through the woods" he answered nonchalantly.

"I think that will be unlikely, Alexander" he countered, "For if there is a general retreat the roads will be blocked with wagons of the commissariat, they are always first away."

"Then what should I do?" asked Alexander.

"Spike your guns, Sir, then ride like the wind with your horse teams, for the Cuirassiers will show little mercy."

Alexander had not realised that the battle was at such a critical stage, as there seemed little to concern anyone in this quarter of the field. As they spoke, Alexander became greatly worried, this officer of vast experience was predicting a disaster and he could feel his confidence sapping away. He became aware that Staff Sergeant John Hall was standing behind the guns with a mallet and metal spikes, to ram into the touchholes of the cannon if they were to be lost to the enemy. 'Spiking' put the cannon out of action for days at least, as the hole would have to be bored out again in a workshop.

They watched the ridge as another mass of French cavalry crested it and swarmed around the expectant infantry squares. Perhaps Gold was right, the number of cavalry appearing over the crest made Alexander wonder if the front line still stood, yet there were no signs of men fleeing. Some of the Belgian infantry appeared to be a little nervous but they stood and prepared to fire at the approaching cavalry.

A noise to the front of the battery made Alexander look to the right and he quickly ascertained that it was coming from infantry formations in the valley. Everyone was convinced that they were French in their dark blue coats.

Alexander gave the order to Fire.

Just as they prepared to apply the slow match to the touch hole of the first gun, Gold cried out, "Cease fire, they are Belgians!"

He was right; the battalion closed and crossed the ridge just in front of the guns on the march to support the front line. That had been close to being a terrible mistake.

Alexander turned his gaze back to the crest but the cavalry had disappeared again! He had no idea where they could have gone.

Alexander drew his fob watch from his jacket pocket; it was nearly three o'clock. He remembered his training, retreat in daylight was much more difficult, the pursuing enemy could not be easily lost, but there was at least another six hours of light to go.

A horseman suddenly galloped up, stopping hard alongside Alexander and Gold. They looked up and were surprised to be staring into the face of Sir Augustus Frazer himself. His blackened face was contorted with worry; his eyes reddened by the smoke of battle making him appear monstrous. Looking more closely, they could make out the smeared smoke stains on his face, he had been crying!

"Are you all right, Sir?" Alexander enquired.

"Norman Ramsay is dead" he replied solemnly.

The news struck hard, Alexander couldn't believe it.

"How?"

"Struck by a ball, during a lull we buried him."

Sir Augustus seemed far away, deep in thought for a few seconds, then snapped himself out of it and bellowed, "Left limber up, follow me as fast as you can!"

Was this retreat?

CAVALRY

It seemed like a lifetime to Johnny Kincaid, despite the terrible noise of battle all around, cannon and musket fire mingled with the cries of the wounded and dying, all he seemed to be aware of was the pounding of the ground as the French horsemen approached, he could feel the earth actually vibrate beneath him. He sat calmly awaiting the sword point penetrating his uncovered breast to send him on his way across the Styx. The pounding grew louder and louder until it became a deafening roar but was suddenly accompanied by the sound of metal clashing on metal, great cries of anguish and pain, then just as quickly the thunderous noise seemed to have abated. Johnny dared to take a peep, he couldn't believe his eyes, the Cuirassiers were gone! What could have happened?

A resounding cheer to his left caused him to look across the front line where the French infantry continued to attack; there was his answer. He watched the Cuirassiers riding like the wind back towards their own lines; they were already passing the sand pit chased by a swarm of red and blue uniformed horsemen of the Household cavalry! The Horse Guards in red and Lifeguards in blue on their huge horses had obviously charged the Frenchmen just before they reached the Rifles and had swept them back into the valley. As he looked toward the Fifth Division still engaged in a firefight, he was in time to see the infantry wheeling back to make gaps in their line. Through the spaces poured the Union Brigade, the charge of the British cavalry smashed into the already shaky French columns. The foul-mouthed Iniskilling Dragoons, the massive Scots Greys with their towering fur hats and the English Royal regiment of Dragoons tore into the massed ranks of the enemy.

The French were taken completely by surprise, they had thought the battle was theirs and had no warning of this attack, the cavalry being hidden behind the ridge.

The attack was frenzied, the cavalrymen struck with their swords as hard as they could, their arms ached from the repeated blows. Swords flowed with French blood; the cavalrymen gave no quarter, simply hacking at anything in their path. The horses became intoxicated, tearing at the French with their teeth and trampling them underfoot. It was a sheer bloody massacre, the French infantry were unable to turn and run for the masses behind barred their way, there was little room in the crush to even manoeuvre their muskets and swords to defend themselves. The screams of their victims raised the blood of the cavalrymen to even greater heights; their faces took on a demonic look as they slashed away without mercy. Many Frenchmen dropped their weapons, falling to the ground in feigned death, hoping to avoid the horse's hooves and survive the carnage. Most stood and received horrendous injuries, heads literally split in two, decapitations, arms hacked off, those slightly luckier receiving horrible gashes on the head, arms or torso as swords cut through the flesh but jarred against bone.

This all occurred in the space of a few minutes, by then the rear of the columns had started fleeing and the masses of French infantry simply dispersed, the cavalry chasing them, all soon disappearing into the high corn. The Rifles like the rest of the Fifth Division cheered ecstatically for the cavalry had saved them from near certain defeat.

A French Cuirassier officer, a mere lad, lay just in front of the battalion, Major Andrew Cameron took pity and stepped out to lift him in his arms, he carried him all the way back to Mr Burke.

A sergeant of the Scots Greys appeared from the cornfields again, brandishing a French eagle above his head, they cheered till they were hoarse; he'd probably get a commission as an officer for that! The Eagle sat atop the regiment's flagpole, the flag carried the names of the great battles in their past, but the little brass eagle was their prized possession as it was presented by Napoleon himself. It meant complete disgrace to lose it; many brave men would have died trying to protect that eagle. Johnny allowed himself a smile and turning to Jonathan Leach commented "That was too bloody close for comfort, I really thought our time had come."

Jonathan nodded, "Very true, but let us now enjoy the fruits of our success."

Three companies were ordered forward again, they moved down the road to recover the sand pit and knoll. Johnny noticed in passing that during the late attack the two guns of Hew Ross's battery left at the abattis had been damaged beyond use and the gunners had gone. As they moved forward, the Rifles encountered masses of French soldiers who were almost dazed by what had happened. Many that had feigned death arose to find British infantry approaching and gladly surrendered rather than face those terrible cavalry again.

Detailing off parties to move further into the valley, Jonathan watched as a handful of Riflemen easily collected a few hundred prisoners. All that could walk were escorted in; some badly wounded Frenchmen were helped in by their comrades. The rest would have to lie out there until the battle ended. The Rifles had to prepare for future attacks and even their own wounded were lucky to get any help back to the surgeons at Mont St Jean.

Johnny Kincaid now had time to check himself over, he was unwounded but his pride was deflated. He couldn't believe his own stupidity in not checking his weapon; if one of his men had been guilty of such a crime he would have been put on a charge and flogged. More to the point, he was extremely lucky to still be alive; his guardian angel must be working hard for him today he thought. He offered up a silent prayer of thanks to his maker. A snort from Beth made him assess his faithful horse as well. He noticed that Beth had been injured in the late attack, her right ear was missing, it had been removed close to her head, probably by a musket ball. Dismounting, Johnny continued to check her over, a musket ball had also caused a furrow in the hindquarter of Beth's left leg, but she was bearing her weight on it and seemed in no discomfort, she had been lucky too.

George Simmons watched as the French prisoners were marched through, tramping sullenly up the road and over the ridge to the rear. He felt proud of his men, moments earlier they had wished nothing more for these Frenchmen than instant death, now they were offering them what assistance they could.

Johnny Castles helped one who was faint from loss of blood and near to collapsing, on the left side of his head all the skin was peeled away from the skull the cranium being perfectly visible; it had obviously been caused by a fearful sword slash.

Palmer helped hold the great flap of skin in place by

wrapping a large grey handkerchief around his head and tying it tight. Another prisoner, only slightly wounded, signed his thanks for their care and took over helping him on, he was his brother, they had fought alongside each other for nine years.

Tom Crawley and Jem Connor stood on the roadside watching them go by, offering those obviously in desperate need a mouthful of water from their own canteens, when they surely needed it themselves.

The men cleared the pit, throwing the bodies out onto the rim of the crater, forming a human rampart as preparation for the next attack.

Johnny watched a detachment of Horse artillerymen come down from the ridge on their horses, with poles bundled behind them that looked just like lances. They were rocket troops! He hadn't seen them in action before so he watched.

The artillerymen halted at the base of the ridge and pulled a number of rocket heads from their saddle packs. Two men could be seen using crimping tools to attach the heads to the long stakes, which formed the tail. Another was laying them on the ground in a neat line facing the French, who could not be seen at all through the high corn. When twenty rockets had been laid on the ground, a trail of fuse was run along the bases of the rockets. It was lit and all the rockets fizzed into life virtually in unison, each wagging their sticks a little then exploding into life. The rockets soared at incredible speed through the high corn towards the French lines. The artillerymen could not see the effect of their fire but fired a few further salvoes, and then having exhausted their stock they retired back behind the ridge.

By now all the prisoners were gathered in and the infantry were back in their positions. It was incredible

Johnny thought, ten minutes ago this ridge was covered by some seventeen thousand French and ten thousand or so British and Belgians. Now only the dead and dying remained. The French had been scattered and had lost about two thousand prisoners he guessed.

The Household and Union Brigades had disappeared toward the French lines and he wondered what had happened to them. The sight of a few bedraggled Scots Greys returning on the road, their horses blown, heads hanging limply, led him to fear that the news that they would bring was not good.

As they passed, Johnny hailed the sergeant leading the group.

"What is become of your Brigade?" he enquired.

The sergeant indicated for the rest to continue back to safety, behind the ridge, whilst he stopped for a moment.

He turned to Johnny, "Wull Sir, efter we smashed through yon infantry, we rode straight across yon valley tae their cannon. Wull we labours into them gunners, hacking them down left and right, didnae spare no horses or drivers even though they's mere laddies. Half those guns will nae bother you agin today, I'll wager."

"But where's your brigade now?" George Simmons interjected.

The sergeant stared George hard in the face with a look of complete contempt for daring to break into his speech. Johnny demurred and he continued.

"Trumpeters blew 'Recall' but nae one listened, as their blood was up, even our reserves got mixed in. Well Boney sent his answer, lancers! Bloody hundreds of them. With oor horses blown it was like sticking pigs, lads didnae stand a chance. Near wiped us out."

With that he turned and rode after the remnant of his squadron. Johnny and George said nothing but stared in horror towards the French lines. All those fine lads on such noble horses destroyed, it was unbelievable. As they continued to watch, small groups of cavalry returned, maybe a third might return all told, but they wouldn't form much of a fighting force again that day.

A few wounded men limped through, some leading their worn horses, many of these showing the scars of battle. As they passed, the lads gave them what help they could.

George was interested to hear one Lifeguard corporal talking.

"Dem Frenchies don't like them bloody rocket fings, when I lays on the ground wounded I could hear 'em. Cursing them rockets as the Devil's weapons and we wus trying to burn 'em all alive! they says."

George smiled, those rockets could go anywhere, and their unpredictability was what made them even more frightening, it would unnerve them if they attacked again, knowing such weapons were ready for them.

There was the occasional sound of a big rocket still roaring overhead, George was attracted by the sound that emanated from the ridge. There he could see more of the rocket artillerymen; these were using some kind of frame. He had heard of these 'Bombarding Frames' before, but had never seen one. Two long iron legs were planted into the ground and attached to them was a twelve-foot ladder. This formed a tripod and by climbing the ladder an artilleryman could place two big rockets in the holders at the top. Once set and attached to a train of gunpowder, they could be ignited from down on the ground. He watched as a pair were lit, they fizzed into action then roared high into the sky; he followed their trails of smoke across the valley towards the French until obscured by the haze of battle. These thirty-two pounder rockets could fly over three thousand yards, causing consternation well behind the front lines. However an officer rode up to the sergeant operating the Bombarding frame and following a short discussion they were removed, obviously someone was nervous where these rockets may land, as they had been known to double back on themselves.

For the next couple of hours little happened to break the monotony for the Rifles, the French batteries had obviously been remanned and fired continuously at the British front line, but there were few targets in their view. Most were speculative shots hoping to strike the units formed behind the ridge, softening them up before any renewed infantry attack. The fire was nowhere near as hot as earlier; obviously the cavalry charge had led to a shortage of gunners to man the great battery properly. The Rifles took their share of this fire, with the added nuisance of skirmishers who had returned into the valley and darted about taking pot shots at anything in view. There were few casualties however and really both sides seemed comfortable with the stand off following the earlier excitement.

The noise from the right of the line became very intense; the clouds of smoke grew thicker and darker, obliterating any view of proceedings beyond a few hundred yards. Obviously, the fighting had switched to the right of the line, but they had no way of knowing what was happening, they simply had to hold their own front and trust that the other divisions would sustain the pressure as firmly.

Mostly, they trusted Lord Wellington to see them through, he had vanished from his observation point at the crossroads, a sure sign that important things were afoot elsewhere, as Wellington had a knack of always being at the scene of greatest danger.

This quiet spell allowed the men to relax a little, but they maintained a constant vigil, as Old Boney wouldn't have finished with them yet.

Harry Smith rode down to the sand pit to discuss the situation with Jonathan Leach.

"All quiet Jonathan?"

Leach turned, "Ah Harry, seems they have more important work elsewhere. How do Sir John Lambert and the Tenth Brigade fair?"

"We have not been called forward yet and have only taken casualties from stray shot, but I dare say there will be plenty of time to make our mark. Indeed, I witnessed the recent attack of the French and their repulse; it seemed close for a while."

"Aye, thank God for the cavalry, I do not think we would have done without them."

Sergeant Robert Fairfoot broke in to the conversation.

"Begging your pardon Soir, but Johnny Frenchman's forming up again."

Spyglasses trained on the French ridge came to rest on a number of dark masses of infantry; they were forming up to attack.

Suddenly a commotion to the rear made them all turn back towards the cross roads, a mass of French Cuirassiers had appeared behind the reserve companies, a moment of extreme danger. Luckily, the reserves commanded by Major Cameron were in the sunken road and the cavalry could not descend the steep banks down to them. Indeed, those behind pushed a few horsemen too near the edge, their horses lost their footing and they crashed down the embankment to the roadway. Men and horses broke their necks or limbs in the fall, those horsemen that survived tried vainly to rise from the ground, but couldn't without releasing themselves from their body armour. They were like so many upturned turtles floundering, unable to right themselves. The Rifles watched in unconcealed merriment, the Cuirassiers slunk away in shame once divested of their shells.

Their way forward was impossible and attacked from the rear by the remnants of the Lifeguards; the mass of Frenchmen sought escape in other directions. Many moved along the crest and found a point at which they could pass over the ridge and return into the valley. One group however, tried to enter the roadway and return via the crossroads. This group ran up against the abattis blocking the road, it was now too sturdy to push aside thanks to George and his men. They were like rats in a trap, the Rifles poured a number of volleys into them and hardly a man or horse survived. It was annihilation; the bodies lay thickly one upon another. Indeed some men and horses died together, they lay stretched on the ground, the horse still as if in the act of running, the rider dead still sat astride, maintaining his grimace of determination even in death.

Drums beating, bugles blaring loudly and a sudden increase in the level of cannon shots brought their thoughts back to the threat in front of them. The columns of French infantry were marching toward the farm and sand pit area. As the columns neared the buildings, the defending Germans poured in a very destructive rifle fire, but the French marched on determined to take this temporary fortress once and for all.

The columns enveloped the three sides of the farm again, but this time they seemed to attack with greater determination and ferocity. A large column also marched on, to the left of the sand pit and then turned to fire upon the Rifles within the hollow and those lining the hedge on the knoll. The Rifle companies fired as fast and accurately as possible, the numbers of Frenchmen falling to their volleys was terrific but greater numbers kept pushing forward, maintaining the pressure.

Johnny Kincaid had watched as a few hundred extra German Riflemen ran down from the ridge and entered the farm on the remaining side free of Frenchmen, to aid in the defence. Lord Wellington and his entourage appeared on the ridge near a single elm tree, he had observed the need to reinforce the farm just in time. His knack for being in the right place at the right moment showed again.

The noise was deafening, the French cannon had ceased firing as the infantry had approached their target, but the British artillery fired as rapidly as they could into the masses around the farm. The continuous firing of rifles made their ears ring; the men had to shout to make themselves heard. The Riflemen were exhausted, parched from the caustic gunpowder in their throats, eyes smarting from the thick smoke emanating from their rifles, deafened, they just kept loading and firing mechanically, their lives depended upon it.

Suddenly a roar emanated from the French, some were climbing over the walls of the farm and onto the rooftops to fire down into the courtyard. The fighting was obviously continuing in the farm but the level of firing from the defenders seemed to be diminishing fast.

A small group of the Germans started to emerge from the rear of the farmhouse and flee towards the ridge; some forty or so ran towards cover in the sand pit.

One of them was obviously an officer, as he ran in with his men Jonathan Leach caught him by the shoulder.

"What is happening at the farm?"

The German crouched gasping for breath, he struggled to speak. Jonathan eyed the cuts on his head, the sweat and smoke blackened face and uniform. After a few gulps of air the officer shouted in broken English.

"Major Baring, vee 'aff lost the farm, they vill attack here next I think."

Jonathan offered him the remnants of his small whisky flask that he had been saving to celebrate his own survival.

The German took it gratefully and sipped it, but ensured he did not use it all, he was only too aware of the sacrifice Jonathan made.

"Vee ran out of ammunition, vee fought with clubs and stones but vee could not stop them!"

Jonathan put a comforting hand on his shoulder, he felt for Baring, he had just seen his battalion destroyed; he tried to understand how he felt. He didn't make the pain worse by asking the question on his lips. Why had no one asked him for ammunition? They had plenty with the reserves, as they used the same weapons. Obviously Baring's requests for ammunition had been sent to his own units, no one had thought of the Rifles.

There was no time to ponder this further; the French had indeed turned their attention fully upon the Rifles now. They appeared from the rear of the farmhouse and fired into the sand pit from the farm's rear garden.

It was far too hot to stay any longer and Jonathan gave the order to retreat again. As before, they raced back to form on the reserves with French musket balls chasing them along the road.

This time the reserves stood firm and the forward companies formed up on them, they would retreat this far but no further. They took stock of their losses, George Simmons had seen Captain Edward Chawner hit in the chest and carried to the rear; Captain William Johnstone was hit in the elbow smashing the bone, that was him out of action following his previous wound at Quatre Bras.

Sir Andrew Barnard slumped to the ground; a shot in his side had disturbed his already weakened constitution. He was escorted to the rear; he couldn't continue to command the battalion.

Henry Lees ran up to Jonathan, "Sir Andrew and Major Cameron are both wounded, that leaves you in command as Senior Captain." Jonathan nodded, he was ready.

Alexander Cameron lay on the ground just to their right, George Simmons went to him. A bugler was already attending him, holding an old handkerchief long since white tightly to the Major's throat. The bugler looked up at George "Shot in neck, Sir, bad" and shook his head.

George understood, he took Alexander's hand for a moment looking on his tortured features, and then hurriedly returned to the front.

Robert Fairfoot scanned the faces of the men; they were still determined to fight. He had seen a number of them fall too, Jem Connor the tailor was amongst them, he had been hit in the chest and lay on the road. Tom Crawley and Johnny Castles ran back down the road, took an arm each and dragged Jem back to the battalion. He looked pale, the wound was bad but they obtained permission to carry him to the surgeons. Whilst the lads pulled Connor back to safety, Fairfoot had recognised the body of a fellow sergeant lying on the cobble stones, Robert turned the body over and was met by the fixed staring eyes of death, it was poor Thomas Morgan the Welshman, with a ball hole drilled very neatly in his forehead.

The French infantry swarmed over the sand pit and the knoll. They moved forward to try and dislodge the Rifles from the hedge bordering the roadway, which now acted as their front line. The battalion had retired far enough and poured in a veritable hail of rifle balls, making any further advance for the French suicidal, but Ross's remaining guns were forced to leave the ridge to avoid being overrun.

A French horse artillery unit moved up to the farm of La

Haye Sainte and pushed two cannon into position to fire upon the Rifles. The gunners set their aim and fired a round each of canister but their first shot was hurried and caused little damage.

This was a serious threat and could not be ignored. Johnny Kincaid picked out Johnny Castles, John Palmer, Thomas Charity and William Mc Nabb; he took them just forward of the battalion, onto the roadway.

"They cannot fire again lads, concentrate on them." He ordered.

The lads knew what to do; at a range of less than one hundred yards their Baker Rifles were highly accurate. Their first shots brought down three gunners attempting to load the cannon. Another volley, which brought down two more persuaded the artillery men that this was not such a good idea and as quickly as they had come they went again, leaving their cannon behind.

Jonathan Leach observed the fighting from the rear of the battalion; his ability to view the scene properly was much improved as he stood on the top of the ridge. He was able to see the men maintaining the firefight and he could see that their fire had clearly dampened the enthusiasm of the French infantry to advance further. Indeed, their officers could be seen vainly trying to drive their men forward with the flat of their swords.

Just to the right of the cross roads, he could see the Prince of Orange clearly organising a counter attack on the farmhouse. The German battalion marched forward in line towards La Haye Sainte, but half way down the slope, a mass of French Cuirassiers hidden by the farm buildings suddenly emerged. Infantry in line were too good an opportunity to miss, they instantly charged and the infantry formation broke as they ran into huddles, desperately trying to form impromptu squares, but they didn't stand a chance and they were overwhelmed in seconds. Jonathan ordered the right hand section of Rifles to fire on the cavalry but they couldn't initially because it was impossible to avoid hitting their allies. As soon as they had over ridden them, annihilating all, the rifles exploded into life knocking many a horseman down in sweet revenge. The Cuirassiers were further threatened by the remnants of the Lifeguards and retired, their bloody work complete.

The Rifles were horrified to observe that the retreating horsemen slowly trotting back took time to halt and drive their swords into any infantryman lying wounded that they passed. That was cold-blooded murder; it made their blood boil for retaliation and the worst culprits became especial targets for the best shots.

The cannon and musket fire was incessant, death stuck out his bony fingers regularly, and his appetite continued insatiable. The constant close calls of death led everyone to become blasé to the danger; they couldn't remain frightened of the whiz of the balls forever.

George Simmons stood laughing and joking with Charles Smith, the Gentleman Volunteer, amongst this madness both had miraculously escaped any injury.

"Well Charles plenty of opportunities for your commission today, indeed if we take many more casualties you may be in line for a Colonelcy!"

Charles seemed shocked by all that he had witnessed but maintained his manly facade. "Is it always like this, George?"

"No, this is one of the hardest battles I've seen, a regular pounding match. I dare say the farmers will welcome this, we'll make good compost, they'll grow a bumper crop here next year!"

The grim humour seemed appropriate for the charnel house they stood in. George looked behind them, there was a regiment lying formed in square, literally dead in formation, the sad remnant of the regiment still proudly standing around their tattered flag.

George suddenly felt a searing pain in his left side, he instinctively held his stomach, the pain was excruciating and he sank to the floor struggling to breath, and all went black.........

ACTION

Sir Augustus Frazer rode off at a gallop; G troop was soon limbered and chasing him. The gun teams rode in single file of sub divisions, the wagons bounding across the fields behind them, drivers and gunners desperately holding on to their seats as they tried to remain onboard. If anyone fell off it would mean almost certain death under the hooves and wheels of the following teams.

By driving Cossack hard with his spurs, Alexander succeeded in catching up with Sir Augustus. Bal ran at full speed and kept up with his master as he rode hard. Alexander noticed in passing that the right sleeve of his jacket was torn open but that there was little blood indicating to him that it was a mere graze. Frazer turned his head to converse with Alexander as they galloped on together. Both urged their horses to close the gap between them for ease of communication, but even with their boots almost touching Sir Augustus had to shout loudly to be heard over the din of battle, which increased markedly as they approached the crest.

"I am placing your troop in the front line to protect the infantry, which is extremely hard pressed. A mass of heavy cavalry has massed across the valley and it appears that your front will be charged very soon after you arrive. The Duke's orders are very positive however, that in the event of their cavalry persevering and charging home, you will not expose your men unwisely defending the guns, for you will certainly be destroyed. Rather, retire at the last moment into the protection of the adjacent squares of infantry, when the French cavalry retire again you may then occupy your battery and reopen firing, for the cavalry will not stop to spike your guns. This order must not be disobeyed!"

Alexander nodded his understanding of the orders and they galloped on, they were now ascending the reverse slope of the ridge and would soon crest it, when Alexander hoped that the battle would be revealed to them properly.

The surgeon Hichens had also caught up and drew alongside Alexander as they crested the rise. The sound of cannon and musketry fire, shouted orders, screams and cries, became much louder, death was now very close at hand.

The smoke was now becoming very thick, indeed as they crested the ridge, little could be seen beyond a hundred yards. The smoke was acrid; it irritated the lungs, burned the throat and was accompanied by an incredible rise in temperature. The air was suffocatingly hot and still, it appeared that all the firing and smoke had produced a localised effect upon the weather; it was like standing next to the blacksmith's furnace on a hot day! The dead and dying lay strewn around, the odd horrific injury had been witnessed over the last few days but now they were plentiful, you could no longer look away, they were all around. Men with limbs shattered or completely torn away by cannonballs, decapitated or literally blown apart, horses sitting with legs smashed or standing with entrails strewn across the ground, patiently waiting for death to call. The troop made the scene even worse, for they had no time to move the injured and dead aside, the horses simply trampled over them, injuring further, cannon wheels crushing all in its path. Everyone tried to look away as the troop galloped on inflicting sickening mutilations, but they simply had to get through. Some of the men genuflected and offered a small prayer for their souls as they neared the fighting.

Strange noises penetrated their ears, a buzzing, like a swarm of bees could be heard in all directions accompanied frequently by a great crashing noise, but nothing could be seen through the smoke.

Hichens looked around continuously in total bewilderment, "My God Mercer, What is that?", then again "What is all this noise? How curious, how very curious!"

Alexander smiled but said nothing; he was too busy assessing the situation.

A great whoosh! And a rush of wind striking his face set Hichens off again.

"There, there, what on earth is it all?"

Henry Leathes took pity on the poor bewildered man.

"It is the passing of musket balls that buzz and the whoosh was that of a cannonball passing close by. It is getting a little dangerous here, indeed I would be careful of stretching your hand out, as it would most likely be ripped off, the balls are so thick!"

Robert Newland joined in, "Hichens, it is far too warm here, you are in grave danger, retire beyond the crest."

Hichens was aghast, "My place is with the troop!"

Robert disagreed, "No your place is to be out of the firing line, as Surgeon we will need you unharmed to care for those that will be injured. It is important that you are there for us, retire just beyond the ridge, the wounded will be brought to you, where they will be safer. Go now before it is too late."

Hichens turned his horse to ride back, his face told clearly that he was not happy with his orders, but all knew that Robert was right.

Sir Augustus pointed out a spot in front of two squares of darkly uniformed troops.

"There is your position, you are to protect those Brunswick squares until the cavalry come close then retire within them." He repeated.

Sir Augustus turned his horse to leave but then shouted a final order, "Be economical with your ammunition, do not waste your shots, replenishment will be difficult!"

He meant impossible.

Alexander took stock of the situation rapidly; he was only too aware that any mistakes now certainly would be fatal to some or all of his men. The responsibility was onerous but he had no time to consider this now, he could already see through odd gaps in the smoke, the French cavalry approaching in the distance.

Alexander arrived only a few moments before the troop and indicated each gun's spot. The position ran along a track way, it was slightly sunken with earthen ramparts two feet high on each side. The guns would set down on the track itself, the wheels were high enough however for the muzzles to fire over the rampart. The ground to the front fell away slowly into the shallow valley between the Allied and French ridges. Alexander could see the formed lines of French cavalry trotting up the incline, moving slowly but surely, to maintain formation.

Looking towards the still arriving G troop, he judged that the guns could deploy just before the cavalry arrived.

He became aware of the two Brunswick squares that he had been ordered to support. Cannonballs smashed into the Germans crashing right through the squares, tearing large gaps in their formation. Alexander could see the officers and sergeants shouting and pushing the soldiers to fill in the gaps that were so dangerous with the cavalry around. Mercer recognised these young lads as the same ones that had fled at the mere sound of G troop approaching them from behind on the retreat from Quatre Bras. Today they weren't fleeing, these brave lads stood, despite the punishment they were receiving. They had never experienced anything like this; indeed their faces betrayed that they were only coping by becoming mere shells, standing like the living dead with little understanding of what went on around them, just like so many skittles waiting to be bowled over.

Alexander quickly decided that these young men would only stand if he helped to protect them, but he felt that the sight of his gunners running from their cannon into their squares would be misunderstood. They were likely to think they were fleeing the cavalry and such a sight could tip the balance against them standing any longer, there was a grave danger that they would run too. Alexander swiftly came to the conclusion that he would have to disobey orders again! His officers and men knew nothing of the order to retire if attacked and he decided to say nothing. He knew that this may put his men at great risk, but he must try, and hang the consequences!

The first gun of Henry Leathes' division arrived and unlimbered rapidly; the men were oblivious to the danger in their front but still worked at top speed, just like in practice. Seconds behind, each gun arrived to be unlimbered in turn; the teams then led off to the rear a little.

Alexander was nervous, he watched them unlimber methodically and quickly, but it still seemed an eternity as he glanced at the French cavalry, now only one hundred yards away.

Alexander bellowed out the order "Load Canister", the

ammunition was dug out of the ready use lockers on the wagons and rammed home on top of the cannonballs already in the barrels, 'double shotting' it was called, particularly devastating at extremely close range. The touchhole was primed and finally gun number one stood ready to fire, the others would be ready soon, but would it be soon enough?

The lines consisted of hundreds of French Cuirassiers with Horse Grenadiers further behind, trotting slowly up the incline on their big horses; they moved at barely more than a walk as the horses carried a great weight with these cavalrymen wearing their gleaming body armour back and front. As the troop was set just below the line of the ridge, it was likely that the Frenchmen had no warning of the cannon facing them.

Alexander bit his lip as he fought the urge to order the guns to fire, he wanted the first discharge to really devastate them, and he had to wait until the horsemen neared the top of the incline. Alexander needed the target to be as large as possible and he cared little if the balls struck either horse or rider, either negated their potential as cavalry.

The Cuirassiers held their swords high and shouted "Vive le Empereur", it was meant to strike fear into the enemy and bolster their own morale. As comrades together they would conquer, that was the message.

As the French horsemen reached the top of the rise they came into view of the Brunswickers. A desultory fire was brought on from the squares, but it was ragged and ill aimed, indeed Alexander knew that the signs of hesitation and nervousness in the faces of these young Germans would not be missed by these experienced French campaigners.

Finally the moment had arrived, the leading files of cavalry were now aware of G troop's presence and he was pleased to see that it had caused some hesitation in the French ranks. Still they came on as the ranks behind pushed the front files, but the front rankers were understandably less keen to proceed as they would bear the fire from the cannon's mouth. Alexander counted himself down; they were less than fifty yards away, three, two, one, now!

He stood up in the saddle and drew a deep breath then bellowed the eagerly awaited order.

"Fire"

The slow match was applied and the first nine-pounder cannon roared, belching flame and smoke. The numerous balls splayed out as they left the muzzle, tearing into the flesh of horse and human. The body armour clanged as the balls struck them and passed right through, they were not designed to protect them from cannon fire!

The shrieks of both injured men and horses was horrible, the confusion in the front rank was palpable as the riders behind tried to negotiate past the injured and dead blocking their way. The horses were unhappy at treading on their fellow steeds and their former masters lying on the ground, the advance became bogged down.

Just as the confusion began to subside and the advance could be resumed, number two gun discharged its container of death. Each gun in turn exploded into life, each one causing further death and injury and increasing the confusion exponentially.

Alexander watched number one gun of John Bretton's division as they completed loading again, they would be next to fire. He watched as John Butterworth used the ramrod to pack down the canister and explosive charge. The Griffith's brothers awaited him finishing and as he withdrew the rod and stepped back, James removed his leather covered thumb from the touchhole and inserted the metal spike. He felt the point drive through the waxed paper releasing some of the powder and inserted the quick match. Removing the pricker, he covered the vent again with his fingerstall to avoid premature firing and indicated to his brother Richard that all was ready. Richard approached with the slow match and James removed his finger and stood back, the burning tip of the match was applied at arms length to the touchhole. As he did so many of the team took a further step away from the gun, some placed fingers in their ears to save their eardrums, their heads turned away from the explosion. The taper ignited the quick match which fizzled into life; the explosion was less than a second away. Alexander watched all this blithely awaiting their fire to observe its effect.

Suddenly, Alexander spotted movement in the corner of his eye, this unexpected manoeuvre made him home in, something wasn't right. He realised that this flicker across his eyes was John Butterworth, the sponge man. John had taken a step backwards away from the cannon's mouth as the match was applied, but he had stepped back onto a large stone, he had lost his balance and began to fall. Alexander realised the danger, but much too late, John's arms extended instinctively to break his fall and at that precise moment the cannon roared into life. John's torso landed on the ground in front of the cannon and all awaited the smoke clearing to see what had happened. As the black fog cleared slowly, the form of Butterworth's body became clear lying across the mouth of the cannon. There was movement indicating that he was still alive, thank God! Through the haze he could be seen raising himself from the ground and lifted his head. As the last of the smoke cleared, John's ashen face bespattered with blood, raised pathetically on two stumps, came fully into view; his two arms had been torn away by the blast!

Alexander was aware of the deathly stare in his eyes as

John looked directly at him, but he was still troubled by the French, who unbelievably still sought to reach them. He had no time to give support to those that fell now; he pulled his gaze away from Butterworth guiltily to observe the troop continue firing.

John Bretton ordered the men to reload again and Thomas Martin was handed a spare ramrod and told to take Butterworth's place.

"We must keep firing or they will overrun us all!" John Bretton shouted to drive his shocked team back into action. John Butterworth was such a mainstay of the troop, a noisy, loud mouthed, hard drinking, rabble-rouser; they would miss his humour and strength of character. Everybody understood the urgency of the moment and returned to their duties but with noticeably less verve.

At first Alexander had noted a small amount of hesitation in the French to proceed nearer the guns; soon he observed that the front rankers that remained were filing back to the rear along the flanks of the attacking cavalry. Those in the centre of the formation now found any direction to escape the deadly firing. There was little room in the dense, tightly crammed mass of horsemen to turn the horses in any direction. They began to fight to get out of the way of the next discharge from the guns. They beat at each other with the hilt of their swords, some fired erratically with their carbines, the formation became a complete mob, all fighting for their own escape route to evade death. The rear ranks that had not suffered and were little aware of the carnage before them still drove those in front onwards.

Some were so desperate to escape and seeing no other route available, they galloped hell for leather towards the guns before they could reload. These men reached the cannon successfully, but had no idea of attacking the gunners, their only raison d'être was to escape with their lives. They rode past the guns to the relative safety behind them and then rode to right or left, braving the fire of the squares and derisory insults as they searched for a point where they could safely retreat into the valley and rejoin their colleagues.

Eventually, the mass disintegrated, the rear eased away having become aware of the destruction, allowing all to retire out of sight of the guns. The mass fled back down the slope, but Alexander fully expected them to try again. Indeed Alexander could see that they had only retired far enough down the slope to reform without interruption from the guns, they were no more than one hundred yards away; indeed the plumes on their helmets could still be observed by the men, they knew they would be back to try again!

There was now time to tend to the wounded and Alexander's eyes sought for John Butterworth, but he was not to be seen. A line of deep red blood leading to the rear, like the trail of a giant red snail, told a story. 'Tuppence' had dragged himself unaided to the rear on his bleeding stumps to seek help from the surgeons.

The guns were reloaded and they then waited patiently for the return of the cavalry. Whilst the French cavalry reformed, their artillery fired from the opposite ridge to weaken the defences. The cannonballs rained down, thudding into the earthen mound to their front, or bounding over the top to smash into the infantry squares beyond, where they maimed a number of men with each strike. The firing was so intense that the men and horses in the battery would have been destroyed if not for the protection of the bank. Luckily little was hit, however one cannonball smashed through the hindquarters of John Bretton's favourite horse, Seth. Man and horse collapsed in a heap, no one rightly knowing who had been hit in the confusion. The two Griffith's lads ran over and extricated John's leg that was trapped under the body of Seth. John was pulled clear and stood dusting himself down, he would just have a few bruises to show for the fall. He pulled out his pistol and holding it to Seth's head he pulled the trigger, Seth sank to the earth. John wiped a tear from his eye then called for his spare, Nancy. He remounted and resumed his duties.

Some of the balls passed overhead towards the Brunswickers, the infantry were in four ranks deep and tightly packed, and so they never just struck one man. Alexander wondered at the stoicism of these infantry that stood and took such punishment, he watched the sergeants once again pushing the men into the gaps caused by the artillery.

The area around the infantry was particularly unsavoury; The squares were surrounded by the carcasses of both men and horses, later cavalry attacks were largely put off by the sights of such carnage, the unmistakable smell of death and the veritable rivulets of blood flowing down the slope. Within the squares was certainly no better, the centre of the hollow formation was filled with the horribly mutilated wounded, combined with the stench of blood and faeces, as no one dared to leave the safety of the square to relieve their natural body functions. Despite these awful sights, Alexander was glad to see that even the nervy Brunswickers were now standing well, the defeat of the cavalry had lifted their spirits.

Whilst the French reorganised, they sent forward a number of skirmishers, these individual horsemen trotted up to within twenty yards of the battery where they halted and took very careful aim with their short-barrelled muskets called carbines, which they carried in a pouch on their saddles. This fire was difficult to ignore, carbines were notoriously inaccurate weapons but at this range, they could hardly miss. The men felt helpless against them, they could not retaliate with cannon fire against such individual targets, it would be a waste of valuable ammunition that they might desperately need later. Alexander could see that this firing unnerved the men far more than anything else; they did not like simply standing there whilst someone took pot shots at them. They were moving back into cover and morale was clearly suffering. It was time for a 'Grand Gesture', thought Alexander.

Alexander urged Cossack forward, up onto the bank and he started riding slowly back and fore across the front of the battery. He feigned a look of complete composure and sought to show contempt for these cavalrymen. A number of skirmishers took up the challenge and hurriedly released shots after him, but miraculously none struck. Alexander swore at them, goading them with cries of 'Cochin'.

Robert Newland shouted "Captain Mercer, come down for you will surely be killed."

Alexander gave Robert a stare denoting total contempt for his daring to suggest such a thing, "I do not plan to hand over command of the troop yet Mr Newland."

This made Alexander even more determined to maintain this act of bravado, despite becoming aware of a particular Cuirassier that had reloaded and was taking a good long aim. The Frenchman sat astride his fine horse no further than twenty yards from Alexander; he was a battle-hardened veteran judging by the scarred cheek and his weather beaten features. At this distance, Alexander could clearly see this old campaigner's blonde hair and fine drooping moustache, his piercing grey eyes and knowing grin, clearly he aimed to make Alexander his!

He continued to ride slowly along the face of the battery, each time that he turned at the end to return he was aware of the carbine still fixed upon him. The Cuirassier took an age, he was determined that this shot would finish the impudent artillery officer. He carefully regulated his breathing and controlled his horse with his legs to maintain its perfect stillness. Up and down he trailed Alexander, determined to pull the trigger at the perfect moment.

Alexander struggled with himself to deny any show of concern over this accursed Cuirassier. He was acutely aware of the weapon continually following his movements and waited for the inevitable shot. As he turned again to face his foe, he became aware that the Frenchman's finger seemed to be tightening on the trigger, the small puff of smoke registered in his brain at the same time that his ears had picked up the buzz of the musket ball's flight. He fought manfully with his body's automatic flinch against the danger, but knew that although he had damped down the reaction, he could not hide it completely. A deep sullen groan behind him informed Alexander that the ball intended for him had missed, but had struck home with somebody else. He glanced over his right shoulder instinctively to see the body of Driver John Miller slump to the floor. The ball had struck the poor man right between the eyes, he was dead well before his body hit the ground and soon ceased its death twitches. Alexander secretly breathed easier and continued his ride. He had made his point and he slowly led Cossack back to his normal position in the rear of the troop.

Sergeant John Nisbitt had been watching the horsemen very closely for the moment that they advanced again. He regularly popped his head above the earthen rampart to sneak a view but lowered it very quickly again before a cannonball removed it! The lads jested with him as only soldiers can.

"Sergeant, can I have your pay book if you catch one?"

"A little more to your left Sergeant, then it's bound to get you."

"A shilling that the next ball gets him."

"I hope not, bugger owes me five shillings!"

The officers let them carry on, the humour was a release for their pent up tension.

Nisbitt was aware of the dangers of lifting his head above the embankment, even though the chances of a hit were poor as they were certainly not aimed at him, it was just that so many were coming so thickly, that one might just knock it off.

He braced himself, tried to erase thoughts of impending death and forced his muscles to push his legs upwards, to stand and edge his head over the top. As he did so he was met by the sight of the cavalrymen commencing a deliberate trot back up the slope towards them.

He attempted to shout a warning, but his throat was too dry from nerves, he swallowed and tried again, he was pleased to hear a loud roar emerge.

"They're coming again!"

Everyone stood to the guns and waited for the order to fire. Alexander watched as the riders slowly rose into view. Still he held the order, Henry Leathes looked at him silently asking if it were not time. Alexander saw Henry's look but continued to wait, now their horses were coming into view, they were no more than fifty yards away. The first volley must stop them; they would have precious little time to reload before they were upon the gunners. The French were approaching a little more warily, aware of the reception awaiting them, and keenly aware that every second's delay brought them nearer the mouths of the cannon where the destruction caused would be horrendous. As they neared, Alexander could see that some in the front ranks were becoming distinctly nervous, unhappy to lead on to the guns; their formation was already breaking down.

Glancing to the rear for a second, he noted that the

Brunswickers were now more confident, holding their fire until the cavalry neared to maximise its effect. He also spotted John Bretton leading Nancy to the rear of the troop, blood streaming from a wound in her neck, obviously caused by a musket ball.

He returned his gaze to the front; they were no more than forty yards away. Now was the time, "Fire" he bellowed and the six cannon burst into life almost in unison. The barrage of shot striking the cavalry was completely devastating to the front ranks again. Both horses and men crashed to the floor screaming in agony, those following on behind flinched from the carnage. The horses refused to trample over the remains of men and horses blocking their way forward. As the gunners reloaded, the French cavalry tried to forge ahead but were brought up hard against the wall of their fallen compatriots.

Alexander continually scanned the view to the wings of the troop to guard against surprise attacks, whilst the guns dealt with the threat before them, but nothing seemed untoward. His gaze eventually returned to the front, he watched as his men loaded and fired their guns incessantly, they were clearly tiring, men wiped their brows of sweat, some had discarded their tight blue jackets to breathe easier or had undone shirt buttons to ease cooling. Their mouths hung open, parched and dry, leathery tongues mechanically ran over parched lips in a vain effort to relieve the desperate need for liquid. Their canteens had been drained hours before and there was no stream or well at hand to quench their nagging thirst. They forced themselves to keep going, despite their fatigue, more than aware that any slackening of the firing would let the French cavalry reach them, which would mean almost certain death to all.

The guns blazed away for a few minutes longer before

the Frenchmen admitted defeat and retired into the valley again out of sight of the guns that had caused such carnage.

The troop knew that the respite would be short as the French rallied and prepared for a further attack. In the lull, the men completed loading, then stood back from the guns gasping for breath, arching their backs in an attempt to relieve their aches.

John Bretton rode up to Alexander to discuss the situation, he was now riding a troop horse, his third horse of the day. Their words had to be shouted to be heard above the din of battle.

"Do you think they will try again, Alexander?"

"Undoubtedly" Alexander replied, "This is obviously an important point to them."

As they continued to discuss the day, their horses nuzzled into each other. John's troop horse stood at right angles to Cossack and laid its head lazily on Cossack's neck. The horse's head lay on his thigh and Alexander bent forward to place his elbow on the horse's head, resting his weary head by cupping his chin in his hand. This had the added benefit of bringing his head nearer to John, enabling him to converse better over the tumult. The horse stood nonchalantly, totally unmoved by Alexander's use of its head for an armrest. All were fatigued, using mutual support to remain on their feet, rather than collapse from exhaustion.

"Are we winning?" asked John.

"I honestly have no idea what is happening beyond this gloomy cloud of gun smoke that lies about us. We must continue to fight here until we receive new orders."

"What time is it?" John enquired.

Alexander peered at his fob watch, "Near Six o'clock I believe."

John looked strained, "How much longer must we endure this?"

Alexander had no time to answer; there was a great whoosh of noise, a violent wind attended by a strong pressure wave, a feeling of complete terror, a drenching in deep red blood that filled his mouth and nose. Alexander slumped onto Cossack's neck, completely disorientated and dazed. Initially he thought he must be dying and was only vaguely aware of concerned voices and helping hands, righting him on Cossack's back. He evacuated the blood from his mouth and nose, it smelt and tasted appallingly, he was still unsure of the source of all this blood, he must have been seriously wounded.

Once upright, his ears slowly ceased ringing, he collected his thoughts and realised that there was no pain, it wasn't him that was hit, thank God, and then it dawned on him.

"Oh God, Not John!"

"It's all right Alexander, I'm all right but we thought that you had been cut in half!" came the comforting reply from John Bretton. John's smile beamed through a face also drenched in blood as he stood on the ground alongside Cossack.

"What happened?" Alexander asked groggily.

"A cannonball, smashed fully into the head of my horse, the one you were resting upon. The ball did not touch you at all and left Cossack unscathed. How it did not touch anyone apart from the horse is astonishing, it's a miracle!"

Alexander smiled, "Perhaps we are not meant to die today!"

John laughed, "I trust you are right!"

THE REAR

The sleepy quiet hollow of Waterloo village was transformed instantly with the first discharge of cannon. It was the starting gun for a race involving all the great mass of various wagons belonging to the Commissariat and the camp followers, setting out on the Brussels road again, to get further away from the fighting. Horses were reharnessed, passengers clambered aboard and soon all were in motion. The road through the wood was narrow, congestion grew rapidly and within minutes there was a virtual logjam of wagons and nothing moved. It would take hours to clear the mess and there was nobody prepared to do it. Everyone was looking out for themselves, frustration led to a number of brawls breaking out.

Eventually Wellington's aides were ordered to sort out the problem, they eventually had the road cleared of abandoned vehicles and things started moving along again slowly as a steady pace away from the fighting was better than being jammed solid.

Occasionally all the jolting on the cobbled roads in these unsprung wagons was too much to bear for some of the badly wounded. They would slip away quietly, but the second it was noticed that they had passed on, indeed sometimes before they exhaled their final breath, they were tumbled bodily from the wagons into the ditches running alongside the road, the space was needed for those still alive. As the wagons rolled on, the sound of cannon fire grew to a tremendous continuous roar. Ned was struck by the number of small groups of soldiers of all allied nations camping out in the woods, what were they doing there? Shirking the fight he guessed.

Every so often riders would fly past shouting that the day was lost and that the French were on their way, spreading fear and consternation throughout the convoy. At one time a whole regiment of Belgian cavalry on beautiful thoroughbred horses passed at a rush, fleeing the fighting. Someone said that they were all Belgian gentry who owned their own horses and were not prepared to lose them in battle! They were roundly booed as they passed.

Ned's head ached, the constant violent jostling of the wagon wore him down and eventually despite the distant sounds of battle he fell fast asleep.

George Simmons came round slowly to find his face embedded in the soft mud where he struggled to breathe, his chest and abdomen were seared by a terrible pain unlike anything he had ever known, he knew that his luck had just run out, he had been hit.

Daniel Kelly and Thomas Treacy came to him and taking hold of his arms at the shoulders roughly raised him up.

"Come on Mister Simmons Sir, let's be having you to Mister Burke" Kelly shouted.

George knew little of what was going on, he was simply aware of the terrible pain and his ardent desire that these men would let him be. They carried him along however, holding him up by the arms, as he had no power over his legs, which just dragged along the ground.

It seemed an eternity to George, but was probably ten minutes or so, before they arrived at the farmhouse of Mont St Jean, which had been turned into a temporary hospital. George was not aware of much he passed, nor cared about anything he saw as he stared at the ground all the way. However, the lack of its two arms made him take notice of one particular corpse, the face showing extreme pain even in death. He had obviously been a horse artilleryman that had just failed to crawl to the farm unaided on his stumps and had bled to death, the sickly pallor of the artilleryman made him more acutely aware of his own predicament. George was not to know that this was the mortal remains of Gunner John Butterworth of G troop.

Many of the surgeons had set up at the farmhouse of Mont St. Jean some hundred yards behind the ridge. It was ideal as a safe and central point for the wounded and not too far from the front line.

The few tables in the house were instantly turned into operating tables; the others used planks laid across barrels as makeshift tables.

Mr Robson, the Assistant surgeon proceeded to examine George, he described his findings as he went. "George, the ball has entered your left side breaking at least two ribs. I cannot tell if it has caused any serious injury within your chest but your lungs appear undamaged, your initial breathing problem is caused by the rib injury being very painful."

He held out little hope for him and felt that George should understand his situation, particularly as he was a dear friend.

George was not really interested in this dialogue, only one question needed answering, "Is it a fatal wound, James?"

James answered very seriously, "I pray that no major damage has occurred internally, but it is very serious George, with our best efforts I hope that the answer is no."

James continued to examine his chest. "There is no exit wound George, your chest on the right side is very swollen." He prodded around this swelling, the pain was excruciating, but as a soldier he was trained not to cry out, George fought the impulse to groan.

"There it is" James announced proudly, his fingers had discovered a hard round object between the ribs, it was the musket ball, he would have to remove it to avoid infection gaining hold.

James fetched one of his razor sharp scalpels and warned George that he would need to extract the ball immediately. He handed George a leather thong, "Here bite on this; it will help you bear the discomfort."

Sergeant Fairfoot appeared alongside him, he had been wounded in his arm again and had been forced to retire; he held George's head throughout the operation to support him.

James made a very deep incision directly below his right pap then pushed his first finger deep into his chest to locate the ball. The pain was almost unbearable for George, who bit hard on the leather strap trying manfully to stifle a cry of pain. James' finger felt the hardness of the musket ball lodged between the ribs. He expanded the incision, allowing him to plunge both his thumb and forefinger into his chest to grasp the ball. He had to use quite a lot of force to dislodge it from its new home. He pulled it out with an air of exultation, "There's the little bugger! And I didn't have to break any ribs George."

George simply collapsed back onto the table and thanked God it was over, he didn't think he could have borne the pain for much longer.

During the operation it became clear that occasional cannonballs were striking the walls of the farmhouse. The wounded became agitated, as it was believed that the French must be approaching and they had no wish to be prisoners or worse. Robert Fairfoot indicated that as soon as the surgeon had finished, he would get a horse and take George to Brussels for safety.

George heard in the distance a voice almost whispering but perfectly audible to him, "What is the use of treating him, he cannot live the night, he is better where he is than to die on horseback." George knew that they were talking about him.

To ease the swelling and despite the already large loss of blood, it was normal practise to bleed patients in the belief that this would ease their sufferings. James held a bleeding cup to George's arm and drained off a quart of blood leaving him feeling very faint. James then applied what dressings he had to the wounds and left him, he had plenty more patients coming in.

James Burke, the Surgeon surveyed the scene in the hospital. There were already hundreds of injured, many had severe injuries from musket balls which caused terrible damage to bone and tissue. They shattered bone into a myriad pieces and the only effective answer to this was immediate amputation. Mr Burke indicated those that were to receive his personal attention for amputation and orderlies held them down whilst he cut the limb away as speedily as possible.

The British surgeons had learned from their colleagues in the Navy that immediate amputation of horribly damaged limbs greatly improved the chances of ultimate survival. The patient was still in shock, which caused the body's blood pressure to drop, reducing the loss of blood during the operation and the body naturally numbed the pain. The surgeon's assistants gave them what brandy or gin they had to deaden the pain further, then he started. His razor sharp blade swiftly cut the flesh down to the bone, his assistants watched carefully to ensure their fingers did not get in the way!

The three cut method was now the modern way of amputating limbs. The first cut was made one inch above the top of the wound as it had been found that directly after injury the area up to two inches above the wound was numb and the muscles were relaxed. The initial cut severed the several layers of skin and nerve endings, the second was through the muscle but angled further up into the tissue above the wound and the third angled even further up clearing right through to the bone. The flesh was by this method cut in an inverse cone shape, allowing the bone to be cut higher up than the skin had been cut. Then the saw, which bit into the bone and the marrow. Ensuring the bone was cut further up than the flesh guaranteed that it did not protrude the stump. Pulling the flap of skin remaining into the centre and sewing up tightly completed the operation. The procedure took minutes and felt like a lifetime to those being cut, but it was the only way known to avoid gangrene.

They at least now had better than a fifty fifty chance of survival and with the bone not pressing on the skin flap, the wound healed quickly and allowed a wooden limb to be attached later. The 'old school' surgeons, who still cut straight across the limb found that the skin contracted and pulled painfully at the stump, the bone grinding on the skin flap made a wooden stump extremely painful, often impossible to use.

Even Lord Nelson, for all his greatness had suffered from this very cause. When his right arm had been amputated above the elbow, the ship's surgeon had simply cut straight across. Nelson's stump had been agony for many months as the bone pressed hard on the stitching; indeed it was so bad at one time that Nelson had thought that his naval career was over. What consequences would have ensued if he had not been fit to face the combined Franco Spanish Fleet at Trafalgar?

The trick was to recognise the wounded limb that was damaged too badly to be saved or that indicated a high chance of becoming infected. The automatic removal of all damaged limbs was no longer in favour in medical circles, as many had previously lost limbs that could have been saved. The main debate was whether to amputate immediately or later when the initial shock was past, as this was thought to reduce their ability to survive the operation in some circles.

The 'do it immediately' school had largely won the argument in France and Britain but the German and Austrian doctors still preferred the old methods. Indeed Doctor Larrey of the French Imperial Guard had published findings to show that after the battle of Austerlitz, of eight hundred immediate amputees he logged, over seven hundred and fifty survived, an outstanding result, the wait and see method saved only one in twenty!

The men were to bear the pain without noise as a point of honour. Alongside George, Mr Burke was working on the soldiers still being brought in. A dragoon was having his arm amputated below the elbow; he was a well-worn old hand who held the damaged arm with his good one to steady it for the surgeon. He lay chewing a wad of tobacco showing no concern throughout the operation. Nearby lay a Frenchman on another table having his shoulder probed for a ball, he was howling with the pain. This annoyed the dragoon intensely and as soon as his arm was severed he took it by the wrist and struck the Frenchman a smart blow across his backside with the bloody end.

"Here" he said, "Stuff that down your throat, and stop your damned bellowing!"

George rested for a few minutes until Robert Fairfoot returned; he had found a couple of horses and was determined to move him away from danger.

"Come on Sir, we must be leaving immediately." He prompted.

George hardly listened, he had other priorities, "Just shut that man up will you!" he said indicating towards a Brunswick infantry sergeant who was clearly dying from a terrible wound to his abdomen and was letting everyone else know with his cries and groans.

Somebody interrupted, "George, do not shout at the poor fellow so, we shall soon all be happy, we have behaved like Englishmen!"

George turned to see a fellow Lieutenant of Rifles, Elliott Johnston, who was also wounded, he hadn't noticed him before. The second horse was for him and with the aid of a wounded Lifeguard, Robert managed to raise them both onto the horses and lead them onto the road for Brussels, George was near fainting from the pain. As they rode off they passed a huge pile of recently amputated limbs standing higher than the window of the farm.

They had not proceeded twenty yards when a stray cannonball bounded by, George heard a sickening sound, he had heard it before, it was the unmistakable sound of a body being smashed by a cannonball. Looking around he saw the already lifeless body of Elliott lying on the ground, the ball had nearly cut him in two. He turned away from the terrible sight, desperately hoping that this was the last of such scenes that he would witness, he had seen enough death and suffering this day, more than he would care to have observed in a lifetime.

Robert Fairfoot led the horse on and soon the scenes of destruction were left behind, except for the odd corpse lying in the roadside ditch along the way obviously thrown from the passing carts. They were already stripped naked for their clothes and valuables by some unseen hand.

One of the first to arrive in Brussels late that morning was Juana; she worried for her 'Enrique' as she lovingly called Harry. She was continuously accosted for news as she rode through the streets, for the sullen sound of the cannon was clearly to be heard from the City walls, but she knew nothing herself and could not offer any words of hope to ease their anguish.

News had started to filter in that the English were defeated and any British families in Brussels were advised to seek safety by moving further off to Ghent. Soon the gentry of all nations resident at Brussels were using any available means of transport to escape the City; Juana was persuaded to go along with this tide and fled with her servant.

Arriving at Ghent late at night there were no rooms available but a kindly soul introduced her to the City Governor's family who took her in. She was thankful for their kindness but could not rest, constantly seeking any news that arrived. She sat at her window all night long watching for new arrivals, which she would call to for news. No good news arrived and she feared for her man.

As darkness fell, the cart of wounded finally arrived at Brussels, Ned recognised the neighbourhood they passed through and bid the others adieu, making directly for his previous quarters but unfortunately found them already occupied. He felt faint, but struggled on to the Place Royale where he had set out from what seemed like a lifetime ago, although it was actually a mere sixty hours before. The square had been strewn with straw as bedding and to soak up the profuse amounts of blood, it was already filling up rapidly with the wounded of all nations. The injured were laid out as they arrived in neat rows to ensure the maximum possible were fitted in, there were already many hundreds.

An alarm suddenly went up that the French were actually at the gates unchallenged and were entering the City. Panic ensued; the scene became one of utter bedlam with all those still able to walk or crawl getting up to move on. However, the panic died down just as quickly as it had set in, once it became obvious that the thousands of Frenchmen walking in were unarmed prisoners escorted by a number of Scots Greys, not a conquering horde.

Ned lay down again and ate his remaining food supplies, a small scrap of bread and half a canteen of wine. He watched with admiration as the women that had remained in the City, helped to tend the injured. Many were ladies of a genteel nature who had to screw up all their courage to work around such appalling injuries; they had never been subjected to such awful sights before. He watched them tending the sick of all nations including Frenchmen without favour, many tearing up their own petticoats to provide clean dressings for the wounds. Local doctors attended to help treat the injured as the army doctors were clearly overwhelmed; indeed all that could be done was done.

Suddenly Ned recognised a fellow Rifleman sitting against a wall, holding a bandaged head. It was Tom Plunket, "Are you all right Tom?"

Tom looked up and smiled in recognition, "Aye, Ned, just a flesh wound."

He then commenced to tell his story as only Tom could.

"The last ting I remember is someone calling out 'Watch out'" he started.

"We was foighting just behoind the chateau, stopping Johnny Frenchman surrounding it. Oi looked up as a French light infantryman stood a mere ten feet away and took aim with his musket. My eyes grew like saucers as the fear grasped me, my sight zoomed in on the fingers of the Frenchman as he squeezed the trigger, I tried to roll away as I heard the sound of the hammer dropping and the musket pop suddenly seemed very distant. A great pain across my forehead and everything went black."

Tom continued "Sergeant Sugden told me the rest of the story afterwards"; he then proceeded to recount the circumstances, as he understood them.

"The news that oi was hit froze the battalion, as I am their figurehead and talisman, they feared their luck was changing against them! They wondered if they would all die in this God forsaken battle!"

He pause momentarily then continued, "After the French retoired, Sergeant Sugden noticed movement amongst the bodies lying on the field, someone groaned. The hole in the sole of moi boot told Sugden all he needed to know. It was me, oi was aloive, and he rushed up and turned me over. Moi face was a mass of blood and gore, but a drop of water from his canteen showed him that it was only a light wound."

" 'You lucky sod! We taught you were dead for sure' Sugden said. Oi was not quite so convinced that I was alright." He held his forehead, which throbbed violently.

"Sugden explained to me that the musket ball had grazed moi head, it's made a furrow across moi brow and he could see to de bone, but oi'll live."

"The others crowded round, really pleased that I had survived. Sergeant Sugden said, 'I'm pleased you are all right Tom, but get yourself to the farm beyond the ridge where the surgeon will attend to you."

Tom had not argued, "oi had no foight left in me today! They patched me up den sent me on my way here."

Tom was as usual full of himself and he had clearly started embroidering his story into one he could relate for years to come to anyone willing to stand him a drink for the privilege, but Ned was pleased to have him as a friend; they would care for each other now.

George Simmons bore the twelve-mile journey from Mont St Jean to Brussels with as much stoicism as he could muster. With every step of the horse, the movement drove the broken ends of his ribs into the flesh turning it into jelly; the pain now grew very intense as the initial shock wore off. Blood oozed out of the wound at every step and George wondered if there was any blood left, he felt weak and faint; the journey seemed to go on for an eternity.

Finally with huge relief they arrived in Brussels and Fairfoot managed to guide George back to his former billet with the Overmars. They took him to his old bed and immediately summoned a physician and a nurse to give him round the clock treatment. All that could be done would be, Robert could stay with him to recover as well.

Mr Overmars looked on George with great pity, all the news from the front was bad and he expected the French at any time, he just hoped that they would leave George to die in peace.

PRUSSIANS

Alexander regained his composure on Cossack's back whilst John Bretton took his fourth horse of the day. Their countenances were now only slightly besmirched in blood since their linen handkerchiefs had been sacrificed to the cause.

As Alexander finished wiping his face, a horseman arrived alongside him; it was Sir George Wood who commanded all of the British artillery in Belgium.

"Damn it Mercer, you have hot work of it here!"

"Yes Sir, pretty hot".

Alexander was pleased by his recognition, but before he could reply further, he spotted the French cavalry climbing up the slope for a third time.

As he passed, he shouted "There they are again; you must excuse me Sir George."

He spurred Cossack forward and ordered the troop to prepare to fire. Alexander watched incredulously at the unbelievable folly of the Frenchmen. They had reformed and slowly walked up the slope again, picking their way between the corpses of their fallen comrades. Alexander admired their bravery, but it was sheer madness, how could they hope to succeed? Both sides were now extremely fatigued but the odds were stacked hopelessly against the cavalrymen. As before, at forty yards the order to fire was given and the cannon spewed out death and destruction again. Dozens more fell with each shot, men and horses crashing to the ground screaming from horrific injuries. The carnage was indescribable, a veritable charnel house, but still they attempted to form up and fill the gaps blasted through them by the cannonballs.

Alexander was now intoxicated with the battle, his cannon firing away, successfully preventing the French cavalry from achieving their victory elated him. With each successful discharge taking its toll on the intrepid cavalrymen, his cool demeanour broke and he shouted with great glee, strong encouragement to his flagging troop.

"Beautiful, beautiful!" he roared, raising his right arm and flailing it about in celebration.

Suddenly, someone grasped his raised arm tightly from behind, Alexander became aware of a shout, "Take care or you'll strike the Duke!"

The Duke of Wellington himself appeared from behind Alexander's right side, riding directly across the front of the troop. The Duke was immediately recognisable by his huge 'beak'; he rode across the guns chased by a small group of aides, the depleted remains of his 'family'. Alexander hastily bellowed out the order for the troop to "Cease Firing", he anxiously turned to ensure that all the guns had heard, as he could not bear the thought of his troop striking his Lordship! The men stopped their actions and bent forward catching their breath, they were completely drained, caring little for the cause of the order to halt, simply grateful for the opportunity to catch their breath and recruit their strength.

A few with an ounce of energy left raised their heavy heads to take stock, to be rewarded by the sight of their great leader. There was no love for the Duke, but they respected him and knew that he had their interests at heart; he spared them as a valuable asset, unlike Napoleon who thought little about the loss of hundreds of thousands. His presence acted like a tonic, the words from Bombardier Thomas Masterson recharged their strength like a bolt of electricity.

"Look to your fronts lads, 'tis old hooky!"

The men's heads raised, slumped bodies straightened, dull eyes brightened, cheering rang out; the man himself was with them!

The Duke of Wellington continued to gallop across the face of the battery, seemingly oblivious to the cheers of the men or to the inherent danger from the French cavalry still picking their way towards the guns only yards away. He simply stared ahead, eyes fixed on his goal, his body automatically imparting his wishes to his fine steed Copenhagen, whilst his mind remained firmly focussed upon the task before him.

Within a few moments, the Duke and his entourage had cleared the face of the guns and disappeared beyond the horizon to the right. The French cavalry were still there plodding forward again, buoyed slightly by the inexplicable silence of the accursed guns.

The order to resume firing given, the guns roared into life again decimating the front ranks of the cavalry that had neared during the short lull. The shock of the renewed fire and the devastation caused forced the Frenchmen to halt. Moments earlier, a glimmer of hope had arisen, thoughts of success had been rekindled, perhaps the guns were bereft of ammunition? Now, surprise at the renewed carnage, linked to thoughts that the British artillery was toying with them, allowing them to advance to point blank range before vomiting forth their missiles of death, led them to reconsider their position. Their confidence was shattered, slowly the futility of the attack seemed to dawn upon them and the advance slowed to a crawl, then stopped. They simply stood there unable to advance and unwilling to admit defeat and retire.

The gunners continued to prime and fire as quickly as they could, their knees buckled from exhaustion and the sweat flowed from their brows, but they would not let up until the French admitted failure. They maintained their impassive line for a further minute or two, suffering terribly from each further cannon shot, the range was virtually point blank and they could hardly miss them. Then, eventually bowing to the inevitable, they turned away and very slowly walked back down the slope, out of the line of fire, this time however, it was obvious to all on both sides that they would not try again.

Robert Newland approached Alexander, "Ammunition is becoming scarce and our reserve limbers are all but empty, permission to retire and seek additional supplies, Sir?"

Alexander knew that he was right; he was grateful for the reminder and nodded his approval silently. Newland eagerly spurred his horse to the rear.

The guns fell silent and the men sank to their knees from complete exhaustion. They desperately craved water to quench their oppressive thirst, knowing that there were no means of obtaining it. Alexander and the other officers also drew breath but remained vigilant, for the battle continued to rage all around and other dangers were sure to emerge.

Whilst they gathered their strength, it became obvious that the presence of the Duke had been occasioned by something important. From their position, nothing could be seen, the thick impenetrable smoke still hung to their front, obscuring all beyond a hundred yards away. Vague feelings that something was afoot was confirmed when a line of

British and Brunswick infantry, some of whom had been the frightened lads they had protected earlier, now marched forward full of determination, bayonets fixed against some unseen foe. The line divided as it passed the battery, reforming in front of the guns and continuing on down the slope to disappear into the smoke in the valley below.

Henry Leathes approached Alexander, "Any idea what is happening?"

Alexander was just as perplexed, "They are probably sent to aid the defence of the chateau," he guessed.

John Bretton pointed to the front, "The smoke is clearing, you can make out the batteries on the opposite rise and large infantry formations advancing."

Alexander realised that without a smoke screen to hide them, the battery would make an enticing target for the French gunners. Indeed, shortly afterwards cannonballs started to bound over the ridge again as the French sought to get their range. Alexander pointed out the advancing infantry. "That is your new target, gentlemen, we must attempt to destroy their infantry."

The men received the order to resume firing with some reluctance brought on by their craving for succour and rest. Their joints, their very being cried out for a respite, but it was not to be. The cannon started to fire again, but the men, despite putting their heart into it, could no longer find the energy to roll the guns back into position after each discharge.

Alexander became aware of a dark mass taking up a position to the left front of the troop, on a rise some five hundred yards away. He could see through his eyeglass that this unit had cannon, which they were rolling into position facing directly at them! Quickly, he ordered the two left hand guns, to face this new threat. This artillery was clearly going to be a very dangerous foe, they appeared fresh, plentifully manned and their position allowed them to fire at the troop from the flank. Here there was little protection from the small earth mound bordering the road, indeed firing across the battery each cannonball had the ability to smash right across the line of guns, wreaking havoc.

Puffs of smoke eventually told that this new menace was now commencing to fire. The cannonballs crashed into the troop immediately causing mayhem. Each ball unerringly struck into the heart of the battery dashing every living thing or piece of equipment in its path. Horses screamed in fright as the iron spheres bounded through, killing and maiming indiscriminately, drivers were brought down as they tried to release the wounded horses from their traces.

Alexander watched in horror as his troop which had survived the trials of the day relatively unscathed, was now being destroyed so quickly. The two guns attempted to quell this devastating fire but with no discernible reduction in shot. Each firing of the cannon rolled the guns further back and the great wooden trails crossed each other as they formed a huddle. No one had the energy to push the guns back into position, even Alexander and the other officers lent a hand at the guns but they could not muster enough strength anymore. James Griffiths let out a short scream of agony as a ball smashed into his torso, his mangled corpse dashed to the ground in a pathetic heap. Alexander watched as Richard Griffiths fell on his knees alongside the remains, tears streaming down his blackened features as he looked down at the gore that moments ago had been his younger brother. The remainder of the gun team watched silently at the moving scene, every eye filled with unreleased tears. Another ball smashed into a wagon, sending a shower of razor sharp splinters flying into the air. One large splinter struck Henry Leathes in the leg, gouging a deep channel in his thigh. Henry fell to the ground clutching his leg, but having it bound with his handkerchief by Staff Sergeant Henry Parsons, he refused to retire and propped himself up on the earthen bank and continued to shout encouragement.

Further cannonballs bounding by took Alexander's gaze away from the distressing scenes toward the opposing battery. Instantly, his eye noticed a tiny speck in the distance, during the split second that it took for the brain to react to this information, the spot grew into a great black orb. Alexander had heard the soldier's stories that you always saw the ball that would strike you approaching, he had always scoffed at them, he wasn't scoffing now! There was not a moment to think further or react before the cannonball whistled past his ear, missing by a whisker. The shock wave struck his temple hard and confused him for a minute or two, unsure whether he had been hit or not. Eventually Alexander became aware of his very near miss and the shattered remains of the troop horse that the ball had struck behind him, nearly cutting the poor animal in half!

A new cry seconds later indicated another man down, this time it was Driver Thomas Dibbin, clutching his shoulder in agony. He was dragged back to safety.

They couldn't stand this level of punishment for much longer, he thought. Shells were raining down on the troop, sitting in the soft mud whilst the fuse burnt down. This added to their discomfiture greatly, the men scurrying away or lying flat until it exploded. Alexander upbraided his men for flinching from the shells. "Get up, get up, we must keep the guns firing!"

Within seconds his own resolve was tested, for a shell landed ten feet to his right, plop! The black sphere sat half buried in the mud, the fuse still visibly burning down. There was no time for heroics such as trying to pull the fuse out before it exploded, he would have to stand there. His whole body wanted to throw itself down for protection, but Alexander couldn't without losing face, he would have to see it through. The fuse burnt for a second or two longer, to Alexander it seemed an age, and then it eventually exploded into life. Miraculously, Alexander escaped unhurt bar a few mud splashes, the point was made but he hoped that he would never be forced to do that again!

An officer rode up wearing a black uniform with silver adornments, waving his hands frantically in a desperate attempt to attract Alexander's attention. His voice betrayed a thick German accent as he shouted in broken English.

"Stop firing, stop, you must stop! Ah! Mine Gott! Mine Gott! What is it you doos, Sare? Vill you no stop? Dat is your friends de Proosians and you kills them! Ah mine Gott, mine Gott! Vill you no stop sare, vill you no stop? Ah! Mine Gott! Vot for is dis? De English kills their friends de Proosians! Vere id de Dook von Vellington? Oh! Mine Gott! Mine Gott!"

Henry Leathes called out "It is a ruse, he's a Frenchman."

But Hincks replied, "Oh no, he is certainly a Brunswicker."

Alexander was sure that he was genuine and pointed to his troop.

"Look at my troop Sir, your Prussian guns have done this! I am returning fire to lessen their destruction of my men."

The German would not accept this.

"Nein, nein, vill you no stop Sare?"

Alexander realised that he would not listen, but he could show him. Ordering the troop to cease fire, he waited for the Prussians reaction. The Prussian gunners no longer under fire themselves, briskly sent over further salvoes. The great whoosh of a passing cannonball was closely followed by two more, each whistling past very close to the

Brunswick officer. Alexander turned back to the visibly shocked German.

"Now, Sir, you will be convinced. We will continue our firing whilst you go back round the way you came and tell them they kill their friends the English! The moment their firing ceases, so shall mine!"

Still he argued, "Oh, dis is terrible, to see de Proosian and de Inglish kill von annodder!"

Eventually, seeing Alexander order the troop to recommence firing, he rode off.

John Hincks suddenly gave out a muted cry and slumped to the floor clutching his chest. Alexander rushed over and with the help of Sergeant Nisbitt; they laid him down comfortably and opened his tunic to inspect the wound. John coughed convulsively, he looked pale and a small trickle of blood ran from the corner of his mouth.

Nisbitt looked up at Alexander, "Don't look good, Sir".

Alexander nodded, he could see the ball hole in the front of John's tunic, it was close to the heart, but there was surprisingly little blood yet.

They struggled to ease the numerous buttons on his braided tunic and white shirt beneath. Finally the chest was bared revealing a large red contusion and a musket ball! The ball must have been 'spent', near the end of its flight and with no real force left within it. It had expended its last ounce of energy ripping through the heavy tunic and had only retained the power to heavily bruise the chest. The wound was minor but painful and had knocked the wind out of his sails; he would have to retire from action to recuperate.

Looking down at John, Alexander wiped his brow and jocularly whispered, "You are a very lucky man, you will outlive us all!"

Alexander ordered Drivers Lightfoot and Bentley to help John Hincks back to Mr Hichens for treatment.

Soon after, the trundling of heavy wagons close at hand made Alexander look to his left rear. A Belgian battery of foot artillery rolled its guns into position and was now adding its weight of shot into the fray. The Belgians shouted loudly as they worked, some staggered and fell, they were clearly blind drunk! Alexander realised that he would have to be as vigilant of them as of the enemy! Whether it was due to the Belgians or the Brunswick officer, Alexander did not know, but he was grateful to finally note that the Prussian battery had ceased firing.

The remaining troopers sank to their knees in total exhaustion, but Alexander could not let them rest now. He quickly ordered that the men be reassigned to guns, it was clear that those left without wounds would barely enable four guns to continue firing. Completing this reorganisation, the guns continued slowly to engage with the French batteries lining the opposing ridge, but their efforts were now less than half hearted.

A lone rider approached, it was General Alava, the Spanish General attached to Wellington. He shouted encouragement to the troop, "Keep firing, the Prussians are arriving, the day is ours."

Alexander was keenly aware of their arrival, it would be helpful however if they recognised who was the enemy!

Suddenly, the valley seemed to fill with soldiers, allied soldiers! Regiment after regiment advanced to pass the guns and march down the slope. Alexander was forced to order the guns to cease fire again to avoid hitting his own troops. Cheering could be heard from the right and it seemed to draw nearer. What on earth could it mean?

FINAL MOVES

The Rifles continued their struggle to contain the French infantry; a stalemate seemed to have settled upon the fighting. Having succeeded in taking the farm and knoll, the French seemed unable to advance any further. The Rifles holding the hedge lining the road some fifty yards back, were able to halt any advance with their accurate fire. On each occasion that some French officer and a few dozen brave souls sought to advance and dislodge the Rifles, a hail of balls rapidly brought down a number and the remainder would scamper for cover again. The less foolhardy French men lined the knoll, kneeling to offer less of a target and attempted to pick off the Rifles in return.

Shortly after losing the knoll some of the Rocket troops had reappeared. The small contingent appeared at the abattis on the crossroads and nonchalantly prepared to place the rockets in the branches to fire them at the columns near the farm. Within seconds of their appearance the French recognised the threat and fired on them furiously. The officer leading the party was hit in the chest virtually immediately and lay wounded. His sergeant had one of his men help him back but forced the remainder to carry on. They pushed their rockets through the abattis using the thickly entwined branches to form an impromptu firing frame. The sergeant took his time over each rocket, ensuring that they were set properly, lying parallel with the ground to avoid it flying skywards wastefully. He seemed totally unconcerned by the musket balls striking the ground all around and seemed to bear a charmed life. Each time two rockets were set; the sergeant coolly stepped back for one of his men to ignite their fuses. The spluttering and shuddering lasted a second or two then whoosh, they were gone. Many flew erratically into the air or to the sides but some went straight towards the French.

The units beyond the knoll were not clearly in sight but the consternation caused was guaranteed, the Rifles were aware how little they would like to be on the receiving end themselves. Indeed, as the train was lit the warning shouts from the French on the knoll could be faintly heard above the continuous din of battle and all heads disappeared into cover until the unmistakable screech of the rocket's flight confirmed their safety again. The sergeant carried on until all the rockets they had brought with them had been fired, he then ordered his men to walk back to their parent unit. He left last, walking back as if having no care in the world, never once did he hurry his pace or look back nervously as he continued his quiet stroll until completely out of sight of his antagonists. His demeanour and gait had given total confidence to his men to see through their task; Johnny Kincaid rode over to him as he strode back.

"Sergeant, I would like your name, because if I survive this battle, I wish to report your brave actions to your commanding officer."

The sergeant looked bewildered, "Jus' doing me job Sir!"

"No sergeant, with your officer down, no one would have criticised your falling back."

The sergeant looked annoyed, "I would never fail to do my duty whilst I still 'ad breff in my body Sir."

"I can see that sergeant and I did not intend to offend your honour, your name Sir."

"Sergeant Daniel Dunnett, Captain Whinyates' Battery, Horse Artillery, Sir. Now if you don't mind Sir, I needs to keep an eye on them rascals."

Johnny let him go and rode back to the front. As he arrived, he witnessed an extraordinary scene that reminded him of the stories of knights of old he had read as a child.

A French officer had stepped out from the cover of the knoll, obviously annoyed that he was unable to drive any of his men forward with him. He stood and gesticulated his anger at the British troops daring them to come and kill him, an obvious attempt to boost his men's morale with an act of bravado. A number of Riflemen levelled their weapons and took aim, the bravery of the man was admired but allowing him to succeed could lead to serious consequences, he simply had to die.

A bellowing voice managed to make itself heard above the noise all around, "Cease fire, do not kill him, he's mine!"

The Rifles remained levelled but no trigger was squeezed, all wanted to know what was happening. Second Lieutenant Allen Stewart, a huge burly Scotsman towering well above everyone else at six foot two, stepped from behind the hedge and strode out to face this audacious Frenchman. It was to be a single combat between these two men, nothing was said but everyone stopped firing and watched the scene unfolding in this amphitheatre between the contending armies. The Frenchman was dwarfed by the huge figure of Stewart but was not to be overawed. He held his rapier sword firmly and stood awaiting his challenger to approach. Stewart drew his great curved sword and strode forward menacingly, the Frenchman did not flinch. Eventually closing, they struck at each other like gladiators in the arena, both knowing it was to the death. Stewart's sword hammered down with immense force, the Riflemen expecting the stroke to split the Frenchman's skull, he parried the attempt with his thin rapier sword, but it would surely not stop the huge blade descending. The metal clang of the swords meeting with massive force was clearly audible and a great gasp went up from all watching as Stewart's weapon broke, leaving him holding a short stub of sword still attached to the hilt! The French cheered, their hero must now surely win, indeed it seemed even more likely as the French officer deftly flicked his rapier and caught Stewart's left arm, cutting through his uniform and causing the sleeve to darken visibly with the letting of blood. Stewart had little chance, indeed he instantly took the only one left to him, and he lunged forward to wrestle with the Frenchman at close quarters, where the point of his rapier could not complete his victory. His size and weight bowled the two over and they fell together locked in combat. Everyone waited for their rising again to continue fighting, but only Stewart rose, very slowly. As he did, the hilt of his sword could be seen buried deeply into the chest of the brave Frenchman, he had won. There was little cheering; Stewart wiped his mouth on his sleeve to remove the Frenchman's blood from his face. Slowly turning with no sign of pleasure, he strode slowly back to the hedge and regained his company without a word said. In fairness to the French, no ball followed his walk back; they would not dishonour his protagonist's memory. Once safely returned to his company the firing resumed, but the French no longer seemed to have the same heart for the fight.

The Duke of Wellington with a small staff appeared

shortly after and in the confidence of this recent victory Daniel Kelly shouted, "Let us attack them, my Lord"

Wellington spoke sternly, but with a feint smile on his lips, "Not yet my brave fellows, but you shall have at them very soon."

They had total confidence in 'Our Addy' as the men called him affectionately, out of his hearing! They didn't idolize him, he was too stern a disciplinarian for that, but they believed in him after his success in Spain.

The firing continued and casualties mounted slowly, Jonathan Leach was hit in the leg though not seriously. Johnny Kincaid rode to the left in an effort to see more of the battle still roaring around them, Beth continuing to carry him despite a further two wounds to her body. The noise was deafening, cannon fire, musket and rifle fire, the shouts of the combatants, screams of the wounded and dying, the nervous neighing of horses, it was a riot of sound, he just wished it would stop.

The thick black smoke from the incessant firing and the burning farm buildings lay around the troops like a blanket, indeed visibility was never now more than eighty yards and often less. They could only distinguish the positions of the enemy by the flashes from their muzzles as they fired. Every throat seared by the heat and smoke cried out for water but there was none to be had. As Johnny rode out to the left he observed the regiments in the rear of the Rifles, many balls had travelled past and struck these units, indeed one British battalion seemed to lie dead in square just behind them. He had thought that maybe the visibility was better over to the left, but found the smoke engulfed everything including the sky. He turned back, now feeling very weary and desperate for the battle to end, it had been such a pounding match, the few uninjured simply seemed to be waiting their turn to be struck. Johnny wondered if this might be the first battle in history when everybody was killed!

These thoughts had to be hidden and he continued to press the men to keep up the fight. Everyone was clearly exhausted and they were finding it extremely hard to muster the energy to reload their rifles each time. Their weapons were now clogged badly with the carbon from so much firing that they hardly had the strength to drive the cartridges home even with their mallets.

All of a sudden a feint cheer was heard far to the right, it grew louder as each regiment took it up, and instinctively all knew it was a British cheer. The French were starting to retire from the knoll and without any orders from anyone all instinctively knew to advance and complete the victory. They knew nothing of what had happened, simply that it was over, tired limbs suddenly gained renewed energy and they ran forward.

Appearing from the smog like an apparition, Lord Wellington materialised, begrimed by the smoke, his great white teeth beaming through the dirt, they started to cheer their hero.

"No cheering lads, but forward and complete your victory!" he shouted.

They needed no further prompting; all ran forward chasing the rapidly retreating Frenchmen, indeed it almost turned into a race.

As they passed the farm of La Haye Sainte, an intense light suddenly blinded them. Bright sunlight! Emerging from the dark oppression of the smoke filled ridge, they were amazed to find a beautiful summer's evening with the golden rays beating down. Glancing left and right Johnny saw the wonderful sight of a long line of British red and Belgian blue intermixed, marching as if on a parade ground across the fields with the whole French army fleeing before it, their dark masses rapidly disintegrating and moving away.

The lads caught dozens of prisoners, their spirit was completely broken, the unthinkable had happened, Napoleon had been defeated. The prisoners were herded together and given full protection; everyone had seen too much death that day.

Black masses to the left made Johnny fear a counter attack for a moment, but a cry went up "The Prussians are here", which instantly dispelled any such thoughts.

Captain Edmund Walcott from Webber's troop rode up to Alexander, his smile beamed through his grimy features, as he waved his arms wildly.

He shouted "Victory, Victory! They fly, they fly!"

The smoke of battle cleared a little and the terrible volume of noise suddenly eased and the far slope could be clearly seen in the evening light. The dark masses of the French could be seen moving away, no, running away! They were fleeing before the advance of the battered remnants of Lord Wellington's infamous army of a dozen nations. Now that the smoke had cleared one could clearly see the sun slowly setting over the heads of the French and over Napoleon's ambitions.

Looking around their ridge, the scene of such constant fighting, incessant noise, smoke and myriad unsavoury odours was suddenly completely calm and silent. Few others could be seen left on the ridge apart from Norman Ramsay's battery, now being commanded by Lieutenant Philip Sandilands, the only officer still standing!

An Aide de Camp rode into the troop calling out, "Who commands here?"

Alexander answered from his crouched position, "Captain Mercer, Sir".

The aide looked earnestly at Alexander, whilst pointing toward the French agitatedly, "It is imperative that this movement should be supported by artillery, your troop must advance."

Alexander stood tall, he stared back at the aide incredulously and spreading his arms wide to emphasise the devastated state of his troop, he replied in a quiet restrained voice. "How?"

Looking around the shambolic scene he continued, "Of two hundred horses, we have lost some one hundred and forty, and as for my men, two thirds are wounded or dead, I have scarcely got the men to man three guns and they do not have the energy left to move the cannon one foot. How do you propose I move the guns?"

The officer had seen enough, the futility of the order was apparent; he simply saluted Alexander, turned his horse and rode away.

Alexander had over stressed his losses but the point was a real one, they were in no condition to move.

The hell was finally over, Alexander slumped on a small hillock to rest his aching bones, and his ears rang from the constant noise making him nearly deaf, immediately his adrenaline ceased to flow, he became extremely weary, and he could barely keep his eyes open. Surveying the battery, he was appalled by the destruction and confusion. Nobody had the energy or the inclination to sort out the mess of the guns that night.

The men that had luckily survived unscathed or with minor contusions sank down where they had stood totally exhausted. But they were now even more aware of their driving thirst and desperate hunger, made worse by the certain knowledge that there was no opportunity to relieve either of them.

This was no moment of exultation after victory, which

had already worn off. Now one offered silent prayers for one's own personal survival and deplored the waste and terrible destruction of war. Despite the overpowering requirement for sleep, the men found that the disturbing sights around them denied them peace. Without saying a word they individually rose slowly and dragged themselves back to clear ground just to the rear of the troop, where the unpleasant sights of mangled friends and comrades could be forgotten. Soon repose grasped them with firm hands, they slept solidly that night.

A Prussian artillery battery halted a little in the rear of the troop, their loud German voices conversing around a large fire they kindled did not disturb the sleeping. A few men sauntered over to offer friendship, with a great hope that they had wine and food to spare! However the Prussians soon showed that their presence was not welcome and there would be no hope of provisions from them. Their language was incomprehensible but the anger in their voices and hand signals did not allow for misinterpretation. The men sullenly returned to the troop empty handed and lay down next to their already slumbering comrades.

Alexander regained a little strength and rose to carry out the essential duty that must be performed each evening, to settle Cossack. He patted the dear horse on the muzzle, Cossack remained alert and bright, but now Alexander became aware of minor injuries. He ran his hands over his withers and legs and counted no less than eight minor cuts and abrasions caused by flying splinters and musket balls, he had been very lucky indeed to escape serious injury. Removing the saddle and tethering Cossack to a wagon with fresh fodder within reach, Alexander now cared only for himself. He copied the others and simply sought a berth for the night without speaking to any body. He decided that a spot off the damp soil would suit his wearied limbs better and eyed the driver's wooden footboard on one of the wagons. It was a bit short, but it looked a wonderful spot through wearied eyes and curling up with the edge of the tarpaulin pulled over him he was soon sleeping deeply with all the cares of the day temporarily forgotten. Bal, still unscathed, curled up on the ground beneath the wagon for the night.

Johnny Kincaid watched the Prussian cavalry sweep across the Rifle's front and on after the retreating French. These fresh troops would decimate any attempted rallying of the French; they would ensure the heavy defeat was now turned into a complete rout and hopefully chase Bonaparte all the way back to Paris. Johnny sincerely hoped so for he was tired of fighting. Passing another house on the French side of the valley, Johnny watched as Wellington met a Prussian officer and shook hands, someone told him it was Blucher, the Old Prussian warhorse, 'Marshal Forwards' as the Prussians affectionately called him.

The Rifles continued their pursuit until encountering a wood a mile or so beyond the battlefield. All the British units were halting here, the men slumping to the ground as exhaustion enveloped them again. Within seconds many fell asleep wherever they dropped down. The Prussian infantry continued to march on and saluted, their bands playing the British national anthem as they passed.

Soon they had all passed and there was a glorious silence as all succumbed to sleep, despite the excitement of the day, their brains closed down and they slept long and deep.

Arthur Wellesley, Duke of Wellington, had enjoyed the moment of exhilaration as he had raised his cocked hat aloft and sent his battered army forward to seal a famous victory. His meeting with the Prussian leader General Blucher, as the two armies converged and celebrated success near the French front line of that morning, ended his role that day. Blucher's fresher troops were to continue the chase that night to prevent the French regrouping.

Weariness descended upon his furrowed brow, he had worked tirelessly since four o'clock that fateful morning to achieve this success and had managed to be at all the various points of danger throughout the day, to ensure the French had not succeeded against his polyglot army. Urging Copenhagen onwards, Wellington slowly rode back across the field of battle, followed at a distance by the remainder of his staff, towards his headquarters in Waterloo. They understood his need to gather his thoughts; he had no wish to converse with anyone for a while.

Wellington and Copenhagen had borne a charmed life again; neither was injured, not even slightly, despite the hail of lead flying through the air at the numerous danger points they were always to be seen at throughout the day. Arthur's visage betrayed red eyes and a face besmirched with the thick black smoke that had shrouded much of the battle, but more telling were the rivulets of tears streaming down his cheeks, coursing strange patterns in the grime. The pitiful sight of thousands of dead and dying carpeting the fields, the cries for compassion and the feeling of total inadequacy to relieve their suffering, backed by the guilt of being an arbiter in this great affair struck him deeply.

Eventually, they arrived at the village of Waterloo, Arthur Wellesley wearily slid from Copenhagen's back and he handed the reins to a groom who would look after his faithful companion. As he trudged wearily towards the door of the public house temporarily turned into Allied Headquarters, he gently patted Copenhagen's rump in a final show of appreciation, before leaving him for the night.

Copenhagen, the placid war-horse that had mildly cantered all day, seemingly oblivious to the danger of both shot and shell, reacted with surprising vigour. His farewell gesture was an extremely powerful kick from his rear legs, which luckily missed Arthur by a whisker! The nearest he had come to serious injury or death had come from his own horse! The irony of it was not lost on Arthur and he smiled slightly as he opened the door to the tavern.

His smile disappeared instantly as he entered the inn and surveyed the scene within. The main room of the tavern was full of allied senior officers sitting side by side with a number of high-ranking French prisoners. The fighting was over, there was no longer any animosity between these men that merely hours earlier had sought to kill each other. They were enjoying their first decent food since the evening before and the conversation was loud and animated. Arthur quickly moved through to the back room reserved for his staff, shutting the door tight against the noise without. His look as he proceeded across the room was unmistakable. Arthur viewed these Frenchmen as traitors to their rightful King; he did not hide his disdain for them. The message was understood, meals were quickly finished, the allied officers made excuses and left, French officers were quietly escorted on the road towards Brussels.

The view within the back room struck Arthur as extremely depressing and tore at his heartstrings again. The large table had been laid to welcome his 'Family' of young nobles, those dashing men that had raced at breakneck speed all day with orders. The room was virtually empty! Almost all his Aides de Camp were still out there, injured or killed. Arthur sat quietly and mechanically consumed a little of the fare placed in front of him, but he continued to stare into the distance contemplating the sad loss of such wonderful young men. With every sound outside Arthur would look up at the door in the hope that one of them would enter, but it was a vain hope.

Arthur conversed occasionally with Alava, his old friend from Spain, now the Spanish Minister to the court in Holland. Alava had been constantly by Arthur's side throughout the Peninsula, but his greatest claim was now to be the only Spaniard to be present at both the battles of Trafalgar and Waterloo! Arthur constantly reiterated his amazement that he had borne such a charmed life again.

He visited Alexander Gordon, a good friend who was mortally wounded and ordered that he should be placed on Arthur's own bed; he would lie out on a put up bed.

The preliminary list of casualties was brought to him in the early hours; it read like a Who's Who of the peerage, every family would mourn some loss.

The tears rolled down his cheeks once more and he offered a silent prayer to God, "I pray that I have seen my last battle!"

He got his wish.

THE AFTERMATH

A dreadful noise disturbed Alexander just after midnight and he sat up, precariously balanced on the footboard to view the scene in the light spread by a near full moon unobscured by even the smallest cloud. The site of battle was even more repugnant, bathed in the cold moonshine. The fields were covered with a carpet of corpses lying in every aspect of death, their bared flesh reflecting the moonlight, for the scavengers were already at work. Local villagers crawling out of the woods now that the fighting was over joined servants, camp followers, and even some soldiers that had partaken in the fighting. They scurried about the field in search of rich pickings off the dead. The quickest way to search them was to remove the clothes from the corpse, the garment would be useful and their valuables could be sought out at leisure. Many soldiers sewed gold coins into their clothing for safe keeping, to be used in time of desperate need. Well, they would have no need now! Officers were particularly good pickings, necklaces were snatched, fancy clothes stripped away for their valuable gold lace, rings wrenched free or if stuck fingers simply cut away so that the rings could be prised off at ease! Sometimes the corpse groaned, not fully dead yet, that didn't bother them, they just got on with the work in hand. If they groaned too loudly, fought back or cried out, they simply finished them by beating out their brains with a stick or simply slit their throats!

Alexander watched these human vermin scurry across the field like scavenging rats, their heads bobbing up and down above the sea of shattered humanity, in search of new victims, whilst avoiding the near approach of those seeking to find and succour their loved ones. The cries and groans of the wounded was heart rending, one could only pity them as there was no means of aiding them, those that survived the cold night and loss of blood, may be lucky to be collected tomorrow and taken to the hospitals, some would not be retrieved for days. Indeed, after such terrible battles, wounded hidden in wooded or less easily accessible areas had been known to be missed and survive for many days before succumbing to a lingering death by starvation. If they were lucky they were found before they had finished devouring the corpses near them.

Occasionally, Alexander spotted wounded men haul themselves into a sitting position, some even tried to raise themselves but always their strength failed them and they sank back down to the ground once more. A few could be seen to repeat the attempt but down they would sink, never to rise again.

In stark contrast, the bright light from their roaring fire, loud talking and laughter from the Prussian battery just behind him, reminded Alexander that all life was not expunged. Slowly he sank back into a sound sleep, not to be disturbed again until the sun smiled.

Waking in the early morning sunlight of Monday 19th June 1815 was a strange experience for Johnny Kincaid. The previous day's occurrences seemed little more than a nightmare that had passed.

The Rifles rose slowly and prepared an inadequate breakfast. They had woken in a beautiful wooded glade with the warming sun's rays peering through the canopy of leaves above. A brook of clean fresh water was discovered nearby and it soon slaked their all-consuming thirst. The clean water was a Godsend, revitalising them and cleaning the grime of smoke and blood from their worn faces and hands. Refreshment made everyone even more aware of the lack of food suffered over the previous days. Sustenance was at hand, the Commissariat wagons had caught up during the night and food was issued rapidly and devoured just as quickly. Sitting beside a roaring fire, fed and watered, their troubles were soon forgotten, this was as good as it got for a soldier.

Everybody wanted to tell of their own exploits and hear every body else's. Soldiers passed from one campfire to another seeking out comrades in other units, sometimes there was a shout of glee as friends discovered each other alive and well, but more often than not they were depressed and saddened to hear of a serious injury or death. Indeed, usually after a battle men would ask "Who's dead?", but it was said that after Waterloo they asked "Who's alive?".

A few good words were uttered for those that were gone then life went on and they were forgotten. That was how it was, it wasn't callousness, it was simply the only way to deal with so much death. Returning to their units, equipment was put in order, weapons were cleaned in case they were needed again and tattered uniforms repaired with a sewing kit, to appear as well as possible.

Soon messengers arrived at camp with orders to detach a number of men with an officer to form a stretcher and burial party on the battlefield. Nobody was keen for such work, to be reminded of the horrors and pain of yesterday. Johnny Kincaid joined the party led by Allen Stewart, which also included Charles Smith the Volunteer, George Kitchen and Thomas Treacy amongst others. They were formed up and marched off back to the battlefield, none envied their task.

Shortly before ten, another messenger arrived to order the battalion under arms to march with the army into France. The fighting wasn't over yet, coupled undoubtedly with many a hard march, the joys of a foot soldier!

As they prepared to set out back to the field of death, Johnny met a British infantryman sitting dejectedly by the roadside; he had obviously been originally dressed in red, but was now encased in thick dark brown mud from head to toe, no vestige of scarlet remaining visible. Johnny asked what had happened to him the previous day.

The infantryman perked up a little saying, "I'll be hanged if I know anything at all about the matter, for I was all day trodden in the mud and galloped over by every scoundrel who had a horse and in short I only owe my existence to my insignificance!"

Johnny smiled and bade him better luck, then rode to join the detachment that had proceeded on ahead.

The burial party cleared the wood. They were forced to leave the road and walk through the fields because of the hundreds of abandoned carriages and cannon all intermingled, blocking the road completely for half a mile. They had been rapidly abandoned as the Prussian cavalry had caught up, it was rumoured that even Napoleon had nearly been caught, only escaping by abandoning his carriage and mounting a cavalryman's horse to ride away swiftly.

Passing this mass of wreckage they observed a number of

Prussian artillery horse teams locating and removing all the captured French cannon. Johnny remonstrated with one Prussian officer but his lack of language and a determination to ignore him by the German, caused him to fail to move him utterly. Somebody was going to be in hot water for letting the Prussians take all the prizes he thought, he didn't want to be the one to tell Lord Wellington!

Now cresting the ridge on the French side they were met with the panorama of the battlefield, the spectacle of devastation shocked them. The wagon jam was nothing to this, last night they had been oblivious to the scenes of suffering as they crossed the fields in the elation of victory.

Bodies were piled everywhere, mangled and contorted dreadfully. Many corpses were already naked, stripped by camp followers or local villagers returning to take anything that they could turn to a profit. In all directions, there were wounded men sitting imploring succour, and as they passed, the lads offered many a mouthful of water to ease their sufferings but they could not help them any further. Their own men lying near the cross roads must be their priority. Injured horses strangely tugged at the emotions more than the men. These poor creatures meekly led into this slaughter, sat silently imploring help, others lying unable to rise simply suffering in silence. One cavalry horse sat on his haunches quietly chewing the grass within his reach. Closer examination showed that it's rear legs had both been blown off by a cannonball! Most looked on with pity, but could not summon up the courage to put the horse out of its misery. Treacy closed up to the horse, putting his head close to the horse's ear and whispering calming words to settle him, he raised his rifle unseen and fired into it's temple killing it instantly, the horse slumped to the ground, all suffering ended. The others turned away, inwardly pleased that Treacy had done the deed.

Proceeding towards the crossroads, they struggled to walk without stepping on some form of human remains. Fragments that once bore human form were scattered everywhere, arms, legs, heads and many pieces less easily identified. It was one huge slaughterhouse; some of the lads retched at the sights and recoiled from the stench of death that pervaded everything.

They encountered robber groups crossing the fields searching for riches; they did not disguise their disgust for them. Many were women, some even children; they quickly searched each corpse for jewellery and coin. Sometimes the corpse emitted signs of life, groaning or even imploring help, few received any mercy beyond their immediate despatch to their maker. Their heartlessness shocked the Riflemen, they were professional soldiers, they only caused death in battle, and they showed compassion once the fighting was over. These peasants and camp followers showed a complete lack of mercy, simple farm folk turned into cold-blooded murderers to satisfy their lust for riches, it was a sickening spectacle.

Johnny's orders were to carry all of their wounded found to the hospitals now set up in Brussels and the surrounding villages. More benevolent locals drove farm carts to ferry the wounded to the hospitals, their compassion contrasting markedly with the carrion of the battlefield. However the fact that many drivers were escorted by an armed soldier to ensure that they completed the journey without dumping their unwanted loads, tempered the feelings of gratefulness for their actions.

Other wagons were detailed to collect the dead; carts loaded the British and allied corpses to be buried in mass graves dug near the chateau and the crossroads. French dead were heaped ready for cremation in huge pyres, the piles rapidly grew mountainous, there were numerous heaps, nobody counted the number of dead but it was certain that it numbered tens of thousands.

Johnny watched as the men helped find the dead and wounded, they showed great compassion for those that they found alive, lifting them to the roadside to await transportation to the hospitals. He noted with pride that this care was applied to the French wounded as much as to their own.

"Sir, Sir" shouted Casima Casima.

Turning over the corpse of a French infantryman, he had stared into the face of a youth with a serenely peaceful look even in death. A simple cursory inspection of the pockets for valuables had revealed a secret. The body was that of a woman! Fully dressed in uniform she must have passed herself off as a man for some considerable time. Talking to other search parties it soon became apparent that this was not the only occurrence of women being found in uniform. They set her body aside and dug a shallow grave to bury the unknown female alone with some dignity.

Surveying the scene Johnny could only contemplate the terrible loss of life and the pain and suffering caused because of the naked ambition of the tyrant Napoleon. He wished that all those that revelled and gloried in war could stand there with him and take in the sights, sounds and smells of death on such an horrendous scale; where was the glory in this?

Leaving the detachment with orders to continue their work until all were gathered in, he happily turned Beth away from the scene of slaughter and rode out to catch the battalion on its march to France to complete the overthrow of Napoleon.

Alexander was reawoken by the bright rays of the early morning sun. He attempted to stretch his legs, which ached from being coiled up tightly whilst sleeping on the board. He pulled himself round to sit upright on the step, his legs dangling down in front of him. He cupped his aching head in his hands and attempted to rub life back into his cheeks. Eventually, he prised open his heavy eyes and he stared down at the ground. He was regaled by the delightful sight of the mangled corpse of Driver John Miller lying directly below the berth he had slept on so snugly that night, the sight made him shudder involuntarily and reawakened all the terrible memories of the previous day.

A groaning nearby, which Alexander had been subconsciously aware of during the night, made him look up. There no more than ten feet away was a Frenchman, wounded by a ball in the right thigh and curiously barefoot. Alexander conversed briefly with him in French; he was extremely gentlemanly and well spoken for a common cavalryman. Alexander ordered two men to aid the brave Horse Grenadier to hobble slowly back to the hospital at Mont St Jean.

Alexander looked himself up and down, he was black from the smoke and his clothes were stiff and ungiving, the blood of Breton's horse having dried hard. His thighs were already chafed from long hours of riding and the rough blood soaked cloth had irritated his skin severely, walking was going to be difficult and painful. Riding was going to be nigh on impossible, he would have to ride side saddle, like the young ladies, a sure source of merriment for his men.

A loud "Ahem", brought Alexander's thoughts back into focus. He looked directly into the face of Staff Sergeant Parson.

"Permission to speak, Sir?"

"What is it?" Alexander asked wearily.

"The lads want permission to bury Driver Crammond, Sir."

Alexander was perplexed, the troop was awash with corpses, "Why Crammond particularly?" he asked, whilst jumping down from his perch and using his arms to straighten his aching back.

Parson answered sternly, "Because he looks frightful, Sir, many of us have not had a wink of sleep for him!"

Alexander pointed toward the men, "Show me, Sergeant."

They walked together to the rear of the carts where the troop was stood in a semicircle looking at something.

Sergeant Nisbitt called out "Make way men".

The group turned and seeing Alexander approach, parted to allow his view of the scene. Nothing Alexander had yet seen or experienced had prepared him for this awful sight.

There lay the body of Driver James Crammond; his skull had been smashed away by a cannonball. However, it had not decapitated him; the ball had only removed the rear part of the head, leaving the front inch of skull intact and undamaged. The visage was complete with piercing eyes and a slight grin, but nothing behind it. The sight was truly repugnant, even to such men as had viewed all the horrors of the previous day with little thought.

Alexander understood and sympathised with their horror, he immediately nodded to Staff Sergeant Parson to proceed.

Three men stepped forward with shovels and dug a shallow grave and poor Crammond, wrapped in his blanket to hide him from view, was rolled into the hole and the sod returned.

Written orders eventually arrived via a dragoon, Alexander read them quickly. They were to proceed after the army with whatever equipment they could supply with horses and men; all other wagons were to be sent to a park in the rear. Ammunition would also be supplied at Waterloo village to replenish the empty chests.

The officers were briefed and soon working parties were formed. Most of the drivers were detailed to capture any wandering horses to bolster their teams; Farrier Job Price would look over each horse, assessing its state and re shoeing where necessary. Collar maker Robert Redhouse and his team sought out undamaged equipment that was scattered about or reclaimed from the dead horses and fitted out the approved horses with saddle, collar and reins. Bombardier Thomas Masterson and his gunners checked over the cannon and collected all the remaining ammunition into a couple of wagons, his count revealed that their guns had fired nearly seven hundred rounds over the last few days.

Whilst they worked, they were all amazed to see the first ghoulish sightseers from Brussels. Their carriages drew onto the battlefield; the heavily perfumed and elegantly attired occupants disembarked looking around in horror at the sights. They were careful not to step too closely to the corpses, as they did not want to ruin their pristine white stockings. They observed the troop as they worked for a few moments without seeking to converse with these wretches clearing up the mess. They then moved on towards the chateau of Hougomont. Now those people really were sick, no right minded person would volunteer to bear witness to these scenes!

The only location from which to obtain fresh water was the well in the grounds of the chateau of Hougoumont, where the right wing of the army had stood during the battle. Alexander accompanied a section of men to obtain much needed water for both men and horses. As they descended into the valley and neared the chateau, the level of destruction became more extreme, even compared with their own experiences. The woods and farmhouse walls were thick with bodies; the gullies were completely filled with them. The trees were smashed and twisted, mere broken stumps remaining, destroyed by the heavy cannonade. As they entered the courtyard, the scenes became infinitely worse. The buildings had been set alight during the battle and many of the wounded, both British and French who had lain within for safety were burned alive. Bodies of the wounded were strewn across the doorways their lower halves burnt to a cinder where they had vainly sought to escape the relentless flames. Further away from the buildings the slightly luckier wounded lay in great numbers around the yard, still awaiting transportation to the hospitals.

Alexander engaged a couple of German dragoons in conversation about their experiences. As he conversed with them, to their rear he could see some Belgian peasants rifling the clothes of a French corpse. Having completed emptying the pockets, they commenced abusing the body, kicking and punching it, obviously in an attempt to impress Alexander as to their hate for the French. They looked to him for approval but Alexander could only look at them with total disgust.

The dragoons turned to see what bothered him and seeing the cause they flew into a rage and drew their sabres, turning the flat side to strike the peasants hard across the back, they roared in pain and scurried away, like the vermin they were.

Walking slowly back up the slope to the ridge with their water supply, Alexander encountered a group of wounded French soldiers, they had been collected together ready for carting off to hospital. An old warrior of a Guard lancer, with a long grey moustache, sat berating his colleagues to stand their discomforts with fortitude, to act like soldiers and particularly to bear up like true Frenchmen. The lancer engaged Alexander in conversation, asking how the battle had gone and praised the English and their allies for their stubborn resistance. He sat waving his arm in the air gesticulating as he spoke passionately. His other arm lay by his side, the hand severed at the wrist and lying on the ground beside him. He also had a dreadful wound from a piece of case shot in his side and another had broken his leg. After a long conversation, Alexander bade him farewell and good luck, the Frenchman handed his lance, still bloody from the previous day to Alexander. He had no further use for it and he would rather Alexander took it rather than the thieving peasants, he said. Alexander gave it to Joseph Millward; he would be his own lancer in future! They returned to the troop, to find that John Hall's team were already back having replenished the ammunition.

The guns and wagons that could not be taken on had been taken to the collection park near the village of Waterloo by Quartermaster John Hall's team. When they arrived at the park it was obvious that a group of senior artillery officers were having a heated argument about something.

John Hall spotted an old colleague, Sergeant Daniel Dunnett of the Rocket Troop.

"Hey Daniel, I see you managed to see your way through again."

Daniel was pleased to see an old acquaintance, "I'm glad your luck held too, John."

Hall pointed towards the group of officers, "What's going on?"

"Summat to do with the French guns left on the battlefield seems Sir Augustus Frazer is mad with Sir George

Wood for failing to collect them. The canny Prussians snatched them all up last night and took them away. Frazer has been to the Prussians to demand our prizes back and they have agreed to send them back tomorrow. Sir George is very lucky not to have to go tell the Duke that he had no prize cannon!"

They both laughed, who'd be an officer?

They shook hands then John's team proceeded back to G Troop. On route Hall found a whole side of venison lying in the mud, which he promptly liberated. His arrival at the troop with the welcome supply of game raised morale considerably. The meat was scraped with a sword to rid it of most of the dirt, a lance shaft was turned into a makeshift spit lying on crossed muskets; upturned cuirasses were used as seats, a battlefield was a source of all sorts of useful items.

By afternoon enough horses had been caught and equipment found to proceed with four cannon, three ammunition wagons and the travelling forge. Then, the best news of all, a long train of wagons creaked along the roadway towards the troop. It was Joshua Coates, the Commissariat and his train of farm carts, a very welcome sight indeed. They had managed to evade the advancing French army and by a very circuitous road finally arrived at the battlefield this morning. The men eagerly accepted their food supplies; there were now adequate stocks for at least five days. Morale rose dramatically as they breakfasted on the excellent supplies.

As Alexander sat and devoured his first proper food for over seventy-two hours, he spotted Robert Newland strolling towards him and realised that he had not seen him since the previous afternoon, when he had gone to look for ammunition.

"What happened to you?" he asked innocently.

Newland looked irritated by the question, "I was with Gardiner and my old troop."

Alexander did not press the point further, but he couldn't understand why Newland hadn't returned. Why stay with his old troop over on the left of the army, where there was little action? The thought that he may have found the heat of battle too much and had found cooler waters, would nag him and colour his view of his second in command for the rest of his life.

Eventually the team were all reassembled and ready to proceed to catch up with the army. Alexander stood up in the saddle. Momentarily he stared around at the fields still scattered with the debris of the terrible struggle, then turning to his troop and raising his arm, he cried out.

"G troop will advance............To Paris!

EPILOGUE

The Battle of Waterloo ended everything for Napoleon. His army was destroyed, the remainder harassed beyond endurance by the Prussians and never recovered. Napoleon and his people's dreams of renewed glory were irrevocably shattered and the politicians in Paris moved rapidly to distance themselves from him, in a belated effort to ingratiate themselves to Louis XVIII who would soon be back on the throne. Napoleon eventually accepted the inevitable, abdicated and attempted to flee to America. The ever-watchful Royal Navy barred his escape and eventually he was forced to surrender. He was taken to the island of St Helena in the South Atlantic, which was turned over to military law as a prison. With enforced retirement, the passion soon ebbed from his ageing frame and Napoleon succumbed, probably to cancer of the stomach, which seems to have been hereditary. Napoleon died in 1821 and was buried on St Helena. Later in 1840, his body was returned to France with great ceremony and finally laid to rest in Les Invalides.

This book has been written because of my life long love affair with the history of the period known as the Napoleonic Wars. I trust that my writing does not glorify war, for that is not my intention. War is undoubtedly horrible, bringing untold misery to all that it touches. Many seem to think that modern warfare is somehow worse than that before, I would question that assumption. Although modern weapons are more powerful in their individual destructive capability, they have the benefit of clinical accuracy, therefore reducing although not eradicating 'civilian' casualties. War in 1815 was carried out at extremely close quarters, the weapons still largely 'hand' weapons, requiring the combatants to be within a hundred yards of each other and certainly in sight. Many weapons, particularly those associated with cavalry could only be used at little more than arms length. Some weapons it is true had progressed to being long range, up to a thousand yards, but, even these were more regularly used at 'point blank' ranges. Death and injuries have always been a horrendous sight no matter the methods used. The difference was the sheer closeness of that scene of destruction, death occurred literally inches from you. Your enemy's death was so close it was personal. With long-range modern weapons, troops are often cushioned from this consequence of their actions.

Indeed to put the level of destruction into perspective one only has to look at the 'butchers bill' for Waterloo. In the three square miles that encompass the main battlefield, the following figures will indicate the level of carnage to be seen.

Troops at Waterloo

British and Allied troops	67,661
Prussian troops eventually involved	51,944
French troops	68,900

Losses at Waterloo

British and Allied killed and wounded
14,400 (21% of combatants) and 4302 horses
Prussian killed and wounded
6,998 (13.5% of combatants) and 742 horses

French killed and wounded

(Accurate figures are impossible as records were lost or destroyed in the aftermath, but were in the region of) 25,000 (36% of combatants, not including prisoners) and 10,000 horses.

This adds up to over 46,000 men and 15,000 horses killed and wounded in such a small space, indeed in some areas the bodies were piled five and six high.

My interest therefore stems from my sheer awe at our predecessors ability to face such barbarity and maintain a level of chivalry unknown in modern times. These men were not just the dregs of prison cells as so often portrayed. The men were enlisted, mostly without coercion, from all strata of the British working classes of the time. Many volunteered to escape from economic hardship; others joined to satisfy a thirst for adventure; many more only thought of the 'Bounty money' paid on joining of up to £40, a small fortune at the time; few joined for sheer patriotism. For this was not a 'National war' for the British as the Prussians saw it, it was just like all previous wars to them, caused by King's falling out. Many were illiterate but quite a few had a basic or good level of reading and writing, keeping records of their adventures.

As is traditionally portrayed, the officers largely stemmed from the middle and upper classes, although the proportion of men being raised up from the ranks was a sizeable minority and grew throughout the period. Officers were generally much better educated and were aloof from the men, particularly in barrack life.

Promotion for officers was still largely by purchase, a huge advantage to the rich. However, the regulations laid down by the Duke of York requiring minimum service in each rank does seem to have persuaded many of the crass fops that used to run regiments as a hobby, to find other forms of distraction for their time.

Indeed, the Napoleonic Wars produced more National Heroes in every European country involved than any other period of history. A simple flick through the great names produces, Wellington and Nelson of Britain; Napoleon, Soult, Ney and Murat of France; Blucher, Scharnhorst and Gneisenau in Germany; Archduke Charles of Austria; Suvarov and Kutuzov of Russia; to name just a few still famous today.

Life on campaign was extremely hard, often long periods were endured with little food and no covering but the stars in all weathers. Here the social barriers eased, the officers and men learnt to help each other, the bond of regiment and company became well established in this long war lasting from 1793 until 1815 with hardly a break. Their hardships sometimes made them callous to death, yet at other times touchingly gentle and supportive. Life in or out of the army was very tough and all were inured to hard struggle, but even here a touch of old world chivalry survived.

Unlike the wars in Spain and Russia, which involved the peasantry and became veritable war to the death, war between the French and British remained a contest between professional armies. This allowed the men to treat the French only as the enemy in full battle, at all other times 'live and let live' was the motto. Indeed the pickets of both armies often shared food and conversation, much to the annoyance of Wellington!

This was really the first Global war, extending to North and South America, Africa and Asia, indeed until 1915, this war was known as the 'Great War'. With the rise of newspapers, letters from the front were regularly printed, again much to Wellington's annoyance as copies of these papers were regularly read by Napoleon and used as a major intelligence source!

This fuelled a demand for more revelations and even before the war ended, memoirs of soldiers and sailors started to emerge. Following the war there was a veritable explosion of books, running into some hundreds. Some are simple narratives of events, largely copied from campaign histories, turgid to read and producing little new, but a number of gems do exist which tell a 'human' story of personal incidents, which give a fantastic insight into this period of history. Their stories fluctuate from riotously humorous stories to the shockingly putrid descriptions of the vile excesses man visits upon man.

These personal histories of men and women just like us, with the same feelings and ambitions, bring those dry pages of history to life for me. No longer is the Battle of Waterloo a simple fact of Napoleon being defeated by Wellington and Blucher. Now the ebb and flow of this momentous day can be seen through the eyes of a handful of the actors in the great scene. Their fears, anguish and elation bring the scene before us and we can form some idea what it was like to stand on that field that day. To feel their pain, their joy and to walk in their footsteps.

The pages you have read are the TRUE stories of those men, all the names in this book were REAL people and the incidents portrayed are ones that they have described. To me, their words resound across the centuries like VOICES OF THUNDER. My involvement has been hopefully to collate all the separate memoirs into one cohesive story that is readable. I have taken the liberty of producing a more descriptive version of the scenes they witnessed, as often to them these scenes were everyday and only warranted a passing word. I have also added much of the dialogue between the characters, which was not usually recorded. That is my contribution, their story is often more fantastical than any novelist dare write for fear of arousing the reader's incredulity. The facts are largely verifiable and I certainly choose to believe them, fact is often more strange than fiction, as they say!

I have supplemented their stories with information gleaned from numerous publications, articles and visits to museums and libraries, ensuring their stories and my additions are all based wholly on fact. In relation to this, I would offer my grateful thanks to Mr Dyer, Curator at the Royal Mint at Llantrisant and his staff for letting me research the original Waterloo Medal Roll, with all it's endless supplements; also the very helpful staff at the Public Records Office at Kew for their help and guidance in trawling through the mass of records available.

Waterloo was a battle of infinite importance; it defined the path of European development and history for a century. Indeed, besides a few small wars, Waterloo led to virtually a century without pan European conflict, a thing unprecedented in previous history. Unfortunately after ninety-nine years, this relative peace collapsed in the greater horror of the '14-18 War.

Waterloo was the first victory of the British army celebrated with a medal for all combatants. Previously, only Senior Officers had received commemorative medals. Those soldiers that had fought so bravely throughout the world between 1793 and 1814 were not issued with a medal, until very belatedly they were given the opportunity to apply for a General Service Medal, when this was inaugurated in 1847, with bars naming each major victory, back to the commencement of the Peninsula War. Even then, only surviving soldiers could apply, not the families of those that had since departed this life. The Waterloo Medal was issued in 1816 to all surviving participants in the battle serving in the army or the King's German Legion; again posthumous awards were rare and only then to families of high ranking officers. Some politicians and others also received a medal, including George Canning, Lady Fitzroy Somerset and the Duchess of Richmond of Ball fame. Each medal required one ounce of finest silver at 5 shillings per ounce. The Royal Mint was supplied with sixty thousand ounces of silver to produce an expected forty thousand medals. The silver was worth some £15,000, a sizeable figure in 1815, a fitting tribute to the men and an indication of the Government's estimation of the importance of the victory.

For those that may have enjoyed my efforts, I continue with a list of the actors in this book and what I have gleaned of their further lives. If you are like me, books that do not tell you what happened to people that you build an affinity with, drive me to fury. I hope this satisfies the curious.

If this book persuades one of you readers to delve a little further into this fascinating period of history, my aim will have been more than accomplished.

SENIOR OFFICERS

Arthur Wellesley, Field Marshal, Duke of Wellington
This was Wellington's final battle, he now turned his hand to politics, something that his dealings with foreign governments in India, Spain, Portugal and the Low countries, had made him extremely adept at. Prime Minister 1828-1829 and in 1834, when the government fell temporarily, he held the posts of First Lord of the Treasury, Home Secretary, Foreign Secretary and Colonial Secretary all at once. In later life he was a great favourite of the young Queen Victoria. He died at Walmer Castle 1852, buried in St Paul's Cathedral.

His home at Apsley House is open to the public. Its address is still as it was in Wellington's time, simply 'No.1 London'.

His Royal Highness, the Prince of Orange (Wounded)
Succeeded to the throne of Holland in 1843 as William II, he died in 1849.

Lieutenant Colonel Fitzroy Somerset, Military Secretary (Wounded)
He lost his right arm at Waterloo, having been struck by a musket ball fired from the roof of La Haye Sainte after the French had captured the farm. Created Baron Raglan in 1852 and as such became a Field Marshal and Commander in Chief of the British army in the Crimea in 1854. Died of

cholera during the siege of Sebastopol. His body was brought home and buried at Badminton. After his death he was unfairly blamed for all the failures of the Crimean campaign.

Major, The Honourable Henry Percy, 14th Light Dragoons (Extra ADC to Wellington)
Sent home with the Waterloo Despatches and made a Lieutenant Colonel immediately. Died in 1825.

Lieutenant General, the Earl of Uxbridge (Wounded)
Wounded in the right knee at the close of the battle, his right leg was amputated and buried under a tree outside the house he was quartered in at Waterloo village. He affixed a board saying, 'Here lies the Marquise of Anglesey's leg; pray for the rest of his body, I beg.' Created Marquise of Anglesey June 23rd 1815, rose to Field Marshal in 1846. Died in 1854, buried in Lichfield Cathedral. His letters were published as 'One Leg'.

Major General Lord Edward Somerset
When bending down to pick up his hat at Waterloo, had the tail of his coat ripped away and his horse killed by a cannonball. Died in 1842.

Lieutenant General, Sir Thomas Picton (Killed)
Buried at St George's, Hanover Square but reinterred at St Paul's in 1854.

Major General Sir James Kempt (Wounded)
Later Governor General of Canada, then Master General of the Ordnance Department. Died in London in 1854.

Major of Brigade, Major Harry Smith (Wounded)
Received a musket ball in the right ankle at Waterloo. Eventually became a Lieutenant General and Governor at the Cape of Good Hope. Victor of the Battle of Aliwal in India. Finally married Juana in 1816 and as Lady Smith, named the town made famous in the Boer War. Harry died at Whittlesea in 1860. His Autobiography was published in 1846.

FIRST BATTALION 95TH RIFLES

Effective strength - 27 officers and 549 men

Total losses at Quatre Bras & Waterloo - 17 Officers (63%) and 197 (36%) men killed or wounded.

Lieutenant Colonel Andrew Barnard (Wounded)
Became Governor of Paris whilst the Allied army occupied France. Eventually became Lt Colonel of Chelsea Hospital, died in 1855.

Major Alexander Cameron (Wounded)
Survived his throat injury, but carried the ball in his neck to the grave. With his previous injuries he was effectively unfit for active service again and he went on half pay, living off his pay plus two separate awards of £500 per annum for wounds received in service. He married into an Inverness family in 1829. Eventually became Colonel in Chief of the 74th Regiment, he died in 1850.

Captain Jonathan Leach (Wounded)
Eventually became a Lt Colonel and wrote his memoirs in 'Rough recollections of an old soldier' published in 1831. He died at Worthing in 1855.

Captain Henry Lee
Went on half pay in 1820, disappears from half pay list in 1827.

Captain Edward Chawner (Wounded)
Retired soon after Waterloo as Captain of the 4th Veteran Battalion, he died in 1826.

Captain William Johnstone (Wounded)
Wounded at both Quatre Bras and Waterloo but survived. Quit the army in 1831 as a Major, became Colonial Secretary in South Africa, but died at sea in 1836.

Lieutenant John Gardiner (Wounded)
Survived, later a Major in the 82nd Regiment, died at Kinoull 18th June 1852, at the same hour as he received his wound at Waterloo.

Lieutenant John Kincaid, Adjutant
Knighted and made honorary Yeoman of the Guard, author of the very lively 'Adventures in the Rifle Brigade', he died at Hastings in 1862.

Lieutenant George Simmons (Wounded)
George Simmons was tended by the Overmar's for many weeks. Within the first four days, the surgeon drew six quarts of blood; he remained extremely weak, not surprisingly. After three weeks he suffered severe convulsions and vomiting, bleeding was carried out again

for seven days, removing (it is recorded) a quart three times a day! (Surely an impossible amount). Two weeks later with little improvement, leeches were applied, up to twenty-five per day. After three days of this his skin was so raw, that he cried continuously from the pain and he attempted to rip the leeches off. Once removed, George insisted that the leeches were destroyed by his servant to avoid them being used again. James Robson, surgeon and friend, advised him that he was unlikely to survive; George thanked him for his honesty but worried for his family in England. Three days later his sheets were covered with putrid matter pouring from the wound. Immediately following the discharge, George felt a little better and started eating again. On October 28th, he landed back in England and miraculously recovered. George eventually became a Major in the Rifles before quitting the army and retiring to Jersey, where he died in 1858. He was the Author of 'A British Rifleman'.

Captain Orlando Felix (Wounded)
Survived his wounds, was a Major on half pay in 1826, returned to duty in 1841 as Deputy Quartermaster General in the East Indies. Rose to Lieutenant Colonel in 1851 and retired on half pay again in 1855, died in 1862.

Second Lieutenant Allen Stewart (Wounded)
Afterwards a Captain, left the service in 1836, died in Norwich Military Lunatic Asylum in 1847.

Surgeon Joseph Burke
Left the army in 1828, died in Dublin in 1838.

Volunteer Charles Smith
Made a Second Lieutenant in July 1815 as he had hoped, but went on half pay as early as 1817. Colonel of

Whittlesea Yeomanry until 1831. He retired in 1837 and died in 1854.

Sergeant Robert Fairfoot (Wounded)
Survived his wounds, subsequently awarded a commission and became Quartermaster to the regiment in 1825, died in Galway in 1838.

John Connor
Wounded in the left breast at Waterloo, discharged in 1816 as 'unfit'. Returned to tailoring, working in Dover and probably died there.

Daniel Kelly
Discharged in 1826, with a 'Very Good' conduct rating. Returned to Rathkeale, County Limerick.

John Castles
Left the army in 1817 at age 41, with a 'Very Good' conduct rating. Listed as a Chelsea pensioner in 1817 and died in Paisley in 1852.

Thomas Treacy
Discharged in 1823 aged 44, illiterate with an 'Irregular' conduct rating, returned to Ireland.

Ned Costello (Wounded)
Pensioned, but returned to fighting in the Carlist Wars in Spain. Became a Warder at the Tower of London. Wrote his memoirs in a very lively book, 'Adventures of a soldier'. Died at the Salt Tower in 1869.

Thomas Maher
Tried and found Not Guilty of murder, returned to the

battalion. The men petitioned his Company Captain, Jonathan Leach, who added him to the Waterloo Roll Call. Eventually he was awarded a Waterloo Medal. A Chelsea out pensioner in Ireland in 1824, he died at Waterford in 1846.

James Burke (Wounded)
Wounded at Quatre Bras, he lingered on to die of his wounds on 29th June 1815.

John Murphy
Rose to Corporal, a Chelsea pensioner in 1831, died around 1847 at Roscommon.

Thomas Charity
Discharged in 1817 aged 34 with a 'Good' conduct rating, but old and weakly and worn out for the service.

William Mc Nabb
Discharged in 1816, old and worn out for duty.

William Smith
Still alive in 1847 as he claimed a Peninsula medal.

Tom Crawley
Still in the battalion in 1818, no further records found.

George Kitchen
Became a Chelsea pensioner but died in 1816.

John Palmer
Discharged in 1818, returned to Abingdon.

Thomas Grindley
Discharged in 1816, illiterate, died in Athlone in 1850.

Thomas Jones
Discharged in 1816, still alive in 1847 as he claimed a Peninsula medal.

George Moore
Wounded at Quatre Bras, survived.

Casima Casima
Deserted in August 1815, perhaps the scenes he had endured had been too much.

2ND BATTALION 95TH

Tom Plunket (Wounded)
He survived, as did his Mary despite her horrendous facial injuries. Discharged with a 'Bad' conduct rating in 1817, as he was insubordinate and too keen on his drink. Tom's previous fame could no longer assuage his misdemeanours. Tom and Mary married but fell on hard times, he sold matches at one time, and he died at Colchester in 1850.

Josh Hetherington (Wounded)
This man obviously existed as he is mentioned often throughout Spain, but wasn't a Rifleman. It seems likely that he survived, as his injuries do not sound life threatening. However, only two Hetheringtons appear in

the Waterloo Medal Roll, neither a Josh. One was in the 69th, which were not in Spain at all; the other was in the 42nd, a Highland regiment. This regiment was in Spain and France, but Josh was a cockney, in a kilt? I don't think so! The search for Josh continues.

G TROOP ROYAL HORSE ARTILLERY AND ASSOCIATED ARTILLERY OFFICERS

Effective strength - 5 officers, 192 men and 216 horses

Casualties at Waterloo - 2 officers (40%) 26 men (14%) and 69 horses (32%) killed or wounded.

Colonel Sir George Wood, Commanding Officer Royal Artillery in Belgium
Became an Aide de Camp to George IV and died a Major General in 1831.

Lieutenant Colonel Sir Augustus Frazer, Commanding Royal Horse Artillery in Belgium
Became a Colonel in Royal Artillery and died at Woolwich in 1835. His letters from Spain and Waterloo were published in 1859.

Lieutenant Colonel Alexander Dickson, Commanding Battering Train (Commander of G Troop, seconded)
Became a Major General, received a 'Good Service

Pension' of £365 p.a., he died at Plumstead in 1840. His letters and notes were published in 1905.

Lieutenant William Bell, Staff Adjutant to Sir Augustus Frazer

William had a very onerous task at both Quatre Bras and Waterloo, constantly passing orders to the various batteries. A few years later he fell from a horse at Norwich and was run over by a Horse Artillery battery at full gallop. He was very lucky to survive, minus one ear! Afterwards General and Colonel Commandant of the Royal Artillery. Died in 1873 at Rippon and buried at Tanfield.

Second Captain Alexander Mercer

Got his own battery immediately after Waterloo, he took Beane's troop as its commander was killed. Became Colonel Commandant of the Royal Artillery, he died in Exeter in 1868. Mercer remained bitter throughout his life for the failure of Wood and Frazer to gain him the knighthood he felt he deserved. There is actually some question as to whether he ever claimed his Waterloo medal, as he does not appear in the medal lists at the mint at all. He retained his dislike for Newland despite never meeting again. Published his memoirs as 'Journal of the Waterloo campaign'.

Second Captain Robert Newland

Went on the Half pay list in 1820, retired selling his commission in 1831, he died in 1861.

Lieutenant Henry Leathes (Wounded)

Resigned his commission in 1819, married and was heir to the family estate of Herringfleet Hall in Suffolk. Renowned throughout his life for his benevolence and philanthropy. In later life he started up a correspondence with Mercer over their Waterloo adventures, which his son had privately published in a small book. He died at Lowestoft in 1864.

Lieutenant John Hincks (Wounded)
Became a Captain, married and retired to the half pay list both in 1826, he died in 1842.

Lieutenant John Bretton
Retired on Half pay in 1820, he died at Lyndhurst in 1852.

Assistant Surgeon Richard Hichens
Went on Half pay in 1816, worked as a surgeon at St Ives, Cornwall until his death in 1866.

Staff Sergeant John Hall
Discharged in 1821 as a Sergeant Major with a 'Good' conduct rating and a pension. Became the Barrack Master at Woolwich for a number of years.

Staff Sergeant Henry Parson
Discharged in 1824 with a 'Good' conduct rating, awarded a pension of 2 Shillings 5d per day.

Bombardier Thomas Masterton
Became a Staff Sergeant, retired at the age of 46 with an 'Exemplary' conduct rating in 1836 because of severe inflammation of the legs.

Farrier Price
Discharged in 1817 on a pension of 1 Shilling per day, recorded as living at Chester in 1828, still living in 1854.

Shoeing Smith John Pettit
Discharged in 1818 on a pension of 9d per day.

Gunner Philip Hunt (Wounded)
Survived amputation of his arm, living at Colchester in 1854.

Gunner John Death
Claimed a Chelsea pension from 1830, still living in 1854.

Gunner James Putten
Claimed a Chelsea pension from 1825, living in Lanark, he died there in 1840.

Gunner Samuel Springley
Claimed a Chelsea pension from 1827, residing in Gloucester, still living in 1854.

Driver Thomas Dibbin (Wounded)
Died of his wounds 29th November 1815.

PERSONNEL SERVING WITH OTHER BATTERIES

Lieutenant William Ingilby
Afterwards a General and Colonel Commandant of the Royal Artillery, died in 1879. His diary of Spain and Waterloo has been published.

Captain Robert Bull (Wounded)
Bull was shot in the arm during the battle. Afterwards he

rose to Lieutenant Colonel; he retired on Full pay in 1834 and died at Bath in 1835.

Lieutenant Colonel James Webber Smith
Afterwards Colonel Commandant of the Royal Artillery, he died at Brighton in 1853.

Lieutenant Colonel Sir Robert Gardiner
Became an Aide de Camp to George IV, William IV and Victoria. Was Governor of Gibraltar in 1848. Became General and Colonel Commandant of the Royal Artillery, he died at Claremont in 1864.

Captain Edward Whinyates (Wounded)
At Waterloo he had three horses shot from under him, he was eventually struck on the leg by a round shot and later severely wounded in the left arm. Afterwards became a General and Colonel Commandant of the Royal Horse Artillery. He died at Cheltenham in 1865.

Lieutenant Colonel Sir Hew Ross
Afterwards he was the first artilleryman to obtain the rank of Field Marshal. Became Lieutenant Governor of the Chelsea Hospital, where he died in 1868 aged 90.

Second Captain William Webber, Beane's Troop (Wounded)
Went on Half pay as a Major in 1826, became a Lieutenant Colonel in 1837, he died at Hexworth House in Cornwall in 1847. His journal of Spain was published as 'With the Guns in the Peninsular.'

Second Captain Alexander Macdonald, Ramsay's Troop (Wounded)

Severely wounded but survived, afterwards became a Lieutenant General and died at Aix la Chapelle in 1856.

Major John Parker (Wounded)
Lost a leg at Waterloo, became Lieutenant Governor of Woolwich Arsenal from 1818 until his death in 1851.

Major Norman Ramsay (Killed)
His body was disinterred after the battle and returned to Edinburgh where he was finally laid to rest. His father raised a monument to him on the field.

Lieutenant Phipps Onslow
Went on Half pay in 1824, he died in 1867.

Captain Samuel Bolton (Killed)
Killed at the close of the battle when firing on the advancing Imperial Guard.

Captain William Lloyd (Wounded)
Died at Brussels on the 29th July 1815 from wounds received at Waterloo.

Sergeant Daniel Dunnett, Rocket Troop
Claimed a Chelsea pension from 1826, residing in Oxford, still living in 1854.

Printed in the United Kingdom
by Lightning Source UK Ltd.
9655800001B/114-209